The Ice Cream Army

Army

Jessica Gregson

Paperbooks Publishing Ltd, Floor 3, Unicorn House
221-222 Shoreditch High Street, London E1 6PJ
info@legend-paperbooks.co.uk
www.paperbooks.co.uk

British Library Cataloguing in Publication Data available.

ISBN 978-1-9065585-0-5

Set in Times
Printed by J F Print Ltd, Sparkford, Somerset, UK

Cover designed by:
Gudrun Jobst
www.yotedesign.com

Front cover photographs courtesy of Broken Hill City Library and
Broken Hill Historical Society

For my parents, Michael and Susan, with all my love and thanks, and in memory of my friend, Paul Mandlbaur.

Chapter One

The ship was huge, a town afloat, cobbled together from smooth, creaking boards tacked together with stinking tar, and thick with seething life: human, animal and vermin. It took all of two hours for the novelty to wear off, after Halim and Irfan had circumnavigated the deck twice, skidding, grinning, in the pools of salt water puddled in the corners; after they'd smoked half a cigarette each, eyeing each other sternly through the bitter, billowing smoke, daring one another to cough; after they'd catalogued and dismissed the few visible women on the ship as too old, too married, too ugly or too protected by a foot-thick wall of male relatives. The ship was not like the elegant ships of Halim's imagination, cutting through the water like silver blades, their intention unmistakeable. This ship was squat and bloated, slouching through the dank, hot water, emitting puffs of smoke like fractious sighs, and Halim felt his exhilaration ebbing away, as the damp ends of his trousers chilled in the brisk wind and snapped icily against his skinny ankles. He could feel Irfan's hot dark stare on his cheek, and wondered which of them would crack first.

Halim was not sorry to say goodbye to Port Said, which had been filthy, sweaty and villainous. It had only been down to luck and fleet-footedness that they had avoided being robbed in the days they'd spent down at the port, waiting for a ship that would give them passage. Halim didn't let himself think back further than that, to the long days of walking, their boots cracked and pale with dust, the sun beating down fit to split their heads open with the sheer heat of it, barely enough breath between them to speak. And further back was unthinkable too, to the round, green hills and to family, hardscrabble and short with expressions of affection, but somewhere that he had belonged in a way that was so deep and so certain that he had never bothered thinking about it until it was gone. They had agreed not to talk about it, he and Irfan, after the second night away, bedding down in the scratchy hay of a disused shed, and both had curled away from each other and taken care not to be heard weeping.

"That's it," Irfan had said the next morning. "Forget it. It's gone – until we can come back home with our pockets filled with money, enough to buy the village if we wanted to, and none of this will matter anymore."

It was seasickness that broke them, uncoiling like a serpent in the gut, thickening the throat, flinging them calamitously off-balance. Hands clammy and cold, Halim noticed with unpleasant surprise the way that his stomach seemed to be moving out of step with the waves that cradled the hull like rough hands. Casting a quick, sidelong glance at Irfan, he found his friend's face set in its familiar expression of stubborn nonchalance. It was the face that Irfan had always made to publicly telegraph that something wasn't bothering him; the same look that his face had worn when he'd been six-years-old and caught stealing grapes from his neighbour Umut, or ten-years-old and staggering to his feet after Halim's father's donkey had bucked him off, or sixteen-years-old, last summer, when Fatma's engagement to Niyazi, the baker's son, had been announced and everyone had asked Irfan in ostentatiously hushed tones whether he minded terribly much. Which, Halim told himself, was just the sort of thing that he wasn't supposed to be thinking about. Irfan's hands were thrust as sturdily into his pockets as ever, and his mouth pursed into its familiar soundless whistle, but Halim noticed with the keen eyes of over-familiarity that Irfan's dark skin was sallow and beaded with sweat, and his breath seemed to be coming with rather steadier determination than was normal.

Casting his eyes around the deck, Halim saw that many of the other new passengers were also looking somewhat disconcerted, fingers tightening their grip on the cold, painted railings, feet shuffling further apart to brace the body, while those who had been on the ship for some time were moving towards the edge of the decks with a sort of practiced weariness. Halim's stomach seemed to be rising unnaturally into his throat, and he took a deep breath and closed his eyes, a near-disastrous mistake that he abruptly regretted as the world seemed to tip immediately upside down in the red, fleshy darkness. He opened his eyes again just in time to see one of the older men, who'd been standing miserably nearby, run, half slipping, to the edge of the deck, bend in half and empty himself into the swirling current below.

Within an hour, they were all at it. All pretence of adult insouciance gone, Irfan and Halim leant limply against the railings, pale and disconsolate, taking turns to heave weakly into the sea below, waves smooth and sculpted like ice. Halim was no stranger to illness, but this was different. As he complained to Irfan in one of the brief periods where both of them were standing upright, normally being sick makes you feel better, but with this, no matter what, the relentless swaying of the ship only made you feel worse.

"There's nearly two months of this ahead," Irfan added, pale and glassy-eyed.

"It'll get better. We'll get used to it."

"We'd better." Irfan dipped his head for a moment, shut his eyes, considering, and then spat feebly into the brine. "We'd better," he repeated, "Otherwise I'd rather still be walking."

*

The boys had grown up in Central Anatolia, their village high and wind-whipped and smothered in snow for four months of the year, the sort of snow that covered the countryside in a milky carapace, iced the roofs of the houses, and balanced like sugar on the crumpled leaves of the grapevines strung over the paths. For four months of the year, the eaves of the houses and the domes of the mosques dripped with jagged icicles like dragons' teeth, and the cold sung in people's ears as the temperature spiralled dizzily down every evening, coating the ground with black ice. The first snow of the season was always cause for excitement, even though Halim and Irfan, at seventeen, were supposed to be too old for snow fights and sledging like the younger boys – there was something about the bright breathless white that seemed clean and sure and exhilarating. But four months of seeing the sky a curdled yellow-blue; four months of watching the steam lift heavily off the roof of the hammam and struggle, labouring under its own weight, into the sky; four months of never being truly warm, of sheltering next to the fire as its smoke grabs your throat, and its heat scorches you down one side, leaving your other side icily untouched, is enough for anyone. By the end of those four months, the idea of somewhere else, somewhere balmy and fragrant, where you never have to ease yourself into prickly blankets damp with cold, where you don't have to live with the faint stink coming off yourself and everyone else through the winter months because everyone would rather wear all the clothes they own than take the time to wash them – the idea of a place like that starts to become appealing.

People had been leaving for years, trickling out of the village in ones and twos, and yet neither Halim nor Irfan had grown up with the idea that leaving was something that *they* could do, much as they liked to talk about it and to listen to stories from people who had been away, however temporarily. Irfan had had Fatma to think about; neither of them could ever point to a time when a decision had been made, or even discussed, but for whatever reason, ever since they were seven or eight, it had somehow become public knowledge that Irfan and Fatma were bound to be married one day. Halim had never had anyone like that – although his eyes had roved around the village, they had never quite settled on anyone – and while he'd always resented the fact that, as the youngest son, he was easily overlooked and expendable, as he got older and noticed the early lines that were forming on his oldest brother's face, and the faint look of longing he saw there when Irfan's cousin came back to the village, full of stories of the way the sun looked before it dropped, fizzing, into the ocean, and the smells of the markets in the big cities, the mounds of spices and the clattering sounds of the foreign languages spoken by the traders, it was only then that Halim started to realise the advantages implicit in his own role in the family being undefined. But then his uncle, cursed with four daughters and no sons, had spoken to Halim's father about the possibility of Halim coming to work with him as a butcher, and Halim, after longing for years for something that made him feel less disposable, found himself perversely resentful of the roots that had suddenly sprouted from him, binding him to the earth where he had been born.

If it hadn't been for Irfan's cousin, five years older than the boys, Australia would never have occurred to them. Too far, too different, too utterly unimaginable. It was one thing to consider moving from one part of the Empire to another, straddling the Mediterranean, living in a world full of fellow Muslims and those others that the Empire had subsumed, and quite another to consider a parched, vast land under a different sky thousands of miles away. But Irfan's cousin, Kemal, whose father had been born in Crete and only came to the village after things started to go bad for the Muslims there, had salt water in his veins instead of blood, and had sworn blind since childhood that as soon as he was old enough there'd be no farming for him. He had no interest in goats or grapes or raising crops, no desire for a solid stone house and a plump glossy wife, but instead his head and his heart yearned for risk and adventure, at least in the abstract. His inchoate longing for difference, which marked him out from the rest of the men in the village, had passed on to Irfan and through him to Halim, as Kemal told them jumbled stories of smuggling and piracy and conquest and warfare, gilded foreign cities, foreign women draped in silks with level eyes and broad, warm smiles. The boys had reached nine or ten before they realised that these stories were largely invented, and those that were not were heavily embellished, as Kemal himself had never been further away than Izmit, and his tales told more of his own imagination than any sort of reality.

Some of his stories had stayed in their heads, though, lodging unshakeably just behind their eyes, impervious to their increasing awareness that Irfan's cousin was a world-class teller of tall tales, the butt of every village joke, and they shouldn't believe anything that came out of his mouth – not at least if they wanted to be taken seriously themselves. But he gave them the idea of Australia: a broad, flat land on the opposite side of the world, full of unimaginable riches and ungodly beasts, at the end of a sea journey past tropical spice islands, dodging sea monsters along the way. Kemal was at least sensible enough not to claim that he'd been there, as even Irfan and Halim, as credulous as they were (and wanted to be), would not have believed him; but in the market in Safranbolu he had met a man, he said, who had gone there, and the stories that he had told about this land of plenty...

"So why did he come back here, then?" Irfan asked, ten-years-old, cocky, and always the pragmatist, at least compared to Halim, who simply listened, dumbstruck and open-mouthed.

"Stupid," Kemal said, equable and dismissive. "He wanted a wife, didn't he? Came back home to find someone to marry. Not many Muslim girls out there, are there? But he was going to take her back there with him – said he'd never come back here to live; the Empire's dying, you know. Out there – that's the future. The ground's full of gold, you can grow whatever you want, and it's all just there for the taking."

Irfan had rolled his eyes, looking at Halim and jerking his thumb towards Kemal, wordlessly asking Halim if he'd ever heard anything so ridiculous, having been taken in by Kemal's fantasies once too often – but they had both believed it, deep down, and they'd repeated the stories to one another so many times that they took on substance, shape, density, becoming more and more real. They had been thirteen-years-old when Kemal had left, his fecklessness and fantasising insuring that none of the village girls wanted to marry him, to which he had shrugged his shoulders, unbothered as ever, gathered up his meagre possessions, and much to his widowed mother's distress, announced that it was time for him to seek his fortune elsewhere.

"He won't make it further than Kastamonu," Irfan had said to Halim, his mocking tones carefully chosen to disguise his envy – and, indeed, it was two years before they heard anything to the contrary, by which point Kemal's mother had, amid much wailing, given him up for dead. But then the merchant had arrived in the village, going from door to door in search of Kemal's mother, and, when she was finally located, solemnly handing her a crumpled, begrimed letter, and a small travel-stained pouch, which she had opened with astonishment, throwing her eyes to the sky and calling out thanks to Allah. Kemal, it seemed, had made it to Australia after all, had found work as a trader, and, owing to his hard work (so the letter said, though Irfan snorted dismissively and whispered to Halim that surely it was just dumb luck), had bought his own land and was living comfortably enough that he could afford to send money back to his dear mother. Ayse basked in the reflected glory of her son's evident success, taking care to remind everyone of how they'd mocked him and laughed at him, but he had had the last laugh, hadn't he?

"I'm sick of hearing about it," Irfan snapped to Halim a few days later, as they sat by the river, taking turns seeing who could fling a pebble the furthest. "He's more annoying now he's gone than he was when he was here, and that's saying something."

"You're just jealous," Halim said daringly – Irfan had a

temper on him that could flare up without warning.

But this time Irfan just snorted, a reluctant half-laugh. "Perhaps," he said. "Even if you take away the bits that he's obviously made up, you've got to admit that he has it pretty good, doesn't he?" He paused long enough to select a suitable stone, draw back his arm, and let fly into the long grass, startling a goat that was grazing nearby. "But anyway," he added, grinning at Halim, "he had nothing to stay for, did he?"

Chapter Two

Halim had always assumed that being sick was the sort of thing that was supposed to stop when there was nothing left to be sick with – as it had always done in the past when he was overfull with summer plums, or his stomach was turned upside down from a fever – but the alarming thing about seasickness was that this was not the case. The nausea seemed to be inextricably linked to the implacable swaying of the boat, like being in some sort of malign cradle. By the end of the first day, neither Halim nor Irfan could bear the thought of their beds, side by side in the colossal, dim and airless dormitory deep in the guts of the ship. The only thing that seemed to help Halim feel slightly less like he was likely to die within the next few minutes was keeping his eyes fixed on the trembling line of the horizon and inhaling deep gusts of the fresh salt air like it was a medicinal draught. Night fell abruptly, the sun swooning suddenly out of its cloud-flecked sky, stars whirling above, a narrow slice of moon. Other passengers started to move inside, but Irfan and Halim exchanged looks.

"I'm not going anywhere," Irfan said darkly. "I'll sleep the whole journey on this deck if I have to, but I'm not going down there."

Halim was in no mood to argue with Irfan's fierce vehemence, even if he'd wanted to. Not only was the thought of the dormitory unappealing in itself, but there was the fact that they were sharing it with a couple of hundred of their fellow passengers. In particular, Halim had noticed two boys of a similar age to themselves, Italians, brothers, their beds next to his and Irfan's, both of whom had, until very recently, been vomiting lavishly over the side of the boat. The younger of the two in particular had disgraced himself when, knocked off balance by a particularly rough and rowdy swell, he had managed to be sick all over himself. The thought of being cooped up for the evening in an enclosed space with that sort of stinking mess made Halim's gorge rise anew.

"How do you think *he* does it?" Irfan asked presently. Halim's gaze had been fixed listlessly on the white-tipped swell, snowy-clean in the faint moonlight, but Irfan's eyes were never still for long and had settled on a nearby man, stood straight-backed and broad-shouldered by the railings. His feet were placed wide apart and his hips set loosely, so that he moved easily with every roll of the ship. His face was serene and relaxed, gazing out over the ocean as if he owned it.

"Don't know. Perhaps he's used to it."

"I saw him at the port, d'you remember? With his family. I think I heard him speaking Turkish with someone."

The last thing Halim wanted to do at that moment was move from the little square of deck that he had claimed as his own, the paint-covered bolts pressing into his thighs and buttocks offering a certain familiarity and groundedness, if not exactly comfort. But Irfan... Of course Irfan wasn't content to sit still, Halim thought with weak annoyance. Of course he had to explore. Of course he had to push back against anything that was pushing him down, instead of just lying back and getting on with being miserable. Sighing, Halim pulled himself upright, gripping onto the salt-scaled metal rail, and followed Irfan to where he was standing, expectant, a peculiar mixture of respect and belligerence, in front of the straight, still man, who took his pipe out from between his clenched teeth, knocked it twice against the rail and, cupping it in his right hand, gave the boys an indulgent smile.

"Good evening," he said. Although his words were curiously

twisted by an accent Halim couldn't place, he was undoubtedly speaking Turkish. Halim had expected to be ignored or, at the very least, spoken to in a tangled flurry of Arabic, of which between them they could cobble together only around fifty words, so the sound of a stranger speaking Turkish, no matter how peculiarly accented, made him feel shamefully tearful.

"Good evening," Irfan said. He seemed to be trying to deepen his voice, Halim noticed with a hidden smile, trying to sound older and sturdier than he was. "The evening is beautiful, isn't it?"

"It is," the stranger agreed, and then smiled a little more broadly. "You boys don't seem to be enjoying it too much, though."

"We feel terrible," Halim blurted out, ignoring Irfan's black look of disapproval. "This is our first time on a ship. They said that we'd be seasick, but I didn't think it'd be like this. Are you used to it? Will we be like this all the way to Australia?"

"I've been to sea before," the man confirmed, "and you will get used to it, but there are a few things that can help." He reached into a pocket, bringing out a knobbly brown root. "Ginger," he explained. Pulling out a pocket knife, he cut off a small piece off for Irfan and Halim each. "It helps with the nausea. You might want to give it a try."

Halim reached out eagerly, and even Irfan took his piece willingly, still shooting daggers at Halim, furious at him for having blown his man-of-the-world demeanour. Having faced Irfan's stubborn rages regularly since the age of four or five, Halim now bore them with equanimity. In his mouth, the ginger was tough and stringy, with a sharp sweet flavour that was almost overwhelming; for a moment, the very action of putting something in his mouth made the nausea rise again, but he swallowed it down, concentrating on the movements of his lips, teeth and tongue, the unfamiliar taste flooding his mouth, and within minutes his stomach started to feel again as if it was a fixed part of his body, rather than a free-floating organ intent only on causing suffering and embarrassment.

"Feeling better?" the man asked, and both Halim and Irfan nodded. The man was in his fifties perhaps, with wiry silver hair that seemed almost stubbornly rooted on his head, and the sort of deeply lined face that came from hard work and weather. He extended a hand. "I'm Yiannis Papadimitriou," he said.

Halim felt his eyebrows rise against his own will, and he quickly turned his face away so that Yiannis wouldn't notice any change in his expression. He had never met a Christian before – he knew that they were common in towns on the coast, where Greek and Muslim families lived alongside one another in relatively harmony, and he certainly harboured them no ill-will, aside from a slightly confused sense that it must be difficult to live with such drastically mistaken beliefs. But he realised then, deriding himself as he did so, that he'd always had the vague idea that Christians would be somehow identifiable, their aberrant beliefs clear from their dress or their posture, or even the very composition of their features. Yiannis, on the other hand, Yiannis looked just like any number of men of the same age that Halim and Irfan had grown up with.

"Halim," he said hurriedly, recovering his composure.

"Irfan," Irfan added, and Halim watched the man's face to see whether their flagrantly Muslim names provoked any reaction. They didn't.

"We're from near Bolu," Halim volunteered, and Yiannis nodded without any real recognition.

"Smyrna," he replied, and then moved slightly closer, looking carefully into their faces, Irfan's and then Halim's in turn. "How old are you boys? Are you travelling with family?"

"Twenty-one," Irfan said, slightly too quickly, and Halim, who'd never been any good at lying, dropped his face to his feet and felt the slow wave of red rise up from his open collar to his hairline. Looking up, he saw Yiannis's eyebrows raised, amused and disbelieving.

"And you're on your own, then?" he said. Halim and Irfan

nodded. "Well, then. Would you like to come and eat with my family tonight? Your stomachs will be empty – " he nodded over his shoulder, indicating the ravenous ocean, which had long swallowed Halim and Irfan's paltry breakfasts, " – and my wife has enough food to feed the entire boat, I think."

Ginger and distraction had worked their magic, and Halim found himself able to leave the deck, breathe the stuffy, thick air inside the ship, clatter his way down the long metal staircases and settle in Yiannis's relative plush first-class cabin with only a very faint clamour of unease from his stomach. Excited and apprehensive, he wasn't entirely sure what to expect of this Christian family and their Christian food, half afraid of finding half a pig laid out and expectant eyes upon him, forcing him to either choke it down his throat and damn himself in the eyes of Allah, or refuse to eat and cause offence. Both options seemed equally horrifiying, but instead, he found Yiannis' wife, Maria, face and hair uncovered, but in all other ways dressed like any other woman from the village where Halim had grown up. Her eyes were diffident but cautiously friendly as she bore bread and cheese and dolma, indistinguishable from those that Halim's mother made. Also present, to his embarrassment and fascination, were Yiannis and Maria's two daughters: Eleni, not much more than ten or eleven and seemingly unfazed by having two unknown boys – *men*, Halim internally corrected himself; *men*, most definitely – in their midst; and Anna, a few years older, hands and eyes fluttering up and down in consternation. Unable to look directly at either of the girls, unwilling to look at Yiannis and Maria and expose his discomfort, Halim's eyes floated around the cabin, desperate for something inoffensive on which to alight. He finally caught Irfan's gaze, sitting across from him, clearly doing exactly the same thing, whereupon Yiannis gave a rough, but not unfriendly bark of laughter.

"Our traditions are different from yours," he said, nodding a little in acknowledgement. "I have Muslim friends from our village, and I know that they wouldn't permit this with their girls. But our traditions are different, and on this ship we're the closest thing to family that you two have. So eat."

Chapter Three

'Family' may have been overstating the case a little. After that first night, full of awkward conversation and crumby, close-mouthed silences, Irfan and Halim weren't invited back to eat again, relying instead on the brackish, tasteless, but filling stew that the ship's kitchens provided, the remnants of the nuts, seeds and dried fruit that they'd bought in the souq in Port Said, and whatever they managed to beg from or swap with their fellow passengers, a polyglot lot of Italians, Greeks and Arabs, who were all equally baffled by one another, but friendly enough. And mostly, during the day, when the seasickness wasn't too bad and Halim was feeling sturdy and robust, he felt certain that this was the way things were supposed to be. Yiannis made friendly conversation when they passed one another on deck – friendly, *adult* conversation, Halim thought – and that was where it lay; they were grown men, independent, not in search of another family to take them in when they'd left their own behind weeks ago. Independence was easy when everything else was easy too, when the only decision that had to be made was how many times they should trot around the deck for their daily allotment of exercise. But when Halim woke in the night to find Irfan shaking and moaning in the bunk below him, all he wanted, more than anything, more than for Irfan to be all right, even, was for someone else to step in and take the responsibility of his friend away from him.

Irfan had been quieter than usual for a couple of weeks. As the ship ploughed on, southbound and unstoppable, he'd seemed paler, too, and while Irfan had always coughed for as long as Halim could remember, a dry-throated tickle that flared up when he was nervous or embarrassed, the racking, shuddering cough that he had picked up on the ship was new, a cough that seemed to rattle his membranes and tear him up from the inside out. Irfan had assured him that he was perfectly fine, it was just a bit of a cough, it was the change of environment and the dusty, thick-aired dormitory, and Halim had believed him because he'd wanted to believe him, despite his friend's uncharacteristic lethargy, his increasing reluctance to explore the ports when the ship docked, with the unconvincing excuse that he wanted to stay on the boat and study the English primer he'd filched off one of the Arab boys when his back was turned. That morning, when they had docked in Ceylon, it had been Halim urging Irfan to come and investigate the docks, instead of the other way round. Irfan, sitting, sweating, on the over-bright deck, had just shaken his head, and when Halim insisted, increasingly concerned, Irfan had just grinned wearily and told Halim to tell him all about it later, and when Halim did return, hours later, having swarmed around the port with a haphazard collection of Italian and Egyptian boys, resolutely refusing to worry, he had found Irfan in the exact same position that he'd left him in the English primer, tellingly propped open at the same page Halim and Irfan had been poring over the night before. In all his life; Halim had never known Irfan to sit still for minutes at a time, let alone hours, and he finally collected his courage and demanded to know what was wrong.

"Do you need a doctor?" Irfan had asked. "There's a doctor on the ship, I can find him for you." But Irfan had put his hand on Halim's arm and shaken his head – his smile hadn't changed, which was a comfort to Halim – and again he had insisted: "It's nothing. Nothing."

At three in the morning, though, with Irfan's face sweat-slicked and scorching, his eyes open and rolling, his entire body shuddering convulsively, it no longer seemed like nothing.

Halim crouched on the floor, fumbling to light a match, a soft globe of brightness that cast Irfan's face in a frightening glow.

"Irfan?"

But Irfan did not answer, nor give any indication that he had heard. Taking his wrist, Halim found it unnaturally, inhumanly hot and dry. A soft flump sounded behind him, of a blanket hitting the floor, and Halim turned to see Gianni propped up on his bunk, looking afraid, speaking in Italian, but his meaning evident from his tone, "What's wrong? He is ill?"

Halim felt a wave of panic break over him. Gianni was fourteen, fifteen at the most; when rollicking around the port earlier, his outthrust chest and pugnacious expression had made him seem well on the way to manhood, but the guttering half-light of the match stripped him of the customary bravado and swagger that all the young boys wrapped themselves in during the day. With his older brother, Mario, still asleep on the upper bunk, Gianni looked like the confused and uncertain child that he was. Halim replied in Turkish, gesticulating as much as possible to ensure Gianni understood.

"Irfan's sick. You watch, please. I..." Halim pointed at Gianni, at Irfan, mimed himself running out the door, and Gianni, scared, nodded.

Barefoot in the passage, Halim didn't even know where he was going until he found himself in front of the door of Yiannis's cabin. Suddenly, he was horrified by the idea of waking a virtual stranger and his family at three in the morning, but one thought of Irfan's flushed face and frantic, blank eyes brought back his resolve, and he knocked once, quietly, then again, more loudly, until Yiannis, worry and anger mixed in his expression, opened the door a crack and peered out.

"Halim?"

"I'm sorry, it's – it's Irfan. He's ill, very ill." The relief of being able to speak his own language rather than having to fashion his meaning with uncertain tools was something to cling to. For a moment, neither of them moved in the humid, sticky darkness, and then Halim said, falteringly, "I don't know what to do."

Yiannis stepped back, nodding the same short, decisive nod he had the first day they'd met. "Wait here," he said, closing the door.

Moments later, both Yiannis and Maria were fully, if chaotically, dressed and standing in the corridor, much to Halim's surprise and confusion. Catching his eyes, Yiannis explained, "I'm going to fetch the ship's doctor. Maria – she knows about these things. Illnesses. She should go with you."

Maria only reached Halim's shoulder, and she barely spoke a word, but, somehow, just the presence of someone older and wiser, someone who knew what to do – or pretended to – calmed Halim more than he could have imagined. As she led the way back towards the dormitory, the cloak over Maria's shoulders flapped and fluttered like a cloud in the shadow. When they reached the hulking rows of beds, Halim was more conscious than he'd ever been of the thick, damp stink of the place and the constant noise, even in the middle of the night, the snuffles and grunts and snores of dozens of slumbering men and women. Halim found both Mario and Gianni awake, watching over Irfan from a wary distance. Conscious of Maria's modesty, the white of her nightgown gleaming in the gloom, Halim frowned at Gianni and Mario, motioning for them to turn their backs as Maria knelt down beside Irfan with comforting certainty and practicality, placing her hand on his forehead and smoothing his sweat-damp hair. It was the gesture of a mother, and Halim felt quick tears come to his eyes – and Irfan, too, seemed to sense a solidity to Maria's presence, as he turned his face towards her. Halim didn't know what Irfan saw, who he thought she was, but he heard Irfan say, carefully and clearly, despite his dry lips and fever-parched throat, "I didn't mean it. I didn't mean to do it."

"Of course you didn't," Maria said soothingly, shooting a puzzled look up at Halim, who could do nothing but look quickly away.

When the doctor arrived, the news wasn't good. Irfan had pneumonia. It seemed likely that he'd had it for days, and had been disguising his symptoms – out of fear, Halim thought furiously, cursing his friend's stubbornness, his determination to show that everything was all right on the surface, that he was a big, strong man, even if things were falling apart underneath.

Irfan was moved immediately into the ship's sanatorium, which was staffed with starched, white-clad nurses and doctors, where the air rang with the stench of antiseptic and the noises of the ill and dying. Despite the staff, Maria, with her quiet persistence, insisted on taking on the bulk of nursing for Irfan, even after the doctors and nurses had assured them that it was uscless, that the pneumonia was building on a case of consumption that had taken root months before, that he was hardly likely to last the next few days, let alone the rest of the journey.

Maria and Yiannis were silent, solid pillars of comfort as Halim blamed himself, went back over the weeks and months and years that he and Irfan had spent together, the cough that he'd developed last winter that had never seemed to go, that Irfan had always brushed off but which had worsened on the boat. "I should have seen," Halim said, again and again, and finally, ultimately, Maria made him understand that even if he had seen, on the ship, or on the journey from Safranbolu to Istanbul, or even back in the village, it wouldn't have done any good.

"You cannot save him," she said with steady certainty, as the doctor took Irfan's pulse and shook his head, listening to Irfan's torn, unsteady breaths, saying that he doubted that Irfan would last the night. And yet, stubborn to the last, Irfan kept breathing, sometimes in silence, and sometimes in distress, fixing his bloodshot eyes on whoever happened to be nearest, saying again and again "I didn't mean to do it," until Halim, broken down, exhausted and in tears, finally told Yiannis and Maria what had happened, why they had had to leave. When Fatma's family had announced her engagement to Niyazi, Irfan had managed to keep his head high and his anger in check until one day, in the market, Niyazi had come past, puffed up with pride. Halim could never remember what Irfan had said, but Irfan's mouth had always got him into trouble. Niyazi had shot back with the words that were designed to hurt most, that Fatma's family would never marry their only daughter off to someone as ugly as Irfan, half his face blotched and angry red from the scald he'd received from upsetting the kettle as a child. "It was a stupid thing to say," Halim told Maria and Yiannis. "Everyone in the village knew about Irfan and his temper." Halim himself had been one of the three who had finally managed to drag Irfan off Niyazi, and they had all waited for Niyazi to spring to his feet, possibly with another carefully chosen insult for Irfan – but he had lain still, and that was when they had noticed the rock clutched in Irfan's hand.

"He ran off," Halim explained. "It wasn't that he was a coward, but he – he really hadn't meant to do it. When I found him, that evening – I'd known where he would go, the same place we used to hide out from our parents when we were children, and so I'd joined the group of people looking for him, to make sure they wouldn't find him – he was so full of guilt. But he didn't want to die himself, and his family didn't want that either, and so they gave us money, and we – we left."

Maria and Yiannis didn't reply at once, and at first Halim thought that he had lost them, that they'd been so horrified at his story that they wouldn't speak to him anymore. But finally: "He needs forgiveness," Yiannis said.

Halim nodded. "Can you…?"

"I'm a Christian. I don't know the right things to say for him. It has to be you."

"But I don't know, either."

Maria put her small hand on his shoulder, a breach of taboo that Halim was well past caring about. "It doesn't matter what you say, Halim. But he knows your voice better than anyone else's. Just... just talk to him."

And so Halim, whose voice had been frozen in his throat by Irfan's bedside, found his tongue loosened, and he talked, the words coming out of his mouth having more to do with his own personal cosmology than with any received Islam. He spoke of the mercy of Allah, of how he can see into our hearts and know what is there and what is not, and he spoke of the afterlife, or his idea of the afterlife, which was framed by his seventeen-year-old experience of the world: freedom, and good things to eat in abundance, and the clarity of light and dawn, and warmth and comfort. He spoke for so long that his voice became hoarse, and he could no longer remember what he had said and what he hadn't, so he repeated things, looped back. The words were the important thing, the shape and the pattern of them, rather than their truth or their meaning; the words, and the fact that it was Halim speaking them. It took Yiannis's hand on his shoulder to halt him, and it was only then that he saw that Irfan's breathing had stopped.

September 10th, 1914

"My mum's going to kill me," the boy in front of Patrick said. His eyes were fever-bright, and he kept tugging at the carefully cultivated patch of fuzz on his upper lip. Patrick didn't believe for a minute that he was any more than fourteen or fifteen, no matter how much the boy tried to deepen his voice and square his shoulders and claim that he was going to be nineteen next month, but he admired the boy's spirit, his willingness to jump into the thick of things, which echoed Patrick's own.

"My mum couldn't care less," Patrick said to the boy, "but my sister – bloody hell, my sister's going to have my guts for garters."

He had written to Maggie just that morning, but he hadn't dared mention what he was planning to do that very afternoon. He hadn't been ready even to imagine the blast of outrage that would come from his sister when she found out that he had volunteered. Even at a distance of hundreds of miles, the heat of her outrage could still scorch him, and he had decided to wait to tell her until he had worked out exactly what his reasons were for doing what he was doing. None of the reasons that he carried in his head right now were good enough: that he was volunteering because all his mates were, or because he was bored in his factory job, same things and same people and same motions day after day after day, or because Sydney was starting to seem too cluttered and crowded and he had started longing for weeks with nothing to look at but the empty sea, or because he was sick of his father warbling on drunkenly about the emerald isle and looking at Patrick askance because he hadn't seen as much of the world as his old man had. None of those reasons were likely to cut the mustard with Maggie, who was firmly of the belief that this was someone else's war, none of their concern, and that Australia was better off out of it. The only thing that he could think of to tell her that he was Australian, and he wanted to show the rest of the world that Australians could handle themselves as well as anyone else could.

Six weeks later, he sailed.

Chapter Four

Halim could never remember much of the journey following Irfan's death. There was the endless rolling of the sea, sometimes silver, sometimes dark, stony grey, sometimes lucent green, sometimes a blank, staring blue. There was the sky, flat white or swirling with clouds, or a high, dizzying indigo, suffocating with a fullness of air. Halim remembered pacing the decks on occasions, the warped boards beneath his feet. He remembered docking in ports, metal thick and heavy with grease, shouts and dust, heat baking or searing, or hanging, choking, in the air; and then the long nothingness between South Africa and Australia, day upon day out of sight of land, until, when the coast of Western Australia trembled like a brown streak on the horizon, he couldn't quite work out what it was. He remembered nights in the dormitory, going to bed as soon as the sun went down, turning his back on what had been Irfan's bunk – now colonised by one of Gianni and Mario's Italian friends – lying in the warm, damp darkness, the gentle murmur of voices around him, speaking in languages he didn't understand. He remembered the few moments when his heart lifted out of its habitual torpor, the first time that flying fish flickered out of the waves, the couple of evenings in the soft dusk light on deck when Maria's soft-voiced folktales, told ostensibly to her daughters, with Halim sitting nearby with a pretence of indifference – he only understood long afterwards that Maria's choice of Turkish rather than Greek for these tales meant that she was telling them to him – spun him far enough away from this creaking, clanking, salt-encrusted prison and reminded him of home. But those memories were just fragments; all laced together, they took up no more than a couple of hours at most. The remaining weeks of the journey were a dull, thick blackness, until, after days of crawling along the dust-coloured coast, the morning came when the sea narrowed itself, squeezing, thrashing angrily, through twin heads of rock, and the ship followed it through, rocking from side to side, hunkered down low over the waves, heading with single-minded determination towards the seething docks jutting out from the city that tumbled down the hills, grey and brown, palled with smoke, gravid with shouts in an angular, clacking language. And with a shocking suddenness the journey was over.

With nothing said, it had been assumed all round that, since Irfan's death, Halim belonged to Maria and Yiannis, at least temporarily. It seemed ridiculous now that he had never asked Irfan to write down the address his cousin had given in his solitary letter home. That was two years ago now, and it seemed probable that Kemal wasn't there anymore, but it would have been a starting point, at least. But the address, clenched firmly in Irfan's tenacious brain, had died with him, and Halim was alone in this city – not only the city, but in this vast, flat, blank continent, sky above like a gaping maw. There was nobody who knew him or cared about him within thousands upon thousands of miles, and the only thing standing in the way of his being swallowed up by the dust and the squalor and the fathomless desert was this strange Christian family whom he never could have imagined befriending months before. He couldn't think, afterwards, how he would have passed through immigration without the guidance of Yiannis, who somehow fixed it so that he could bypass the dictation test that was bedevilling many of Halim's fellow passengers. When Halim went to ask Yiannis what he had done, Yiannis just winked, shook his head and said, "Don't you worry about that, Halim. It just means you're part of our family, for a while, at least."

The alleys leading up from the port were hot and damp, a rich stink in the air, men and women brushing together in the street, the women bold-eyed and smiling, men raucous and swaggering. Maria and Yiannis and their girls were among the last of their family to cross the ocean. A young man, after glancing curiously at Halim, fell on Yiannis's neck at the docks, voicing extravagant, elaborate greetings. Then he shouted, in a language that Halim didn't know but assumed was Greek, and it seemed like dozens of men came running out of the seething mass, hefting Yiannis and Maria's trunks and cases – Halim kept a tight hold of his own meagre bundle of belongings – and leading them through the knotted alleyways to a house.

Tall and narrow, decorated with iron curlicues, crammed in between two identical houses as if jostling for space, the house extended a long way back. When the five newcomers arrived, they were met by a multitude of women, black-clad, shouting their thanks to the heavens, and men, tired-looking and shy-eyed, clasping hands and beating one another's shoulders. These were Maria's brothers and cousins, Yiannis's sisters, aunts and uncles; the scene was both familiar and unfamiliar to Halim, and he felt a sense of consuming emptiness growing in his throat, pushing down into his stomach and up into his mouth. For weeks, he had wished himself off the boat and safely arrived. He had sensed that once the voyage was over and he had left behind the boat that had been the scene of his troubles, the thick, dark fog that hovered at the edge of his vision would lift. Now, he found himself wishing fervently for the confines of the ship, the sea bright and brash around him, that known, floating world, rather than clinging to the edge of this vast, harsh continent.

He was introduced gently and kindly by Maria and Yiannis, and he was received gently and kindly but with a degree of shy, slanting curiosity. Every time he looked up, eyes seemed to slide away from him, and he was greeted with smiles from those in the family who spoke only Greek, and pleasantries from those who spoke Turkish, but no more than polite, routine enquiries. His village and family seemed to squat in his chest, next to his heart, unacknowledged amid the familiarity that surrounded him, and he longed to be asked where he was from, what his family were like – his life story was standing on the back of his tongue, ready to spill.

The house was close and damp and too warm. There was a garden behind it, small and square, a half-glazed window opening into it from the kitchen. Halim looked, looked again – there was a face at the window, young, male and laughing. It was one of the boys he recognised from the quay, the ones who'd lifted the trunks as if they were nothing. He looked away for a moment and, when he looked back, a hand was raised, waving, beckoning, holding a cigarette between two skinny fingers. Halim followed.

The garden had seemingly become the sanctuary for the young men who were bored with the adult, or responsible, or womanish talk inside. Four men, all around Halim's age or slightly older, sprawled loose-jointed on upturned crates, smoke twisting up to the sky, and Halim felt his chest relax slightly. The boy who'd been beckoning at the door turned and grinned, stretching a long arm to hook an empty crate into the circle where they were sitting.

"You all right? You looked bored in there. Thought you might want a smoke."

His Turkish was even harder to understand than Yiannis and Maria's, grammatically confused, and riddled with pauses as he seemed to search for the words that kept eluding him – but Halim was powerfully grateful for the effort. A cigarette, wrinkled and tightly rolled, appeared on Halim's right and he took it, muttering his thanks. He'd never quite got the hang of smoking. He had only done it at Irfan's insistence, because that's what grown men did, and he had given it up with some thankfulness after Irfan had died. Still, as soon as the burnt, bitter taste hit the back of his throat he felt somehow better than he had in weeks, reminded, suddenly, of who he'd been.

"You want a beer?" one of the group, Christos, asked. Halim shook his head too quickly, realising as soon as it was done that they'd think he was childish, or that he was judging them. But Christos just shrugged. "No worries. You a Muslim?" and when Halim nodded, he jerked his head towards the young-looking boy beside him. "So's Mostafa there. From near Smyrna too, though. All of us are. Or were. Still, these things don't matter so much out here as they did back in the old country."

The boys all spoke the same broad, slangy type of Turkish, interspersed with words that Halim couldn't understand, which he took to be Greek, and a few English words that he knew from the boat. In their way, they were just as foreign to him as the Italians he'd met on the ship, or the Irish family hanging their sheets in the neighbouring garden, close enough that Halim's back was splattered with droplets. But they were from the same part of the world as he was, and that lent a degree of familiarity and shared association that he immediately knew he wouldn't have with anyone else out here, and so he relaxed, back curving, listening to their conversation about people he didn't know and things he didn't understand, his cigarette curled into the cave of his palm, the evening air hot and heavy on his back.

"So Uncle Yiannis said they met you on the ship," Christos said at last, turning towards Halim with open, idle curiosity. "You travelling alone?"

"I wasn't. I was with my friend, but he got sick and died."

Halim was glad that he didn't want sympathy, because it didn't seem to occur to any of the boys to provide it, other than a slight frown and shrug from Christos, which Halim interpreted as *hard luck, but these things happen*. Rather than resenting their hardheartedness, Halim found himself bolstered by it.

"Did they make you do the language test?" Mostafa asked, striking a match off one of the rough bricks that made up the wall, and lighting the sad scrap of a cigarette that dangled from his lower lip.

Halim was confused. "What do you mean?"

"It's the policy," Mostafa explained. "Meant to stop men from the islands coming across to work cheap, and Chinese, too. They make all new immigrants take a language test, but the trick of it is that it can be in any language they want. Say you're Italian – they don't like the look of you, they give you the test in German. That sort of thing. Europeans are generally all right – they don't mind those – but anyone whose skin is a bit darker can run into problems." He looked at Halim curiously. "You didn't have to do it, then?"

"No, no one asked anything. Yiannis said –" He flushed suddenly, remembering what Yiannis had said about family. "I think Yiannis must have fixed it for me."

Stephanos looked at him appraisingly. "You got lucky, mate. You can get out of the test by paying a bond to the immigration officials, and that must've been what Yiannis did – for you, as well as for his family. He must really like you." Halim, acutely embarrassed at this casual discussion of Yiannis's largesse, was relieved when Christos cut in and changed the subject.

"So, you looking for work, then?"

Halim nodded. "Yes, I will be. My friend, the one who died – his cousin's out here, we were going to go and meet him, hope he could help us get work, but I don't know his address or anything, and he didn't know we were coming. Irfan knew where he lived, but he didn't have it written down and he didn't tell me. I didn't think to ask."

"What's the name of the bloke?" Stephanos asked. "Not too many Muslims around here. We might know him."

"Kemal. His father's name was Ibrahim, I think."

Most of the boys shook their heads, looking blank, but Mostafa looked up, eyes sharp. "Short bloke? A little fat? Round face with thick eyebrows?"

Halim nodded warily. "Yes, but –"

"Talks a lot of shit? This bloke, the one I'm thinking of – I've never heard anything like the stories he'd come up with!"

Halim laughed, and Mostafa grinned and shrugged. "It might not be the same bloke. This one I'm talking about, he's not in Sydney, anyway. I met him when I was out working in the mines in Cottier's Creek. Not too many Muslims out there, you have to stick together."

"Oh," Christos said, surprise in his voice as he turned back to Halim. "You going to work out in the mines then?"

Halim shook his head. "We weren't planning to. My friend said his cousin was a trader, going round to different towns, selling things. We thought maybe he could help us get the same sort of work."

Mostafa shook his head. "Maybe. Bloody hard to get hawker licenses, though, unless you buy someone else's – which is what your Kemal probably did. If it is the same bloke as I'm thinking of, he seems like the sort of person who can talk his way into anything."

"Or some of the Italian boys on the ship were talking about getting work in the colliery…"

"The colliery?" Stephanos asked, and the boys all groaned. "Oh, God. You don't want to do that. Tough work, awful pay, and dangerous, too. You'd have to be crazy. Lots of new immigrants start off there, but move on as soon as they can find anything better. Bottom of the pile, the colliery is. You did it for a while, didn't you, Christos?"

Christos nodded. "Yeah, when I first arrived, five years back. Horrible. See this?" He rolled up his shirt sleeve, exposing a jagged, ugly scar that was hard for Halim to look at. "That's what I got from the colliery. No way I'd ever go back to that. If you've got any chance to do something else, you should take it."

"So what do you do now?"

Christos grinned. "My fiancée's father owns a tailor's shop and I help out there. He's got three daughters, and he's getting me ready to take the business over from him."

"He got lucky," Stephanos said to Halim, elbowing Christos in the ribs. "She'd never have looked at him back home. But here, the parents are always so keen to marry their daughters to people from the same place, so even someone like Christos is in with a chance, especially once he'd saved a bit of money from working in the colliery. The rest of us have to put up with the tough jobs."

"What is it that you do?" Halim asked. Stephanos was tall and broad, unlike the slimmer Christos, though he had gathered that the two were brothers.

"I work down at the docks. Me and Costas. Costas has been here for a few years longer than me, and he helped me get the job. It's hard work," Stephanos displayed the palms of his hands, torn and bloodied with blisters, "but it's good to work outside, and it keeps me strong."

"I keep telling them," Mostafa said, leaning forward, "I keep telling them that they should try working in the mines. Out where your mate's cousin is, there are plenty of mines – silver, zinc, and lead; lots of work, and the money is good, so you don't have to live out there permanently. I was there a couple of years back. It's hard work, too, but worth it."

"No need for me," Christos said, slightly smugly.

"Nor me," added Stephanos, and Costas nodded. "I like my job, and I like the city."

"You like living with your mama, you mean," Mostafa said dismissively, but Stephanos only laughed.

"Well, why not? Good food and clean clothes without having to worry about it."

"If it's so good," Halim dared to ask Mostafa, "why did you come back?"

Mostafa grinned while the others laughed. "I'm getting married, that's why," he explained. "Working out there for a few years earned me enough money to set up on my own. A mate and I have got together and we're setting up a fish shop. There's a little flat above it where I'll live when Khadija and I are married. She's from India, Muslim of course; her father came to Australia as a cameleer, and I met their family when I was out in Cottier's Creek. So, you see, the mines worked well for me."

The conversation drifted off again for a while, discussions of girls that Halim didn't know, and their various merits; if it hadn't been for the unfamiliar accents and the lingering heat in the air, when Halim closed his eyes he could have been back in the village where he'd grown up, surrounded by Irfan and the other boys, assessing the village girls for the thousandth time. He allowed himself to drift, the moon a bright penny in the sky above them, until the conversation finally circled round again and Mostafa asked Halim, "Where will you be living now?"

Halim shrugged. "I don't know exactly," he said hesitantly. "Maria and Yiannis said that they would… they would find me somewhere more permanent to live for the next few days, until I find some work, and somewhere else to stay. It is kind of them, but I'm not sure where exactly they intend I should be…" He was surprised at how unconcerned he was about this uncertainty, as if he'd surrendered himself on the high seas, to be disposed of as Yiannis and Maria wished.

A look was exchanged between the other boys and there and then Christos said, "Well, why don't you stay with us? We don't have much room, but if you don't mind a bit of a squash, you're more than welcome to kip down with us for a while."

Chapter Five

Christos, Mostafa and Costas lived in a single room with a single window looking out onto a flaking brick wall. The room was redolent with the smells of three – now four – young men: sweat and cigarettes and unwashed clothing, smells that made Halim feel both at home and alienated at the same time. But for the unfamiliar surroundings outside the front door, into which Halim ventured with mixed excitement and trepidation, the overwhelming maleness within his bedroom mean that he could have been back in his village, sharing a room with his brothers, listening to them talking about girls (favourably) and work (unfavourably). In that context, the fact that Christos and Costas were Christians ceased to matter entirely. Although the Greeks tended to speak their own language when Halim and Mostafa weren't present, they switched effortlessly to a strange melange of Turkish, Greek and English whenever they were – Halim often felt as if he were picking up as much Greek as he was English – and their strange language, as well as their ease at dealing with Muslims like Halim and Mostafa meant that the Greek community around them, from the islands of Kythera, Ithaca and Kastellorizo, regarded these strange Greek-Turks with a mixture of confusion and suspicion. As far as Halim was concerned, he didn't feel as if he were among Greeks, Christians and strangers; it was only when Mostafa and Halim were preparing for the first daily prayer at dawn, as Christos swore and yanked his pillow over his head, and Costas danced around their kneeling bodies, dressing for the start of the day down at the docks, did the difference become clear. And, occasionally, Halim wondered whether, if Mostafa hadn't been there, he would have stopped bothering to pray himself – his duties to Allah were suddenly seeming a lot less pressing than his duties to himself.

The room was at the back of a house belonging to a cousin of Christos's fiancée, which was why Christos availed himself of the luxury of the single, metal-framed bed while the others slept on rugs on the floor. The rest of the family seemed to regard the boys with amused indulgence, feeding them if they were there (though more often than not Costas and Mostafa were not, and when they were, Stephanos was almost always with them, another mouth that the family fed uncomplainingly) and largely keeping out of their way. Halim was uncertain whether Giorgos and Katerina ever knew how many men were living in that one room. A couple of days at least passed before Giorgos blinked at him myopically, saying, "Hello, I don't think I've seen you before..." Halim blushingly introduced himself, whereupon Giorgos smiled kindly and vaguely and went on with whatever he had been doing.

Giorgos and Katerina had two sons and three daughters, the youngest two of whom were still living with them, and Halim was trying his hardest not to find their proximity shocking. "It's different here," Mostafa told him, again and again, "It's more free. And they're Christians, anyway." The girls largely kept themselves to themselves. Katerina took in washing and mending to help with the bills, and the oldest remaining girl, Agape, helped with the business; she was engaged in all but name, to a man whom Halim hadn't met, but who was apparently working in the outback on a sheep farm, trying to earn money for the eventual wedding.

The youngest girl, though, Fotini, was a different proposition entirely, and Halim could not make up his mind whether to be horrified at, afraid of, or charmed by her behaviour. At seventeen-years-old, she was the only one to have been born in Australia, and though there was barely more than eighteen months separating her in age from Agape, who had been a baby when her family moved to Sydney, the mere fact of being Australian seemed to have wrought some sort of change in Fotini. For a start, she refused to stay at home and help her mother and sister with their washing and mending; instead, she had persuaded a cousin who owned yet another of the fish shops that seemed to power the Greek community in the city to give her a job there, and she came home in the evenings smelling of frying batter, salt dusted over her clothes, her shining hair caught up in a hairnet until she set it free with a sigh of relief as soon as she came through the front door. Although she spoke the same strange mixture of Greek, Turkish and English as the rest of the household, Halim had the impression that she did so unwillingly. Often when her parents would speak to her in Greek, she would answer defiantly in English, as if determined to make them forget the old language and embrace the new, and her Turkish was even more circumscribed than that of the boys, though her certainty of purpose was such that Halim never found it difficult to understand her when she spoke. And that was the other thing that was different about Fotini – she talked to the boys. She was never quite so daring as to enter their room – that would have been a step too far – but when the boys were in the kitchen, fumbling to put together some sort of breakfast, inky black coffee for the Greeks and bitterly strong tea for Halim and Mustafa, Fotini would sit at the table, chopping nuts and rolling pastry for the endless sweets and cakes she made to sell in the fish shop; or she would lean against the garden wall while they were having a smoke break. The boys laughed at her jokes, but Halim could tell that she made them uneasy; they liked the fact that she spoke to them, didn't hide herself away like her older sister, gave them something pretty to admire at the end of the day, but at the same time there was a pervasive sense that her behaviour was beyond the pale, and they sometimes discussed this among themselves in the evenings, in their room, settling down for the night.

"If she were my daughter…" Christos would say ominously, but surprisingly it was Mostafa who protested.

"They're different from us. Fotini was born here. It's right that she's different."

"Still," Costas said, making a rare attempt to break the silence, "I wouldn't want someone so bold as my wife."

*

Halim's search for work was not easy. Christos and Mostafa were unable to help him; Stephanos and Costas promised that they would watch for openings down at the docks, but Halim saw them eyeing his slight stature and skinny arms with uncertainty, and seeing the size of the two of them, and how tired they were every night when they came home, covered in sweat and bruises and cuts on their hands, despite his insistence that he would manage, he doubted that he would last more than a day even if they found him a job. He spent his days going from factory to factory and from shop to shop, but despite trying to cram as many English words as possible into his head every day, his language abilities were limited, as were his contacts, and he came home each night unsuccessful. Yiannis and Maria asked their assortment of shop-owning friends and relatives, all of whom seemed sympathetic to Halim's situation, but all seemed to have a long lists of brothers, brothers-in-law, cousins and nephews whose needs for work were more pressing than Halim's. Meanwhile, he couldn't help but notice Mostafa's clothes, which were finer than those of the rest of the boys, and his plump, self-satisfied air as the preparations for his wedding moved on and his business started to burgeon, and noticing these things, he started listening a little more carefully and sitting up a little straighter whenever Mostafa mentioned his time back in Cottier's Creek and the work that he had done in the mines. It didn't sound like a lot of fun, but then he'd never expected a job to be fun, and any job that brought the sorts of rewards that Mostafa was obviously enjoying had a great deal to recommend it.

In the end, it was Fotini who decided it, coming home one evening with the smell of smoke and vinegar on her skin, her eyes bright and eager, to find Halim slumped at the kitchen table, staring disconsolately into his tea. They had barely spoken to one another directly before, Mostafa and Christos taking the bulk of the banter with Fotini, but she always seemed to pay sharp attention to what was going on, and often seemed to know more about Halim's unsuccessful job search than he did himself.

"No luck today?" she asked that evening, settling the kettle on the stove and sitting down opposite him, elbows on the table, propping her face in her hand, looking at him intently. He found it difficult – he wasn't used to such things – but he forced himself to look her in the eye.

"Not today, no. Nobody wants someone fresh off the boat in the factories. They say my English isn't good enough to work in a shop, and I don't blame them. I'm starting to think that the colliery is going to be my only option."

Fotini shook her head vehemently. "No, no! You mustn't. Jack, one of the blokes who used to come into the shop, he died there last year. Too many accidents there, always, and the pay is so bad. I don't know why anyone puts up with it."

"Because they have to," Halim snapped, a little bitterly. "Your family has been kind enough to let me stay here cheaply, but my money's running out and I can't stay here forever. I didn't come to Australia to spend the rest of my life sharing a bedroom with three men from Smyrna. I need to make some money of my own, somehow."

"You've barely been here a month –"

"It's been six weeks now, and that's enough. That's more than enough." Since Halim was a child. he had never been idle for this long, first the lengthy boat journey and now these days of searching fruitlessly for work, and it was weighing on him heavily, chipping away at his idea of himself. "Anyway," he added, looking up at Fotini, "you of all people should understand. You choose to work outside of the house. You know how important it is."

Fotini laughed. "My parents say that I will never marry a Greek man now. No one will want a girl who's worked in a shop."

"And what do you tell them?"

"I tell them that I don't care. I'm Australian, anyway – why do I need to marry a Greek? Greek men are more than happy to marry Australian women, and I could do the same. Someone fresh of the boat from Smyrna, or one of the Kytherans in Redfern – he'd be just as different from me as an Australian. At least with an Irish man or something we'd have religion in common, although my parents would probably collapse and die if I married a Catholic!" She laughed again, and Halim joined her, not entirely sure what they were laughing about, but her cheer was infectious. He could already feel his spirits lift a touch, as if she was tugging them up with one of her long-fingered hands.

"Do you have to stay in Sydney, anyway?" she asked after a while, pouring him another cup of tea. The boiling water sloshed over the edge of the cup and onto the bleached wood of the table as Halim pulled his hands back to avoid a scalding, and she grinned and apologised.

"Well, no. But I don't know anyone anywhere else. I'm having a hard enough time getting a job here, and I have Christos and Stephanos and Costas and Mostafa helping me, and all their families, so how would I get on anywhere else?"

"Haven't you been thinking about what Mostafa did? Going out to Cottier's Creek and working in the mines?" And as soon as she said it, it became a real, tangible option, crystallising out of the shimmering, half-imagined impossibility that it had been hitherto. He shrugged.

"I've thought about it…"

"Mostafa was saying that your friend – the friend who died – he has a cousin who was out there. Maybe he could help you get a job."

"Maybe. It seems a bit of a risk, though. I don't even know if this man that Mostafa knew is Irfan's cousin, and whether he'd help me even if he was… and he's a hawker, anyway, nothing to do with the mines."

"Still," Fotini said, cocking her head to one side, eyes bright as a bird's, "it's worth a try, isn't it? We could all help you with the train fare. You could pay us back once you've mined enough silver to make yourself a rich man. And if it didn't work out, you could always come back, couldn't you? No harm done." She smiled, a smile that was swift and melting. "I could write to you, couldn't I?"

Chapter Six

The train was as unfamiliar as the boat had been, clanking and puffing, a thread of metal pushing its way through the countryside. It left on a Sunday, allowing them all to come to see him off, Christos, Stephanos, Costas, Mostafa, even Yiannis and Maria. Fotini had insisted on coming as well, as the train was departing before the start of her shift, and her banner of glossy hair attracted looks, both admiring and disconcerted, from the crowds on the platform. Just as she had said, they had clubbed together to buy his ticket. He had promised, again and again, that he would send back the money as soon as he was able, but Halim could tell that they were humouring him even as they agreed. "There's something about you," Stephanos had said, with a mixture of wonder and envy, "something that makes people just want to help you out." Halim wasn't sure what that thing was, whether it was some sort of benign helplessness in the face of the world, and in many ways he wished himself rid of it, wished he could be large and imposing, blankly unbothered by life, in the way that Stephanos and Christos were. But, still, he supposed this quality had its uses.

Maria and Katerina had packed him food, a massive hamper that was unwieldy to carry, more food than he could possibly eat, borek and leblebi and halva; and with it swung over his arm, Halim felt somehow emasculated, childlike and proud all at once. Though neither Maria nor Katerina were his mother, they nevertheless had that motherly quality of caring for his well-being more than they did for his delicate, young man's pride, and he managed to ignore the amused glances of Christos and Stephanos – not to mention the other, burlier young men on the platform – as the women fussed and clucked around him, bathed in the steam from the engine, ensuring that he was clean and tidy and had everything that he needed. Fotini stood back from this too; she had already given him a large paper bag of baklava, transparent with grease, that she had taken – legitimately or not – from the shop where she worked. The thought of all that sugar made his stomach tip slightly, though he knew that he'd be grateful of it during the journey.

A whistle blew, and there was a commotion on the platform, knots of people unravelling, some withdrawing, some retreating onto the train. Halim leapt for the doors himself, went to his compartment and pushed his way to the window, to wave at the people cluttering the platform below. He was surprised to see Maria weeping into a handkerchief and realised, dimly, that despite the comfort of Yiannis and her two girls, she was far away from home too, and that she may have become as fond of him as he had become of her. The train hissed and began its inexorable backwards slide, and then suddenly there was Fotini, right below the window, hands upraised, eyes wide. "Take this!" she gasped, and thrust a small parcel, wrapped in a handkerchief, into his hands. Halim had nothing more than an infinitesimal impression of a cool, dry palm, work-roughened, before she dropped back, arms lowered, head on one side, watching him leave.

The train moved slowly, burrowing through the ramshackle outer suburbs of Sydney, houses being thrown up out of the ground like weeds, train tracks in the long grass like silvery spider webs, and he found himself surprisingly pleased to be leaving. The city had been harsh to him, a beast on his back, and when, at the end of October, the Ottoman Empire had declared war on Britain and its allies, Halim had sensed a growing unease among his Christian friends. Without him in their midst, they could claim to be as Greek as the Kytherans or Ithacans, but with Halim came a risk of being seen as the enemy, and he hoped that a country town, less frantic and desperate to prove itself than Sydney was, would be more forgiving.

The city opened out to a yawning plain, all the colours muted, dry, dusty grass that rustled like paper, trees that seemed more solitary and solid than the trees Halim had seen back home, white trunks, bark peeling like skin after a burn, leaves hanging down like rattling fringes. Then, in the distance, mountains – nothing like the mountains that Halim had heard about at home, with their dramatic grandeur, perilous peaks, forests caught between their limestone folds – but impressive in their way, too, the gentle incline giving way to mile upon mile of nothing but trees, blue-green towards the horizon, like an inland ocean, and the sound was like an ocean too, as an invisible wind tossed those millions of leaves. The day was warm, the window in the carriage was open, and the smell that the breeze brought in was sweet and tangy, honey and mint. The train swayed, the wind hushed the clatter of the wheels on the tracks, the sky turned a deep, mournful blue, streaked blood red in the west, the stars blooming one by one. Halim slept.

His sleep was light and easily disturbed by the murmuring of the other passengers, the clink of the drinks trolley mixing with the bright, vivid images of his dreams, but still he slept as the afternoon gave way into evening and night, the tension of the last few weeks rising off him like steam. It was many hours before he woke properly, the sun having looped below the horizon behind him and then risen again, its rays striking him in the face, lighting the inside of his head warm red. When he opened his eyes, raising his hand to shield them against the glare, he saw that the landscape had changed again. Now it was dry and dusty, the ground baked hard, flinging the early sun's heat back towards the sky, trees standing against the gathering light like skeletons. He had no idea where he was, and turned to the man next to him, a gruff, elderly man who seemed kind and had exchanged a couple of smiles with him when the train was first sliding out of Central Station. "Cottier's Creek?" Halim asked, tentative, and the man nodded.

"Three more hours," he said and, with clumsy kindness, wanting to ensure that Halim understood, he pulled his watch out of his pocket, pointing with a blunt, ragged finger to the eight.

By the time the train pulled in to Cottier's Creek, the sun was high and bold in the sky again, and the station was nearly as chaotic as Central Station had been back in Sydney, people running to and fro, trunks being hoisted onto the platform, people clutching other people in tearful greeting and farewell – the only difference being that this time there was no one there for Halim. He hadn't expected anyone, of course, but still, it made him feel a little emptier inside, his body trying to fold in on itself. As he stood on the platform, he noticed that even the men who had been travelling alone seemed to know where they were going, striding off alone in all directions, while he stood by his suitcase and his ludicrously oversized hamper of food (of which he'd eaten next to nothing, wary of the train's sway following his prolonged experience with seasickness), waiting for the crush to die down, for a bit of quiet and space with which to get his bearings. Though of course all that happened then was that he was alone, with no better idea of where he should be heading.

"They call it the Ghan Town," Mostafa had explained to him back in Sydney. "It's on the edges of the town, where the Afghans live. They're camel drovers out there, see. Yes, I know – " Halim had tried to interrupt – "but Arab, Persian, Afghan – it's all the same to them. Dark-skinned and Muslim. They don't make problems for us, the Australians, but they're not very interested in the history of where we all come from."

The Ghan Town, Halim reasoned, was where Irfan's cousin was most likely to be, if he was there at all – and if he wasn't, the Ghan Town would be where he would be most likely to find someone who would understand him – someone who spoke his language, or even a fellow Muslim would do. His Arabic was virtually non-existent, but he had a vague, muddled idea that Allah would take care of things, providing some sort of warm fellow-feeling between displaced, misplaced Muslim brothers. But he didn't know where the Ghan Town was or in which direction he should walk.

It was the man from the train who helped him in the end. It seemed that he'd met an acquaintance at the station and stayed to talk for a while, and by the time he was ready to leave, there was only Halim left, alone, scanning the horizon for a clue to where he should go.

"You Afghan?"

Halim knew he should just say yes; the man's intentions were obviously good, and it would be easier to claim to be Afghan than trying to explain his origins, but he couldn't help his natural truthfulness and his battered sense of pride in where he had come from.

"No, not Afghan. Speaking Turkish. Ottoman. You know?"

The man with the beard looked relieved. "Turk? Wait here."

Halim didn't understand his words – the man's accent was thick, and much of what he said was swallowed immediately by his beard – but he understood his gestures, hands out flat in front of him, urging Halim to stay put, and so he stayed while the man vanished out of sight. It occurred to him that perhaps he shouldn't be so quick to trust this man, whom he had met only hours ago on the train and exchanged fewer than ten words with, but he had no better bets in this town, and so he stayed.

The man with the beard had been gone for ten minutes, and Halim had nearly given up. He sat slumped on his suitcase, nibbling on one of the pieces of baklava that Fotini had given to him, contemplating just striking out in a random direction and hoping for the best. But then there was the sound of footsteps, not one set but two, and around the corner came a dark-skinned man in his fifties, short and round, wearing a short-sleeved checked shirt and looking damp and flustered.

"You speak Turkish?" the man asked, speaking fluent, if unfamiliarly accented Turkish himself, and Halim felt his heart soar up inside his chest as he rose to his feet, smiling irrepressibly.

"Yes! Yes, I'm Halim. From near Safranbolu."

"Süleyman," the man said, smiling too, but more cautiously. "You've just arrived?"

"Yes, just in from Sydney. And I only arrived in Australia a few weeks ago."

Süleyman's smile grew broader. "Well. Welcome. I'll be pleased to have another Turkish speaker around."

Chapter Seven

Süleyman, it turned out, was an ice cream seller, with his own pony and trap, and he easily loaded Halim's cases onto the back of it, taking him clopping through the town, the horse's hooves throwing up dust, the wheels singing in the sand. He took Halim back to his small clapboard shack, on the edge of the Ghan Town, alive in the morning light, sheets flapping and lanterns flickering under the still-visible sliver of the moon.

"I lived there when I first arrived in town, years ago," Süleyman explained, "at first in a tent, and then in a humpy – a bark house, you know – but when I got some money together I wanted to build my own place. Some people thought I would move into the town, but I wanted to stay close to my friends out here."

"It's a nice place," Halim said politely. It wasn't *not* nice, it was just that it had the unmistakeable stamp of the bachelor, a strong emphasis on the functional and the good-enough. All attempts to beautify it – like the dusty chintz curtains at the window, and the scrap of checked cloth that served as a tablecloth – seemed tacked-on and half-hearted.

"Well, it suits me."

Opening a trunk, Süleyman brought out an armful of blankets and folded them, piling them on the floor in the corner of the living room thickly enough to form a comfortable bed.

"You can stay here for a while. Until you find your feet."

"You're very kind."

Süleyman shook his head. "It's my duty. And besides, it's no

49

trouble. It will be nice to speak in Turkish again."

Halim smiled at this. He had never really thought, before he'd left his village, about the importance of language, and he was fortunate enough to be able to pick up new languages quickly, so communication was becoming less and less of a problem – and yet something inside him had relaxed the moment he'd heard Süleyman speaking with such ease the language they'd both grown up with. It had given them an immediate familiarity that stretched across the gulf in age, experience and background that should have been between them, and Süleyman evidently felt much the same way.

"Does no one else speak Turkish here?"

"Not for a few months. They're almost all Arabs here, but decent men – those old divisions don't matter so much here when we've got religion in common.Why, were you expecting to meet someone?"

"My friend's cousin, Kemal. I was told that he might be here."

"Ah, I know Kemal. He was here quite recently, then he moved on. Went north, I think. The hawkers never stay for long, it's part of their job. I've heard that there's good money in it – Kemal used to talk about sending a lot of money back home – but it's not a life that suits everyone. I like to put down roots; all that wandering's not for me."

"I was hoping that he could help me find a job, perhaps working with him, or in the mines."

Süleyman shrugged. "You'd be lucky. Hawkers' licenses are damned hard to come by these days, unless you know someone who's giving it up and you're willing to pay for his old one. And the mine, it's so tied up with the union. It's easy enough to get a job if they want you to have one, but if they don't, there's no chance – and I don't mean to offend, but they tend to choose men who are a bit bigger and stronger than you are." Seeing Halim's face fall, he added swiftly, "We'll find something for you to do, don't worry. We can talk about it later. Now, you need to get some sleep – you must be tired from your journey – and I need to go out on my rounds. There's water in the pail over there so that you can wash. I'll leave you to it, and see you this evening when I'm back."

In the almost claustrophobic silence born of utter stillness, Halim washed his face in the tepid water from the pail, made wudu and, guessing at the approximate direction of Mecca, prayed with an impious haste, eager for the chance to stretch out his cramped limbs and catch a couple of hours' sleep in the approximation of a real bed. Reaching into his case for his nightshirt, his knuckles brushed against something wrapped in linen, something that fell to the floor with a dull thump, and he recognised the parcel that Fotini had thrust into his hands the morning before, which he'd tucked into his bag to keep safe, not wanting to open it in the heated crush of the train carriage, under all those curious Australian eyes. Wary, trepidatious, he unwrapped the cloth and felt the cool, smooth metal against his hand, the dusty crackle of paper. Fotini had scratched out the words in her unschooled hand, the Latin script that, though increasingly familiar, still looked strangely angular to Halim compared to the smooth loops of Arabic that he'd been taught, picking out a characteristic maelstrom of Greek, Turkish and English. Fotini's spelling was guessed-at and haphazard, but Halim caught the shadow of her speech in the shapes of her words: 'I hope you won't be offended by me giving you this, but it would make me feel better if you would accept this gift, and I trust that it will keep you safe.' And in his hands, chilly and angular, a small, standing crucifix.

*

Halim woke to the sound of cocks crowing, throwing their voices proudly to a sky that was just starting to lighten, pale threads of cloud strung over the brightest fading stars, winking through the window above Halim's head. He lay quietly for a moment, listening to the clanking and banging sounds coming from Süleyman's room next door, and the muttered imprecations of a man desperately trying to keep quiet but – Halim remembered Süleyman's big feet, his disproportionally long arms, his exuberant and grandiose clumsiness – constitutionally incapable of it. Halim levered himself upright and into his clothes in the silence born of a lifetime spent sharing rooms, and grinned at Süleyman when he finally poked his head, cautious and apologetic, around his bedroom door.

"Good morning."

"I'm sorry – did I wake you?"

Halim shrugged. "Not really. I suppose I wasn't really that tired – I slept so much during the day yesterday." He hadn't realised until he'd stretched out on the musty blankets that Süleyman had laid out for him quite how tired he had been, not from the train journey, but a bone-deep, soul-deep weariness that had built up in him during the blank, overlong days on the ship following Irfan's death, and the clutter and clatter of Sydney, the constant strain of politeness with Maria and Yiannis's extended circle of friends and family; even with Christos, Stephanos, Mostafa and Costas he had never felt himself totally at ease next to their expansive, dismissive confidence. The luxury of a room to himself – albeit a living room – and the relative quiet, after weeks of Christos's snores and Costas's sleep-talking – "talks more asleep than he does awake," Mostafa grumbled to Halim one morning – meant that Halim slept soundly that day. He had barely been able to rouse himself when Süleyman came home in the evening, beaming after a day of non-stop sales, and Süleyman had kindly refrained from pressing Halim's sleep-addled brain into any taxing conversation, but had merely boiled up some rice over the gas stove, urged Halim to eat it, and then gone outside to sit on the veranda to smoke, while Halim slept again.

"I'm sorry about yesterday," Halim said now. "I hadn't realised how tired I was until I lay down. In Sydney, I was living in a room with four other boys, and with all the worry of trying to find a job, I never slept very much."

"It's no problem. You needed it and, like I said yesterday, it's good to have you around. You're welcome to stay here until you find your feet…" He broke off suddenly, laughing at Halim's astonished face. "What is it?"

"Is that – it's – "

"The ezan, you mean? Yes, of course. Didn't it wake you yesterday? With so many Muslims here, it makes sense for us to have a mosque, a muezzin and an imam."

For a moment, the two of them sat silently at the table, Süleyman smiling at the way Halim's head was tilted, listening to the way the call to prayer unfolded like a ribbon, curling over the roofs of the tents and the huts in the dusty dawn, before nudging Halim out of his reverie. "Well, come on then," he said. "If it means so much to you…"

They prayed together in companionable silence, Halim vaguely conscious of the creaks and pops that Süleyman's body made as he bent, knelt and rose, and the unselfconscious way in which he closed his eyes and moved his lips. Praying with Mostafa had always felt full of sidelong glances; the way that Mostafa had rolled his shoulders back and the loose tilt of his hips had seemed like visual disclaimers: *don't think this means anything to me, I'm doing it because I have to, but no more than that.* – it had made Halim ashamed of his own unexamined but fervent faith, the central place of Allah in his heart and in his head and crowded around his every action. He already felt more comfortable with Süleyman, thirty years older and with his strangely-accented Turkish, a man he'd met only the day before, than with the boys that he'd known in Sydney. As the two of them rolled up their prayer mats, Halim looked out of the door to the porch which stood open to the lightening sky, and saw the flicker and bob of lights in windows, guttering through the flaps of tents, and the silhouettes of men standing, bowing and kneeling.

"I never thought that there would be so many…" Halim said to Süleyman, as he lit the gas ring with a hissing whoosh, blue flames cradling the burnished swell of the kettle bottom.

"Yes. Lots of Muslims out here. Started off with the Afghans – that's what they call this place, you know, the Australians, they call it the Ghan Town, from the Afghans – they came out here to work as camel drovers last century. Then others followed – Syrians, Indians, some Egyptians – some working on the camels, some as traders, some working in the mines, some doing whatever they could to get by. When I first came here fifteen years ago, there were people coming fresh off the boats to try their luck in the mines, but things have slowed down a lot since then, what with the White Australia rules – you know, the dictation test, designed to keep non-Europeans out, though they don't seem to know quite what to do about people like us, or some of the Syrians and Lebanese who've lived in Europe for years and years, and of course anyone who can pay a big enough bond to the immigration officers to get out of the test – and then the union took control of the mines. Bloody hard to get a job there now, unless the union like the look of you, and you, I'm afraid you won't have much of a chance, what with your English – "

"My English isn't so bad – I speak some already, and I'm learning fast!"

"I'm sure you are." Süleyman's tone was sympathetic. "But there are men who've been here months waiting for an opening, doing odd-jobs in the meantime, and every one of them speaks better English than you. And, I don't like to say it, but they look tougher than you do. Stronger. Have you ever done physical work before? It's harder than you think it is, I'm sure."

Halim looked down into the murky depths of the tea Süleyman had placed in front of him, bitter and sugar-swirled. "I know I don't look like much. Being on the ship for so long, with no exercise, it wasn't good for my strength. But I'm not weak. And I'm young, and healthy – I can learn, and build up my strength."

"Could be," Süleyman said diplomatically. "But still, it

wouldn't hurt for you to have something else that you could do, in case a job in the mines doesn't work out. I'm assuming that you don't want to head back to Sydney?"

"I can't afford it," Halim said truthfully, but there was more to it than the money; the thought of going back to Sydney and admitting to Maria and Yiannis, to Stephanos and Christos, to Fotini, that he had failed and he needed their help again was too defeating. It was intolerable. Australia had been nothing but a series of failures for him so far, but all around him he could see people who had made the country work for them. Even Süleyman, despite the flimsiness of his cottage: he had a home and a living that was nothing to be ashamed of – and at some point, Halim knew, he had to pick one thing, one place, and hold onto it until it gave him what he wanted. When he thought of Sydney, he knew with a grim certainty that he didn't want to go back, not yet, anyway. The camp, with its low tents and dust and the ezan, no matter how hoarse the muezzin's voice, or how often he stumbled over his words, was more comfortable and comforting than the hard-edged metropolis with its unfamiliar stink, the southerly wind hurtling in from the sea every afternoon, shaking the chimneys, the narrow streets like ravines, the nonsensical rattle of unfamiliar language, the vast, roaring ocean lapping at the end of every road, rushing in over hills and valleys, flinging itself at the wild, blank sky. Cottier's Creek, Halim thought – it was manageable.

"I want to stay," Halim said. "There's bound to be something that I can do here." Süleyman nodded, pleased.

"Good for you, boy. It's good to choose one place and make it work; I see too many new migrants who want everything to be perfect, and they keep moving on and moving on, looking for something they're never going to find. And besides, what with the war, you're better off out here. Less likely to be any trouble. We'll work something out for you, as long as you're willing to work hard. Tell you what, I'll take you to meet the Imam – oh yes, we've got one, he was sponsored to come out from Punjab years ago, to give the community spiritual guidance – he's bound to have some ideas."

When they walked through the camp that morning the sun had lifted itself high enough to slant over the roofs of the tents, striking the plumes of dust lifting from the ground and making them solid, beating heat out of the hard ground. Men stood outside tents and humpies, rinsing out bowls and flinging the water into the dust, squatting on their heels and exchanging morning greetings over a glass of tea, and Süleyman seemed to know them all, waving to one, clapping another on the shoulder, and once, being kissed extravagantly on the cheeks by a tall, thin man who, when introduced to Halim as Sadiq, one of Süleyman's oldest friends, grinned widely, his smile dividing his grizzled face, and kissed Halim in his turn. Occasionally, Halim caught sight of a woman; a couple of children, chasing one another and shrieking, ran across their path, but, "Mostly," Süleyman explained, "it's just the men. Some of them have families back in the cities, some even back in the old country, but most don't choose to bring them here. They don't think it's a place for them." He shrugged, inclining his head towards a nearby tent, outside which a morning game of backgammon was leading to raised voices and elaborate threats. "They're probably right."

The mosque was little grander than Süleyman's cottage, cobbled together from boards and bits of canvas and a rickety two storey attachment that served as a minaret – but there was no mistaking its intention, and the bare patch of earth outside it was scrupulously clean; even now, a boy younger than Halim was attacking it vigorously with a broom made of twigs, brushing away the dust on top of dust.

"Salaam aleikum," Süleyman said.

"Aleikum salaam," the boy responded, smiling, and, having exhausted his meagre Arabic, Süleyman switched to English, a tumble of sounds out of which Halim could only understand a few words and his own name. No matter how much his English was improving, he was easily thrown by an unfamiliar accent, and every new person he met seemed to speak it slightly differently. But the boy nodded at Süleyman's words and set off at a run, kicking up sand from his bare feet, only to reappear, moments later, with a tall, elderly, bearded man clad in a pristine dishdasha.

"Tariq, the Imam," Süleyman explained, and stepped forward to clasp his hand, as Tariq gazed at Halim with interest. A few more words in English, and then Tariq smiled widely. "Welcome," he said in English – a word that Halim could understand no matter the accent – before pulling Halim into an embrace that made tears, foolish and unbidden, spring to his eyes; he was careful to knock them away before either man could see.

The three of them sat under the canvas shade of the porch, close to the ground on low stools, sipping thick, sticky tea that the boy had brought them before returning to his enthusiastic sweeping, and smacking away the flies that tried to dip their feet into the syrupy runnels that slipped down the outside of their glasses. Halim felt warmer and safer than he had at any point since leaving his home. His friends in Sydney had been kind to him, of course they had, but there had always been a sense that they were waiting for Halim to prove himself worthy of their interest and investment in him; their pioneer spirit and determination was confident and unforgiving of failure. With Süleyman and Tariq, it was different; he felt that he could fit into this community, find some way to serve it, and that it would close itself around him, taking care of him.

Süleyman was deep in conversation with Tariq, and Halim had all but forgotten the purpose of the visit and was lazily drawing shapes in the sand with his toe, when Süleyman turned to him and switched back to Turkish.

"I've been explaining your situation," he said. "How you came here for the mine, and he agrees that that's not likely to work out. Unfortunately."

The Imam nodded in friendly incomprehension, sensing that it was expected of him, and Süleyman went on: "It's not the end of the world, though. There are many things that you can do here. The question is finding the best fit for you. What would be easiest, I know, would be to take you on to work with me, making and selling ice cream, but there's not enough work for two. Barely enough for one, some of the time. There will be times when I would be glad of your help, especially in summer, but you'll need something else to do. Now, what did you do back home?"

Halim shrugged. "The same as everyone else. I helped with the herds – goats and sheep. I can shear," he added hopefully, and Süleyman translated for Tariq's benefit, who nodded thoughtfully.

"That will be useful at some times of the year," Süleyman explained, "but not all the time. I suppose you could try and get work as a farmhand – there are certainly enough farms around here – but again, there are many men who want that kind of work. It's not so easy to get." Halim appreciated the lack of mention of his puniness, but he knew both men were thinking it. "Now look, what else can you do?"

"I was apprenticed to my uncle for some time – he was a butcher." Halim began to explain, but was cut off by the instant interest that flared in Süleyman's eyes.

"A butcher?"

"Yes, but – " He couldn't finish; already Süleyman was explaining to Tariq, and the same excitement that had been evident in Süleyman had jumped to Tariq like a bushfire.

"Listen," Süleyman said at last, "you know how to cut halal meat?"

"Yes, but – "

"But nothing! Halim, this is wonderful! There hasn't been a halal butcher here since Sadiq's uncle died nearly two years ago!" Tariq was also smiling with evident enthusiasm. "Those who are devout haven't touched any meat in all that time. Those of us who are less devout..." He grinned, and cut his eyes towards Tariq. "Well, I'm not so religious that I'd happily go without meat just because it hasn't been killed the right way. But I'd be a lot happier – everyone here would be – if we could buy halal meat again. People try and do it themselves, but they all know that they're not doing it as well as someone who's been trained. Of all the things that you could do for the community here, that would be the best."

Halim flushed, suddenly unhappy. As the youngest boy in his family, he'd been the obvious one to be sent to be apprenticed by his uncle, who was cursed with four daughters and had no one to take over the family business, and as much as he'd tried to hold his head high and be proud of having a job that differentiated him from the rest of the village, he'd hated it, every second of it – the cries that the goats and sheep made when led to the slaughter, as if they knew what was coming, and he knew they did; the tough, slimy feel of the cold meat under his hands; the abattoir-stink; the ache in his muscles after a long day doing battle with dead things. In private he'd begged his father not to make him do it. "Why me?" he had asked, even though he knew the answer. It was the same reason for all the unpleasant things that had ever been foisted upon him – because he was the youngest. He'd hated it so much that he'd stopped eating meat himself, unable to think of the mutton he held in his mouth without thinking of the shrieking desperation of the sheep that he'd cut it from, and he'd been passionately, pathetically glad when his cousin Döndü had married a man who showed a far keener interest in taking over the family business than Halim ever did.

"I hated it," he said at last to Süleyman. "I didn't come all this way to go back to that."

Süleyman sighed. "And you didn't come all this way to end up homeless and penniless either, did you?" he asked; a question for which Halim had no answer.

Chapter Eight

"You don't have to decide straight away," Süleyman said when they got back to his house, with Halim still indecisive and downcast. "I told Tariq not to mention it to anyone else. Don't want to get their hopes up, don't want them putting pressure on you."

Süleyman was trying to be kind, Halim knew, but he also knew that Süleyman was baffled by his behaviour. Meat was meat, as far as he was concerned; you eat it, you should be prepared to kill it and cut it up, and he'd be quite happy to do it himself if only he knew how. Süleyman was the sort of man whose open-handed, bare-faced honesty didn't allow for any sort of self-deceit, or any sort of squeamishness, which he counted as the same thing. He made excuses for Halim's youth, but these would only stretch so far before he started to lose patience.

"It's just..." Halim began, seeing it was time to start vocalising the conversation that he'd been having in his head. "It's just that, I thought it'd be different here. When I left my village, I thought I would get away from having to do things that I didn't want to – I was the youngest, always having to do the things that no one else would. I thought that leaving home, going so far away – I thought that I'd have more freedom. That I'd only have to do things that I wanted to do."

"It's impossible to go that far away," Süleyman said. He couldn't help a grin at Halim's naiveté, but he hid it as well as he could. "That's life, son, doing things that you don't want to, just so that you can get by. Do you think that most of the men here like going down the mines for hours and hours a day?"

"But I would – "

"You try it for a week, and then you'd see. It's not some sort of idealised man's man's world. It's hard work, exhausting and dangerous. You know how many men die down there every year?" Halim shook his head, wide-eyed. "Well, I don't know exactly, either, but it's a lot." Changing tack abruptly, he went on: "Look. Let me tell you something. I'm not planning to be here much longer."

"What do you mean?"

"I've been here nearly fifteen years now. Never planned to stay. I'm from Crete, did I tell you that? I'm a Muslim, of course, but that's where I grew up. I left after the massacres in 1898, and I went to Smyrna for while – should have stayed, maybe – but I couldn't settle, travelled around, finally got passage on a ship that was bringing some camels and drovers out here, and I tagged along, even though I know nothing about camels and like them even less. Horrible, filthy, bad-tempered beasts, they are. When the killings started... well, I just wanted to get as far away as possible."

Halim didn't know what to say, but Süleyman didn't seem to expect any sort of response.

"It was fine at first, and I was glad to start again, but after a while you start to realise that, no matter how decent people are, there's nothing like your own people. So for the past few years I've been saving my money, planning to go back. I've got nearly enough now, enough for the boat, and enough to set up a house and a small business, near my sister, outside Denizli. I just want to be sure that I have enough not to have to struggle when I go, and so I just need to have another good year here, maybe two, and then I'm leaving."

Halim nodded. Süleyman's Spartan living conditions made a little more sense now, and he was impressed at the man's dedication and restraint; the idea of having savings was so alien to Halim that he couldn't imagine not wanting to spend them straight away, or to send them home so that everyone would know how successful he had become.

"But – "

"So what I'm saying is this. When the time comes for me to go, I'll want someone to take over my business. It's a good business; it's served me well, it's easy to learn and it makes good money. And if you were prepared to stay out here, do the butchery for the Muslims in the Ghan Town, I could teach you what you need to know, and you'd be ready to take over by the time I leave. And, meanwhile, if you really don't fancy the butchery lark as a long-term job, you could find someone else in the camp and teach it to him. Pass the skills along. I bet Hafiz – the boy who was sweeping outside the Mosque today – he'd be keen on learning the business. You being the butcher wouldn't have to be anything more than temporary. Now, what do you say?"

Halim didn't know what to think. The idea of returning to butchery still made his gorge rise and his shoulders slump, but then the prospect of his own business at the end of it – long before he would manage to earn enough to set up on his own – it was unimaginably appealing. He thought, briefly, of how it would feel to tell them back in Sydney, tell them that he'd set up on his own, he had his own ice cream business and his own house, and that he'd done it on his own, too, without having to be helped by a convenient father-in-law, like Christos. And he thought, then, of being able to write a letter home to his mother, to tell the village that Halim who had fled with Irfan, Halim, who had always been dismissed, overlooked, with kindness, yes, but still seen as irrelevant, Halim whom the village would have long given up as lost, had made himself a success in Australia. The idea was intoxicating.

"Anyway," Süleyman continued, before Halim had marshalled his thoughts enough to be able to answer, "give it some thought. Meanwhile, I've got to pick up some milk from the Bells' farm. Would you like to come with me and give me a hand?"

*

That was the shape of Halim's first week in Cottier's Creek. Up at dawn, he prayed with Süleyman and then followed him for the rest of the day, helping him with the things that needed to be done – collecting supplies of milk and sugar, turning the great churn to make the ice cream, and helping him sell it in the town. This was always the part of the day that he liked the best, clip-clopping through the wide, shady streets, lined with brick buildings that told of the town's newfound prosperity, on the back of Süleyman's cart, scooping ice cream from the cart into cones in great sticky hunks, taking the money from the customers, handing the ice cream to the children who clamoured for it, soft white hands reaching. He would never quite dare to take the money from adults, especially the women, but Süleyman was so at ease with the townspeople that he never had to. Just spending time in the company of English speakers meant that Halim was picking up more and more of the language, but the cadence of Süleyman's speech in the conversations he had with his customers told him more about the cordial relations that they shared than any of the individual words he managed to decipher.

People varied, of course. Süleyman would point out the women who gripped the arms of their children a little tighter as they passed the cart, ignoring their imploring looks. "Not everyone in this town wants to buy from us," Süleyman said in explanation; his tone was light but he wouldn't meet Halim's eyes. "Sometimes the children will come on their own, but their mothers tell them to keep away." But with others, relations were relaxed and even friendly: the young men who were on their way to the pub after a long day's work, and who'd punch Süleyman chummily on the arm, trying to cajole him into giving them a larger scoop of ice cream than usual; some of the younger mothers, who pressed coins into the hands of their children and urged them forward to lisp out their requests and carefully count out the change. One of the latter, Süleyman told Halim, was Maggie, who would come past the cart every day. In her late twenties, freckled, with her face usually split with a slightly wicked grin, she lived in one of the larger houses towards the end of town, and every time Süleyman would drive his cart by, she would come running down the path with a sort of sloppy, ramshackle grace, a baby tucked into one arm and Peter, her three-year-old boy bouncing on her other hip. Peter would stretch out his sticky fist shyly, exposing the bright coin in the centre of it, and it would be left to Halim to scoop out the ice cream for him, placing it carefully in his little hand, responding with "You're welcome," to Peter's carefully schooled, "Thank you".

Maggie and Süleyman always talked for a while, she leaning her hip against his cart, absently jogging the baby, Mary, up and down, though always careful to keep her in the shade. She'd tried to talk to Halim, too, the first time they'd been introduced, but realising from his downcast eyes and shy smiles that he understood little of what she said in her sharp, flinty accent, she now limited herself to grinning at him every so often while in full flood of her conversation with Süleyman, and sometimes taking Mary's pale, starfish hand in her own and making the baby wave.

"She's bored, and she's lonely," Süleyman explained after the second time this had happened. "She came to the town a few years ago, to teach in the primary school – she's Irish, from a big Catholic family in Sydney, and you know what that means – well, maybe you don't. But it means that the same people who don't like buying from us don't like her, either."

"Even though they're all Christian?" Halim asked, and Süleyman nodded grimly.

"Even though. But she got lucky – she fell in love with Charlie McGill, and he with her – you know, from the McGill farm I told you about it, the one that's the closest to the centre of town, where Sadiq sometimes works. Well, she had to give up her work when they were married, of course, especially when Peter came along, but Charlie's rarely home these days – he's always working out in the paddocks with his father and brothers, or going off to Sydney, Melbourne and Adelaide to sell things from the farm – and she has nothing much to do. She has nurses for the children and she's not the type to want to sit around embroidering all day. It's too quiet a life for a woman like her."

Meanwhile, as he accompanied Süleyman while he was working, Halim kept the thought of butchery in the back of his mind, and he was surprised to find it growing on him. The thought of the process itself still didn't fill him with delight. He wasn't sure if he could ever quite get over his natural antipathy towards blood and flesh and dead meat, but he had come to realise that perhaps being a butcher on his own in the camps, somewhere where people would be grateful for his services, and where he could work for himself, not constantly under the critical eye of his uncle, who was always ready with a cuff around the head if Halim made the slightest mistake... perhaps it would be different, and perhaps it would be something that he could do willingly, if not quite happily. It wasn't in his nature to capitulate immediately, though. He forced himself to go town to the mine once and then twice, when the bell was squalling its insistent demand for change of shift, but nerves had the effect of robbing his mind of its carefully-learnt English. As Süleyman had predicted, the few stuttering words of English he managed to produce got him nowhere, and he went away suffused with embarrassment and empty-handed.

The second time he went, it was near dusk. Still smarting with angry shame at the way the forman - twice his size, with arms as big around as Halim's waist - had raised his eyebrows and laughed when Halim, his carefully learned introduction forgotten, had stammered, "Please...work...", Halim decided to walk for a bit through the town before returning to Süleyman's.

Evening heat was rising off the streets like mist, the warm sound of voices was uncoiling around the pairs and groups of people taking the evening air, and the occasional cascade of laughter and shouting burst out when the door to the pub banged open and one of the men stumbled his way down the steps and onto the street. Something in the quality of the air, the heavy purple twilight which lay on his shoulders like a mantle, was enough to calm Halim down, and he felt the last remnants of his shame trickling out through the soles of his shoes. *So what?* he thought. *So what if they don't want me in the mine?* And the idea of working for himself blossomed and ballooned within him as he thought of the smug grins he could give to the Ghan Town men who worked in the mines, trotting down to the pit at the claxon's squall, as obedient as dogs to a whistle, while he didn't have to move for anyone but himself. He would do it, he decided, the decision having sneaked up on him throughout the week. He would go to Tariq tomorrow and tell him that he would be the butcher for the Ghan Town, and that would be it. He wouldn't have to jostle and fight for prestige and recognition, for a role was there, ready and waiting for him to step into it and wrap it around himself. He had a smile on his face without realising it, a smile that was contagious and spread to the faces of the people who passed him, and his smile widened when he caught the eye of two of the young men who he recognised from the ice cream stall, and one of them nodded his head and grinned: "G'day".

Up ahead on the other side of the road he spotted a familiar stance, Maggie's hip-tilted lean, in full conversational flow with one of her friends, the silhouette of Mary in the crook of her arm, Peter's shadow squatting in the dust beside her, playing with a ball that he was pushing back and forth from hand to hand. As he approached them, Halim watched as Peter leant further and further, following the trajectory of his ball... and Halim's smile dropped from his face as he realised that the drumming noise he could hear was the sound of a buggy coming around the bend at quite a clip, and in perfect, inexorable timing, just as the pair of horses came into view, Peter gave his ball such a punt that he had to trot into the middle of the road to retrieve it. Halim saw Maggie's eyes widen as she realised what was going on. Her chest hitched as she shouted Peter's name, and she thrust Mary, unthinking, towards the woman she'd been talking to. Halim saw Peter look up, all trusting, towards his mother's voice, start back towards her, then turn to collect his forgotten ball. Then Halim ran, faster than he could remember ever running before, out into the road, sand scuffing, Peter's warm body curling under his arm, the crashing roar of the horses, screams from some of the women by the side of the road and a stream of words from the man driving the trap, none of which Halim could understand, but which he doubted were complimentary. And then he was sat on his heels, Peter shouting and squirming by his side, safely by the side of the road. He was breathing so hard he felt his lungs would crack.

Maggie bent before him, coaxing Peter away from his grasp, her eyes round and wet, crying, "Thank you, oh my God, thank you, oh my God," over and over again. Halim knew that he should tell her that she was welcome and walk nonchalantly away – that was the sort of thing that the man he aspired to be would do – but his legs were liquid beneath him, and he doubted he had enough breath left in his body to get to his feet, even if he felt that they would support him, so he just smiled vaguely in Maggie's direction and put his head down on his knees to regain his composure. Something cool nudged his cheek – a glass of water, brought out from the nearby pub; then a man was holding out his hand to shake; the driver of the trap, he saw, looking contrite, mumbling apologies that Halim couldn't hear, though their intention was clear enough, and then Maggie was back again. Peter wriggling in her arms, as whole and alive as ever, had helped her regain her composure. Her broad grin was back in place, and she extended a hand to help Halim rise.

April 24th, 1915

Patrick had heard the news, of course, but he didn't really know what it meant. The greatest combined naval and military operation in history, they were saying it would be, but that didn't mean anything to him. Maggie would always tell him, in frustration and amusement, that nothing went into his head unless he could see it, hear it, or touch it, and it was true: not until his boots hit the sand on the beach and he was in the thick of it would he be able to understand. The Major had spoken to them earlier, full of jokey warmth, clearly trying to keep their spirits up, but Patrick's spirits felt unquenchable, and he longed for more information, anything about what was waiting for them tomorrow. Bloody Turnbull had started up again on his harmonica, *Nearer my God to Thee* for the umpteenth time, and Patrick walked away, turning his back on the bloody sunset, to fill his mess tin with more bully beef and water for the morning.

Chapter Nine

Maggie grew up dreaming about escape.

She considered herself to be the first real Australian in her family. Her parents had migrated, separately, from Kerry and Cork in the 1870s: her mother aged fifteen, her parents dead and in the care of her three older brothers; her father at nineteen, alone and brave-faced – or at least that was the way he always painted himself in the stories he told the children in the evening, usually when he had a few glasses of his home-made poteen inside him. He told them that he'd come to Australia to get away from Ireland, the cold and the rain, the poverty and the desperation, and seek his fortune in this sun-browned land. Yet Maggie started to wonder, once she got old enough to think about these things, if that was the case, then why did he never stop looking back? It was as if both of her parents, unwilling pioneers, had arrived in Australia and immediately, deliberately, turned their backs on its vastness, clinging to the edge of the country as if they would take the first opportunity to leave it. In the rabbit warren of inner Sydney, the dank, dripping streets, steamy heat and the omnipresent ocean, the only people they associated with were the other exiled Irish, of whom there was no shortage, and some of Maggie's earliest memories were of trying to fall asleep in the bed that she shared with her three sisters, squirming this way and that to avoid an elbow in the face, or a knee in the kidneys, the door half open to the glow of the gas lamps, and the sounds of drunken singing coming through – songs about place she'd never visited, but which loomed large in her imagination, the Mountains of Mourne, mist-soaked and grandiose, dropping into a frothy ocean; the fields of Athenry, lush, green and vivid with flowers.

It wasn't until she started school that she realised the position of Australia relative to the position of Ireland, which until that point she'd assumed to be a day's trip away, as if Australia was some sort of detached, floating county, perhaps a little way south of Cork. She hadn't believed the teacher at first, and had argued with her until she'd earned a quick, light strike with the cane on her pink, plump hand, which had been more painful for the blow to her pride than for its actual sting. When she came home that day, her father had reacted with rage towards the teacher who dared to strike his daughter, but after a few days the story became family currency, trotted out at regular intervals as proof of Maggie's naivety and stubbornness. The caning convinced her, though. Many times during the following days she would find herself gazing avidly at the map that hung in her classroom, trying to work out the exact distance between her current location and the places that her parents spoke of with such gluttonous nostalgia, imagining their past lives and their journey to Australia in their separate, rickety vessels, clinging tenaciously to the curve of the world.

The exile mentality seemed to seep through the food and drink of the family, infecting Maggie's three older sisters and two older brothers, all of whom identified themselves resolutely as Irish, not Australian, and who laid claim to the same misplaced melancholy as their parents. Their social circles were confined by choice to the children of their parents' admittedly extended Irish expatriate network. When the oldest sister, Mary, became engaged to Seamus Hannigan, they spoke with no trace of irony of bringing forth another generation of Irish children. Maggie was bright, logical and ever aware of potential contradiction, so she couldn't help pointing out, whenever voices were raised to lament their separation from Dublin or Galway, that none of her brothers or sisters had even set foot in

Ireland, let alone had any real claim on Irishness.

"You wouldn't understand," said Dolores, the second eldest. "It doesn't matter where you were born. It's about – it's about the way you think, the things that you enjoy, the people you know." And in that moment, Maggie made up her mind that, from that moment on, she was resolutely Australian.

She did her best to pass this idea on to her younger brother, the only one who came after her, whispering denials in his ear whenever any family member started waxing lyrical about the old country in their presence, showing him the map and trying to make him understand, at a far younger age than she had been, where they had come from and where they were.

"Ireland's in the past," she told him, again and again. "Australia's where we are now." He always nodded, looking sober and attentive. She was never certain how much of her lectures actually penetrated his mind, but, as she got older, she hoped that at some point the things that she said would provide a sort of ballast to counter the hyperbolic imaginations of the rest of the family, conjuring forth images of a lost Eden when she knew that all they'd really left behind was famine and hardship.

She was never sure what it was that had triggered rebellion in her – perhaps it was something to do with being the youngest girl, the least regarded member of the family – for at least Patrick, young as he was, was a boy, hardy and longed-for, designed to leave the family home and achieve, unlike the girls, who were bound to be parasites until they were of an age to marry. Maggie was constantly trying to work out a means by which to fight her way out from under the weight of expectation and friendly neglect that were the hallmarks of family life, but it took some time until she could work out the way to do this. The two paths that had always been shown to her, as a girl, were marriage and motherhood, or the church – the third option, spinsterhood, a lifetime spent caring for her parents as they aged, and then eking out some sort of paper-thin living once they'd died that left her penniless and purposeless was one that she intended to avoid at all costs. She considered marriage for a while, as a girl of nine or ten, the idea of a man to come and take her away from that overcrowded, noisy house – but then Mary married. The family went to visit her marital home and Maggie found it little different from the one that she'd left – a room of their own, yes, but that room was attached to Seamus's family house, teeming with brothers and sisters and cousins, the noise constant and unabating, far from the calm and quiet sanctuary that Maggie had dreamt of.

The church, then: she knew that that, at least, would be quiet, and for two years, aged ten to twelve, she fabricated a passionate religious devotion, going to Mass six days a week, her knees bright pink and polished as a mark of her piety, announcing her vocation so long and so loudly that even she almost believed it. Her family never knew quite how to react to this. Having a nun as a daughter and sister had been something that had never quite occurred to them, and, to be honest, it struck most of them as somehow strange and aberrant, but none of them could have openly admitted this, and so they warily admired Maggie's outward demonstrations of faith, barely wrinkling their noses at the scent of incense and candle wax that trailed from her whenever she entered a room, impregnated into the warp and weft of her clothing, the very follicles of her hair.

When she was twelve, she changed schools and, with it, her entire outlook. All the teachers that she had had before had either been men and therefore impossible to aspire to, or the sort of ancient, dried out old woman that seemed so different to Maggie that they were virtually another species. At high school, though, there was Miss Nolan – in her twenties (not young by Maggie's twelve-year-old standards, but young enough to be familiar), a long plait of heavy dark hair, a lazy grin and the sort of quick mind that Maggie most admired. It had never occurred to her that teachers could be anything but male or ancient, that they could be anything she herself would aspired to be, but that first day in Miss Nolan's classroom she sat erect and mesmerised at her scarred, ink-stained desk, unable to take her eyes of the teacher as she moved around the room, writing on the board with chalk that somehow never flaked onto her dark blue dress, slapping the board with her long, vicious-looking pointer, dealing with questions from the class with ease. Unlike Maggie's primary school teachers, who were either fearful and therefore despised by their classes, or ruled with a rod of iron and were therefore loathed, Miss Nolan walked into her classroom with the assumption that it was her domain, where she set the rules, and she dealt with any infringement on these rules, any insolence, with a sort of scornful disbelief that left those responsible for the infraction red-faced and ashamed. Within weeks, the entire class would have laid down their lives for her without a second thought. *That*, thought Maggie, staring up at Miss Nolan with an adoration that verged on idolatry, *that is what I want to be.*

Her previously much-vaunted religious vocation was promptly discarded without a backwards glance. The priest eyed her more in sorrow than anger when she put in a perfunctory appearance at Sunday Mass with the rest of her family, urging her to remember her earlier zeal and fervour, but she shrugged his concerns off with barely a second thought. Now, every atom of her being was concentrated on pleasing Miss Nolan, excelling in her schoolwork – she'd always known that she was a clever girl but, drawing on newfound reserves of patience and determination, she found herself a hair's-breadth away from brilliance – uncomplainingly taking part in extra-curricular activities, getting to school early enough to open the windows in the classroom and put a bunch of flowers on Miss Nolan's desk, an act of worship to which she never admitted, although she knew that everyone in the class, Miss Nolan included, knew that it was her. Normally bold and fearless, it took her months to pluck up the courage to talk to Miss Nolan outside of the classroom, to say anything more than a muttered 'good morning' if she wasn't giving her the answer to a question posed in class, but eventually she gathered her courage up. She waited after school until the classroom was deserted, before approaching the desk behind which Miss Nolan sat, calmly grading the essays that the class had handed in that day. The teacher looked up when she heard Maggie's footsteps, and smiled – for the first time a smile of real warmth and humour, rather than the somewhat theatrical smile behind which she hid during lessons.

"Maggie. What can I do for you?"

And Maggie asked, her heart in her mouth: "Can you tell me what I would have to do to be a teacher like you?"

Chapter Ten

Once Maggie had realised that learning and, eventually, teaching, was to be her way out of her choked, chaotic family home, she never once looked back. Her family was baffled as every evening she brought home piles of books, straining her eyes in the dim, flickering light of the gas lamps to read and study. When her marks were invariably top of her class she was looked upon with vague pride that was overlaid with confusion. There was no history of this sort of behaviour in the family. Maggie's parents' families' paths had been either farming or emigration and, without considering otherwise, their children had adopted those low expectations of a life spent scraping a living from the world however they could, marriage at a young age to the first suitable person who came along, and then the production of children to follow the same pattern and face the same fate. There had certainly been no history of academic achievement within the family, no idea that school was anything other than something to be endured for as short a time as possible before moving on to some sort of money-earning enterprise.

As soon as Maggie got into her mid-teens, her parents' amused appreciation at her achievements abruptly ran dry. She was of an age now to be earning a living and contributing to the household, rather than wasting her time poring over books and sitting, rapt and silent, in dusty classrooms. The money for school fees was unequivocally withdrawn, and Maggie, who had previously looked fondly on her parents despite her desire to escape, started looking upon them as the enemy. Luckily, her prior achievements had not gone unnoticed by her school, and they proved to be on her side, securing a fund of scholarship money to pay for her fees, ensuring her position was secured. This solved the immediate problem, but the issue remained that Maggie was now expected to earn her keep and contribute to the running of the household, and so for her last three years of school she rose every day at five and rubbed her hands raw washing clothes and mopping floors in a local boarding house, arriving in school at half-past-eight and going straight from the school gates back to the boarding house every evening for another shift, which allowed her to bring home enough money to hand over to her parents to cover her keep. She did this with her teeth gritted, stubborn and uncomplaining, her eyes fixed unwaveringly on achieving the age of eighteen, when teachers' college blazed like a beacon on the horizon.

When the longed-for time finally came, teachers' college was a revelation. As she had hoped and prayed and worked for every day for the past six years, she was granted a full scholarship that not only dealt with her fees but provided her with a place to live. It was a small, dark room with a narrow cot in lodgings shared with other students. Her mattress was lumpy and smelled of old cabbage, the bed rattled and shook whenever she turned over, and the windows in the room refused to shut properly, shaking fearsomely every evening when the winds turned and the southerly roared through the city. It was freezing cold in winter and sweltering in summer, a haven for flies and mosquitoes that filled themselves so full with Maggie's blood that by morning they were barely able to lift themselves off the ground.

Maggie loved it. For the first time in her life she had privacy. She could use the toilet without one sibling or another bellowing on the other side of the closed door, demanding access. She could take her time in front of the mirror every morning, making sure her hair was neat and tidy, trying out the fashions of the day without one of her sisters mocking her and accusing her of having tickets on herself. Best of all, her bed, uncomfortable as it was, belonged to nobody but her; no sisters moaning and complaining when she came to bed late, shifting over begrudgingly; no one sneakily trying to warm their cold feet between her warm calves; no conversation when she wanted to be quiet. She luxuriated in her freedom every night as she climbed in between the sheets, patched and worn but always clean, and even if they weren't, it would have been no one's dirt but her own. She read for at least an hour every night before putting out the light, gleefully imagining the cries of irritation and anger that such behaviour would have provoked at home, and every morning she would wake early, with the light, listening to the sounds of her fellow students moving up and down the corridor outside, taking turns to use the bathroom, their courteous and quiet good mornings and thank-yous, the swish of their skirts and, eventually, the quiet knock on the door from Lizzie who slept in the next room, letting Maggie know that the bathroom was free and it was her turn.

The other girls, too, were nothing but a source of pleasure. Although she had wanted nothing else since the first moment she had started in Miss Nolan's class, she had found herself, in the days when teaching college had solidified from a dream into impending reality, facing the idea with some trepidation. She had eyed up her clothes – clean, yes, and neatly mended, but unfashionable, obviously cheap and much-used – and realised they would not do. She was as familiar as anyone else from her part of the city with the disdainful looks of the wealthier girls when they passed in the street, looking down on her dress, the slapdash way she dressed her hair next to their sleek coiffures, the unfettered way in which she moved her body next to their tight-laced corsets and poker-straight carriages, her hurried and harried manner next to their studied languor. Teaching college, she feared, could mean years of sharing space with those very same girls, enduring their scorn and mockery, friendless and ignored. When she arrived, however, she quickly realised her mistake. The girls with the nineteen-inch waists and the perfectly trimmed hats would never have lowered themselves to employment; instead, the girls that she found there were girls similar to herself, who had grown up in damp, overcrowded houses in Sydney, or in the baking vastness of the countryside; girls who needed to earn a living, bright, studious girls who often wanted to escape their pasts just as much as she did. For the first time in her life she had friends – real friends. She'd been popular at school, it was true, at least with those pupils who didn't regard her with envy, muttering "teacher's pet" behind her back, but she'd never had the time to associate with them outside of school, and so nothing had ever progressed beyond friendly acquaintanceship. Now, at last, she had confidantes, girls with whom she could stay up late into the night talking, sometimes about their work, but sometimes about romance and clothing. At this place of higher learning, she was finally learning how to be a normal girl.

But when the time came for graduation and jobs were on offer, she found all her fellow graduates falling over one another for jobs in the city, if not in Sydney then in Melbourne or even Adelaide. The countryside held no appeal for them. Those who had grown up in the city had no desire to leave it, and those from the country spoke about the unimaginable boredom, the smallness of the society, the trials of always being the subject of talk and speculation, every move scrutinised by people who had nothing better to do. Those who were unsuccessful in the city and were forced to take the country jobs complained about it unceasingly, the successful ones consoling the less successful, assuring them that jobs within the city were bound to come up before too long, that they'd be able to move. Once again, Maggie found herself swimming against the tide. She had never wanted anything but a job in the country. She had no desire to stay in the city, every corner of which spoke to her of confinement and looking backwards. She thought of her parents and her older brothers and sisters, hands linked at the edge of the continent, looking back towards where they had come from – or where they imagined they had come from, in the case of her siblings – backs turned in fear from the broad land around them. And so without ever really articulating it or realising it until it was challenged, she had fixed her sights on exactly the opposite, the centre of Australia, burrowing her way into its heart, having it surround her.

The Cottier's Creek job was the one that she wanted as soon as she heard about it. Lizzie herself had grown up on a farm near Cottier's Creek, and she had told Maggie about it, her face creased with dislike as she described the punishing heat, the drought, the flies, the dust storms, the unforgiving glare of the sun, the small town atmosphere, the small-mindedness, the endless scrutiny... Lizzie had no intention of ever going back; she'd rather die, she told Maggie melodramatically, and yet it was the town that had paid for her fees at college. The local school teacher was nearing retirement, keen to hand the reins to a younger woman, and the town's eyes had fixed on Lizzie, while she wriggled under their glare, desperate to escape.

"So I'll do it," Maggie said, barely even thinking about it, and Lizzie's eyes widened – this, clearly, was an outcome that she had never expected, especially given her unfavourable description of the town and the job. Maggie had graduated within the top three of her class; she had her pick of the jobs; she could have walked into the best school in Sydney and been welcomed with open arms, and yet here she was offering herself to a small, rural primary school that was bound to never offer her the chances and the challenges that she had always claimed that she wanted. Lizzie and Maggie had been best friends for three years now, and she was a decent enough person not to jump at Maggie's offer, insisting that she think it over for at least a few days before rushing into things, but the next morning Maggie woke from dreams of the desert, living under a great broad sky that she had only ever viewed in chinks between the cluttered buildings of the city, and to Lizzie's bafflement and delight, Maggie announced that her mind was made up; they could write to the school that afternoon.

For Maggie, arrival in Cottier's Creek was like coming into bright sunshine after years spent in the half-light. The narrow streets of Sydney had been like living underground; even the expanse of the harbour had been fenced in by the houses that surged down the hills to the lip of the water; there was never enough room, never enough space, the sunlight slanted obliquely through the canyons between the buildings, seldom striking anything directly. The job in Cottier's Creek came with lodgings with the headmaster of the school, Mr Heysmand, and his wife, a prim, frowsty woman in her forties, who was laced so tightly into her corset that her flesh seemed to rebel and sneaked out of her clothes in other ways, bulging at her neck and wrists. The two of them met her at the train station. The journey had taken nearly two days, and when the train finally came to a halt, Maggie had her face pressed to the window and was gaping unashamedly at the bitter brown fields, the blue hazy mountains and the limitless horizon.

After greeting her, the couple led her down the main street to their home. Maggie screwed up her eyes against the intensity of the light, which seemed unnaturally vivid, and by the time they reached the house, which was only a two minute walk away, her legs were shaking so much that she could barely climb the five wooden steps to the veranda. Mrs Heysmand led her to her room, Maggie saw bare, scrubbed boards and a narrow bed covered with an inexpertly made quilt, the remnants of someone else's life. As politely as she could, knowing that she was bound to offend but unable to muster the energy to care very much, Maggie ushered Mrs Heysmand out of the room, stammering that she was tired and needed to lie down. As soon as the door was safely shut, she moved as quickly as she could to the window, slammed the shutters closed, stripped off to her underclothes and lay down on the bed, her head pounding, her body surfing on wave after wave of intense nausea. She ignored the insistent knock on the door summoning her to dinner for as long as she could, but finally after several minutes, she managed to lever herself up off the bed and make her way over to the door, part-covering herself with a shawl, and explained in slow, halting sentences to the grim-faced Mrs Heysmand that she was unwell, that it must be the after-effects of the journey, and the heat, and yes, it was a lot hotter than it had been in Sydney, and she was unused to it, and yes, of course she would have to toughen up and get used to it as best she could. Afterwards, she couldn't remember half of what she'd said to the hatchet-faced woman standing at the door, who seemed to be trying to force her way inside, other than she'd simply agreed with anything in order to secure herself some peace and to close the door, and then stumbled back to bed.

For hours, she remained in a fugue state, not waking and not sleeping, hallucinations dancing in front of her eyes whenever she opened them, her body burning with heat, the sun having floated in through a gap in the shutters and taken up residence in the corner of her room, scorching the curtains. Her head throbbed unceasingly, her eyes stung, and every noise was agony. She held on for as long as she could, but when she heard the click of the Heysmands' bedroom door closing for the night, she hauled herself to her feet, went out of the back door and staggered down the path to the outside toilet, where she locked herself in for upwards of an hour, her stomach seized up in an agony of cramps, helpless with sickness. By the time she felt well enough to leave, her entire body felt raw and wrung out and there was barely any strength in her limbs, but the pain in her head had lessened a little, the heat that had flushed her skin had subsided, and once back in her room she flung the quilt over her damp, goose-pimpled body and fell almost instantly into a thick, intoxicating sleep.

She woke at dawn, the threads of her sleep still tangled around her, slow-moving as treacle, but her head was clear and her body prickled with restless energy despite her sleepiness.

The clock beside her bed said half-past-five, and she slipped out of bed, hurriedly dressed herself, and moved as quietly as she could through the house until she stood on the back veranda, looking out over the edge of the town and the hills, beyond the houses and the station and the road that snaked out to the farms, to the collection of tents and huts that crouched by the roadside, where fires flickered and the occasional shadow moved about in the half-light. Maggie felt renewed and almost reborn after the intensity of her physical reaction to the town and to the desert; she had a vague feeling that she had alienated Mrs Heysmand forever through her perceived rudeness and evident physical weakness, but that didn't matter. The blank morning sky and the muted tones of the desert were a fresh start, a new phase of her life that she could direct any way she pleased. The children in Cottier's Creek were different from those that she had been used to in Sydney.

They were quieter, more docile, and the sly mischief that characterised many of the city children that she'd encountered during teaching practice was absent. She would have thought that she would be relieved by that, and be pleased at the freedom to turn to write on the blackboard without fearing that revolution was fomenting behind her back, but, strangely, she found that she missed the turbulent energy. These children, with their placid obedience, bored her, and instead of having to calm them down, as she had had to do often in Sydney, she started to try and find ways to liven them up.

It was easier than she'd expected, once she worked out what the problem was. Most of them had spent their educational lives under the iron hand of Miss Morrison, who had now gone to Adelaide for her retirement, and had had mischief schooled out of them. Contrary to a fault, Maggie actually started to encourage acts of minor disobedience, rewarding the cheeky with a smile of complicity rather than a stroke of the cane, and soon the children started to smile and laugh in class; her questions were no longer greeted by a sea of blank faces but a forest of waving hands, and the young boys fought among themselves for the privilege of carrying her books when they met her in the street on their way to or from school.

Her methods were met with far from universal approval. Mr Heysmand started making hinting remarks about the noise level that emanated from her classroom, which she blithely laughed off with an explanation of youthful enthusiasm. One of the young mothers complained that, since Miss Morrison's departure and Maggie's arrival, her daughter had started answering back at home, questioning her mother's rules, demanding to know why things were so. Unapologetic, Maggie explained that this was the sort of attitude that she was encouraging in her class; that in her opinion, unquestioning obedience was bad for children, who were, after all, adults in training, needing to learn the skills that would help them survive in the adult world. Maggie's steadfast belief in her own rightness, her direct gaze and her unflappable, city-schooled manner made her difficult to resist, and soon most of her detractors were sufficiently bowled over by the strength of her personality so they kept their complaints down to a subdued muttering, while publicly averring that they didn't know what teaching was all about but that, with her fancy city training, Maggie was bound to be doing wonders for the school.

Education had been her own salvation and, with the heady zeal of the converted, Maggie was determined to pass this salvation on to others. As a result, she was enraged when the importance of education was ignored by parents, who would often allow their children to miss school for the most spurious of reasons – to visit relatives, perhaps, or to help around the house or on the farm. In the case of the latter, even when the children were able to make it to school, they were often too tired to be of much use. When Paul McGill had fallen asleep at his desk three times in a single week, after helping with the sheep shearing before and after school, Maggie was filled with crusading fury. Of course she had worked while she had been at school, but she had had no choice. In contrast, the McGills were one of the wealthiest landowning families in the town. They had plenty of hired labour to help with the shearing and no need to put a ten-year-old boy – not to mention a ten-year-old boy who was already behind in his reading and arithmetic – to work.

Despite the insistence of Mrs Heysmand that this sort of thing was never done, on Sunday morning Maggie dressed in her smartest clothes and, after Mass in the small Catholic church on the edge of town, waited outside the grand Anglican church to try and catch hold of Peter McGill, Paul's father. The old man was nowhere to be seen, but on asking, a man in his early twenties was pointed out to her as Charlie McGill, Peter's oldest son and Paul's brother. Head up and fearless, Maggie marched up to the handsome, laughing young man and demanded a word. She barely waited until they were out of earshot from the rest of the crowd before letting loose about Paul's academic achievements – or lack thereof. She spoke fervently about the importance of education, pushing her point, while Charlie stood gazing at her with good-humoured attentiveness. Despite his polite, well-bred manner, she couldn't quite shake the notion that he found her somehow entertaining. When she finally stuttered to a close, having lost her composure in a most uncharacteristic manner, he smiled, warmly and widely, and apologised with what seemed like gratifying intensity. "None of our family were ever keen on the books," he explained, "and we all know that Paul will work on the farm when he's old enough, so I suppose we've always assumed that those things are more important. But you're right, it's rude for him to be going to school in that sort of state. He should at least be able to stay awake and pay attention, even if he's never going to be top of the class. I'll talk to my father about it."

Chapter Eleven

To start with, Maggie found Charlie's interest in her nothing more than an amusing diversion, and never dreamt that it meant anything more to him, either. The McGills were one of the wealthiest families in the surrounding area, staunch, Scottish Protestant landowners, while Maggie was an Irish Catholic from Sydney, brash, outspoken and overenthusiastic, worlds away from the carefully schooled, delicately brought up girls who were raised in Cottier's Creek for the sole purpose of finding an appropriate man to marry. Besides, she was a working woman. She had bidden goodbye to the prospect of marriage with little regret when she had gone to teachers' college, and had no intention of changing her mind now. The children were coming to life under her hands, she was making her mark on this town, she fell asleep every night planning her lessons for the next day and woke up every morning still thinking of them. Even the severely banked reserve of Mr and Mrs Heysmand, whose disapproval wafted across the dinner table every evening, was not enough to dent her spirits. She had an image of herself for the first time, an idea of where she was going, a picture of herself at sixty, a white-haired schoolteacher, stern but well-loved, her high standards bringing forth generation after generation of bright, intellectually engaged young adults. Whenever she caught herself thinking this way she would laugh, mocking herself for her pride and her hubris, but nonetheless the image remained.

At first, Charlie's courtship was gentle, barely noticeable, but

Maggie did start to notice *him*. Perhaps not every day, but certainly once or twice a week, he would be there outside the school gates when the bell rang at the end of the day, instead of the maid and groom that Maggie had been used to, with his horse and buggy, jumping down off the box, beckoning at Paul across the school yard, and waving at Maggie once he was sure that he'd captured her attention. The first few times she noticed him, she was able to laugh it off, excuse it as coincidence – perhaps he'd been coming to pick up Paul for weeks and she'd never noticed him before she'd spoken to him that morning after church. But before long, she was able tell the days of the week by his movements; every Monday, Wednesday and Friday without fail he would be there, waiting outside the school gates, often before any of the other parents or siblings had arrived, and always there was that jaunty wave, always that smile.

Afterwards, she felt that the fact that she didn't care, the fact she had no intentions of trying to catch the attention of a man with a view to marriage, was what cemented her appeal with Charlie – she saw him as nothing more than a possible entertaining diversion. She had no second thoughts about talking to him for the second time, after he'd been coming to the school for about two weeks. As soon as the last of the children, who often clung to her after school, asking question after question about the lessons of the day and their homework, had headed towards their parents, she crossed the yard towards him, her boots tapping on the warm, soft earth. Seeing her approach, Charlie helped Paul up onto the cart, spoke a quiet word to him and then turned back towards Maggie.

"Well, then? Has he been behaving himself better?"

Maggie nodded, smiling. "There's been a big improvement. No more sleeping at his desk, and his work's getting better. He's a bright boy when he puts his mind to it."

"That's good news. I spoke to my father. He hadn't realised how much of an impact the farming was having on Paul's schoolwork – he wants the boy to do well. Although he's bound to end up on the farm – if he wants to, of course, though he says he does – there are things that he can learn at school that will help him as much as knowing how to shear a sheep. Mathematics, of course, to do the accounts. My father had to realise this, and now, I think, he's got his priorities right."

"I'm glad. Paul seems to enjoy school, and when he's well rested and on good form, he's an absolute pleasure to have in my class."

"And we do appreciate you taking the time to talk to us about it."

"I'd do the same for any of my pupils…"

"I'm sure you would." He grinned, head cocked on one side, squinting into the late afternoon light. "You're a very dedicated woman."

She grinned back. "I like to think so."

He half turned away from her, and for a moment she thought that that was it, that he was leaving, but after a moment of hesitation he turned back, seeming to heft his courage into his mouth.

"Listen," he said, "they're showing *The Story of the Kelly Gang* down at the new picture house on Saturday afternoon. A matinee performance. I was wondering if you'd like to come with me?"

For a moment she deliberated. A matinee performance in the picture house, which had only opened in the town a few months before, which still had novelty value and was therefore bound to be full of Cottier's Creek residents…Appearing at such an event on the arm of one of the McGill boys was exactly the sort of thing that Lizzie had warned her about while complaining about her small town upbringing. She knew that doing such a thing was bound to open herself up to the sort of gossip that breeds in the sticky humidity of a small town, the sort of gossip that could be friendly or malicious but either way was unlikely to much help her cause. She considered this for a moment, weighing it up and then decided that, really, she didn't care. Her heart and mind had been invested in nothing but her work for over a year now, and with a sudden internal lurch of excitement, she realised that perhaps for a little while it might be nice to have something else to think about.

"I'd love to," she said, and Charlie's face brightened immediately. He was the sort of person, Maggie realised, who showed his feelings on his face, and that realisation only endeared him to her.

"I'm so glad. I'll meet you at your house at two o'clock, shall I, and we can walk down together?"

By half-past-one on Saturday afternoon, Maggie was ready, dressed in her finest dress, her hair carefully arranged, pinned up on the back of her head with tendrils over her forehead and cheeks in a way that she knew was most becoming, and she was compelled to give herself a stern talking-to in the mirror that was nailed on the back of her bedroom door, narrow and dim enough to dissuade vanity. It was perfectly fine to make a friend in Charlie. Friends in Cottier's Creek, real friends, rather than the sorts of friendly acquaintances that she had in the mothers and sisters of her pupils, had proven hard to come by, purely thanks to the fact that she had significantly less time on her hands than most of the other Cottier's Creek women. She was impressed by Charlie's good humour, his quick intelligence, his willingness to smile and to laugh. But it could be no more than that, of course. Work was – work had to be – everything to her. She knew that she got a degree of satisfaction out of it that she sensed could never come from any more domestic pursuit – and, she told herself harshly, she mustn't get ideas above her station. Charlie seemed to like her, it was true, and she had a realistic enough opinion of herself to realise that she was personable and friendly enough to catch the attention of young men, but there was no way that it could be more than that. Charlie McGill was the sort who could have his pick of the local girls, he was young, handsome and the son of one of the richest families in the area, so there was no way that he could form any sort of genuine, serious interest in someone like her. Friendship was all that she could expect from him – which was good, she warned herself, because it was all that she wanted.

She had prepared mentally for scrutiny at the matinee, but not the amount of interest the two of them attracted, she in her best outfit with her hair in a carefully slapdash style, and Charlie looking smarter than she'd ever seen him, with his hair carefully combed and flattened, a neat blazer over his normal uniform of trousers and shirt. All eyes appeared to be on the two of them and within minutes of arriving, she had already identified four families that she knew. Children from her class were staring at her, wide-eyed with shock at seeing their teacher out of the classroom, dressed up to the nines, while their parents eyed her up with a mixture of wariness and surprise. Nervousness lurched inside her. With her foot on the bottom step of the picture house, she stopped dead – only momentarily, she thought, an infinitesimal pause, as her pride was such that she could never have brought herself to tell Charlie that she'd changed her mind. But, with his hand on her arm, he noticed her halt and turned to her, eyebrows raised in enquiry. She did her best to smile, but he saw through it and his face softened immediately. "They've got nothing better to look at," he said, his voice low. "If they want something to talk about, I don't mind giving it to them."

Chapter Twelve

Maggie had never been courted before. When she was sixteen or seventeen, one or two of her brothers' friends had expressed an interest, flirting clumsily with her whenever they came to the house to meet John Paul or Seamus, but they'd always been easily laughed off – big, boorish men, with jobs in breweries or at the docks, men who could barely string a coherent sentence together, let alone read. Maggie's response to their hopeful, ham-fisted overtures had always been to briefly look up from whatever book she happened to be reading, fix them with a withering stare, and look down again, leaving them wordless and flushed with anger. Later, at teachers' college, her friends had talked about the boys that they liked, and at the end of each year there had invariably been two or three girls who dropped out to marry. But although Maggie had occasionally obliged when a friend had needed her as a companion and chaperone, and had endured the attentions of whichever over-eager university boy had been deemed her partner for the evening with as much politeness and charm as she could muster, she had always been so focussed on her studies and on the glittering idea of a career that it was virtually impossible to drag her attention away.

Charlie was different, though. He was far from a bookish man, but he had a lithe, supple intelligence and an intense interest in the world around him that meshed well with Maggie's own. A few weeks of his company had left her both charmed and intrigued, and he seemed equally fascinated by her, listening to her with an intensity that she had rarely seen on the face of anyone but her pupils, often referring back to something that she had casually mentioned days before, making it clear that he was paying attention to the things that she had said and thinking them over when they were apart. The more time she spent with him, the more she felt her spirit lightening, and she realised for the first time how single-minded she had become in the past few years, so focused had she been on her studies, her work, her pupils.

Cottier's Creek wasn't a town that offered a great deal in the way of entertainment, so their meetings tended to be limited to visits to the cinema, evening walks through town, and the occasional glass of lemonade at the local café that catered for those genteel enough not to be interested in the raw joviality of the local pub. A couple of times he had offered to take her for an evening drive in his wagon, and she had always refused, certain that the Heysmands wouldn't approve, fearful that any rendezvous out of plain sight of the rest of the town might possibly put her reputation at risk; she cared little for her reputation for her own sake, but she was savvy enough to know that it was vital if she wanted to maintain her job. But Charlie only became more and more persuasive as time went by, and Maggie became more and more tempted. There was only so much that they could talk about in the cinema or while walking through town, where every way they turned there was an eager face with an eager ear at their elbows, scavenging for any scrap of gossip they could pick up, and so finally she agreed.

That evening, she waited for him on the veranda as the evening thundered in, purple as a bruise, ignoring the disapproving stares emanating from Mrs Heysmand in the kitchen – they were somehow tangible enough to be felt through the wall, even when Maggie's back was turned. Until then she had been able to convince herself that Charlie wanted nothing but friendship from her and that to believe otherwise was risking too much – but that evening, as they rode along the road out of town, Charlie was uncommonly silent, so silent that Maggie's throat stopped up too, the words that normally rose all too readily to her lips running dry. Just past the last of the large houses, the road rose slightly, offering as much of a panorama as Cottier's Creek could muster, the lights of the town bobbing and blooming like flowers. It was a warm evening and as Charlie reined in the horses, rolling to a halt under one of the large, spreading jacaranda trees, Maggie could hear the whine of a mosquito near her left ear, distracting her so much that when Charlie bent to kiss her, it took her so much by surprise that she didn't have time to feel nervous.

Maggie had never been kissed before – or at least not properly. One of her fellow pupils had tried once, when she was at secondary school, in the dark of an alleyway while walking her home after a school dance, but there had been no tenderness in it, nothing but adolescent awkwardness, like being slapped with something wet, and Maggie had been too shocked and astounded to do anything but burst out laughing, which brought down a stream of shame-driven invective onto her head. But this… this was totally different. Charlie's face warm and smooth near hers, the gentle, familiar smell of soap and his hair cream, and she couldn't help herself from smiling into his mouth and kissing him back, before the mosquito landed on the back of her neck and she jerked away with a cry of annoyance, squashing it with a slap. For a moment Charlie stared at her, almost angry; then she collapsed into helpless giggles and he followed suit.

Maggie enjoyed the subsequent kisses as much as she had enjoyed the first one, and noticing the way that Charlie's breathing quickened and deepened, and the urgent way he put his hand around the back of her neck, drawing her closer, she gathered that he felt the same way. By the time they finally broke apart, almost an hour had gone past. When he told her the time, she panicked. "Quick, you must take me back," she said urgently. "The Heysmands will make my life a misery if I miss supper." He acquiesced, spurring the horses into a swift trot, pulling up to her front door with two minutes to spare before the Heysmands' cook beat the gong to summon the household for dinner. Nonetheless, by the twitching of the flowered curtains Maggie knew that Mrs Heysmand was poised at the front door, waiting avidly for her return. Red hot annoyance surged through her. *To hell with it*, she thought, and turning back to Charlie, she gave him a brazen kiss on the cheek before jumping down from the box. She mounted the stairs two at a time, only turning back when she reached the front door, to see him gazing after her, grinning broadly.

They met again two days later, and as they were walking arm in arm down the main street at dusk, Maggie bolstered her courage enough to ask, having first ensured that no one was close enough to overhear: "What do you like about me, Charlie?"

His first response was to laugh. Then he looked into her face and, realising her question was serious, his smile dropped into a frown of concern.

"Surely it's obvious?"

"Not really. I know I've only lived here for a couple of years, but I know enough about how things work in this town to know that you could have the pick of all the local girls out here. Why not... why not Esther Campbell, or Arabella Webster, or Meg Clarke? Any of those would be over the moon to have you, and they'd be bound to make your life a lot easier than I would."

He ticked them off on his fingers. "Boring, boring, boring. None of those girls have anything to talk about other than the latest hairstyles from Sydney or Melbourne, or – or whether pink or red roses are better for trimming your hat. I don't have anything to say to those girls, and they don't have anything to say to me."

"But your family..."

"My family doesn't have to marry them." Unable to hide his feelings, Charlie stopped short as soon as he realised what he'd inadvertantly said, and despite the ferment of excitement and anxiety that the implication of his words churned up inside her, Maggie couldn't help laughing at the dumbstruck expression on his face. Moments later, he seemed to relax a bit and gave a breathless chuckle as he took her arm again and they walked on.

"See, that's why I like you."

"Because I laugh at you when you make a fool of yourself?"

"Something like that. You're – you're just good fun. You make me laugh, and you make me think. I've only known you for a few months but already there's no one I'd rather spend time with than you."

He paused for a moment, gathering his courage, and then, with uncharacteristic diffidence, he asked, stammering a little: "So... would you?"

She caught his meaning and, though tempted, wasn't quite cruel enough to pretend to misunderstand and force him to spell it out.

"I – I don't know, Charlie. I never thought I would marry. I love my work, I love my independence, and I'd have to give that up. It'd be hard for me. And I don't know if I could be the sort of wife that you would want, or need. I've got no experience of running a household. I wouldn't know where to start. I'm outspoken, I'm no good at pretending to like people I don't like... You need someone diplomatic, someone well brought up – "

"But – "

"Quiet, I haven't finished. I've got no money, I'm not from Cottier's Creek, I'm three years older than you and, worst of all," she dropped her tones to a mocking hush, "I'm Catholic. And Irish. I really can't see your staunch Presbyterian parents approving of that, can you?"

"It doesn't matter what they want."

"Oh, of course it does, you love-struck fool."

Charlie fell into mutinous silence. Maggie followed suit, her eyes fixed on the dents her boots made in the sandy path, uncertain of what game she was supposed to be playing here, why she suddenly seemed to be working so hard to dissuade Charlie from proposing. It was an unfamiliar idea, certainly, one that she'd never properly considered, but perhaps that was no reason to dismiss it outright; perhaps she should at least do him the courtesy of considering it.

"Listen," she said at last. "I'm not sure about this, not by a long shot. But you know how fond I am of you, I hope, and – well, if you'll think about it, properly think about it, what it would mean, and how it would work, then I'll think about it too."

He grinned, his mood lifting in an instant. "I've already thought about it," he said.

"No, you haven't."

"And now that I've done it once and you didn't bite my head off, I'm not going to stop asking,"

"Ask away."

"I will."

"Just don't expect a quick answer."

"I won't. I know how stubborn you are."

They smiled at each other, his face full of boyish eagerness, and she knew at that moment that, whatever her protestations, he was bound to wear them down eventually.

*

Maggie dealt with the wedding with a mixture of humour and bemusement; she sometimes thought that she couldn't have got through it any other way. It had taken Charlie nearly two months to wear her down with weekly proposals, becoming more and more elaborate as time went on, and after a couple of these, both of them accepted the proposals for the jokes that they were. Maggie knew that she was going to say yes eventually; Charlie knew that she knew; it was all just a matter of time. By the second month, all the consideration that Maggie was giving it was around the timing of her acceptance; given the increasing grandiosity of Charlie's gestures, she realised that he was enjoying the game as much as she was, and didn't want to stop him short, but also didn't want him to end up making a fool of her. In the end, it wasn't even one of his proposals that she responded to. He was walking her home from yet another showing of the only film that was playing in town, when he drew her into an alleyway to kiss her – risky, but she was nearly past the point of caring – muttering in her ear as they pulled apart, "I wish you'd just say yes, you know." That was when she replied with, "all right then, yes," before her mouth had even given her brain a chance to think about it. He pushed her away. For a moment she was confused, wondering if she'd somehow offended him by acquiescing too soon, but his expression was thunderstruck rather than angry.

"Are you serious?"

"Yes, I think so."

Slowly, his expression broke into a grin, and he rubbed his hand over his face. "I was beginning to think you'd never say yes."

"I've been enjoying the proposals. Didn't want to stop you too soon."

Charlie frowned, suddenly worried. "Do you – should I ask your father, do you think? That's what I'd do if it was one of the girls around here, but I know you city girls do things differently…"

"Good Lord, no. Don't bother with that." Maggie giggled, thinking of the perplexity with which her father was bound to meet a request for his daughter's hand. "All of my sisters just announced that they were getting married. No one's ever asked my dad's permission. He wouldn't know what to say. Anyway, he always used to say that it was a relief that anyone would take us off his hands…"

"Don't say that," Charlie said, his face suddenly stern – it was in moments like that that she saw the man inside the boy he still mostly was, and she loved him for it – "any man would be lucky to have you. I'm lucky, unbelievably so." Maggie opened her mouth, accustomed to countering any compliment with a joke, but before she could speak he reached out and put his finger to her lips, which surprised her into silence. "And don't make some sort of self-deprecating joke, either. You're going to have to get used to compliments, because I'm going to give you plenty of them."

Maggie had dreaded making the announcement to Charlie's parents. They'd met just twice before, both times in town, when his mother, Elizabeth, had been polite but cool, and his father had ignored her almost completely, but they'd evidently prepared for news of an engagement. As hard as they'd tried, Maggie and Charlie's courtship had been far from a secret, and Elizabeth was well enough bred to be able to put a brave face on it and feign delight. However, Charlie's father, Peter, reacted with his customary sang-froid, which upset Maggie a little, despite telling herself that she shouldn't be so silly, and Charlie's soothing words of excuse: "He's just shy, that's all. Not used to meeting new people. It's nothing personal, I promise, he'd be like that with anyone". However, she found herself taking comfort in Elizabeth's excitement, real or otherwise, as a sign that she was being welcomed to the family.

This comfort started to dissipate, though, as it became clear quite how grand a wedding Elizabeth was planning for her eldest son. After quickly ascertaining that Maggie's mother was unlikely to have a particularly strong interest in organising the proceedings – at which she drew a small, but perceptible, sigh of relief – Elizabeth threw herself into the planning with gusto. The McGill farm had a small chapel on the grounds, which at least solved the issue of whether they should go with St. Andrew's, the large Presbyterian church in town, or St. Thomas's, the smaller Catholic church, which even as a somewhat lapsed Catholic, Maggie would have fought for. She had every intention of asking Father Matthew to quietly bless their union afterwards, and Charlie had no objection to this – but St Andrew's, filled as it was with the local Protestant aristocracy, would have been beyond the pale. And then there was the question of the dress... Maggie would have been perfectly happy with something plain and simple; she had never been particularly physically confident, and had no desire to draw any attention to herself, but once again that was unacceptable to Elizabeth, who insisted on a lavish white dress. Initially, she tried to urge Maggie into her own dress, which still hung, pristine and crisp as snow, in her closet, but Maggie was broad shouldered and robust, and Elizabeth's twenty-inch waist couldn't go near her – which, Maggie thought wryly to herself, was probably part of the point of making her try it on. A dress was ordered from Sydney instead; a pitched battle was fought, in the most gentle of possible tones, between Maggie and Elizabeth regarding exactly how many frills and furbelows were to be permitted, the result being that neither of them got what they wanted, Maggie finding the dress far too fancy, and Elizabeth dismissing it as dowdy and plain. But despite all of this, or possibly because of it, Maggie felt her treacherous heart warming to Elizabeth, with her passionate interest in society and fashion that was so at odds with Maggie's detachment. Elizabeth's no-holds-barred involvement in the wedding looked to Maggie like the obsession of a woman with far too little to do, whose youngest child, Paul, was already starting to push her away in his struggle for independence, and once the vital issues of venue and dress were decided, Maggie was happy to let Elizabeth have free rein with the issues of catering, flowers, decorations and bridesmaids, which fascinated her and interested Maggie not one jot.

It was with a certain amount of trepidation that she extended invitations to her family; she was terrified of them declining the invitation, but equally scared of them turning up. In the event, the invitation was sent, and the expected response came, written on cheap, flimsy paper in her mother's childishly careful handwriting, which twisted Maggie's heart. They were very sorry but it would be impossible for them to attend – Maggie felt a nauseating mixture of relief and sadness at this news – but they would happily send their son, Maggie's brother Patrick, to represent the family.

It was Patrick's face, even more than Charlie's, that Maggie drew comfort from on the day of the wedding, as she advanced step by trembling step down the aisle of the McGill family chapel. Although only a few metres long, it felt like a marathon journey as she walked down it on the arm of Mr Heysmand, who, with mixed embarrassment and reluctant pride, had agreed to give her away in the absence of her father. Ahead of her were Charlie's two sisters, Rose and Violet, sixteen and fourteen, giggling in their pink, flouncy dresses and flirting with any young man that caught their eyes. Behind her were Alma and Diana, Charlie's two young cousins from Adelaide, swelled up with pride at the privilege of carrying her train. Not given to nervousness, Maggie's heart bounced inside her and suddenly stuck in her throat at the sight of all those faces turned to hers, the church so superficially familiar but lacking all the touches that she was used to in St. Thomas's. For a moment, she was perilously close to turning and running, seeing so clearly in her head the image of her, white dress and veil trailing behind, dashing across the stubbled brown fields. But then there was Patrick... He had arrived only the day before and was staying at the hotel in town, but she hadn't had time to see him before the ceremony. He was twenty now, far taller and more serious-looking than she remembered, but at the very second that Maggie hesitated, he caught her eye and his face transformed. For a split second, he rolled his eyes back into his head and poked out his tongue. It was the very face that he had pulled as a child when she was annoyed with him and he was trying to make her laugh, and as she fought back her grin, his face returned to normal, but for a surreptitious jerk of his thumb towards the elaborate hat of Arabella Webster beside him, and a roll of his eyes. *Don't you let these toffs intimidate you*, his look said, as clear as a bell, so Maggie squared her shoulders, straightened her back, and fixed her eyes on the still, straight figure of Charlie by the altar. That was what mattered; not the rest of the McGill family or the curious, speculative crowd, or the minister who stood awkwardly at the end of the aisle, evidently uncomfortable with marrying a Catholic bogtrotter from the Sydney slums to the son of one of the town's best families. She could step on her skirt; she could make as many mistakes as possible during the ceremony, stumbling over her words or forgetting one of Charlie's middle names; she could make a fool of herself and end up the talk of the town for the next six months, but none of that mattered, save for the fact that by the end of the day she and Charlie would be husband and wife.

*

Maggie had known that everything would change after marriage, but she hadn't expected how suddenly the changes would come about. They had timed the wedding to take place at the start of the summer break, allowing Maggie to teach out the school year, so she had expected a more gradual transformation, but overnight it was as if something had shifted, both inside her and within the town. People looked at her differently when she walked down the street, and she started carrying herself differently in response, without even noticing the change at first. She had always walked quickly, her movements lithe and supple, both out of a desire to get where she was going as swiftly as possible and to avoid notice, but now she started moving more slowly, with a sort of deliberate dignity, carrying the weight of the eyes that were on her. Her clothing changed, too – she had money, now, for the first time in her life, and Charlie was more than happy for that money to be spent on dresses, ordered in from Sydney, Melbourne and Adelaide alongside Elizabeth's, made to her exact measurements. It was such a change from the hand-me-downs from one older sister or other, which were darned as many times as they needed and taken in or let out to fit. Maggie had never had any interest in clothes, but with the arrival of these fine dresses, cut to flatter her décolletage and her plump shoulders, Maggie started to realise that much of this disinterest had been enforced; she hadn't been interested because she couldn't afford to be interested, whereas now, bit by bit, she started to bend her head over the fashion plates in Elizabeth's magazines, offering more and more of an opinion when Elizabeth suggested colours and fabrics and cuts, taking more care in dressing her hair, and showing an interest in matching hat trimmings. There was something pleasurable in the feeling of being encased in fine materials, and something even more pleasurable in the way that Charlie looked at her, eyes wide and admiring, when she put on her light green muslin or her blue poplin frock for a journey into town.

It was the change in living arrangements that affected her most, though – the move from the Heysmands' house, which had been austere and cramped, not in terms of space but in terms of scrutiny, where she had felt their eyes on her every move and their unvoiced disapproval seeping through the cracks in the floorboards and impregnating itself into the plaster on the walls and the thick floral curtains. Even the pressure of living with her parents-in-law couldn't compare to that, and she found, to her growing surprise, that the more time that she spent with the McGills, the more she started to like them. She had been right in her original assessment of Elizabeth, who was bored and class-bound and in turns horrified and intrigued by her new daughter-in-law's more liberated and outspoken ways. Despite their differences, the two became unexpected company for one another. At first, Maggie tried to urge Elizabeth into reading and Elizabeth pushed Maggie towards needlepoint and embroidery, but soon they were sitting down together in the evenings, working at their respective pastimes in a silence born of friendship. And Charlie had been right about Peter and his shyness. The first night that they'd all sat down together for dinner, he'd barely said a word to her, as usual. Every time she'd looked in his direction, he'd cut his eyes away from her, and yet at the end of the meal, as they were rising from the table, he had managed to hold her gaze for more than a split second and gave her a smile of such diffident warmth that she had quite melted towards him.

Best of all, living with Charlie was a delight. For the first couple of months, she couldn't think of a time when she'd been happier, even during those first heady weeks at teaching college. He both challenged and entertained her by turns. His adoration of her was evident, but he also saw her clearly for who she was, refusing to tolerate any sort of pretence from her, and with every day that she woke up next to him she felt her love for Charlie, which had started off fragile, insubstantial and, if she was honest with herself, something not to be trusted, growing stronger and tougher, more reliable and more resilient. Love had always seemed to her to be a silly and ephemeral thing on which to base any major choices, and she had second-guessed herself every step of the way in her relationship with Charlie, but marriage had changed something between them; it had given her something tangible to point at and hold on to; it had made something real out of something that had simply arisen, unbidden, between the two of them.

It wasn't without a twinge of mixed envy and anxiety, though, that she greeted her replacement's arrival in Cottier's Creek. Out of friendly fellow feeling – and more than a touch of curiosity – she had gone with the Heysmands to meet the girl off the train, and she couldn't help feeling a mixture of relief and disappointment when she realised the inadequacy of her successor, a small, pallid, anaemic-looking girl who limped off the train, head lolling with exhaustion. She warned herself not to judge too soon, and tried to attribute the girl's lack of vitality to the length and rigour of her journey, and the possible effect of homesickness. After all, she told herself, many girls in her position had never been away from home before and not everyone had her drive towards independence. But when they met again the next day, Maggie having invited her round to the McGill farm for afternoon tea, her initially negative impression was confirmed. Alice Crawford seemed barely able to lift her voice above a whisper, and her pale eyes seemed to be constantly swimming with unshed tears. Fighting down her frustration, Maggie did her best to draw Alice out, but her questions were met with shrugs and monosyllables more often than not. When asked why she had decided to teach, Alice had shrugged and replied with, "I don't know. My sister did it," and Maggie was unable to stop herself assuming that it was the default choice of an unmarriable girl. When asked what she thought about Cottier's Creek, and whether she was looking forward to starting the job, the ever-present tears in Alice's eyes threatened to brim over. She hadn't wanted to come here, she said; it was too far, she missed her mother, she had wanted a job in the city but there had been no jobs to be found – or rather, no employers willing to take her, Maggie thought, reading between the lines. The city children that Maggie remembered would have devoured her, ill-fitting dress and all, and it was clear to Maggie that, far from being the thrilling blank slate that Cottier's Creek had been for her, for Alice, Cottier's Creek was a prison sentence, something to be endured in the hope of getting time off for good behaviour, a job offer back in Melbourne, or a marriage proposal from a decent man. When Alice finally trailed off home after an hour or so of strained, lurching, one-sided conversation, Maggie found herself regretting for the first time her policy of enlivenment towards her former pupils. Now, not only were they going to charge straight over the hapless Miss Crawford, but they were bound to be bored, frustrated and disappointed by someone who was that weak-willed.

On the first day of the school year, Maggie woke up at dawn, the sky only half-light. Unable to stay in bed, she crossed to the window and Charlie woke. "What is it?" he asked, his voice muddy with sleep, but she didn't know how to answer, just glanced back at the bed and her drowsy husband, his hair sleep-tangled, and then stared out of the window, down the hill towards the town where she could just about pick out the lights of the school room. Charlie, ever quick on the uptake where Maggie's moods were concerned, slipped out of bed and padded over to where she stood by the window.

"I know you're going to miss it," he said. "I'm sorry that I had to take you away from teaching; I knew how much it meant to you, and I wish that it could be different. But – "

"I know, the people here wouldn't accept a married teacher," she replied, parroting the explanation that he'd always given her, even though both of them knew that it was more than that. Charlie himself, despite his love of Maggie and her unconventional nature, had a streak of iron-hard, inflexible conservatism running down his spine, passed down to him from his squatter grandparents who had worked themselves into threads to carve out a semblance of their respectable, upright, Protestant background in the vicious Australian bush; and even if the town had been clamouring for her reinstatement, the idea of a working wife would have filled Charlie with horror. He never would have allowed it.

For the first month or so, Maggie had to stop herself every morning from just taking a casual wander into town, dropping into the school and having a little look at what her pupils – she still thought of them as hers – were making of Miss Crawford, but she knew that Charlie was watching her, sensing her impatient impotence with a wry grin, and providing her with as many distractions as he was able, given the time he had to spend working the farm. Every time Maggie set aside her book with decision, gathered up her skirts and went to cram her hat over her unruly hair, Charlie would appear as if from nowhere, fabricating a reason for Maggie to come with him to inspect the storehouse, or suggesting a jaunt that would somehow inevitably take them to the opposite end of town from the schoolroom. Maggie had to content herself with questioning

Paul as subtly as she could manage, trying to find out how he was enjoying school this year, but Paul was not a particularly loquacious and perceptive boy, and a shrug and an answer of "it's all right, I suppose", were as much as she could prise out of him – and even she wasn't certain what answer she wanted. If he'd told her that he loathed Miss Crawford and the place hadn't been the same since Maggie left, then she would have berated herself for abandoning her students. If he had spoken favourably of Miss Crawford, she would have felt supplanted, and so after a while she stopped asking at all, though she could never resist offering to help Paul with his homework, allowing herself a tiny, vicarious taste of teaching through coaching his addition or subtraction, or listening to his halting reading aloud.

Chapter Thirteen

When pregnancy came, Maggie welcomed it as much as a distraction from thoughts of teaching as she did for its own sake. Despite her lapsed Catholicism, there had been lines she hadn't been prepared to cross before her marriage, behaviours too deeply ingrained into her, and the prohibition of sex outside of wedlock was one of those. A few weeks after the wedding, Charlie pointed out that they seemed to be making up for lost time, and so the pregnancy shouldn't have been the surprise that it was. But Maggie somehow allowed herself to shrug off the mild yet persistent symptoms that she had seen in her elder sisters so many times, and to deflect Charlie's eager questioning, until two months had passed and her belly and breasts were swelling enough that she had to let out her dresses, whereupon she was forced to admit that Charlie was probably correct in his suspicions. The news was met with joy by the whole McGill household, particularly from Charlie, who had a wide-eyed, uncomplicated longing for fatherhood, and from Elizabeth, longing as she was for a new project – a baby to look after as Paul was distancing himself from her every day. Even Peter gave one of the longest speeches she had ever heard him make – all of two sentences, back to back – when telling her how glad he was to be expecting his first grandchild.

Maggie's own joy was somewhat more circumspect. She'd never had the strong longing for children that she'd heard other women speaking about. She and Charlie had spoken about it shortly after their engagement, and he had confirmed what she had always suspected: that in his position as the eldest child of a landowning family, children would be less of a choice than an imperative – children, and preferably sons to carry on the family line and take over the farm in the fullness of time – and she had acquiesced with a shrug. Just as surely as engagement led to marriage, marriage led to children in the world as Maggie understood it, and by accepting to marry Charlie she felt as if the decision was already made. But now that she found herself pregnant, it struck her at last quite how different a child of one's own was from simply looking after other people's children all day. And at first, this wouldn't even be a child, it would be a baby, loud and demanding and uninteresting, as she'd always felt about her sisters' children, and she'd be solely responsible. Of course Charlie would say he'd help, and so would Elizabeth, and there would be nurses and servants, making things a thousand times easier for her than they had ever been for her mother or her older sisters – but despite all of that, everyone knew that the main carer was the mother; it was all up to the mother. Maggie held on to her uncertainty for as long as she could, battening it down behind glassy smiles, but she became increasingly snappish and short-tempered, changing the subject whenever anyone mentioned the baby, coming dangerously close to losing her temper with Charlie because, in his straightforward pleasure in the idea of impending fatherhood, he could barely bring himself to talk about anything else – and finally, the day that she found her belly too swollen to allow her to fit into her favourite blue poplin dress, Charlie found her curled up on their bed, shaking with silent, desperate tears.

For all his faults – Maggie had mentally castigated him again and again in the past few weeks, irrationally furious at his seemingly deliberate inability to see behind the façade of happiness that she had put up – Charlie was faultless when a problem was laid clearly in front of him, without obfuscation. He took Maggie into his arms, soothing her, even as she struggled against him half-heartedly with a child's embarrassment at being seen in tears. But when she started to subside, sniffing and hiccupping and laughing at herself slightly hysterically, his calm questioning began to lay her fears out in front of her, like playing cards turned upright. At last she began to see how much of her ideas of motherhood – and her subsequent anxieties – had been related to her view of her own mother, of how hard she'd worked, and how bitter and cramped and small her life had always seemed to be, how much pleasure and interest and stimulation her life had lacked, and how little enjoyment she had ever had in her own children.

"I didn't even realise," Maggie said to Charlie. "I didn't even know that was what I was thinking. I know that it won't be like that for us, or for me..."

"I hope you do," Charlie said, looking worried. "I don't know how much I'll be able to help myself, not when he's very small..." Charlie had referred to the baby as 'he' from the very start, which Maggie found oddly touching and so had never bothered pointing out his assumption – "but my mother will help, of course – she's desperate to help – and we have the maids, and the cook – it will be completely different for you here."

Maggie never spoke of her anxiety to anyone but Charlie, but Charlie himself must have mentioned it, because over the next weeks and months she noticed Elizabeth's behaviour becoming more tender towards her. They had been increasingly friendly since the wedding, but now there was something motherly in Elizabeth's demeanour, a genuine kindness in her eyes when she looked at Maggie that had been absent before, and Maggie realised that, for the first time, Elizabeth saw that the two of them were on the same side; the last lingering doubts that Elizabeth had harboured, that Maggie wasn't an appropriate match for Charlie, and the jealousy that Elizabeth would never have admitted to but that Maggie dimly sensed whenever Charlie smiled at her, had finally dissipated. By the time the end of the pregnancy drew near, Maggie felt more of a McGill than she had ever felt a Sullivan, the tail end of a long line of children that had been surrendered to, rather than ever actively wanted. All her life she had failed to understand the importance of family. Aside from her bond with Patrick, she had never really grasped why people valued some people more highly simply because they shared a modicum of blood. But in the final weeks of her pregnancy, heavy and lumbering in the height of summer, too hot and uncomfortable to move, with Elizabeth tirelessly fanning her as she lay in the shade of the veranda, Charlie rubbing her feet in bed at night, in spite of his own exhaustion, Paul haltingly reading aloud to her as the evenings finally drew in and lifted the heat off the day, and Peter making a special trip into town to buy a tub of ice cream from the Turkish ice cream seller, because it was the only thing that she could consider stomaching as the sweat ran off her in rivulets, she understood at last that for some people, for her at least, family was who you choose, and who chooses you back.

She had been prepared for the birth, long and arduous, painful and humiliating, and yet at the same time the most real, genuine thing she thought she had ever done. She had been prepared to love the baby: Elizabeth had told her in the last few weeks that the love was indescribable, on a different scale to anything else that she had ever felt, and Maggie had nodded and smiled and rationally, intellectually, taken the information on board, but nonetheless she was completely and utterly unprepared for the intensity of emotion that she experienced when the baby – a boy, Peter Patrick, they had decided on the name months before – was laid on her chest, swaddled in white linen, his face puckered and crumpled, hands curled in on themselves like autumn leaves. If she hadn't been told that what she would feel for the baby was love, she wouldn't have been able to identify the emotion, so different it was from any other experience of love that she'd had, intense to a point of being almost sickening and painful. She'd always thought of love as a positive emotion, a pleasant feeling, but this wasn't pleasant; it was a cramping, an itching inside her skin, handcuffs slamming down over her wrists, chains cinching in around her torso. She'd thought that she'd surrendered her freedom when she married Charlie, and she'd done so willingly – or mostly willingly – but she had never realised quite what it meant to be beholden to another person until she found herself wrapped around the tiny finger of her son.

Afterwards, Maggie always had difficulty remembering the next couple of years clearly. Little Peter was an angry baby, twisted up with colic and gasping and wheezing with croup. Maggie felt his suffering as if it was her own. Her own lungs turned to water, her own guts twisted up in pain, and for the first six months she barely slept. To Charlie's dismay, she refused to leave the baby overnight in the care of the nurse that they had painstakingly employed from Sydney. Nancy was a cheerful, broad-faced young woman, hardy enough despite one leg crippled by polio. She was trustworthy enough for Maggie during the day, but at night all the visions of ghouls, goblins and banshees that Maggie's parents had tormented her with as a child, which she hadn't thought about for years, came roaring back, hooting and gibbering. It wasn't as if Maggie believed in them, not really, not for herself at least, but Peter was different, a precious, tiny, helpless little scrap of flesh and bone; anything could happen to him, natural or supernatural. For the first few weeks, even though their bedroom was at the other end of the corridor from the nursery and she shouldn't have been able to hear anything, Maggie was tormented by the ghosts of Peter's wails, flung like gossamer through the house, lurking in every corner and, roused by a phantom cry, Maggie would pad barefoot down the heavily waxed hall into Peter's room, to find the boy silent and slumbering in his cradle, or, more often, Nancy, eyes bleary with sleep, rocking him as he howled – a vision that always filled her with a surge of unreasonable jealousy. After the third time that this had happened, Maggie insisting that the obedient but evidently puzzled Nancy hand Peter over to her, as much for Maggie's own comfort as for his, the damp warmth of his flesh through his cotton nightshirt acting like balm on her burning skin, slowing the skip of her heart, Maggie surrendered at last to the inevitable, told Nancy that her duties would henceforth end at night, and moved a bed into the nursery so that she could sleep near Peter and have the satisfaction of knowing all the cries that she heard were real, not imagined.

Maggie fell pregnant for the second time when Peter was only nine months old, and both she and Charlie had to laugh. They had had scarcely any time together since Peter's birth, especially with Maggie choosing to sleep in the nursery rather than in their bedroom at night. In fact, when discussing it they could only remember two times when they had had the time and inclination for making love, but clearly one of these had done the trick, and Maggie now faced a second pregnancy with a mixture of terror and excitement: excitement because she knew what to expect this time – she knew the intense ferocious love that motherhood brings, she knew the rapt fascination of holding a sleeping baby, and she wanted to experience them again – and terror because she knew how much having Peter had exhausted her, and the idea of doubling that amount of exhaustion was unimaginable. But after her baptism of fire with Peter's anger and illness and fussiness, fate smiled on her. The second time around, her pregnancy coincided with Peter getting over the last, lingering traces of his infant colic, and transforming from a fractious, screaming baby into a charming one, smiling and plump, engaged by the world and able to entertain himself for hours. As for Mary, when she was born she was as different from Peter as could be, quiet and calm without being the docile sort of baby that Maggie found irritating. At only a few weeks old, she was already sleeping through the night and through much of the day as well, and one day, as Maggie sat on the veranda with Mary in her arms and Peter at her knee, banging brightly coloured blocks together, she realised with a start that she was no longer managing her children, but actively enjoying them.

The main change in her life, now that Peter was a bit older and growing out of his difficult phase and Mary was proving to be such an easy baby, was the difference in her mobility. With Peter just about able to walk, staggering about on fat, bowed legs, and Mary slung over her hip, she could manage a trip into town on her own. Even better, now that Peter was as happy and healthy as he was, she felt comfortable about leaving her children for the first time, as Nancy obviously doted on the two of them and Elizabeth, too, craved their company. Peter was the darling of the family, as the oldest grandchild and the first boy of the next generation, but Elizabeth clearly harboured a soft spot for Mary, with her easy charm – and when Nancy inconveniently took to her bed with a cold on a day when Maggie was longing for some time off, rather than feeling put upon, as Maggie had feared, Elizabeth seemed not only delighted but actively flattered to be trusted to take care of such precious bundles. When Maggie returned after a couple of hours spent in town looking at the shops and having tea with a friend, she found Elizabeth aglow with happiness, with Mary asleep over her shoulder, and Peter at her feet producing an elaborate painting, despite the fact that more of the paint seemed to be on his own arms and legs than on the paper.

It was around this time that Maggie started to become friends with Süleyman. She'd known who he was for years – everyone in the town knew Süleyman, with his round, genial face and his cart, painted with scenery of mountain and lakes that took on a near hallucinatory quality out there on the edge of the desert. Maggie had been interested in him in the same way that she was interested in everyone, wondering where he had come from and how he had ended up in Cottier's Creek selling ice cream, but she never thought to give him much more than a friendly smile and a few words when they were exchanging money, or a wave when he passed in his cart – not until she was a mother. One of the strange things about becoming a mother, she had said to Charlie once, was that you start to judge people differently. In the old days, when Maggie met someone she would form a rounded impression of them, taking in their appearance, their intelligence, their friendliness and charm and native wit. Nowadays, though, she found herself pleasantly disposed to anyone, irrespective of their other qualities or lack thereof, who liked her children and was liked back, and between Süleyman and Peter it had been something akin to love at first sight.

The day that Süleyman and Peter first met, Maggie hadn't seen Süleyman in months, though she heard him pass the house most days, the bell of his cart clinking, announcing his presence. Most days it was Nancy or one of the maids who would go down to the end of the path, open the gate, and buy some ice cream for the while family, but that day Nancy was in the middle of bathing Mary when Süleyman came up the road. Looking out of the window, Maggie could just about see Süleyman, sitting straight-backed on the rear of the cart, Sena, his horse, pawing at the ground, emanating a sort of quiet, still patience that she, as someone with the natural patience of a grasshopper, couldn't help but envy.

"I'll go," she said to Nancy, who looked up in surprise, but nodded; Maggie hoisted Peter into her arms, trotted with him down the stairs – while he squeaked with pleasure – and down to the gate, where Süleyman caught sight of her and raised his arm in a surprised, pleased greeting.

"I haven't seen you in such a long time," he said, in his careful, accented English. "I thought maybe you had left the town."

"Oh! No, I've been right here." It was as if a gulf had opened up between them. Maggie had never thought much about it, but realised then that, despite the rumour mill that ran ceaselessly through Cottier's Creek, there was a whole part of town – the part of town that lived in the flapping white tents beyond the station – who knew nothing of the details of her life, and probably couldn't care less.

Süleyman frowned. "You were the teacher, weren't you?"

"I was, but I married – three years ago; more, now." She

jiggled Peter in my arms. "This is my little boy. You don't think I have time for work when I have one of these? And another little girl back in the house, too."

Looking at Peter, Süleyman's face split wide into a dazzling smile, one that was echoed by Peter himself, who instantly put his arms out, fingers extended like branches, and started to crow with delight.

"How old is he?"

"He was two a couple of months ago. His name's Peter."

"Peter," Süleyman repeated, and then asked: "Do you mind?" indicating the steps of the cart with one hand. When she shook her head, he leapt down with unexpected agility for someone so rotund, and approached, holding his hand out to Peter, his face solemn though his eyes were creased with laughter. Unhesitating, Peter reached out and placed his sticky palm into Süleyman's, who gently clasped the boy's hand in his and pumped it up and down once, twice. "Pleased to meet you," he said gravely, and Maggie couldn't help but laugh. Still holding Peter's hand, Süleyman turned to Maggie. "I love children. In my culture, children are very important – but out where I live..." he shrugged. "Too many men on their own; not enough children. I miss seeing them, at this age."

"Would you like to hold him?" Maggie asked. The words were out of her mouth before she fully realised what she was going to say, but the look of happiness that crossed Süleyman's face instantly made it impossible for her to take them back. Indeed, Peter seemed to sense what was happening and leant precariously out of her arms towards Süleyman, arms outspread like wings. Süleyman took him, lifting him with a gentle, fluid ease that Maggie had rarely seen in men. Charlie's father, Peter was seemingly unable to lift Little Peter without treating him like a piece of fragile glass, and even Charlie had taken some time to get the hang of it.

"Do you have children?" she asked.

"No," Süleyman answered, with a slight shake of his head,

before turning back to Peter and asking eagerly, "Would you like to see the horse, then? Would you?"

Peter let out a squeal of delight, and Süleyman carried him over to where Sena stood, now snorting with impatience, ears dancing about on her head, eyes rolling slightly. It occurred to Maggie that she should probably be worried, but the way Süleyman had draped Peter over his hip, casual yet firm, held such assurance that she couldn't help but trust him. And indeed when Süleyman spoke a couple of words to the horse in an angular, slithering language that Maggie couldn't place, it stilled immediately. Peter reached out his starfish hand, face rigid with fascination, and touched the smooth, shiny coat of the horse's neck, damp with summer morning sweat, the smell of which seemed to stay on Peter's hand for the rest of the day, the sharp tang of salt and the sweet smoke of hay. In that moment, Peter and Süleyman became fast friends, and Maggie with him.

She told Charlie about it that evening, couched in carefully casual tones that would be certain to provoke no alarm. Charlie was easy-going at heart, and certainly bore no malice towards the darker-skinned men who lived on the edge of the town, but he was prone to the occasional panic-laced worry when it came to his children, and Maggie didn't want to say anything that could concern him and initiate some sort of ice cream moratorium. Maggie told stories well, her body taking on the shapes of the tale, and Charlie laughed at her description of Peter's gleeful face, the way he had strained to reach the horse as if his very life depended on it. But that night, in bed, Maggie found herself thinking again and again of the one part of the incident that she hadn't told Charlie, because she hadn't known how – the almost imperceptible pause between her asking Süleyman if he had any children, and his answer in the negative. His face had gone blank, just for a split second, just for the time that it took to remember something unrememberable, and to telegraph the message: *don't ask*.

Chapter Fourteen

The best thing that Süleyman had discovered over time, the best lesson that he had learnt, the best skill that he had – better than his spoken English, his ability to read the Koran, the way that he could make ice cream that was so sweet and creamy that it would torment people in their dreams – was the ability to make himself forget. It wasn't a total forgetting, of course – they were always there, with him, a slightly uncomfortable presence just under his skin, or the mere shadow of a wraith at his elbow whenever he turned around too fast – but those things were bearable; he could live with that sort of gentle manifestation in the way that he couldn't live if dragging around every day the leaden weight of his loss, the hard, painful immovability of his grief and anger that could lodge in his gullet or in his gut, leaving him uncomfortable and dyspeptic for days, unable to swallow more than a small glass of oversweet tea. That was the pain that he forced down, forced back every day, the reason that he practiced the memory games that he did, imprisoning his vanished family in a corner of his head, bowed down, battened down, only let out on the rare occasions when his mood was soft and gentle enough, the edge taken off with raki or a smoke of the nargileh; at those times he could sometimes bear to remember the past.

He had never really meant to tell Halim. In general, he had found that his story was the sort of thing best kept to himself, both due to the difficulty of the telling and because of the way that it changed things in the person who heard it, the way that their eyes shifted, the way that they never seemed able to make Süleyman the butt of their jokes again, which was something he loved. He felt that he was born to play the fool, but telling the story seemed to create distance around him, leaving him standing alone amid his loss, and while he knew that part of it was because people didn't know how to treat him, what to say and how to avoid making the pain any deeper – while all the time he wanted nothing more than for them to treat him the same as they always had, pretend that the messy, incontinent grief running through his past didn't exist – he also knew that part of it was an unwillingness to catch his bad luck, which everyone knew was as infectious as scarlet fever, turning people black and rotten beneath its ink-dark shadow.

He hadn't meant to tell Halim, but there was something confessional in the boy, something about the way he was happy to sit in silence, feeling no need to fill the air with words – the sort of quiet, still demeanour that drew conversation out of a person. Halim had told Süleyman about where he came from, stories that sounded to Süleyman like an idyll, despite Halim's occasional distaste – the cramped quarters, the hot offal stink of his uncle's butcher shop – and he could taste Halim's curiosity about a man from another part of the Empire, sharing a religion and a language over such a distance.

It was hard to look back with any degree of objectivity, but Süleyman could just about remember a time when he'd felt his life was as idyllic as the life that Halim had described – a childhood spent in the fields in summer, under a sky as wide and warm as a blanket; the warm, moist heat of animals; the slightly claustrophobic love of his family – all sisters and then him, alone and yet never alone, cosseted yet, he felt, never understood. Süleyman had married young. He looked at Halim, seventeen and still a boy, and half-laughed, realising that at Halim's age he had already been married for a year and was the father of one, with another on the way. His wife, Aygen, had been a cousin, a narrow-faced girl with whom he'd played as a child, whose hair he'd pulled and who had always annoyed him by going off crying when he suggested his roughest, most adventurous games. Aygen had made a far better wife than she had a playmate, and when the time came, he had found himself entranced by her soft, undulating body, the curves that grew as she got older into a generous cascade of flesh, as if she was bursting out of herself, and Süleyman had loved her for it. She had made the best kuzu güveç he had ever tasted – better even than his mother's, he told her with a sly grin early in their marriage, and she'd smiled, both believing him and not believing him at the same time – and she made the best bread, too. She grew herbs in small pots in the sunny courtyard of their little house; she milked the goats without complaint; but best of all, Aygen seemed designed to do little other than to make children, gestate them, bring them into the world silent and stoic, and then raise them with a light heart and a heavy hand. She was the sort of mother that Süleyman's own mother had been, the best sort.

The first child was a boy, whom they called Süleyman after his delighted father, and the second, a year later, was also a boy, Karim. The third was a girl, Feride, then came two more boys, Orhan and Ziya, and then for the first time, late in the evening, curled together in bed, Süleyman pressing urgently against Aygen's ample flesh, she put her hand flat against his chest. "No," she said. Then, smiling into his offended face, she went on: "I need a break," and, with her long, probing fingers – the only part of her body that had remained slim through the intervening years – and her full, wide mouth, she proceeded to make him almost glad that she had had enough of children for now.

Neither of them had ever given any thought to what it had meant to be Muslims; the fact of what they were was simple enough to be unquestioned, it ran in their veins, the black ink of the Koran instead of blood. Süleyman had never been particularly religious but the mosque, with its delicate minaret like a finger pointing out Allah, was the centre of his world. He had always had Greek friends for as long as he had been alive; the subtle differences between them were as all-pervasive and as unremarkable as the difference between men and women. But things change, he told Halim that evening, years later, in the suffocating desert hush of Cottier's Creek; things always change, and as his children were growing, he started to realise that the gap between the Greeks and the Muslims was growing, too – that faces that had previously been kind or at least indifferent were now hostile. The other Muslims noticed it also, and they started to talk. The Empire was crumbling, they said; its time was over, they said (though some of them averred that its time had been over a long time ago); opinion was split as to what they should do next. Yes, they spoke Turkish, but the centre of the Empire was as alien to them as France or Norway. Crete was where they had lived, often for generations, and there were those who insisted that they stay, mark out their part of the land, and prove that they belonged here as much as anyone. Others decried this idea as lunacy. The thing to do, they said, was to leave, to travel for as long as it took to reach Istanbul and rest safe in the arms of a country that they knew would take them in. It was funny, though, Süleyman told Halim, that the people who advocated the latter course of action were the richer ones, those with the money to leave and start up anew, or at least those with family elsewhere. Most of the Muslims weren't in that position; most of them held whatever meagre wealth they had in their land; for most, the idea of packing up and leaving the place where they had been born, where their fathers and mothers and grandfathers and grandmothers had been born was as unfeasible as it was unimaginable and undesirable. And so they stayed.

Süleyman's greatest fault, he had always joked, was his optimism, and never did his joke prove truer than in that particular case. Certainly, things had changed – he knew that, he would have had to have been blind not to see that – but it was still home. The man whose looks cast daggers across the street to him when walking through the village was still just Philo, whom he'd played with as a child, throwing sticks at rabbits. The woman who turned her back on him in the market was still just Elpida, to whom he'd professed arbitrary and undying love at the age of eight. Yes, they were acting differently now, but it was bound to be temporary. Things would get back to normal before too long.

But Aygen started having nightmares. This was the part of the story that Süleyman found hardest to tell, even harder than the parts that should have been harder; he had to stop and swallow against his rising nausea and his rising tears. Aygen, his gentle, laughing wife, who had slept soundly beside him for years, had started to thrash about in her sleep, moaning and writhing, calling out words, sometimes nonsense and sometimes simple denial: "No! No!"

At first she claimed that she didn't remember the dreams; she plastered a brave face on every morning, trying to cover her pallor and the deep bruise-like circles under her dark eyes, but Süleyman was unconvinced, until one evening, late at night, the children in bed, Aygen sat at the kitchen table for longer than she ever had after a meal, eating a last piece of bread crumb by crumb, ignoring Süleyman's repeated suggestions that they go to bed, and eventually she broke down. With tears rolling down her smooth, round cheeks, trying her hardest to keep her shaking voice low so as not to wake the children and frighten them, she told him that she was dreaming of death, death and blood, avenging angels with swords that reflected the sky, their multiple feathered wings pummelling the air like thunder, slaying and maiming and bringing about interminable suffering. It was unbearable, she said; she couldn't bear to go to bed, she couldn't bear to sleep. She knew that he was going to say that she was just being silly, but she knew, she had a feeling, she was surer than she'd ever been in her life, that something bad was going to happen, and she knew, oh, of course she knew that he didn't want to leave; it was the last thing that she wanted, too, but she couldn't shake her dreams from her head, the way that they lurked just behind her eyes throughout the day, and she knew what they meant, and she knew that something bad was coming. Süleyman held her while she cried, and, unable as he had always been to refuse her anything, he agreed: if that was what she wanted, if she was so sure, then they would leave – not straight away, they didn't have the money for that, but he would start saving, and before too long they would go.

Things had been turning for a while, with the subtle certainty of a change in the wind, but when it came to it, Süleyman was still woefully unprepared. He had always respected Aygen's wishes – she was normally so unquestioningly compliant that he found himself willing to concede to her on the rare occasions that she expressed them directly; he still laughed away her fears, refusing to believe that anything bad could happen to them on their home soil, but somehow her fear was infecting him, perhaps creeping its way across the pillow at night as they slept, perhaps clinging to the tea glasses that they drank from together, and all he knew was that, before long, his fear of leaving teetered and then toppled into a fear of staying. He was saving as much money as he could, from the sales of milk and vegetables at the market, but now, of all times, trade was dropping off due to the growing anti-Muslim feeling in the village. It was the first time that money really mattered to him, yet it was unforthcoming, and cracks of panic started to appear just under his skin. Aygen would surprise him sometimes sitting at the kitchen table, smoothing and counting out the soft, tattered notes that they kept hidden in a jar, and sometimes he would surprise her doing the same thing, but no matter how many times they checked, the money never grew any faster, and Süleyman started to cast around for other things that he could sell.

They were never going to be in time. In early spring, Süleyman had to travel to the nearest town, Agios Stephanos, in order to sell some goats. It was a slightly desperate move, and Aygen had pleaded with him not to go, afraid that it would be a wasted mission for him, and more afraid, a fear that she could barely admit to, that something would happen when he was gone. But he persuaded her with soft talk of the possible profits – if the trip went as well as he hoped, it could be the difference between staying and going for them, enough money to for the whole family to take the boat away from the island. Süleyman had initially hoped to save enough to allow them to set up somewhere new, but the increasing tension in the village and the surrounding area, and the increasing fear in Aygen's eyes, made this a vain hope. If they only had enough to get them away, then that was that, they would have to leave with what they had, and take their chances. Süleyman was still young, he was intelligent and he was strong; so what if he had never done anything but work as a farmer? So what if he had never been further than twenty miles from the place that he was born? He would manage; he would make a new start for his family. He closed his eyes and his heart to the thought of his mother, alone now, his father having died years before, who could not be persuaded to leave, insisting that she would die where she was born and that any other earth would surely reject her body. Two of his sisters and their families had already left, and if he and Aygen and the children could only make it so far as where Lale and her husband Shevket were living near Denizli, then that would be enough, at least for now.

But when he came back from town, his pockets weighed down with money, his heart lighter than it had been for months, he found the village burning and his family gone.

That was how he phrased it when speaking to Halim, years later, as darkness gathered in the house and their tea cooled on the kitchen table in front of them. Süleyman looked down at his hands – hard, gnarled; farmer's hands, though he hadn't been a farmer for years – as Halim stared at him, watching every movement of his face for a clue, trying to work out if he meant what Halim thought he meant.

"Gone?"

"Gone."

"But – gone how?"

And Süleyman snapped, anger rising quickly up his throat like bile: "How do you think? I had a family, and I don't have a family any more. They are gone."

He didn't want to tell Halim. For some reason these details were intimate, and he would have sooner talked about Aygen's sexual practices than he would describe to him the mess he found when he returned to his house, the way that Aygen's dress was arranged, making it clear what had been done to her; the hot, metal stench of blood; the children clustered together, their expressions living but their eyes lifeless. Horrible as they were, they were his memories; he had not carried them around inside him, having them tug him, gasping and retching, from dreams, just to share them with a boy who had never lost anything real in his life.

The problem with forgetting, with making yourself forget, is that there tends to be collateral damage, and with all the effort of thrusting those images out of his mind – an imperfect job at best – Süleyman sacrificed the next few weeks, even months of his life. He could piece it together, afterwards – flashes and flickers of memory, like the sun glinting off glass – standing in the back garden, digging, because he had to bury them as quickly as possible, that was the Islamic law; being approached by Dimitri, who had been his neighbour since he was a child; the look of sick pity and shame on Dimitri's face which meant that, even though he was the enemy now, Süleyman couldn't bring himself to leap at him as he wanted to do. Dimitri saved his life, Süleyman explained to Halim. He never knew why, but for some reason Dimitri hadn't succumbed to the madness that had gripped the rest of the Greeks in the village – a madness which, he later understood, had leapt from place to place, as in Muslim villages Greeks were slaughtered, and vice versa.

Dimitri still saw Süleyman as human, and he helped him, hid him in his house for a week – two weeks, maybe a month; time ran through Süleyman's fingers and it could never be any more than a guess – and then helped him, when the time was right. When things had calmed down – though only temporarily – he gave him enough food to tide him over for the journey to the coast, walking through the night and sleeping wherever he could, and then the boat, with only the clothes that he stood up in and a spare shirt of Dimitri's, stained by mud and sweat and dew. Then there was Smyrna, louder and more frightening than anywhere that Süleyman had ever been, an alien beast of a city that stripped him bare and took him apart and put him back together, different, stronger but harder.

The last thing he wanted to do was to travel east, find his sister and lay his tragedy out in front of her like raw meat, and so he chose to sink into anonymity, working down at the docks, moving crates. For the first few months, his hands were a mass of blisters, red raw and bleeding, his muscles corded and shrieking every morning when he woke up. He slept in a boarding house for men like him, poor, silent, desperate men who never asked each other about their pasts, who only wanted to work as hard as they could and get as far as possible away from whatever demons were snapping at their heels. Süleyman took to drink and then gave it up as quickly as he had started. He'd been told that drink made you forget, but all it did was make him remember, and worse, it made him talk, telling his story again and again to faces shocked or indifferent, and every time he told his story, the words running over the places in his mind where he stored the exact slant of Aygen's smile, or the smell of his children's sun-warmed skin, it became more real, it anchored him to his past and made a lie of the stories that he told himself when he was sober: that he was no one, he came from nowhere, he had always been this man in this place, there had been no happy wife, no light-hearted children, no goats, no pots of herbs, no warm wooden house draped in vines, no village in a valley, no parents, no family, no community, no homeland. If he had never had them, he could never have lost them. It had taken him years, Süleyman told Halim, years until he could trust himself to take a glass of raki or two without it prompting a precipitous fall into the pit of memories that he had learnt to skirt so carefully.

Smyrna had been the perfect place to bury himself, until one morning he woke up and unaccountably found it suffocating. Then Süleyman started to drift. Finding a job here, a friend there, he made his way gently south and east, where the land became hotter and sandier and drier, further away from the altar of Empire on which his family had been sacrificed. When the offer came to work his passage to Australia on a ship full of tough-skinned, hard-eyed cameleers and their hissing, spitting charges, Süleyman didn't think twice, although he'd never heard of Australia, and even when he was told about it – a new land, far away – it seemed impossible to the point of myth. He had given up on the idea of the Empire, the imagined village that he and Aygen had wrought from nothing in their nightly conversations about leaving, where he would buy some land and she would raise their children, and life would be like it was before, only they would be somewhere that no one could take away from them: those ideas had belonged to the man that Süleyman had been before, and the people who had belonged to him; they had nothing to do with him now.

The journey was painful and sickening, the hardest work that Süleyman had done in his life. He suffered from claustrophobia, down in the belly of the ship. He had never realised how important the sun was to him, and the sky; he felt that he could cope with any sort of pain, any work, no matter how hard, as long as he could breathe fresh air and feel the wind on his face. He hated every second of it, and yet still he never regretted his choice and never looked back. The journey was a divestment, as Süleyman shed layers of himself, almost unawares – first the silent, tough mantle that he'd slipped on in Smyrna, to protect him from himself and from others; then the bitterness and rage and pain that lay underneath; he stripped himself back and back until he was as raw and fresh as he had been as a child. The grief was still there, it would never go away, but he had burrowed through it now, come up with something deeper and more real; he'd come up with himself, a harder, truer idea of himself than he ever would have discovered had he stayed happily where he had been born. And then he built himself up from scratch, a layer of courtesy, a layer of compassion, a layer of conscientiousness – until he had reinvented himself as a man that he could bear being, a man that he had chosen to be, not the boy he'd been born as or the man who was what life had made of him. He decanted his memories and his past carefully, very carefully into a part of himself that stood just outside of him; he knew they were there, treasured, but kept at arm's length; they cost too much, and were too fragile and precious, for him to carry around every day. The final evening on the ship, before they docked in Sydney, Süleyman spent an hour in the tiny, stinking bathroom, leaning over its dim scrap of mirror. He shaved for the first time since he'd left Smyrna; he cut his hair as best he could with the knife he carried with him; he slicked it down with water and combed it with splayed fingers; and then he smiled, the first smile that he had attempted in a long time, a smile that cracked the corners of his lips until they bled and made his jaw ache, but still he smiled, he smiled, he smiled. This was who he was now.

July 15th 1915

Patrick wouldn't have believed that it would be possible to be bored at war, but he was. The initial, visceral horror had long since worn off, the echoing, clenching fear had died back to a dull throb in his belly, and even the most terrible things had become normal. The night before, the medical officer had been caught by a shell blast, his feet blown away, no hope for recovery, and while Patrick had been sad for him – he had been a good man, a kind man, and perhaps more importantly, had a seemingly endless collection of dirty jokes which he had told in a deadpan manner guaranteed to cadge a laugh on even the grimmest day – the sadness had been distant and muted, as if belonging to someone else. He wrote to Maggie religiously every Friday, but his letters contained nothing but the minutiae of his life and routine, the time of his breakfast, the contents of his lunch, who he had talked to while on guard in the evenings. Her letters came back, begging for more news: how was he feeling, and what was he seeing, and what was really happening out there? But how could he tell her? He had never had the facility with words that his sister had had, and he had no way to capture the exact tenor of a man's cries when his arm was blown off, or the precise smell of the mixture of blood and smoke that came after a shelling, or the look of dragging despair and tedium that he saw on his own face when he could be bothered to look into a mirror to shave it. And if he couldn't capture those things, if he couldn't tell it right for her, he didn't want to tell it at all.

Chapter Fifteen

Summer in Cottier's Creek was a breath of hell, desert opened wide like a yawn, the wind hot and sand-licked, the sky bright as death with the heat bouncing off the roads, earth packed tight and close. Halim's body ran with sweat from morning to evening, and he started to realise the point of it for the first time, waking up in the middle of the night in Süleyman's house, the air packed around him like a malign presence, hot and dense, and Halim would welcome the trickle of moisture down the back of his neck, an instant of coolness before the heat locked its arms around him again. There was something about this sort of weather that could make a man slightly unhinged. There was the faint metallic taste of panic in the back of Halim's throat every day that he opened his eyes to another blue, breathless sky and the sun as heavy and relentless as blows on an anvil. It had been November when Halim first arrived, and it wasn't until March that the summer, which had felt like a great, held breath, started to exhale a little, sending a cooler breeze coiling around the houses, through the great trees beside the roads, rattling the canvas and the flimsy wooden boards of the Ghan Town, toppling dry leaves; and Halim, who had felt as if he were wading through honey for the past few months, sticky and slow-witted by the end of the day with the weight of the sunshine and the newness scraping him raw, was given enough time and respite and breathing space to declare himself happy.

His English had gradually developed. Süleyman's house was littered with scraps of paper, phonetically spelled words, laboriously sounded out. Halim had spent the past few months, whether churning milk for ice cream or hanging, legs dangling, off the back of Süleyman's cart, or disjointing a sheep, mouthing words to himself, practicing them at any opportunity, whether talking with Süleyman's customers or with the other men of the Ghan camp, with whom English was the only shared language.

The butchery had come back to him with surprising ease. The first time, as he held Tariq's sheep in his hand, mute desperation in its eyes (which he told himself again and again that it couldn't feel; the sheep didn't know what was happening; it didn't feel the same way that he, Halim, did), springy layers of wool tight and bunched against his palm, he felt sick. He felt these things: the wool of the sheep, the tilt and strain of its sinews as it pulled away from him, the sand thin and scratchy beneath his sandals, the push of the wind against his white cotton shirt; and equally he felt these things: the weight of expectations of the people of the Ghan Town, some of whom had come to watch the slaughter; the eyes of his ancestors, living and dead, peering around each other's heads, judging his performance, keen to be disappointed; and Allah, broad and diffuse, wide and intent and unhurried, his eyes (such as they were) as sharp on the movement of Halim's knife as they were on every other Muslim around the world at that moment. Halim had held the sheep's head as firmly as his shaking hand would allow; and he had cut, numb, bloodless lips dedicating the sheep to Allah in words that were no more than routine, rhythmical sounds at that moment, meaningless, the tap of his tongue against lip, tooth and palate, the hissing exhalation of air as the knife had moved through the arteries and veins, the windpipe and the gullet, stopping short of the spinal cord. The sheep's blood had pattered into the dust like rain, like giant scarlet coins, and a woman from the camp, one of the few, silhouetted bright against the opalescent sky, opened her throat and cried out, ululating with wordless joy. It was that noise that had brought Halim back to himself and his place, and it was that moment that he remembered, cast back and clung fast to when the carcass was slippery under his weak boy's fingers, the knife treacherous in his hands, the flies battering around his face, blind and vicious.

Being a butcher had given him instant status, and he soon leant that this was as good as currency, or better – though the butchery brought him that, too. His Arabic still went no further than the Koran, and his English, while improving daily, was still too rudimentary to understand most of what the Ghan Town men said, for their accents were thick and fluid, and their speech was peppered with slang, both English and Arabic – but there were ways of communicating without words: the sleepy clack of counters on a backgammon board; the trill of amber tea poured into a tea glass; the chink and tumble of coins. The butchery was not making him rich, not yet, but he had sent the money for his fare back to Yiannis and Maria in Sydney (and received a letter in return that seemed to vibrate with restrained gladness for his good fortune); and he was able to pay Süleyman a nominal rent for the patch of boards that he occupied each night, the use of the bedrolls and blanket, the endless cups of tea and the bread and potatoes and yoghurt that accompanied the meat that he himself could offer. They had quiet, hurriedly-eaten meals each evening, heads down close to the bowl, fingers pursed around their bread, chasing every scrap of oil and juice from their plates.

They lived in two worlds, though, at least two. It was easy to forget that at dawn, with the shadows of the tents gentle and familiar against the lightening sky, the faint freckle of the fading stars, the singing sand and the voice of the muezzin looping over the camp – but Halim remembered it every time he helped Süleyman with his work, and that was most days. Süleyman would saddle up his horse, Sena, the silver of her bit and bridle gleaming like clear water – Halim was charmed and mystified by the horse, the clean warmth of her sweat and the copper shine of her burnished flank – load up his cart and if Halim wasn't busy with anything else, off they would go together, Süleyman sat up the front, supple leather reins caught around his calloused hands, moving easily with the dip and sway of the carriage, as the wheels slid and out of potholes in the road and as Sena flung up her hooves behind her. Süleyman always looked comfortable wherever he was, but a look would come over his face when he was seated at the front of his cart; his features would settle into a look of nobility and repose that, Halim reflected, would have been risible and sad if it had been deliberate. But it was just Süleyman, the most at home he ever was. Halim never knew what Süleyman thought about while he was sitting there – perhaps nothing more than keeping his eye on the road, or adding up his accounts in his head – but wherever his mind was, it made him unusually disinclined to talk, and, after a few uncomfortable attempts, with Halim pointing out landmarks and respectfully demanding explanations and translations, which came in terse monosyllables, if at all, Halim gave up and settled happily into his position at the back of the cart. He faced where they'd come from, watching the wheel tracks unspool, his body as ungainly as a sack of potatoes as he jounced from side to side, shoulders curled in and every vertebra cupped cosily on top of the other, deliciously slumped.

These were his favourite moments of the day, when the tracks of the wheels scrolled away from the camp, the tents fluttering smaller and smaller behind, their colours leaking into the heat-shimmer of the desert light. Soon, the cart mounted the tarred road of the town and the horse's gait smoothed; the wheels always shuddered, as if they hadn't quite expected this, and then shimmied into a rhythm, spinning in time; and houses loomed on either side, stark and blind-eyed, sharp-leafed and pock-marked lawns too tough and hardy to be comfortable, and top-heavy trees, holding their arms over the road. Halim was always particularly fascinated by the places he would never dare explore – by the town church, its boastful spire trying to pierce the sky, silent and as still as a museum bar Sundays, when it was decorated by women in their best dresses, children skittering up and down the flaking sandstone steps; and by the town pub, the church in reverse. Its balustraded balconies stretched along the corner of Main Street and Zinc Street like a pair of open arms to welcome the town on the days that the church would not, and for every drunk ejected, body curled like a baby as he tumbled down the steps, there was always one or more willing to take his place – all men, sweaty and red-faced, unadapted to the climate; faces like slabs of meat; eyes that seemed mean and watchful but were (often, mostly, Süleyman explained, and Halim tried to tell himself) simply closed and withered by the strength of the sun.

The women, though, Halim was more comfortable with – the women, the children and the young men, those whose faces were still open and ready to laugh, not shut in on themselves under the merciless desert sky. When they collected milk from Mrs Bell's farm for the ice cream, Halim always worked hard to make conversation with the maid, Millie, who laughed and blushed, rolled her eyes and never said much back, and with Mrs Bell herself, who was brusque and red-faced and pleasant, never afraid to correct Halim when he stumbled over a word or used one incorrectly (more than could be said for some of Süleyman's customers, who smiled politely and let Halim get away with any sort of gibberish), and whose open-throated caw of a laugh was somehow impossible to take personally.

He spoke to the customers, too, especially to the children, squatting in the sand, so his face was level with theirs, looking into their large, guileless eyes, which were often of that pale, helpless blue that ended up swallowed by the face as they got older, the skin colluding to protect those delicate organs – and their fine, white skin, sometimes red and flaking from the sun, sometimes spattered with a collection of freckles as if splashed by weak tea. The children knew him now, though not by name.

They didn't hide behind their mothers' skirts anymore but staggered out, mouths wide in gummy smiles, plump arms outflung, pressing a sticky coin into Halim's hand, fingers splayed to receive the ice cream cornet that Süleyman handed to Halim, and which dripped, cool and sweet, out of reach, until their mother gave the distracted smile and nod that said it was all right. The youngest of the children – those of three or four – had an English vocabulary around Halim's own level, and it was an embarrassment-free trick to pretend to be helping them, pointing at something unfamiliar; "What's that?" – excavating the real words, the parade of consonants and vowels that underlaid their blurred, lisped enunciation.

The women who came to the stall were almost always friendly, offering Halim smiles that ranged from tight and shy to broad and – he thought with concern – bordering on coarse, but he was always happy to leave the conversation to Süleyman, while listening intently for words he could ask Süleyman about later. Aside from greetings and thanks, the women never attempted to speak to him directly, apart from one blazing, crashing exception, and that was Maggie. From the moment that Halim had pushed Peter out of the way of the horses, Maggie seemed determined to force her way into his acquaintance, and to forge a friendship despite the gulfs of language and culture that stood between them. Lacking a common language, it seemed, was of little concern to Maggie; she certainly wasn't going to let it stand in her way, and when she realised, back in November, how strained and broken Halim's English really was, rather than giving up, as most people would have, and turning her attention to Süleyman, she seemed to latch onto Halim as her personal project. Every time she saw him, she was determined to teach him something new, offer another word for him to add to his arsenal. The first time she'd done this, showing him a cabbage in her basket and making him repeat the word over and over until his tongue had negotiated its careful way around the unfamiliar syllables without upset, he'd grinned and shaken his head after she'd gone, and had thought no more about it. But the next time they met, Maggie had fixed her eyes on him, narrowed and stern under the broad brim of her hat. "What's this?" she'd asked, pointing to the cabbage that she carried, and he realised then that she took him seriously, that he wasn't just some sort of endearing amusement to her.

*

And then one day the air shifted and everything suddenly seemed to feel different. Neither Halim nor Süleyman could identify it at first; something lay hunkered over the Ghan Town, a storm cloud, invisible, thick with tension and foreboding. They didn't speak of it, breakfasted as normal, saddled up the horse and cart in unnatural silence, and still the air felt heavy. There was no change in the behaviour of the other men they saw, who nodded and smiled as normal, but something was seeping into them, through the air and the earth and in the dry, brittle wind, and Halim didn't like it at all.

It worsened the closer they got to the town. Halim had to look up again and again to check that the sun was still hammered like a blank disc to the cloudless sky, for it felt darker than usual, the dense feeling of crowded air that comes before thunder. Süleyman, too, was starting to show his unease; he was stiff and tense as he gripped the reins between his slippery palms, jerking unnaturally from side to side with every step the horse took – and even the horse, normally placid, seemed susceptible, her shining coat shuddering and jerking with irritation, kicking out her hooves at the shadows they passed.

Maggie was waiting for them as they turned onto the main road. It took Halim by surprise – her house was at the other end of town – and he could see at a glance that her arms were empty: no children clamouring for sweets, and she never bought ice cream for herself – out of concern for her figure, she'd told Halim once, puffing out her cheeks in a mimicry of fatness, laughing. There was no laughter in her face today, though; as soon as she caught sight of the cart she raised her arms and waved, but the wave wasn't friendly, it was urgent, and Halim's heart lurched and banged behind his ribs. Cursing softly to himself – again, unlike him, Süleyman was normally good-natured – Süleyman dragged on the reins and the horse slowed from a fretful trot into a sulky walk, and then a halt, stomping and sighing like a petulant child. Seeing them stop, Maggie approached at a near run.

Halim understood barely any of her words which come out in a half-whispered rush, but he understood Süleyman's reaction: lips drawn back, eyes round, hand rubbing distractedly through his stubbled hair. Maggie gesticulated as she talked, her arms bouncing around like accents on top of her words – she was a thoroughly physical person, Halim realised, seeing her for the first time unfettered by children. After a few minutes she stopped, her arms hanging helplessly by her sides, hands open like a supplicant, and Süleyman rested his head on his hand, screwing his eyes up against the light.

"What – what is it?" Halim asked at last, and Süleyman turned towards him, the look on his face almost surprised, as if he'd forgotten Halim's existence.

"It's the war," he explained.

The war. Halim had been conscious of it, of course; that complex skirmish going on across the ocean, back in that part of the world that he'd left so far behind. Occasionally, he and Süleyman would talk about it; Süleyman's voice always sounded worried, but Halim realised now that whenever he'd thought about it, it was with a sense less of concern and of sorrow than of secret self-congratulation, that he'd come so far away from such barbaric mentality. The fighting in the Empire was far from his family, and he had not paid enough attention to try and make sense of the complex tangle of assassinations, tested and torn loyalties, battleships and the serried ranks of his countrymen lined up on a cliff-edge, staring down the

Mediterranean. It made little sense to him, and he was happy that way; it allowed him to feel superior to it.

"You're going to have to start caring," Süleyman said, and though he hadn't said anything, Halim knew that something in his body had betrayed his insouciance. Süleyman didn't look angry, though; merely weary. In short, stark sentences he spelled out for Halim the story of the Gallipoli landings – Gelibolu, Halim though vaguely, mentally placing it somewhere near Smyrna - and the men who had washed up on that unfriendly shore, who had scrambled up the beach, pushing their way up the cliffs, only to be cut down by the men at the top – Muslim men, and the men on the beach, they'd been Australians and New Zealanders. Still it didn't make much sense to Halim; what had it to do with him? And this time Süleyman's exasperation showed through.

"Australian men, Halim. Some of them men from this town, from around here, and they've been killed by our people. How do you think that's going to affect us, boy? We're not going to be too popular around town for a while."

Maggie stood watching them, her face still but her hands in constant motion, picking at the dry skin around her nails, smoothing the creases in her skirt. Halim caught her eye and offered her a shy grin; she smiled swiftly in return but it was gone from her face as quickly as it had arrived, no more than a pleasantry; her mind was evidently on other things. Süleyman looked back towards her, indecision warring over his features; Halim could practically see the parade of his thoughts as they passed through his mind.

"Wait," Süleyman said to Halim, and turned back to Maggie, bending low towards her, his words offering her something with a quiet, urgent courtesy. She let out a short laugh, surprised and frightened and pleased all at once, and took a half step back. Süleyman's face fell for a moment, but Maggie seemed to collect herself for she gave Süleyman a firm, decisive nod and his face flooded with relief, and she marched to the back of the cart, where Halim was sitting. When she extended her hand to him, Halim wasn't sure what to make of it. Doubtfully, he gave her his hand to shake, but when she felt his loose grip she laughed and shook her head. She cast her eyes down for a moment, and then up again, her hand patting the smooth boards next to where Halim was sitting. "Help me up," she said, miming a lift, her foot on the spoke of a wheel.

Incredulous, Halim half turned towards Süleyman for confirmation. "She's getting onto the cart?" And Süleyman nodded curtly.

"We need to find out as much as we can about what's going on. It's impolite for us to expect her to talk to us out here in the street, in the sun, with people around. She will come and drink tea with us."

By the time they arrived back at Süleyman's house, Halim was suddenly, violently aware that he admired Maggie McGill more than anyone else that he could think of. The way that she had climbed onto the back of the cart, her hand warm and dry in Halim's grasp, and settled herself beside him on the soft wood without a trace of awkwardness; the look on her face as they travelled back towards the camp – while Halim felt that he could shrivel up in horror at every stare they attracted, simply wither up like a leaf in autumn and bounce away into the gutter, Maggie's face showed nothing but amusement and a kind of friendly hauteur, as if there was no place to which she was better suited, no place that she would rather be than the back of an old ice cream cart, driven by one Turk and sat next to another. In the time that they had spent talking by the side of the road, a small crowd had gathered over the other side of the street, Mr Thompson leaning on his front fence, and Mr McBride from next door, silent and watchful if not entirely unfriendly, and so Maggie's journey hadn't gone unnoticed. Not only that, but it became clear just from those few moments what the attitude of most of the town was – wary, if not outright hostile – and while Halim couldn't quite fathom why Maggie had chosen not to share it, he recognised her stance for the act of reckless, slightly prideful bravery that it was.

Halim poured the tea himself, careful as a child at a tea party not to jolt the delicate tea glass that Maggie was holding, pushing sugar towards her. She seemed nonplussed for a moment, and Halim suddenly remembered Mostafa telling him back in Sydney, grimacing, that Europeans don't drink their tea like Muslims; they dilute it with milk and barely use any sugar at all. For a moment he could have kicked himself, but then Maggie shovelled two spoonfuls of sugar into the syrupy tea, stirred it with the filigree spoon, and lifted it to her lips.

The conversation limped forward, awkward in process – while Maggie usually spoke slowly and carefully enough for Halim to be able to understand, urgency doubled the speed of her speech, so Süleyman had to translate for Halim, who was constantly frustrated that only fragments of what Maggie was saying seemed to filter through Süleyman's brusque prose – but not in feeling. Maggie sat in the rickety chair, her elbows leaning on the table, as if she belonged there, and that sense of comfort calmed Halim and Süleyman, both uncertain of the protocol of the situation, propriety balanced with hospitality. Maggie told them all that she could, her voice rising with excitement and asperity. Thousands of men killed; "men," she said, "but boys, really," Süleyman explained – just mown down, and Süleyman couldn't understand it either, and made her explain again and again: why there, why did they land there, "surely it was lunacy?" And Maggie shrugged, blowing a loop of reddish hair out of her eyes: surely it's all lunacy, she said, and Halim didn't need Süleyman's translation to understand her meaning that time.

"She says that people are angry," Süleyman explained to Halim, "people in the town. They're angry with our people. The names of the men who have been killed – they haven't come back yet, but some of the men from the area are over there, and there's a large chance that some of them won't be coming back."

"It's not our fault," Halim said. Anger was rising within him, a confused and painful anger: anger at his country for dragging him into this squabble, when he was in the middle of trying to make a new life for himself – and anger at this new country, the country that claimed to be welcoming to all, for tethering him to the place that he'd come from. As a man, just one man – or two, counting Süleyman – caught between continents old and new, he could hear the clash and grind of bedrock in his imagination, and for a dizzying vertiginous second, knew that he didn't stand a chance.

When Maggie seemed to have exhausted the information she had available, the three of them fell silent. Halim felt empty and discombobulated, as if he still didn't understand the gravity of what had happened and how things had shifted and changed; he'd felt so far away from his country for months now that he couldn't work out how to make it relevant again.

Süleyman's worried expression hadn't budged from his face, and after a while he looked up at Halim and tried a smile. "Well, at least you'll be all right," he said.

"What do you mean?"

Süleyman spread his hands and shrugged, inclining his head towards the window and the Ghan Town outside. "Your work is here. If you wanted to, you could survive out here in the camp, you'd never have to go into town. It's not like that for me. I need people to like me, or at least to be well-disposed towards me. I can't afford to try and hide from this."

Halim flared. "I'm not trying to hide!" And Süleyman nodded quickly, placating.

"I know you're not. But you have to understand – "

"Do you really think that it will matter so much?"

"You saw the way that they looked – the people by the road, when we were talking to Maggie. They didn't look as if they were just going to ignore this, to let it pass."

"How do they even know where we're from? We're all Ghans to them, aren't we?"

Süleyman lifted his empty hands in supplication. "Where you come from doesn't matter, until it does. Trust me, I've lived this before. Greeks and Muslims lived together in Crete for years until someone made it a problem, and as soon as the line was drawn, everyone knew what side of it everyone else was on." His face suddenly seemed drawn and weathered, older than his years – Süleyman wasn't a handsome man, but his genial, open demeanour kept him youthful-looking, at least while his mood was buoyant. To see him look so old frightened Halim, and reminded him of the few times Süleyman had spoken of his past, before he'd come to Australia and Cottier's Creek, of his enduring pride in the Empire and in the Sultan, and his commensurate humiliation when he'd been driven from his home and Crete had been lost to Greece. Süleyman was seeing Crete overlaid onto the Australian outback, Halim understood suddenly, and it was scaring him.

Süleyman turned back to Maggie and spoke a quick question, watching her intently while she answered, before turning back to Halim. "She says that some of the men have already started talking about joining the army. The men who never would have thought about going to war before – the adventurers, those who fancied a bit of a lark halfway around the world, those have already gone. But it's more serious than that now." He paused for a moment, then added, "Her brother is already there, did you know that? And her brother-in-law, and her husband is talking about going now, too. Soon they'll all be at it, all the young men in this town."

"But it's not their war, it's not their fight! Why should they go and die for some – some king of a country so many thousands of miles – "

"Because that's how young men are when it comes to war. It's how it always is, no matter where you are."

Maggie spoke again, urgently, and Süleyman shook his head – again she entreated, and this time he looked away, before standing up sharply.

"What's she saying?"

"It's silly. Inviting trouble."

"What's inviting trouble?"

"She thinks that I should go out on my rounds as normal, try and sell some ice cream. Show my face around town."

Halim shrugged. "And why not? She's right. You'll have to do it sometime – like you said, you depend on them. You need their custom. Unless you're going to give up, hide away out here in the Ghan Town and try to sell ice cream to the stingy bastards out around here – or go into business doing something else – "

"Don't suppose you need an apprentice butcher, do you?"

" – then the best thing is to go back out there today. Show them that you're still the same person that you were yesterday, and last year, ever since you've been in this town – and why are you smiling?"

"Either your English is a lot better than you're letting on, or you can read minds. That's more or less exactly what she said."

"And she's right." Halim stood up, squared his shoulders and looked at Maggie. "We will go," he said in English, bravely, his voice wobbling only slightly. A broad, warm smile slid across Maggie's face.

"Me, too."

Süleyman turned towards her quickly, spoke; at her reply he flung his hands into the air in comical mock-despair, turning away.

"What did she say?" Halim asked, but Süleyman only snorted. "Crazy woman," he muttered under his breath, and Halim turned to Maggie, entreating: "What?"

She spoke slowly and clearly, directly to Halim. "I will come too. On the cart, with you."

*

It wasn't the best day of business they'd ever had, Halim conceded, but that evening when they came back to Süleyman's house he felt as euphoric as if they'd just sold enough ice cream to make both of them millionaires; looking over at Süleyman, quiet but grinning like a dog, he imagined that he felt the same way. Maggie's children were being looked after by her mother-in-law, and she'd used her free day to come around with them, legs in her long muslin skirt dangling off the back of the cart, swaying as it jolted from side to side. Normally as Süleyman and Halim trotted around the town, ringing the bell, children and adults would come out into the street and flag them down, but today there was nothing, until Maggie put her foot down. "Stop here," she had said, and when Süleyman, so staggered by her behaviour that he seemed unable to do anything but obey her wordlessly, had complied, she hopped down from the back of the cart, strode up to the nearest house, and emerged, moments later, holding a perplexed-looking Mrs Campbell by the shoulder. Mrs Campbell, looking none too happy about it, nonetheless handed over her money and received her cone, licking at it half-heartedly while Maggie made casual, elegant-sounding conversation, from which Halim could only identify the occasional word.

"About the war," Süleyman whispered to Halim when they had a moment unobserved, "she's talking about how terrible it is, but how of course innocent people shouldn't be blamed for the actions of their leaders – and she's agreeing, Mrs Campbell; I'm sure she doesn't even know what she's agreeing to!" And after Mrs Campbell left, sated and sticky of hand, Maggie started to go from door to door, reappearing from some, furious, red-faced and tight-lipped, but from others, more often than not, with a slightly awkward looking woman or boy clasped firmly by the shoulder or the hand, persuaded into buying appeasing ice cream from the two Turks in town. It had been a warm day, word spread, and by late afternoon, although they had done nowhere near their normal amount of business, a small but mostly cheerful-looking queue had formed in front of their cart, handing over money and taking their ice cream without any coercion other than Maggie's approving gaze turned on them, one by one.

"She was amazing," Süleyman said at last, breaking the pleased silence that had stretched between the two of them. "Amazing woman. I don't know if I could have her for a wife, someone like that, but still, amazing. Formidable."

"Why do you think she did it?" Halim asked, marvelling. "She didn't have to help us. She had no reason to. No one else would've done it…"

"She'd always been friendly to me," Süleyman said, "And you know that she's especially fond of you, ever since you saved her little boy. But it's more than that, too," he added. "There are some people in this world who are always on the sides of those who are down on their luck, and who get joy from fighting for them – both to help people, and to make themselves feel good. I think Maggie is one of those people."

*

And then the town was quiet, as if it were waiting for something, breath held. At the time, they had thought that Maggie's intervention had saved them, that they'd somehow be overlooked, but after the initial euphoria had worn off, Halim started to realise, watching Süleyman come in in the evening, face downcast, that perhaps all she'd been able to do was buy them some time. Business was bad. There were still some loyal customers – Maggie herself, of course, Mrs Bell who sold them the milk, one or two old men in the town, and some of the women – but they were in the minority. There was no open hostility – *yet*, Süleyman would say, his voice doom-laden – but some of the women who used to send their children over to buy from Süleyman's cart now pulled them closer to their side when the cart was spotted, their walk quickening, the children stumbling to keep up, looking longingly over their shoulders at the source of their former gastronomic pleasures. And the women, Süleyman pointed out, they were the least of his worries. It was the men, and most of all the young boys, those in their late teens and early twenties, those anxious for adventure, those who hadn't mustered the courage to join up yet, or who were unable to do so for physical reasons, of because their parents prevented it, needing their help on the farms – those boys who were bursting to prove their bravery, desperate to somehow bring the war within their grasps and thereby win it.

Halim wasn't able to accompany Süleyman every time he went out with his cart, and neither of them would have wanted it. It prickled Süleyman's pride to feel that Halim needed to look after him. In any case, Halim had his own nascent business to run that was unaffected by the town's burgeoning hostility, but that didn't stop Halim from feeling guilty when Süleyman reported back on the events of his day – the ten-year-old boy, always friendly before, who'd flung a stone at Sena when Süleyman's back was turned, and had just stared sullenly when Süleyman had reproached him; or the adolescent boys who would gather, arms folded, across the street from Süleyman, watching and waiting, passing a limp cigarette back and forth. The change in Süleyman was dramatic and immediate, the ever-present smile vanishing from his lips, and his shoulders rearranging themselves in a way that spoke of anxiety – and Halim knew that for everything that happened to Süleyman in Cottier's Creek, there was an answering, echoing experience from his past in Crete that made disaster seem inevitable to him.

"I was a fool," he said to Halim one evening. "A real fool. I had the chance to go to Istanbul after I left Crete; why didn't I take it? I should have learnt then, that should have been enough for me – people should stay with their own kind. If they don't – it all seems fine at first, of course, and it can be fine for a long time. But then one thing goes wrong and everything falls out of place."

"That's not true," Halim said robustly – but mostly because he wanted it not to be true. In reality, he wasn't sure. He would never have admitted it out loud, but he had noticed that the people in the Ghan Town had started to draw away from him and Süleyman slightly. It was nothing that Halim could put his finger on, and nothing that couldn't immediately be denied in high dudgeon if Halim were even to hint at it, but while everyone seemed as friendly as they always had been, behind the smiles was a frisson; eyes darted away from the two of them; invitations to breakfast, which had always been forthcoming, especially to Halim (perhaps hoping to be rewarded with choice cuts of meat), started to dry up. It was as if the others in the Town were keen not to be associated with the two of them, not to be mistaken for their compatriots, for Turks, and as much as it niggled at Halim, as much as it struck him as unfair, he couldn't say he blamed them, as he might have acted in the same way himself.

Süleyman had no such compunction, however, and spoke bitterly. "Zein and me, he's from Syria, but we've been friends for years, ever since he arrived in town seven years ago, didn't speak any English, and I helped him out, lent him a bit of money while he was waiting for an opening at the mine. And then when I was in the store yesterday, buying some flour and sugar, I heard him talking to Jack, the owner – Jack's nephew is away with the war, you know – telling him how terrible it was, what happened at Gallipoli, and how he'd never liked the Turks, how all Arabs feel that way, especially those who lived under the Empire. And the worst of it is that he knew I was there, the bastard, he knew that I was hearing it, and he didn't care."

"You can't blame them," Halim began, although he did, in part, but Süleyman broke in: "Yes I can, and I do. We'd be all right here if we stuck together; there are enough of us, it would help things, make them better. You'd think that there would be some solidarity in Islam, at least – we're all brothers under Allah, after all – but no."

"He has to look out for his own family, do what's best for them…"

"Doing the right thing is the best thing for them. Standing by his friend. I fed him, Halim, him and his family, when they first came here and didn't know anyone. I helped them, and now – what will his children think, what can they be learning from his behaviour? That it's all right to turn your back on your friends?

Look what Maggie's done for us, someone who hardly knows us, who's only bought ice cream from us, who's a different culture and a different religion and who lives at the other end of town. If she can stick her neck out for us – she, who doesn't have any reason to, and who has more to lose – why can't Zein?"

Maggie seemed to be the saving of Süleyman's peace of mind. Every time he went out with the cart, without fail she would appear, head up and smiling, often with at least one other person in tow, whom she would gently bully into buying ice cream while keeping up a flow of friendly chatter, distracting them from the group of disgruntled-looking young men, Süleyman's constant uneasy companions on the other side of the street. Sometimes she would come to the house in the evenings, too – uninvited; neither Süleyman nor Halim would ever be so forward as to invite a lone woman back to their scrupulously clean and neat but undeniably Spartan residence. But a few evenings every week there would come a bold knock at the door, and there would be Maggie, usually bearing some offering as an excuse for her visit – a bag of potatoes, or some tomatoes from her garden – which would oblige Süleyman to invite her in for tea.

Süleyman seemed to shrink into himself in her presence, with a mixture of pleasure and shyness, and Halim wondered sometimes whether Süleyman wasn't perhaps a tiny bit in love with Maggie, rather than just being simply grateful for all her assistance. On the evenings that she would visit, the three of them would sit around the table – the door to the back porch always kept open, so that anyone passing could see them sitting there in plain sight, proving that nothing untoward was going on, as Süleyman would have died rather than tarnish Maggie's reputation – and they would talk and talk. It was mainly Süleyman and Maggie doing the talking, of course, Halim's understanding being limited, but he would listen as hard as he could, turning each new word over again and again in his mind, committing it to memory. On the occasions that Maggie would visit and find Halim there alone, the visits would take the form of impromptu English lessons. They would sip their tea out on the veranda, watching the evening activity in the camp and on the main road out of town, the roar and leap of the cooking fires and the flickering of candles, as Maggie scratched notes on pieces of paper, grammar, verb conjugations, vocabulary, and Halim repeated them as many times as she asked, just to please her. The more time they spent together, the more he seemed to get an understanding of her that went beyond Süleyman's view of her as a champion of the underdog. When they sat together on the veranda, she would lean out at every noise, following its direction, straining to see; when she spoke to Süleyman, while Halim couldn't understand much of what she was saying, he couldn't miss the interrogative inflection of her voice, the number of questions that she asked, and so he became aware of the strong, lively curiosity within her. He realised that her willingness to fight their corner within the town was only partly altruistic, and the most part was because the two of them were a gateway into another world for her, one that she longed to explore. Oddly, this realisation, the revelation that Maggie was involved with them because she wanted to be, rather than it being down to some sort of unselfish saintliness, relieved Halim, and he felt his bones melting, muscles shifting, relaxing into her regular presence.

Then one evening Maggie came when Süleyman was there, and coming off her was more than her usual friendly, swift-moving energy; there was some sort of need that Halim was immediately alert to, and that altered the electricity in the room – she was the most vital person that Halim had ever known. Along with her customary offering of food – a bunch of carrots this time, which Halim eyed dubiously, not entirely sure what they would do with them – she was clutching something else in her hand: a letter, the paper thin and delicate as cobwebs. Barely pausing for their normal pleasantries, polite enquiries about one another's health and the state of her family, she thrust the letter at Süleyman. "From my brother," she explained, that much Halim could understand, and then "...Turks."

Süleyman shook his head, his face sad. "She wants me to tell her about Gelibolu," he explained to Halim, who was watching avidly. "Her brother is there, with the war. She wants, she wants – oh, I don't know, I suppose she wants to get an idea of where he is, of what he's doing, of whether the things he says in his letter are true. But I've explained to her – I'm from the Empire, I speak Turkish, but Gelibolu and that area is as unfamiliar to me as it is to her. So silly."

"I could tell her," Halim said, excited. "I haven't been to Gelibolu, but I know people from that area. I know my English isn't good, yet, but it's improving – this could be a good way for me to learn..."

Doubtful, Süleyman relayed Halim's words back to Maggie, evidently expecting a refusal, but immediately her face blazed with enthusiasm. Her eyes never left Halim's face as Süleyman explained, "She says she will teach you properly. Proper lessons. She used to be the teacher in town here, before she married, and she would like to do some proper work again, I think."

"Really? Then – " Shy, uncertain of what her reaction to his question was likely to be, Halim struggled to find the right words to frame the idea that had sprung into his head, fully formed at that very moment, the idea that could, he thought, be their salvation here in the Ghan Town, protecting him – and by extension, Süleyman – from the Arabs' desire to distance themselves: "Do you think that she would be willing to teach more than just me? It's just – I know that there are other people out here in the camp who would like to learn. Zein's brother, some of the women – even the men, the men who can speak English – some of them might want to learn to speak better, the ones that learnt English down the mines, at least, or they might want to learn to write and to read. Can you ask her if – if she would be willing to start a class?"

Chapter Sixteen

When confronted with Maggie McGill, people were sometimes charmed, sometimes horrified, sometimes baffled, but never entirely unmoved, and it was generally accepted that, when faced with Maggie with a bee in her bonnet about something, an idea that she'd decided needed to be carried out, anyone was bound to be powerless against her breezy, iron determination. Although she never spoke of it, Maggie had always mourned the fact that she had had to give up her work. She loved her children, of course, loved being a mother, and largely enjoyed the running of a household, but even with all the tasks that those jobs entailed – and Maggie threw herself into such things more than most – she found herself left with too much time for herself: hers was a busy mind, and it needed filling with something more than just the routine tasks that keep a household ticking over. And now there was the worry about Patrick... Patrick, who had been gone for four months now, but until the Gallipoli landings Maggie had been able to think of his deployment as a lark, something to smile and roll her eyes about, one of those strange things that men tended to feel that they have to do, more about fun and adventure than danger. The true nature of war – of this war – had been brought home to her by the reports of the casualties at Gallipoli, the mechanical way that the men had been put forward for sacrifice, without a thought for their humanity. She believed that Patrick was all right, because they hadn't heard otherwise – not yet, anyway, but the lists of dead and injured were trickling to a close and he wasn't among them – and because she had to believe it; this boy, two years younger than her and the closest to her of all her six siblings, who had clung to her through childhood because their parents and older brothers and sisters were far too busy to be interested in the two little ones, and to whom she had become a sort of surrogate mother; the thought of anything happening to this boy was utterly unbearable. She knew that she was lucky in that Charlie seemed immune to the battle-fever that was sweeping across the country, and had never expressed any sort of interest in joining up, and while she was thankful every day that that was a fear she need not face, she occasionally found herself wondering, traitorously, whether perhaps she could bear the loss of her husband above the loss of her brother.

She had space in her head, then; she had drive and determination and the sort of will that was like a tsunami when faced with it; and she had things from which she wanted to distract herself, and so it didn't surprise Halim too much that, within a week, Maggie had secured one of the rooms in the town's primary school to hold English classes three evenings a week. She came to Süleyman's house one evening to find Halim, and took him there, showing him what she'd done. He had to stoop to get through the low door, and he laughed to see the miniature desks and chairs in their neat rows, facing the blackboard at which Maggie stood with a grin, evidently enjoying his amusement.

"Sit down!"

Without even realising it himself, Halim had reached a stage where, despite his remaining confusion when Maggie and Süleyman spoke together, his mind unable to keep up with the ceaseless torrent of sound, he was able to understand most of what Maggie said, when her conversation was directed straight at him and she spoke simply and clearly. Obedient, he sat at one of the desks, folding up his long, skinny legs as best he could, his knees poking up around each side of the desk lid.

Maggie let out a laugh: "Perhaps we'll see about getting some larger chairs."

The room smelt of chalk dust, ink and an indefinable sour-sweet smell that seemed to be characteristic of classrooms everywhere. It made Halim nostalgic for the madrassa where he'd first learnt the mesmeric looping verses of the Koran, and he wished that he had the words to explain to Maggie what it had been like.

"My school," he started, diffident, "my school was like this."

"In your country?" she asked, with immediate interest. "What lessons did you do there?"

"Not like here. It was – " he paused for a moment, lost for words. "It was a school for Islam. For religion. But schools – " he spread his arms, indicating the room around them " – schools are the same everywhere."

Maggie smiled. "Your English is getting good, you know. You're a quick learner. You shouldn't be as shy as you are – the only way to improve is through practice. Keep talking, talk as much as you can..."

"I make many mistakes."

She shook her head. "Mistakes don't matter. The children I used to teach would sometimes be like you; they would rather do nothing than do something if they couldn't make it perfect. But mistakes are the way that we learn."

*

Süleyman had been dubious about the whole English lessons plan from the outset, but faced with the combined enthusiasm of Maggie and Halim he was helpless and agreed to go with Halim to speak to Tariq, to get word out throughout the camp, to help Halim get across the points for which his currently fractured English was insufficient.

"Tell him it's about unity," Halim urged Süleyman when, faced with Tariq's placid gaze, he ran out of English words. "Tell him it's good for the community, that it will help to get people together, people from different countries, and it will help us get along better with the people in the town."

Süleyman rolled his eyes, clearly seeing the classes as being merely about learning English, despite Halim's lofty ideals, but dutifully passed his words on, and after a long, contemplative pause and an excess of beard stroking, Tariq gave an almost imperceptible nod. Nonetheless, for Maggie's first class, a Monday evening an hour after the children had left school, with dust storms looming fractiously in the late afternoon sky, the only person there at the appointed hour was Halim himself.

Characteristically, Maggie was undaunted. "It'll pick up," she said staunchly, "they'll come," and, with Halim crammed behind one of the minuscule desks, his insides lurching with disappointment and embarrassment – both for himself and for her – she turned her back to him, picked up a piece of chalk in her long fingers, and began. Wednesday was more hopeful. There weren't the multitudes for which Halim had been hoping, but two others were there. The first was Zein's brother, Salman, who had been living in Lebanon for years before he came to Australia, but despite his perfect French, his English was even more meagre than Halim's. The second, much to Halim's surprise, was Zeinab, the wife of Omar, a woman he had barely seen out of the shack in which she and her husband lived, let alone out of the Ghan Town. Swathed in veils, hands, face and feet invisible, looking almost as if she was gliding, shy but straight-backed, she came into the room, bowed slightly to Maggie who was standing at the board – Halim noticed the expression of shock that flickered across Maggie's features, and remarked with pride at how swiftly she wiped it clean, to be replaced with her customary welcoming look, Zeinab chose a desk over the other side of the classroom from the two men, sitting in attentive silence. And Saturday was better still – Halim, Salman, and Zeinab had brought with her two of the few other women who were resident in the camp, floating through the town like dark ghosts. Even among just five of them, the variation in levels of English was obvious, but Maggie managed as best as she could in the two-hour lesson, adapting materials for the weaker students, concentrating on the huddle of women by the window, then moving back to Halim and Salman, giving them extra vocabulary, ensuring they weren't bored. At five on the dot the lesson ended; the women departed, murmured thanks coming from behind their veils; Salman scuttled out behind them, his head bowed with shyness, and as Halim levered himself up from the diminutive desk, Maggie collapsed into the chair behind hers, letting out a gushing sigh and fanning herself with comic exaggeration. Halim offered her a grin.

"I thought twenty six-year-olds were tiring," she said, speaking carefully for his benefit, "but that was nothing compared to this."

"It was very good," Halim said, his voice warm. "They are learning. It is good, especially for the women."

"I hope so," Maggie said doubtfully. "Can I ask..." she motioned with her hands in front of her face, a visual description of a veil. "What is this?"

"It is for – " he couldn't think of the word for modesty, and so improvised as best he could. "To stop men from seeing them. Women like that would not usually come out of the house. I am surprised to find them here."

"You're surprised that their husbands would allow it?" Maggie asked, and Halim nodded.

"Yes. But I know their husbands. They are men who work very hard, in the mines. Perhaps they want their wives to learn, and then they can take the lessons home with them."

"It's good of their husbands. It can be a problem with us, too – the husbands not wanting the wives to go outside of the home. My husband is very reasonable." She laughed suddenly, "Well, he had to be, to marry me! Many people in the town think that he's mad, to allow me to do something like this."

Chapter Seventeen

The visit from the public health authorities came towards the end of September. It was something that neither Halim nor Süleyman had expected; they had both been keeping their heads down as much as possible, at least as far as business permitted. Maggie's support had stopped the town erupting into any sort of outright hostility towards them, and Halim made sure to never miss her evening English classes, feeling somehow that being visible in the town was important, making sure that no one got the idea that he and Süleyman thought they had anything to be ashamed or afraid of. But both of them felt that the truce was held by a hair's-breadth, and that stepping even a fraction of a toe out of line could bring all sorts of unpleasantness raining down on their heads.

The problem remained, however, that neither of them were sure exactly where the line was. They knew who their allies were – Maggie, Mrs Bell, some of Maggie's close friends and the younger children in the town, who put ice cream ahead of international events in their own personal hierarchies of importance. They knew who their enemies were, too, mostly the boys and men who were too young or too cowardly to fight in the war themselves, and so wanted to feel as if they were doing something close to home, as well as those who were distrustful and intolerant of any sort of difference, and leapt gleefully on any justification for their beliefs. It was the rest of the town, who as yet seemed to have made no firm decision either way, that Halim and Süleyman were most worried about – and the rest of the Ghan Town, too. After the Gallipoli landings, there had been an initial scramble away from the pair of them, as the men who looked superficially similar to Halim and Süleyman strove to prove how far from them they really were, but things had normalised somewhat since then. There was still a degree of wariness on both sides, but Süleyman was glad to see that his long residence in the town counted for a grudging degree of loyalty, and Halim's meat was his own ticket to continued acceptance. But their fortunes still hung in the balance, dependent on those people who didn't know what to make of them, and both of them were treading very, very carefully, anxious to avoid doing anything that would inflame things more.

The room where Halim did his butchery had been specially and hurriedly constructed next to the mosque, with solid floors, wooden walls and a canvas roof to keep the sun off. Halim had never thought much about it – it was simply the space he needed, conveniently located near to the centre of the Ghan Town, so his customers always knew where to find him; not the most sophisticated building in the world, but more than enough for Halim's needs, not to mention a great deal cleaner than his uncle's butcher shop back in his village. Halim always took pains to wash and scrub the floor after slaughter, and it was only slightly bloodstained; he had gauze netting to keep the flies off the meat while it was hanging, waiting to be bought, and he went to the trouble of buying blocks of ice in order to keep the meat as fresh as possible.

The Australian men in suits weren't happy with this, though. When they arrived, at first Halim was puzzled: Australian men at his shop? Did they want to buy meat? Why would they be interested in halal meat; were they thinking of converting to Islam? Should he fetch Tariq to talk to them? The men came closer, stepping inside, as Halim stood up; he saw one of the men put his sleeve over his mouth and nose to stifle the robust, cloying smell and felt a burning twist of anger mixed with shame; anger at the man's rudeness, and shame because he knew that the smell was oppressive, the heavy stink of blood (he realised, suddenly, why it was that Süleyman never came here if he could help it) and a faint hint of shit, a smell that he would have wrinkled his nose at too, months ago, but that now he didn't even notice, a smell that was probably clinging to his clothes while he walked around oblivious, seeping out of his skin and hair as he sat with Maggie in the evening, conjugating verbs or telling her as much as his halting English could manage about the place where he was from, the place where her brother was fighting. Covering his distress as best he could, Halim walked over to the men, hand extended to shake – he'd just washed it, had just been shaking the last drops of water from his fingers when they'd arrived – but, to his bafflement, they simply looked down at his glistening palm and then up again at his face without moving. Nonplussed, he dropped his hand to his side and waited. This was evidently not going to be a friendly visit.

"You the butcher then?" the first man asked. Halim's English had improved enormously over the past few months, helped by the necessity of communicating as much as by Maggie's assiduous coaching, but he still had trouble when someone spoke quickly, or if their English was heavily accented; still, he caught the word butcher, and nodded.

"Yes, Muslim butcher."

For a moment no one said anything, and then the other man spoke. His words ran into one another in a way that Halim found incomprehensible, but the look on his face – a kind of sneering disgust – was hard to misinterpret. Feeling sick, Halim held up a hand to stop him.

"Please. My English is small. I don't understand. I fetch my friend."

The men stepped back from the door, letting Halim pass. He walked with all the dignity he could muster to the edge of the dusty square by the mosque, not wanting to show them how much they had rattled him, then as soon as he was out of sight he broke into a run, dodging between the tents and humpies, curling round the few people who were walking the paths in the middle of the day, heart drumming against his ribs, praying that Süleyman would be in. Bursting through the door, which bounced off the wooden wall behind it, he was unspeakably relieved to see Süleyman standing at the churn, head down and sweating, his hair in his eyes. He looked up at the noise, his face going from annoyed to concerned in a moment, raising his arm to push his damp hair out of his face.

"What is it? What's happened?"

"Men!" Halim gasped, then shook his head, took a couple of deep breaths and started again. "Two men have come to my shop. I don't know what they want – they speak too fast – I need you to come and translate for me."

"Now then, calm down." Süleyman put a heavy hand on the back of Halim's neck. Halim had sometimes been irritated in the past by Süleyman's fatherly attitude towards him, but now he was grateful for it; it was frightening how quickly he could be knocked off-kilter out here – he could be feeling confident and sure of himself, grazing the border with cocky, but one thing going wrong could instantly slap him back down to earth, make him brutally aware of every mile that stood between him and everything that was easy, comprehensible and familiar. Just having Süleyman at his side at times like this steadied him, made him more certain. The fact of having a countryman close, someone who knew where he was from and what it was like there made him feel more real. Without a countryman around, Halim sometimes felt that his life before Australia would seem like a hallucination, something so unimaginably different that it couldn't possibly have happened. When he woke in the night, he often found himself uncertain which of the images in his head belonged to memories and which to dreams, and at times like that he couldn't be sure if his feet and a ship and a train had brought him from a village on the other side of the world, or if he had been dreamt into being by the vast undulating body of the desert itself.

Back at the shop, Halim listened to Süleyman speaking to the Australian men. Looking down, he caught himself twisting his hands in nervousness. The supplicant nature of the gesture irritated him and he forced his hands to his sides, only to find that they had jammed themselves back together when next he looked, wringing and twisting again. Süleyman seemed to be arguing with the two men, his voice low and angry enough that Halim probably wouldn't have been able to make out his words even if he'd understood them, but the men seemed certain of their position, cold and unbudging. Finally, Süleyman turned to Halim and tried his best to explain.

"They say they're from the public health office."

"What does that mean?"

"It's – it's an organisation that looks out for the health of the town. They say that you're breaking rules here, breaking health rules."

"What?" Halim was astonished. He was always so careful, keeping his knives as sharp as possible, scrubbing the floor every night with lye, throwing bucket after bucket of water over it until the last traces of red were gone, washed away clear, doing his best to keep the flies off – and the flies, well, if they were complaining about the flies, he'd seen the butcher in the town, the one that the non-Muslims used, and he knew for certain that if places with flies were a problem, that butcher would have had a visit from these men a long time ago. It was suddenly imperative that he make his case to the men directly, without recourse to Süleyman as a translator:

"My shop is clean! No one gets sick from the meat that I sell them! No one! I do not break any laws!"

"You need a license, mate," the first man said. His face was marginally kinder than the second man's, who persisted in looking around Halim's shop-cum-slaughter house with an ostentatious expression of disgust.

Halim didn't understand, and Süleyman explained. "A license. These people have to decide whether or not you are allowed to kill animals and sell meat. And they didn't know of you before now."

"Well, they know now," Halim retorted in Turkish and then turned back to the men. "I can get license? From you?"

The first man's face seemed to be getting gentler, with a pity that scalded Halim's pride anew and made him draw himself up as tall as he could, soldier straight. "Not on these premises, mate." And then, when Halim's face creased at the unfamiliar word, he explained: "Not here. It's not clean."

"Is clean!" Halim pointed to the bucket of lye that sat in the corner and the stiff-bristled broom with which he scrubbed the floors every evening. "I am clean man! This is clean shop!"

"Not clean enough," the other man muttered, but before he could go on the first man turned to him and gave him a quelling look.

"Here," the first man went on, pulling a piece of paper out of his back pocket and handing it to Halim: "This is for you. For court. You – " Helpless, he turned to Süleyman and shrugged. "You can explain it to him, right?" but before Süleyman could answer, Halim had snatched the paper out of the man's hands, staring down at it with a concentration that feigned comprehension.

The two men walked away in silence and Süleyman and Halim stood and watched, Süleyman scowling and Halim feeling his heart shaking, a tremulousness that he couldn't bring himself to show on the outside. He wished that he could grab onto Süleyman's rage and use part of it; it seemed a far more useful, practical emotion than the baffling mix of fear, hurt and confusion that was throbbing through him. He didn't understand why he had to take things like this so personally, feel them as a judgement on his intelligence, his character and his very personhood, while Süleyman was sure enough of all those things that he could throw criticisms back as anger. Fundamentally, though, the two of them wanted different things from Australia – Halim was still hoping that it would take him in and swallow him up so that he could become a part of it, whereas Süleyman had long ago accepted that that would never be so and had stopped wanting it, hoping only to milk the country for what it was worth and then return to a homeland that he had never set foot on. The two Australian men were nearly out of sight when the smaller one, the crueller one, with his pinched, pained face, pulled on the sleeve of the taller and spoke in clear, carrying tones: "Filthy buggers, aren't they?"

Halim didn't understand the words, but he understood the derisive, sneering tone well enough, and Süleyman clearly understood both. Incandescent fury blazed across his face. "Hey!" he called, and the men turned, the taller one at least having the good grace to look ashamed, and Halim remembered that he hadn't laughed at the other's remark, or even agreed with it. But this seemed to make no odds to Süleyman, who strode across the square until he was toe to toe with the smaller man. Süleyman was smaller still, but broad; Halim had always thought of him as tubby, with a sort of jovial, harmless roundness, but with this anger lighting him up from the inside he suddenly looked fearsome and imposing, cords of muscle standing out on his arms, shoulders thrown back so he looked solid, as barrel-chested as a boxer.

"Don't you dare talk that way about my people," he said, with slow venom that was easy for Halim to understand. "You know nothing about us. Nothing."

"I know enough, mate," the smaller man replied. His tone was snarling; he was clearly responding to Süleyman's challenge by raising his own hackles, even as his taller colleague put a soothing hand on his arm and muttered, "Calm down."

"What do you know?" Süleyman asked, guttural with rage. "You lot – you, you ignorant people, you've never been outside of this country, probably never been outside of this town – "

"Maybe so," the man said, and he rocked on his toes, as if

hiding a delightful surprise, "maybe so, but I read the paper, don't I? I see the films. I know what you lot are. Bloody murderers, bloody murdering our boys – "

"It is a war! Our side is being killed, too – "

"Your side?" The man looked round, his face incredulous, as if playing to an imaginary audience. "Your side, you say? That just goes to show, doesn't it? You come here, live here for years, work in our towns, take our money – but that's where your loyalty lies, doesn't it? And we know it, the government here knows it. You know what they're doing to your kind, to the Huns and the Turks? They're rounding you up and putting you in camps – "

"No – "

"And they're bloody right to, aren't they? *Your side*. If you're so bloody loyal, what are you doing here, eh? You should go home." He turned and looked at Halim for the first time. "Both of you. Go home."

As he turned and walked away, Halim could see his colleague remonstrating with him. Süleyman started to go after him, still clearly boiling with rage, but Halim went to him and took his arm, gripped it, hard enough to bruise, and eventually Süleyman subsided.

"They're not worth it," he said, convincing himself rather than Halim, and Halim agreed, though he worried about Süleyman's defeated tone of voice, the slump of his shoulders.

There was nothing for it but to go home, where Süleyman read the paper that the men had handed to Halim, explaining that he had to appear in court the next week and until then he wasn't allowed to work. Süleyman made tea while Halim sat, dejected, at the table.

"What do you think will happen?"

"What, in court? I don't know. Could be lucky. Could just be a question of making a few changes to the way you do things, you know, be a bit more modern, and they might let you set up shop again."

"And what if they don't?"

"If they don't?" Süleyman sighed, resigned. "We'll cross that bridge when we come to it, my boy. There's no point worrying."

Halim was silent for a moment, and then: "And what about the other thing he said?"

"What other thing?"

"About – about the camps? About putting our people into camps?"

"He was just making that up to frighten us. That sort of thing wouldn't happen here." Seeing Halim's sceptical expression, Süleyman said fiercely: "Listen to me. Whatever people might think, whatever people like him might say, this is a reasonable country. They know that we're not a threat to them – we can't be, so far away from the battlefield. They've got nothing to gain by doing anything to us, nothing at all."

*

The morning of the court date was unusually cool and windy, the roads choked with dust that Halim could feel on his teeth whenever he closed his mouth, dust that came off his skin like grease and settled into his hair, obdurate and unmoving. Maggie had agreed to come with them – well, agreed wasn't quite the right word. She'd insisted on attending, despite Halim's misgivings; he wasn't sure if he wanted her there to witness his humiliation if things went badly. In the end, though, the hearing was briefer than Halim could have imagined. A magistrate, imposing and bewigged, read the charges, which Süleyman explained to Halim: he had broken the law by killing and selling meat without inspection from the proper authorities, and doing so without a license and on unapproved premises; did he plead guilty?

"But I'm not guilty," Halim said to Süleyman, his tone urgent. All desire to try and speak English for the sake of the court had fled; he had never been gladder of Süleyman's solid bulk beside him, and his calm, steady voice using the words that came so much easier to him.

"I know you're not, not really – but their rules…"

"Can you explain to him, though? Explain to him about Islam, about our religion, and how meat must be…"

So Süleyman tried. He was a persuasive speaker, Halim could tell even when he couldn't understand the words, and the magistrate's face did soften slightly, but still he shook his head, and Süleyman explained: "He understands about the religion, but still, according to their rules, you are guilty."

Halim was silent, mutinous.

"It will be better for you," Süleyman cajoled, "better if you plead guilty. They will make allowances," and Halim shrugged, suddenly every inch the sulky child; Süleyman had to fight back irritation mixed with fondness: half man, half boy.

"He pleads guilty," he explained.

Halim was given a fourteen shilling fine, which made his eyes go round with horror, but as Süleyman pointed out in a murmur, it was a damn sight better than two weeks in jail, which would have been the alternative option, and Halim shrugged again. He felt hot and humiliated; he could feel Maggie's eyes on him, and refused to look her way, knowing that she was only going to offer him unwanted sympathy when all he wanted was to get out of there as quickly as possible.

In the corridor outside, Halim was trying to shrug off Maggie's apologies and concerns, and Süleyman was trying to placate them both as best he could, when he suddenly went still, his eyes cold. Halim looked behind him to see the man from the shop, the taller, kinder one, but, still, not someone that either Halim or Süleyman were well-disposed towards.

"What is it?" Maggie asked, and the only thing that Halim could think to say was: "It was him…" He wanted to walk away, but yet again Süleyman seemed determined to square up to him, though this time his belligerent pose was disarmed by the man extending his hand to shake.

"Look," he said, "I'm sorry about this, and I'm especially sorry about my colleague last week. He shouldn't have said those things, and I should have done more to stop him."

There was a thick-aired pause while the man's hand hung, white like fish belly, in the air. For a moment, Halim hoped that Süleyman would bat it away, or simply turn his back – he remembered the scorching humiliation of having his handshake rejected by this same man the week before. But Süleyman couldn't do it. Polite to the core, he clasped the man's hand. The man then turned to Halim and proffered his hand, and Halim knew that there was no way that he could turn it down when Süleyman had accepted. The atmosphere palpably relaxed.

"Listen," the man went on, "I have an offer for you…" He went on at such speed that Halim was lost, though both Maggie and Süleyman looked intently interested.

After he was finished, Süleyman turned to Halim. "We might have a solution for you," Süleyman explained. "This man says that he can help make arrangements at the town abattoir, where the other butchers work. You should be able to use their facilities and sell the meat back in the camp." Süleyman gave a half smile, and tilted his head to indicate a bearded man, standing back from the crowd, but watching their conversation with interest – and with a jerk of his heart, Halim recognised the man who had helped him on the train when he'd first arrived in town, the same man who had introduced him to Süleyman in the first place. "That's Mr Cartwright, over there, who runs the abattoir. Mr Cartwright understands, this man says, about the religion, and he knows that you're working for our community. I think he's all right, this one."

"It'll be all right there?" Halim asked, and Süleyman nodded. "I won't be breaking the law?"

"Not at all."

"I'd have to talk to Tariq, to be sure that it is halal to slaughter animals in a place where people do not slaughter in a halal way." He caught Süleyman's frown, and the man and Maggie's looks of confusion, so added hurriedly. "But thank him, please – and Mr Cartwright too, of course. It is kind of them to help. I appreciate it."

Chapter Eighteen

The abattoir was a long, low building on the outskirts of the town, banked with dust and sand, and Halim eyed it with a degree of trepidation. It was one thing to go through the town selling ice cream with Süleyman, or to sit in the school room in the evenings with Maggie reciting vocabulary and the class chanting words back to her, and quite another to integrate himself so completely. He couldn't help being slightly afraid of the men in the town, the red-faced ones who rolled down the wooden steps of the pub at closing time, the ones fighting on street corners as the evening swept in, the ones that had started loitering near the ice cream cart when Süleyman and he were working, their faces like fists, vibrating with tightly banked and threatening energy. His thoughts swung, pendulum-style, from one idea to another: he wanted to fit in, to become a proper Australian; he wanted nothing more than to go back to Sydney and get drawn into the friendly brawl of Maria and Yiannis's extended family, or even to go further, back home, back to the village, back to the shame he had left behind and to whatever shy, tremulous cousin his parents could find for him to marry, back to where he started from so that he could pretend that this strange, frightening interlude had never happened.

The Australian men all looked so big. He knew, when visually measuring the tops of their heads against the bricks of the wall, that they weren't much taller than he was himself, but they invariably seemed surrounded by an invisible aura of strength, confidence and swagger, the sort of unconscious arrogance that can only come from being in a place where one's right to belong could never possibly be questioned. Five of them were ranged up against the outside wall of the abattoir when Halim arrived, enjoying a smoke break, passing the soggy butt between them. They were talking, laughing and spitting occasionally on the ground to rid their lips and tongues of shreds of tobacco, and for a moment all Halim wanted to do was turn tail and run, back to the Ghan Town. Damn the laws, he'd happily take the risk of being reported and caught and fined again if he could avoid running this gauntlet. But he squared his shoulders as much as he could and when their eyes settled on him, as he'd known that they would, he told himself again and again that they were just curious, curious, that was all, not unfriendly, not hostile, just curious, because he was different.

"Hey, mate," one of them called out, and Halim turned. He recognised this boy, no taller than Halim himself, only in his mid- to late-teens, he thought, whom he'd often seen in town with what he'd assumed to be his younger brother and sister; he and Süleyman had sold them ice cream often enough. The boy was even skinnier than Halim himself, pale and freckled, sandy-haired and blue-eyed with a strangely twisted back, as if he'd had an accident when he was a child and had never grown properly since. But his face was open , uncomplicated and even kind; if he was to be hailed by anyone, rather than allowed to simply pass and be left alone, this was the best person Halim could think of. The boy limped up to him, and extended his hand. "I'm Daniel," he said, and his tone was friendly.

Halim took his hand and shook it, feeling the tight knot of fear in his chest and belly unravel just a touch. "My name is Halim," he said, but the boy laughed.

"I know who you are. Mr Cartwright told us to watch out for you."

"I will come and work with you," Halim said tentatively, and Daniel nodded.

"Yeah, that's what he said. You need a special place, right?

Cause you lot do things differently to us, don't you? Funny rituals and things."

Halim gave Daniel a quick look out of the corner of his eye, but Daniel didn't seem to be making fun, simply making an observation, and, if anything, his face was a little curious.

"Yes. We have rules about meat. It is our religion. I worked out at the camp" – Halim extended his arm, pointing towards the low hills on the horizon – "but I was breaking the law, they said. I didn't know I was doing anything wrong."

Daniel shook his head. "Public health, wasn't it? Stupid rules. You weren't hurting anyone, were you? Didn't make anyone sick from your meat?"

"No!" Sensing a sympathetic audience, Halim warmed to his topic. "No one was ill. I made... I made good meat. Clean. My shop was clean. But the men said that it wasn't right. And the mag – the man in the court – "

"The magistrate," Daniel offered.

"Yes. He made me pay a fine."

Daniel shrugged and gave Halim a friendly clap on the shoulder. "Hard cheese, mate," he said, which Halim didn't understand, but the cheerful commiseration in his words was clear enough. "Still, you're all right now, aren't you? Come with me, I'll show you the area where you'll be working."

Inside the building, Halim surveyed the space, the hooks hanging from the ceiling, the freshly scrubbed stone floor, the lights and the fans that kept the air moving, and, best of all, the large ice room, all with an approving eye. He still resented the men who had come and told him that he was breaking the law when he knew himself that he hadn't been doing anything wrong, that he'd been acting in accordance to the will of Allah – but, he grudgingly admitted to himself, if this was the price that he paid for making the mistake of not knowing enough about Australian laws and regulations, if that behaviour got him access to this place, it wasn't too bad.

He would never have admitted it, but the situation he'd been in before had been far from ideal. The tarpaulin that acted as a roof had served its purpose in keeping the sun off, but had failed utterly in keeping the little room cool, and Halim had spent his days sweltering in a lather of sweat. He'd had to stand the door open to avoid roasting himself alive, which meant that any gust of wind from the wrong direction brought in a spray of sand that stuck fast to the floor, whether it was damp with water or with blood – and the flies had been an infernal nuisance; he'd tried every trick he could think of, but all too often when he glanced over at the sides of meat that he had stacked up in the corner, he'd find them dotted with flies. If he was scrupulously honest with himself, he knew that the fact that no one had become ill yet was more about good luck that anything else; it was probably all a matter of time. This new place was an enormous improvement, and he couldn't help but be a little thankful for it; he could see now why Tariq's face had lit up when he and Süleyman had told him of Mr Cartwright's suggestion.

Daniel was watching his face anxiously, and Halim realised with a gratified thump of his heart that Daniel wanted him to like the space; he wanted him to be happy.

"Is it all right?" Daniel asked, and Halim nodded, smiling.

"It is very good. It is better, much better, than the place where I was working before."

It was nearly six o'clock in the evening – normal knocking-off time for the rest of the abattoir staff: it had been thought prudent that Halim not be working at the same time as the rest of them, and Halim couldn't help but agree; it also made it less likely that his meat could be contaminated by the haraam meat that was prepared there. By rights, Daniel, dressed in his street clothes, scrubbed and clean and smelling of carbolic soap, should have been raring to get home – or to get to the pub for a drink, though Halim guessed that Daniel wasn't that sort of boy – but still he stood, half shy, in the doorway, shifting his weight from foot to foot, and after a while Halim became impatient, unsure how much more pleasure in his new surroundings he was supposed to show. "It is all right?" he asked Daniel at last, and Daniel flushed, looking slightly embarrassed.

"It's all fine," he said, lowering his eyes, and then said quickly, as if rushing his words out before he thought better of them: "Do you mind if I stay? I'd like to see how you do it. How it's different, you know." For a moment Halim thought he must have misunderstood – why would this boy be interested in the Muslim way of slaughter? – and the look of discomfort on Daniel's face grew. "It's all right," he said at last, "I'll go – "

"Wait," Halim said, and Daniel turned. Halim asked, with honest curiosity: "Why do you want to stay? Why are you interested?"

Daniel reddened again. "Well, it's something different, isn't it?" he said, sounding almost sulky. "All the other boys, other people my age, they're talking about going off to war, going off to Europe or Gallipoli to fight. I keep thinking about all the different things they're going to see, and I'll never get a chance to do that, will I? Because of my back, that's obvious. But I'm interested in different things, aren't I, just as much as the rest of them. I'll probably never get to leave this town, so I suppose I'm just interested in the different things that are already here."

It was a long speech, and Daniel spoke quickly. Halim understood little more than half of what Daniel was saying, and yet he understood that his interest was sincere – and there was something touching about the boy, with his candid, affable face and his crippled back. Halim remembered the way he'd stood awkwardly on the end of the line of men smoking outside, included only by dint of his presence there. In Daniel, Halim sensed someone who was almost as much of an outsider as he was himself.

"It's all right if you stay," Halim said, and Daniel grinned.

"Great! I can help, if you want…"

"No, no, don't help. It's not – " He struggled to find the words to explain, and settled on, "It's not right in our religion, if you haven't learned how. But I don't mind if you watch."

Daniel shrugged. "Whatever you say, mate."

*

Halim went home that night buzzing with an excitement bordering on joy, and a certainty that at last, despite all his misgivings, things were going to be all right after all. For the first time since coming to Cottier's Creek he had a real, proper friend – not someone from the Ghan Town, who was bonded to him through common religion and background and not much else; nor Maggie, for as fond as he was of her, there was an imbalance in their relationship, she as teacher and he as student, that meant they could never be genuine, uncomplicated friends. But Daniel was different. He had no need to feel any obligation towards Halim; quite the opposite, and yet nonetheless he was interested, and out of that interest a real liking was developing.

Daniel had stood quietly at the side of the room when Halim had led in the first sheep, watching closely as Halim lowered his eyes and clasped his hands, speaking the words to dedicate the animal to Allah. He kept watching as Halim deftly flipped his knife under the sheep's throat, severing its carotid artery with a graceful ease he had never realised he possessed until he knew someone was watching. With spare, precise movements Halim turned the animal on its back, cut it from groin to sternum to remove the offal, before starting to skin it. By the time he was disjointing the meat so that it would be ready to sell; he was moving with a well-practiced fluidity and had practically forgotten Daniel's presence, until finally, finished, he took a step back and heard Daniel whistle with dumb approval.

"Whoo-ee!"

Halim turned and grinned. It had been a long time since he'd been admired by another man for any sort of physical prowess, but Daniel's raised eyebrows and unselfconscious smile made him remember how, as a child, his light, skinny frame had meant that he'd been the best in the village at climbing the tall trees that no other boys dared climb, and, scrambling down the trunk with a bird's nest clutched in one sweaty hand, he had always been met by almost identical expressions to the one that he was seeing now.

"It is good?"

"Mate, I've never seen anyone do anything like that. It's different here. One bloke kills the animal – " He mimed a shot in the head, and Halim nodded, " – and another bloke skins it and another bloke takes it apart to sell. No one could do the whole thing like that, and so quickly. It's amazing." He seemed to think for a moment, and then asked: "Why d'you do it with the knife, though? We have guns – special guns, for killing animals…"

But Halim was shaking his head. "It's not allowed, that way. We cannot eat an animal that has died from a blow, and we must have the blood to come out of the body. This way is the right way – for Allah."

"For Allah?"

Halim reddened a little, embarrassed, though Daniel didn't seem to mind displaying his own ignorance. "Allah. It is the name of our god."

"Oh, I see. So Allah likes you to use the knife, eh? And what about that thing that you said at the start – what was it?"

"It is like a prayer: bismillah Allahu akbar. It means, it means that the animal is for Allah."

"In Turkish?"

"No, it's Arabic."

"But you're not an Arab, are you? They said you're a Turk…"

"Yes, I speak Turkish. But Arabic – it is the language of our religion."

"Huh." Daniel looked doubtful and impressed at once. "There's a lot of rules in your religion, aren't there? Not so many in ours."

"What – what is your religion?" Halim asked, shy. He had never had this sort of a conversation with an Australian before, and wasn't sure what sorts of questions were appropriate, though he had an inkling that, judging by Daniel's frank interrogation style, he wasn't one to be bothered by a lack of propriety.

"Presbyterian, I am, like most other people around here," and then, when Halim looked puzzled, Daniel added: "Christian. Kind of Christian, anyway. It's not like your religion, though. Doesn't tell us what we're supposed to eat, or how we slaughter our meat, nothing like that. Just, you know, Ten Commandments and church on Sunday. No more than that."

The two boys stood looking at one another for a couple of moments, and then Daniel jerked his head towards the open door behind him.

"Fancy a smoke-o?"

Halim hadn't smoked since Sydney, but he felt that it would be rude to refuse. The acrid taste in his mouth and the choking sensation in his lungs brought back bright, vivid memories of Irfan, but instead of making him sad, he felt that this was somehow right – Irfan was gone, but he was standing there with another boy now, someone who could turn into his friend. He couldn't help letting out a short burst of coughing, though, and Daniel turned to him.

"You not used to tobacco, then? Is that against your religion, too?"

It was clearly meant to be a joke, but it disquieted Halim slightly; he had never been entirely sure on the Prophet's views on smoking, and although he was certainly not as devout as he could be, neither was he as relaxed as Süleyman, who enjoyed the occasional alcoholic drink in the evening, and spoke mournfully of the proper anise-flavoured raki that he hadn't had for years, and which he missed furiously. Seeing his expression, Daniel's face changed: "It isn't, is it?"

Halim shook his head. "No. I don't think so, anyway."

"But drinking is, isn't it? Never seen any of your lot down the pub."

"Drinking is not allowed, you're right – but some of us drink anyway. We don't go to the pub, though. We think that we wouldn't be welcome there."

Daniel shot him a quick look out of the corner of his eye, before replacing the drooping cigarette back on his lower lip. "Yeah, that makes sense. Not too tolerant of difference around here, are they?"

Halim detected a note of bitterness in Daniel's voice; there was something sad in the boy's swagger, as if his ego was making promises that his body couldn't follow up on. "What happened to your back?" Halim asked at last, uncertain whether the question would be welcomed, but wanting to know nonetheless.

"Riding accident, when I was six. My dad works as a jackaroo – you know, working on farms, helping herding the sheep and the cattle and all that. Wanted me to follow in his footsteps, like my two older brothers. Put me on a horse that was too big for me, it ran off, I fell, and now here I am." He forced a grin, but his eyes were defensive, as if expecting mockery. It occurred to Halim that growing up with a physical disability like that in a place like Cottier's Creek, where brazen, unashamed physicality seemed to be an intrinsic part of all the men's make-up, would have been a very difficult path.

"Is your family here?" Halim asked, and Daniel shook his head.

"My mum died when I was a kid. Dad and my brothers – they go where the work is. They used to take me with them when I was younger, but I couldn't work in the places where they'd go, and so when I was old enough to start working myself I got a job here. I board with Mr Cartwright. He's a good bloke, and I get on with his wife and kids; they feel more like my family now. I sometimes go with the kids to buy ice cream off you and the other bloke." Daniel shrugged and looked at the ground, inching his toes into a pile of sand, evidently keen to turn the subject from himself onto something more interesting. Halim felt a sharp stab of pity for him. "What about you?" Daniel asked. "Is your family here? The other Turk, the one with the ice cream – I've seen you with him. Is he your dad?"

Halim let out a laugh, and stubbed out the last of the cigarette on the sole of his shoe. "Süleyman? No. We didn't know each other until I came here. I came to Australia alone – " He found himself reluctant to mention Irfan, although Daniel reminded him strongly of his friend, his stubborn, forced confidence plastered over his physical shortcomings " – all my family is back in my village. I came to Sydney first, but it was hard to get a job, so then I came here. I had heard that a friend was here, but when I arrived he had gone north. So I met Süleyman and he helped me. I stay with him in his house, but he isn't my family." Halim paused for a moment, considering it, and then reiterated, "I don't have any family here." For the first time in a long while, the words felt more of a liberation than a loss.

Daniel didn't seem interested in his family, though; his ears had pricked up at the mention of Sydney. "You were in the city?" he asked, his voice raw with excitement. "What was it like? Why the hell would you come here if you could stay there instead?"

Halim shrugged, baffled slightly by Daniel's enthusiasm. "It's hard to get work there," he explained. "It's big – it's too big. Too many people. Here is better…" but he could tell that Daniel wasn't taking his words in.

"Sydney," he muttered, half to himself, and then turned back to Halim. "I've never been, but I'd love to go. I want to live there, there or Melbourne. Maybe Adelaide. Get a job in a shop, maybe a tailor's shop. Bet no one there cares about this sort of thing, do they?" He indicated his twisted back. "Nah. No farms there, men don't need to be tough and strong like they have to be here. Yeah, that's where I want to be." He looked at Halim with critical disbelief. "You're not really serious, are you, that it's better here? You'd go back, wouldn't you, if you had the chance, or the money?"

Halim started to say no, but then, unbidden, he remembered

Fotini, her velvet hair and the sweet smell of her rosewater scent that followed her around wherever she went. He couldn't help it; his mouth had quirked up at the corners before he realised what it was doing, and Daniel's sharp eyes missed nothing.

"What are you smiling about?" he demanded, and then: "Oh, I get it! There's a girl, isn't there? A girl in the city?"

Halim wasn't quite sure what to say. Fotini had written to him once or twice, and he had written back. Her last letter had been two months before, sharp with concern as she had heard that Germans had started to be put in internment camps, and feared that the same would happen to Turks – and implicit in her words, underlined by what she didn't say, was the fact that this fear only applied to him. She and her family were safe, she knew, because, as Christians, they could easily say that they were Greek, oppressed by the Ottomans as much as anyone else. He and Fotini were still friends, but there was nothing more between them, only the gulf of religious difference that the war was widening – and yet he found himself nodding, grinning at Daniel's whoop of mixed admiration and envy. After all, who could say what would happen with Fotini once the immediate disaster of the war was over?

"It's always the quiet ones," Daniel said, jostling Halim with a friendly elbow, and Halim felt pleasure, slow and sticky-warm like treacle, spread from deep inside him, winding its way around his joints and down into his limbs.

Chapter Nineteen

By the weekend, Halim's light-heartedness had crept into Süleyman's bedroom and infected him, too. As he made the tea in the morning Halim heard him humming; Süleyman was far from being a musical man, and in reality his humming was more akin to a tuneless series of grunts, but Halim knew him well enough by now to take it as a marker of happiness, and to add his slightly more tuneful voice to Süleyman's, until Süleyman realised that he was being mocked and swatted Halim playfully with a dish rag. They ate breakfast together exchanging companionable remarks about nothing in particular, and when Süleyman went outside after breakfast to saddle up the horse and cart, bridle chinking in the crisp morning air, Halim heard him start humming again.

"Listen," Süleyman said a little later, after Halim had given him a hand loading the ice cream onto the back of the cart, "why don't you come out with me today? You've got nothing much else to do, have you – and there's a new picture playing at the picture house, should be a good turn-out of people, very good for business. What do you say?"

For weeks, the only things that could entice Halim into the town had been the English classes with their small but steady core of attendees. Maggie had insisted that they keep coming regularly, that making themselves visible to the townsfolk made it seem as if neither side had anything to fear from the other, and while Halim had continued to attend, his head held high on his rigid neck, Zeinab and her friends walking beside him for protection, he had loathed himself for desperately wishing that he didn't have to run the gauntlet of hard stares and cold shoulders that the town had to offer. He had vastly preferred the occasional afternoon when Maggie had managed to come and visit them out at the Ghan Town, and the three of them had sat quietly on the veranda, Maggie reading one of Patrick's letters sentence by sentence, Halim stretching his English to its limits, trying to expand on Patrick's sparse descriptions of the places and the people he was seeing, Süleyman listening hungrily.

But the faint pall of fear that had hung over him for the past weeks had dissipated since the start of Halim's work down at the abattoir and his burgeoning friendship with Daniel, and suddenly, the idea of a brisk clop down the lane into town, and a few hours spent watching the townsfolk walk by, tricked out in their weekend finery, sounded appealing. That afternoon as he sat, legs dangling, on the back of Süleyman's cart, he found himself thinking that the town had never looked better. The spring had brought about a change in the quality of light; the sky no longer looked so glaring and hostile, and the lingering wintry chill in the air added a clarity, sharpening the edges of the trees and houses alongside the road. Halim could have been imagining it, but he felt that there was a slight thaw in the mood of the town, too. He caught sight of some of the young boys who had stalked the ice cream cart before with their closed, arrogant faces, but while they had inspired a spasm of fear in him before, today they seemed hardly more than children, trying to lash out at something that was too big for them to grasp. Bolder than he'd felt in weeks, when he caught the eye of one of the women who'd bought ice cream from their cart before Gallipoli but who'd intentionally or unintentionally boycotted them ever since, Halim couldn't prevent himself from raising a hand in a lazy wave and, to his gratification and amusement, automatically and seemingly almost against her will, her own hand raised in counterpart.

Maggie was at the cinema when they arrived, Charlie on her

arm, and she greeted them with a little cry of pleasure, rushing over to the cart. "It's good to see you here! I was thinking that you wouldn't come."

Saturdays at the cinema had previously been one of Süleyman's most lucrative days of the week, but while he'd managed to build up the confidence to ply his trade around the town since the hostility following the Gallipoli landings, the Saturday cinema slot had felt rather too much like walking into an ambush.

Süleyman shrugged, trying to hide his delight at her enthusiastic welcome. "Well. It seems that things have calmed down a little. It's been a few months now, and nobody's done anything bad to us – so I thought that perhaps it was worth a try." He frowned a little, glancing over at Charlie, who was standing on the porch of the cinema, smoking a cigarette and determinedly refusing to look in his direction. While Süleyman and Halim had never been friends with Charlie, not in the same way that they were with Maggie, he had always been friendly towards them. His refusal to greet them seemed ominous.

Maggie shook her head. "Don't mind him. He's just – " She sighed a little. "He's just a little anxious. His younger brother's over there, you know – not in Gallipoli, but in Europe. We haven't heard anything from him for some time, and Charlie – well, Charlie wishes he could go himself, but his father won't hear of it – says he needs him here to run the farm, and that's true – and of course I don't want him to go, especially with the children being so young. But I think he feels – oh, I am sorry, but I don't think he's prepared to be friendly with you at the moment."

She looked so shame-faced at the admission, clearly loving her husband, wishing that she could truly excuse his behaviour, and Süleyman, no matter how he felt about Charlie's behaviour (and, if he was honest and dug down deep enough inside himself, he wouldn't blame Charlie for his antipathy), had to be seen to forgive.

"It's understandable," he said. "I know that many people feel that way."

"But it's unfair," Maggie burst out, her voice low and intense, glancing over her shoulder to ensure that Charlie wasn't watching what she was saying. "It's not your fault – "

"Still," Süleyman said, placating. "I think that perhaps if I were in his position, I might even feel the same way. Anyway," he said, his voice brighter, "what's playing today?"

"*The Swagman's Story,* I think it's called. I've heard it's very good – Arabella Webster saw it when she was in Adelaide last month. And of course the newsreel at the start."

Within fifteen minutes, the choked knot of people outside the cinema had vanished; the film was about to start, and Süleyman had only sold two ice creams but, he explained to Halim, that wasn't a problem; people weren't allowed to take ice cream into the cinema, and so it was interval when they did the really big business, then and after the show. The street was deserted, other than a dog nosing around in a pile of rubbish; Halim found himself looking at the cinema longingly, wondering what was going on inside.

Süleyman nudged him. "Have you ever been?"

Halim shook his head. "No. Of course there was nothing like this back at home, and then in Sydney some of the boys I knew used to go, but I never had the time or the money…"

"Shall we go in, then? I do, sometimes. The ushers don't mind me going in for free if I just stand at the back." He hopped down from the cart and gave Halim his hand so he could jump down beside him. Nodding to the bored-looking boy who stood at the cinema door, he explained, "This is a friend of mine – all right if he goes in?" and the boy nodded back, not bothering to speak, then stepped away from the door and drew back the curtain. Süleyman motioned Halim towards it. "Go on."

"Aren't you coming in?"

"I need to find somewhere to tie up Sena, don't I, and make sure the ice cream's in the shade."

"I can help you – "

Süleyman shook his head. "It's no problem. A one person job. You go in, stand at the back by the door – I'll join you there," and as Halim stood there, hesitant, he flapped his hands, shooing him: "Go on! You'll miss the start."

Pushing his way into the thick, throttling dark, Halim felt almost suffocated, before he turned and saw the light of the screen. He'd had an idea of what to expect, but still he couldn't help his mouth dropping open slightly – the size of it; the energetic plinking of the piano; the way that the images were moving, as if giant people were trapped in a celluloid cage; the motes of dust caught in the stream of light that ran from the projector, drifting their languid way to the floor. A grin spread across Halim's face, invisible in the darkness – it was amazing, and for the first few minutes he was so overwhelmed by the experience that his mind couldn't quite settle enough to make sense of the images that he was seeing, the words flashing up as undecipherable as hieroglyphs. All he could think was that he never wanted to leave.

The hush of Süleyman's whisper at his elbow startled him so much that he jumped, and Süleyman had to put a steadying hand on his arm. "It's me," he said, his voice low, although plenty of the couples in the cinema seemed perfectly happy to discuss the action on the screen in conversational tones. "How do you like it?"

"It's miraculous!"

Halim caught the glint of white in the half-light as Süleyman grinned. "Fun, isn't it? I should come more often. It's good to see it through your eyes. Easy to get too used to this sort of thing." He looked back towards the screen, squinting slightly. "What's it like, anyway?"

"I don't know." He looked back at the giant, grainy image of men marching, comically fast, in black and white. Realisation dawning, he said, "I think it might be about the war."

Suddenly the experience was tarnished. Halim could hear a

threat in the urgent trill of the piano, a martial note in its clanking chords, and he could sense the ripple of pride in the people in front of him, their backs straightening as their attention to the screen grew more rapt – a pride that made him uneasy. He didn't understand many of the subtitles: he recognised the word 'Australia', which he'd seen Maggie spell out on the blackboard so many times; he recognised 'enemy' and his stomach churned a little in fear. Pulling at Süleyman's sleeve, he brought his lips close to his ear. "Maybe we should go…" But Süleyman was frowning, all his attention directed forwards, his feet broadly planted, immoveable. Halim recognised that stance from the day that he'd confronted the man from the public health office, and he didn't like to think about what this attitude of Süleyman's could mean.

The images of marching men gave way to shots of men standing, wearing the battered hats that Halim had learnt to associate with Australia, and the audience broke into a spontaneous spatter of applause. And the next shot: Halim had just about enough time to decipher the word 'Turk' from the subtitle, and then there they were, his countrymen, dressed for battle and marching. His heart lurched at the sight, and began to canter when he heard the audience's reaction to it: the hoots and whistles, boos and catcalls. A close-up, now, on an individual soldier, and he couldn't help feeling shame and anger at the picture that had been chosen, of a scrawny, half-grown boy with patched clothing – poorly equipped, he looked too weak and afraid even to hoist his rifle.

Süleyman snorted with disgust beside him as laughter bubbled up from other parts of the audience. Süleyman's hand was on Halim's arm now, his fingers gripping with a convulsive violence and Halim was desperate to leave, to get Süleyman out of there before he caused any trouble, or before trouble was caused for them. Flickering, uncertain, the image on the screen changed again to a great close-up of the Ottoman flag and the booing broke out anew; something hit the screen with a patter like rain, and Halim saw out of the corner of his eye one of the ushers marching down the aisle to remonstrate with the boy who had thrown whatever he'd thrown. From the flag to a shot of a mosque, a minaret, a muezzin with his head thrown back, mouth open in a silent cry, his face creased with the intensity of his faith; then a shot of the faithful in the mosque, kneeling, bending again and again to the floor, and bursting up from under the sick fear lining his gullet Halim felt anger, real, excoriating anger directed at the screen, and at the audience, their faces twisted with mirth, rocking back and forth with laughter that they couldn't contain, grotesque caricatures of themselves.

Mock his country, yes – he didn't like it at all, but he could cope with that; mock his people, all right – but mock his religion? Halim had never given much thought to his faith beyond taking it for granted, the low, steady vibration that underpinned every aspect of his life; and now, suddenly, these fools, these arrogant barbarians, were laughing at the thing that was laid most closely around his heart, the one thing that kept him upright and straight-backed when everything else that made him who he was had been stripped away. It was simply intolerable. With a strength he hadn't known that he possessed, he wrenched his hand out of Süleyman's grip, turned and made his way towards the exit.

Blinded with fury, he barely saw the hulking shape of the usher until he had knocked into him with his shoulder, but he heard the irritated whisper, "Watch it, mate," and his anger boiled over. With a shout of rage that he barely recognised as coming from his own throat, he was on the usher, the usher who was a head taller than him and built like the side of a house. Halim's fists were flailing and he was somehow desperate for the man to hit him back, to give him any excuse at all to kill him. Hands grabbed ineffectually at his wrists but he shook them off; a muttering grew to a grumbling, hissing roar in his ears, and then suddenly, startlingly, the lights were on. Halim blinked, stilled, raising a hand to shield his eyes, to find Süleyman beside him, holding him by the shoulder, the manager of the cinema standing by the door, looking appalled, and the entire audience twisted around in their seats, some standing, craning their necks to see what was going on.

The manager spoke to Süleyman, his tone low and angry; Süleyman shot something back. Halim couldn't catch a word of it; it was as if his rage had stripped all English words from his brain. Then the large usher spoke, shrugging; he was a dull, friendly-looking man who looked less incensed than puzzled by Halim's behaviour. The next moment the two of them were out in the street where the clear desert air was burning Halim's lungs as he drew in great breaths of it, fighting down his emotions. Anger was unusual and unfamiliar to him; he felt drenched by it, his limbs weakened and rubbery.

"Come on," Süleyman said. They were the first words that had penetrated Halim's ears since they'd left the cinema. Süleyman's face was tight and closed, a door slammed shut, and for a moment Halim was unsure where Süleyman's antagonism was directed: at the patrons of the cinema, for their heretical laughter, or at him, for causing a scene and losing Süleyman sales. In silence, they mounted the cart, Süleyman on the box and Halim squeezed in beside him, somehow reluctant to be too far away. With tightly banked rage, Süleyman lifted the reins and spurred the horse on to a trot, and they lurched their way away from the cinema, and out of town. Halim closed his eyes and only opened them when Süleyman said, minutes later, his voice stretched taut: "Bastards."

"I'm sorry," Halim said, not knowing what else to say. "I didn't mean to cause a scene," but Süleyman shook his head impatiently.

"You did what I should have done. How dare they, how dare they?"

"I don't understand it. Why were they laughing?" Süleyman's rage had somehow leeched Halim's from his veins, and all he was left with was a dull stone of incomprehension in the pit of his stomach.

"They're fools. Fools and buffoons. They laughed at our country, our people, our army – "

"They laughed at our *religion*." This was the part that Halim couldn't comprehend – that someone could dare to mock Islam. "Why would they do that? We would never think to laugh at their beliefs. I don't agree with them, but I respect them – we are all people of the Book, isn't that so? The Imam says so."

Süleyman swore softly under his breath, a muttered litany of curses, then turned to the side to spit. "Look at this place," he said, at last, arm waving to encompass the town, the hulking silhouettes of the mine equipment, the towering slag heaps and the desert beyond. "Look at it. These people, they live here, they drink and they fight and they scratch a living out of this land, and they dare to laugh at us, at our country! Let me tell you, this place was nothing, nothing but a desert and some kangaroos and a few tribes of black men a hundred and twenty years ago, and what were our people doing then? Our empire, the Ottoman Empire, it was the centre of the world." Süleyman shook his head, letting out a hissing whistle. "They'll never accept us here. About time we face it. We need to make some money, serious money, and get ourselves back home."

*

Maggie sat through the rest of the film and the main feature following it hating herself with a fury she had rarely felt before. Why had she stayed? She'd seen the faces of Süleyman and Halim when the lights had come up, Süleyman's wordless rage, and Halim's expression of furious humiliation – *Halim*, she thought to herself, a boy who had never shown any anger, any hostility, a gentler boy you couldn't hope to find, and there he was, launching himself at that brick wall of an usher, all because of the film that she had just sat through with not a murmur of protest. She was proud of her country, it was true, proud of the troops who were fighting, but she was a bright woman; she knew propaganda when she saw it, and she had an idea, thinking over the footage that she'd been shown, of the intense effect that it must have had on the two Turks, two men who had been trying as hard as they knew how to fit in with the town, but for whom some insults were too much.

When the lights came up at the end, she and Charlie left the cinema in silence. Looking at the grim set of his face she relaxed a little – he felt the same way as her, it was clear from his demeanour; he was just as disgusted as she was by the film and by the town's unthinking acceptance of it. But as they left the picture house, walking towards the wagon that was waiting for them in the shade of a jacaranda tree, he spoke, shaking his head: "I've been an idiot, Mags. I haven't taken this war seriously enough, not at all – I laughed at Martin when he signed up, thought he was just going for a lark, ignoring the important business of the farm. But he's the one who's doing the important business, isn't he?"

Chapter Twenty

When Maggie knocked on the door that evening, it was the first time that Halim had seen Süleyman any less than delighted to see her. They had both spent the afternoon slumped in separate states of despair; Halim had thought that a visit from Maggie would raise Süleyman's spirits, but instead he seemed to invite her in only grudgingly, stomping about the room as he boiled the water for the tea, while Maggie sat at the kitchen table rubbing the tips of her fingers nervously against the soft grain of the wood. Halim, meanwhile, could barely bring himself to look at her out of shame at having lost his temper in front of her. The anger that he had felt that afternoon was still within him, flickering like a guttering flame that only needed a breath of air to flare into life again, but his overwhelming feeling by this point was a sense of shame and humiliation. He couldn't get the memory out of his head of the moment that the lights had come up, the shattered silence in the room, the blank, uncomprehending face of the usher that he had tried so impotently to batter. He felt sure, thinking about it now, that the man hadn't fought back simply because he hadn't needed to; he had never felt threatened by someone as small and as weak and as insignificant as Halim. The thought burned and sickened him.

"I came to say I'm sorry," Maggie said at last when they were all sat around the table, glasses of tea in front of each of them that no one had any intention of drinking. She said it bravely, her head up and her eyes looking directly at Süleyman and then

Halim. "I shouldn't have just sat there this afternoon. I should have said something, I know I should. That film– "

"Why did you just sit there and watch it?" Süleyman asked. His voice was husky; Maggie seemed surprised at the interruption, which was so far from Süleyman's habitual quiet courtesy, and Halim hoped that she understood that Süleyman hadn't meant to be rude; he was simply very upset.

"I – I don't know. It was stupid of me. I suppose I didn't want to upset Charlie, and – and I didn't want to cause a scene. Not in front of all those people."

"But after all we've told you about our country, you know what they were saying in that film, you know it's not true?" Halim asked.

Maggie nodded, but her face was uncertain. "I do know that. But – you have to understand, both of you, that this is war that we're talking about. I know that the bad things that the film was saying about your people aren't true. But it is also true that the Ottomans are our enemy now, and people are going to be upset by that."

Neither Halim not Süleyman spoke. The word 'enemy' meant so little to Halim that he couldn't quite make sense of it: the very idea that one country could be the enemy of another, and that that could impact on the small life that he had cobbled together for himself. The three of them sat in loaded, painful silence as the dusk seeped into the room, until the looping call of the muezzin coiled its way in through the open windows, which seemed to wake Maggie from her reverie.

"I should go," she said.

"Thank you for coming," Süleyman said at last. "It does mean a lot to us."

"But not as much as what I could have done," Maggie said, nodding as if she was agreeing with something that Süleyman hadn't said. "I do understand, and I am sorry." She turned to Halim, and smiled with a heartbreaking uncertainty. "Halim, will I see you on Monday? For the English class?"

For a moment, Halim couldn't think what she meant, so far was the English class from the thoughts that were at the forefront of his mind; when he realised what she was talking about, he couldn't help a surge of annoyance that she was asking him about something like that at a time like this.

"I don't think so," he said, with unnecessary brusqueness, feeling a guilty pleasure as her face fell. "You know I have to work in the evenings now, at the abattoir."

"But last week – "

Halim shrugged, with a carefully studied nonchalance. "Last week was different," he said, and as a hot flush poured over Maggie's face he knew he'd hit his mark.

She nodded at both of them, unsmiling now, turning to go, and neither Halim not Süleyman could muster the energy to get to their feet and open the door for her. All three of them seemed to sense the change between them, the way that the chasm that had been breached between two Turks and an Irish-Catholic girl from the Sydney slums had opened up between them again, space yawning and infinite. As if recognising the finality of the moment, watching Maggie's broad, straight back descending the steps from the veranda, Süleyman brought his palm down flat onto the tabletop. "Well," he said. "That's that, then."

*

By Monday afternoon, Halim found that the burning, acidic feeling he'd had in his guts had returned, the one that had been assuaged for a week through his friendship with Daniel Brewer, and he wanted more than anything not to go to the abattoir that evening, to just forget about his business and walk as far away from it as possible. He could even see it in his head, a vision of himself striding through the darkened desert, bone-dry spinifex whispering at his ankles, the sand kicked up in a light spray, and stars tangling with his hair. But it was impossible, he knew that; if he really did want to leave – and that seemed more and more likely to be his only option following the scene at the cinema – he knew that he needed money, and for money he needed to work. Head down, he strode down the road, hands crammed deep into his pockets; something in his demeanour made sure that he was avoided by all who saw him, at least until he reached the gate of the abattoir, where Daniel and his few counterfeit friends stood as usual, sucking on soggy cigarette butts and watching the world go by.

Halim quailed – these boys had never bothered him before, but they seemed like the type that would, and he wasn't naïve enough to think that his nascent friendship with Daniel would be anything that could protect him; quite the opposite, it would only put Daniel in the firing line. Praying to be ignored, he pushed past them, in through the gates, and to his relief none of them moved towards him. The only thing that was out of the ordinary was the noise that one or two of them made as he passed, a soft hissing noise, quiet enough that in other circumstances Halim could have believed it was only the wind in the dry leaves of the trees. Moments later he was inside, and as usual, Daniel was at his side.

"G'day."

"Hello," Halim said stiffly. He was starting to wonder whether friendships were like unnecessary possessions, nothing but excess weight, something that should be discarded in case he needed to cut and run. He avoided the blue beam of Daniel's stare, as he knew he couldn't resist the pathetic entreaty in the boy's gaze, the desperation for contact that belied his tough-guy stance.

"You all right?" Daniel asked at last, pushing through Halim's barrier of unfriendliness. "I mean – I heard what happened in the cinema on Saturday."

"Yes." Halim carefully shaped his mouth into a pretence of a smile. "I think everyone in town has heard what happened."

"Well," Daniel seemed uncertain what to say. "I heard it was a stupid film anyway. No point getting upset about it, is there? All that's happening all the way over there, isn't it? Not here."

As usual, Halim was only able to pick up one out of every

few words that Daniel said, but the gist was clear enough, and he had almost begun to soften, when Daniel said, as if this was the crucial point of his argument, "And, I mean, you're not like the rest of them, are you?"

For a moment, Halim was perfectly still, considering. Then he spoke, quietly. "What did you say?"

Daniel's face creased in incomprehension. "Just – you're not like the rest of those Turks, are you? You're different, what with living over here and all – " and Halim turned away, started to walk, his heart banging in his ears, almost drowning out Daniel's plaintive voice: "What'd I say? Come on, Halim, what'd I say?"

Anger was better than fear, Halim told himself; it poured though his veins like liquid fire, speeding his pulse and sending steel through his limbs. He worked faster than he ever had before, not thinking about anything but the meat in front of him and the high-pitched whine of tension in his ears. He was almost enjoying the emotion, which at least made him feel powerful, not hopeless and unmanned, as the fear did. He had finished his work in record time when he turned and saw the men standing in the doorway, still as moss, just standing, watching, eyes as blank as their faces.

For a moment, his mind running untrammelled, Halim thought of the knife that he had just laid down, and two thoughts battled with each other in his head: the atavistic desire to protect himself, no matter what the cost, and the rational part of him that denied what was going on, said *no, this isn't happening, this is just some sort of joke they're playing, that's all*. The rational part won; he left the knife where it was – for even if they were planning to hurt him, he didn't want to escalate things, didn't want to scare them into hurting him more – and with his head down, he slowly, carefully stacked up the meat that he had cut onto the tray that he used for carrying it out to Süleyman's cart, right outside. Keeping his hands busy seemed to stop them from shaking – and still they watched, motionless, silent, nothing moving but their eyes. *Four of them*, he thought to himself, and his insides seemed to dissolve – *four, and I can't even handle one!* – and then *easy, easy, nothing's happened yet*. Climbing to his feet, he held the tray in his hands and approached the door. For one astonishing, impossible second it seemed like things were going to be all right, as the two boys in front parted to let him through, and then there was a movement swift as quicksilver and he realised that no, they hadn't been letting him out, they'd been letting someone get to him.

Halim closed his eyes and waited, as dumb and resigned as the sheep he'd had under his knife only an hour before, waited for the pain that he knew to be coming, but it didn't arrive, and when he opened his eyes the boys were drawing back, grinning like devils, watching his reaction as Halim looked down on the meat that he was holding in front of him, now covered and stinking with a mixture of offal and shit.

Delicately, Halim put the tray down on the floor, straightened and stood, his hands uncoiled in front of him. His mind was suddenly as empty as his hands; something bad was going to happen – something bad was already happening – and all he could do was stand and wait for it. He heard Daniel's voice as if it belonged to another world, the dry, lurching patter of Daniel's shoes pelting through the corridors of the abattoir, calling his name: "Halim! Hey, Halim!" and then the dull thump of the feet that were pursuing Daniel. Rounding the corner, all four boys turned to look as Daniel swung, lopsided, into view. "Halim, get out of here," he yelled, his voice as high and clear as a whistle, moments before a mammoth shape landed on him from behind and simultaneously the first fist sank deep into Halim's belly, pushing the air our of his mouth in an undignified whoop.

The beating seemed both to go on forever and to be over in a trice. Halim knew that there was no point fighting; knew, as a veteran of dozens of fraternal conflicts, that the best thing to do would be to hit the floor at the first blow and lie there looking wretched until they gave up and went away. And, yet, he found himself bracing himself, placing his feet further and further apart in a fighting stance he'd unconsciously borrowed from Süleyman, rocking with each blow like a pendulum but refusing to go down until one of them, infuriated by his stubbornness, actually kicked his legs out from under him and his cheek met cool stone. Faintly, he could hear Daniel's yelps of protest as the man who'd been chasing him laid into him, and he supposed, when he really thought about it, that he should feel guilty, but he couldn't quite gather the energy together.

Afterwards, he could never quite pinpoint when it had ended. He wasn't sure whether he had lost consciousness, but one moment the room was thick with the sound of five men panting and grunting with exertion, the dull smack of a boot in his ribs, and the next moment there was nothing but the moans and whimpers coming from Daniel, lying a few feet away, the sluggish push of blood through Halim's veins, the pain ringing through the cage of his bones, and a sharp taste of metal in his mouth.

The floor was cool and seemed to be moulded specially to fit the shape of Halim's fallen body, beguilingly comfortable, and yet somehow it seemed imperative to Halim that he get up, move, get out of there, go home. Slowly, hearing the crack and pop of his joints knitting themselves together, he stretched his arms out in front of him. They seemed reasonably undamaged, other than a few bruised fingers from when he'd made the mistake of trying to use his hands to shield his body from their boots. Levering one hand under his body, he managed to haul himself into a sitting position. The world rocked alarmingly; for a moment it was as if he was back on the ship again, falling through time and space; he could almost hear Irfan's voice in his ear saying *get up, idiot, you're fine, it's hardly anything*. "You're dead," he told Irfan sternly, and sure enough the world gradually righted itself, the walls around him solidifying from wide sky and open sea. Turning his head to one side he spat, blood. On his knees now, his back yowling in protest, he put one foot on the ground and then the other: standing! He paused for a moment to congratulate himself on this epic achievement, and then started to shuffle towards Daniel.

Daniel's eyes were squeezed tightly shut, but when he heard Halim's footsteps coming closer he opened them, gazing first at Halim's boots within inches of his nose, then shifting his head carefully so he was looking up at his face.

"Hello," Halim said gravely. For some reason the situation was suddenly striking him as inexplicably funny, and it was all he could do to keep the laugh out of his voice.

"Christ almighty," Daniel said. His voice was cracked but steady. "Don't tell me I look as bad as you do?"

When Halim had persuaded Daniel to his feet, the two of them tottered together, arm in arm, to the on-site bathrooms. As Halim retched painfully into the sink, noticing with detached interest the streaks of blood in his vomit, Daniel laid a tentative hand on Halim's back, and Halim didn't shrug him off. When he was finished, subsiding into coughs that sent electric sparks of agony through his chest, they both leant in towards their reflections in the full length mirrors and examined every cut and bruise.

"Blimey," Daniel breathed. Halim knew how he felt. He'd been in fights before, plenty of them, part of the natural rough and tumble of growing up in a big family in a small village, and of being best friends with the most notoriously quick-tempered boy for miles, but there had never been anything like this. The worst he'd experienced had been no more than a black eye or a split lip, and now here he was, in the bathroom of an abattoir, dripping fresh blood from his nose into the sink, and looking at a face that resembled nothing as closely as the now ruined joints of meat he'd stacked up earlier. His face was purple and lumpy with bruises, his left eye was swollen completely shut, and all the skin had been scraped off the right side of his face from forehead to chin – from being kicked about on the rough stone floor, he supposed. Opening his mouth, he found his tongue bitten and his gums bleeding; baring his teeth he found two of them loose. Unmindful of Daniel's curious look, he coaxed his recalcitrant fingers into unbuttoning his shirt, tugging off his vest, and found bruises like ink stains spreading across his torso; breathing was difficult and painful. Altogether, he couldn't think of a time when he'd seen a bigger mess of a human being. Then he caught Daniel's eye in the mirror and revised his opinion: a bigger mess of a human being other than Daniel, that was.

Daniel gave him a rueful grin. "We're in a state, aren't we?" he asked, and though Halim didn't understand his words, his meaning was clear enough. He nodded, grinned back as far as he was able – which wasn't much; just the act of trying to smile reopened several cuts on his lips and sent blood oozing into his mouth again – and, dipping the edge of his vest into the water, tortuously slowly, he started cleaning as much blood off himself as possible.

Half an hour later, still looking as though they'd been dragged around a field by an angry horse – Daniel's choice of colourful metaphor, and once he'd had it explained to him, Halim agreed that it was appropriate – but slightly more presentable, they shuffled their way outside into the cool evening air, the last of the sun glancing over the town. Half expecting the cart to be stolen, Halim was relieved to find it still where he'd left it, the horse bobbing her head with impatience, patting the ground with her hooves.

"Can I give you a lift?" Halim asked Daniel, who, frankly, didn't look as if he could make it to the gates without keeling over, let alone to his lodgings, and Daniel nodded gratefully. Walking round to the back of the cart to help Daniel on, Halim realised that his instincts had been correct and the cart had been tampered with as well: there, squatting malignantly in the middle of the cart, was the head of a pig, its eyes dull and milky, a halo of flies around his head. After the beating he'd just taken,

Halim couldn't even be bothered to be outraged, but let out a hissing sigh. Daniel, on the other hand, looked horrified.

"Oh, Halim. God, I am so sorry."

"Why?" Halim forced the words out through his shredded lips. "You didn't put it there."

"No, but – I told them about the pigs and your religion. They said they were interested to know, like I was. I never thought they'd do something like this – " Listening to himself, he gave a huffing laugh, and indicated his battered face. "Well. I never thought they'd do something like this, either."

They hadn't spoken about it yet. "What did they do to you?" Halim asked. "Where were you when you came running?"

"Thompson – he's the big bloke that was chasing me – he was told to take care of me. Knew that if I was aware what they were up to, I'd try and warn you. I knew I couldn't fight him off, not properly, so I waited till he thought I wasn't struggling anymore, then – wham! – kicked him a good one in the nuts and took off." Daniel gave an appreciative chuckle. "Maybe this whole thing's worth it just for that moment. Bloke's been winding mc up for ycars. Was lovely to see him down on his knees in the dust, singing soprano."

For a moment, they looked at each other frankly and openly. In silence, Halim forgave Daniel for his earlier remark, searching underneath the words and grasping the essential kindness that had been intended – and then a gust of wind made them both shiver, reminding them of the time.

"Come on," Halim said, indicating the pig's head. "Would you mind? I can't touch it."

With the straightforward lack of squeamishness of an abattoir worker, Daniel leant forward, took the head by its jowls, and heaved it off the cart. As he stumbled away to dispose of it, Halim filled a bucket from the outside tap and rinsed the place where the head had sat, again and again, until the blotch of red where it had lain was invisible to anyone who didn't know it was there. Daniel came back, stumbling like an old man, letting out little grunts and expletives with every movement that Halim found unaccountably hilarious, and had to suppress giggles as corrosive as bile. When he had control of himself again, he gave his hand to Daniel, helping him onto the back of the cart, and then clambered up himself, too weary and hurting to bother with the elegant jump that he normally tried for. He took the reins in his aching hands, and the horse was persuaded to move.

For a moment, neither of them said anything; then Daniel's voice came shrilly from behind him: "I was right, you know, Halim," he said. "You're really not like the rest of them," and Halim had to rein in the horse as he bent over the box, crippled with spasms of joyless laughter.

October 20th, 1915

"Six months," Collier said to Patrick, shaking his head, and he didn't have to say any more; it was all that most of them were thinking about, that it was nearly six months that they had been there, no change, no advance, and talk all the time that the Turks were reinforcing their positions and digging in ever deeper. Patrick was more afraid of dysentery than he was of the Turks these days, as it seemed to be causing far more damage among the men; dysentery, and his own men, for there had been an awful case a few days before of a man shooting his mate dead while cleaning his rifle in the trench. Compared to that sort of behaviour, the Turks were starting to look more and more appealing. Patrick sometimes felt that he couldn't stand to look at another can of bully beef, and so he'd had a rare flare of joy when he'd heard that the Turks in the trench opposite, not more than twenty metres away, were willing to trade it for cigarettes. Patrick had never really got a taste for smoking, either, but the smell of the cigarettes did a lot to dampen the noisome stench of the trench, and the fag ends were also useful for burning off lice and fleas.

It was that sort of detail that he omitted from his letters to Maggie. He did tell her, though, that the Turks weren't bad chaps at all; he thought she would like to hear that. He didn't tell her how bloody unnecessary the whole battle felt to him these days.

Chapter Twenty-One

Maggie had never thought of Charlie as an angry man. Certainly, he'd lost his temper around her; he had a short fuse, and was liable to snap and shout when things didn't go his way, but he always burnt out quickly, subsiding into laughter and sheepish apologies as soon as the initial burst of rage was gone. This was different – this was deeper and more corrosive, and Maggie didn't know what to do with it, how to deal with it, or where to put it. It frightened her.

The telegram came at the start of October, and she'd be lying if she said that she hadn't expected it. It was clear from what they were hearing through the newspapers and the radio how the war was going over there. It was a bloodbath, a shambles and that made her flare with anger – that grown men should be toying so much with mere boys, using them as pawns across the chessboard of Europe, sacrificing them at the altar of imperial expansion and national pride – and she was particularly angry about the Australian side of things, that this country that had been supposed to be bold and brave and new had been dragged back into petty-minded squabbling over the other side of the world. And, worse, that the boys and men seemed too willing to wade into the thick of it, bayonets swinging and guns blaring their ugly shouts to the sky. It sickened her.

In some ways it had brought them closer when both Patrick and Charlie's younger brother Martin were away at war together, especially when Martin was sent to Gallipoli, too. They both knew that the chances of them bumping into one another on the Gallipoli peninsula, let alone the chances of them recognising one another in their camouflage fatigues, given that they'd only met once, scrubbed and shining in their formal finery at Charlie and Maggie's wedding, were slim to none, but that didn't stop Charlie and Maggie from fantasising about it, imagining the two of them, who meant nothing to one another but so much to Maggie and Charlie, sitting together on the beach at Suvla Bay as the sun went down, sharing a cigarette and maybe a bottle of grog that they'd somehow got their hands on, gossiping about the family that they half shared, watching each other's backs. It was a comforting thought, a false idea that perhaps someone was watching out for their loved ones, even though they both knew that it was impossible.

The day that the telegram arrived was unseasonably cold, a chill frosting the air, the southerly wind slicing through clothing and flesh to the bone, and when Maggie saw the post office cart drawing up at the gate, and the sombre face of the postman as he came up the path, all her limbs turned to water with a combination of horror and relief. She knew that it must be Martin because, if it was Patrick, she wouldn't be the one to be told. Despite the fact that his letters came mostly to her and not to their parents, their parents were still his next of kin and they were the ones who would be notified in case of any disaster. Somehow, that the dreaded telegram had arrived here seemed to be protection against anything happening to Patrick. She knew it was nonsensical but on some level she believed that it was a balanced proposition – one or the other could be killed or wounded; both surviving unscathed would seem unnaturally lucky, and both being killed or wounded unnaturally cruel. She knew that, in some way, Charlie felt the same way – that despite all their cosy imaginings about the two boys looking out for one another so far away, at some point, one of them would have to be sacrificed so that the other could live.

She was the only one home – Peter and Charlie were out in the fields; Elizabeth visiting a friend on the other side of town

– and so, with shaking hands, she took the telegram, thanking the postman with blank and bloodless lips. This was her punishment, this was her penitence for that flicker of gladness that Patrick had been spared, that the burden of telling the family had fallen on her. Ignoring the postman's look of overweening sympathy, she closed the door and opened the envelope, and for several long moments she couldn't make sense of it, because it wasn't what she was expecting. Scanning it again and again for the word 'killed', her eyes finally were snagged by the word 'wounded' and stuck there.

In some ways, Maggie said to herself throughout that long afternoon, waiting for the family to come home, planning out the best way to break the news, in some ways, this could be the best possible outcome for now. A tragedy, of course, for a boy so young to lose a leg, and a double tragedy for someone as active and vibrant as Martin had been – but at least it was a reprieve; it got him out of the action and would get him home and safe with no shame upon him; there'd be a living badge that he'd done his duty, and he'd have no accusations of cowardice to fear. In some ways, Maggie thought, though she knew she would never voice these thoughts to Charlie or to anyone else, in some ways maybe Martin was even the lucky one, luckier than Patrick (whose letters still prickled with schoolboy enthusiasm; despite all he had seen and experienced and continued to see and experience, there was a blazing, irrepressible part of him that couldn't stop thinking of the war as a game, and it made Maggie's heart hurt), who was still in the thick of it. Martin was safe, protected and taken care of now, but Patrick was out there alone, a tiny speck of humanity in that vast, swarming miasma of violence and blood and death, and at that moment she felt suddenly, violently, that she would sacrifice her brother's legs if she had to, if it would bring him home safely.

Maggie had expected that the news would be hard to take at first, but that before long they would see the positive side of it, and Elizabeth certainly seemed to, when she came home. Weeping helplessly when Maggie put her arms around her and told her the news, she choked out through her tears: "Maggie – am I a terrible person for being relieved that he's coming home?" and Maggie assured her that no, no she was not, it was only natural to feel the way that she did.

Peter and Charlie were always going to be harder nuts to crack, and indeed both of them met the news with silence and stoicism. Peter was still, stiff as if frozen, and after a moment got up with a jerky movement as if it pained him, stumping heavily out of the room as Elizabeth followed. Charlie, on the other hand, turned the colour of chalk – she had never seen him look sicker, even when he'd been felled by pneumonia the winter before and spent his days and nights battling for breath. Peter and Elizabeth gone, she struck them from her mind – her husband was her concern and she sat with him, knee to knee in the overly-formal parlour room where she'd waited to tell them – why had she waited there? She didn't know, other than the gravitas of the occasion had somehow called for it – waiting for him to speak as the minutes ticked by. She couldn't quite bring herself to touch him, take him into her arms as she wanted to do – there was some sort of forceful, flickering energy coming off him that warded her back.

When he spoke, his words were the last thing that she had expected from him.

"I've got to sign up," he said. At first Maggie thought that she had misheard, but he nodded to himself as if he had come to some sort of internal decision, and turned to look at her. "There are recruiters coming through town in a month. I'm going to sign up."

"Charlie – "

"I have to, Maggie. It's the only thing I can do."

"But Charlie, the children! Your parents! They've already had one son injured. How could they stand it if it happened to another?"

"But that's why I have to go, you must understand. For Martin, of course. I have to go, and – and finish what he was doing."

"And get revenge, you mean! This is madness! What about – what about the farm, then? Surely now your father needs you more than ever – he needs one able-bodied son to take over the work…"

"Paul's growing up, now, though – he'll be old enough soon enough."

"And then he'll probably be off to war like the rest of you fools!"

Charlie battered on regardless, as if he hadn't heard. "And there's my cousin Jim from Adelaide, he could easily help out, he'd be happy to; he's itching to get out onto a farm. And anyway, I shouldn't be worrying about the farm at a time like this – the war, this is war! It's far more important."

"Charlie," she stood in his path, stopping his fevered pacing, and gripped his arms in either hand. "What's come over you? You never cared much one way or another before, did you? You thought it was a lark – you thought it was Martin off having a lark, getting a free trip to the other side of the world – "

When he looked at her, the blankness of his eyes frightened her. "Because it's real now, Maggie. Suddenly it's real to me. Martin – I grew up with Martin, I know him, and I know that this is the worst thing that could have happened; I know that he would rather be dead than for this to happen. He said it to me, in exactly those words, just before he left. I asked him if he was worried about – about something happening, about not coming back – and he said no, he wasn't worried about dying. He said that there's nothing to worry about, dying like a hero – but the only thing that he wouldn't be able to bear would be to be crippled. And now – "

"But he'll change his mind, Charlie! That's just the sort of thing that young men say; you know that. Patrick told me the exact same thing. But he'll cope, he'll get used to it, and he'll end up glad to be alive…"

Charlie shook his head with a bull-headed certainty that made Maggie feel sick with panic. She tried to remind herself that this was his grief talking, but over and over again in her mind's eye she kept seeing Charlie in a uniform, herself left alone with the children, and, before too long, the inevitable telegram coming to her door, and she couldn't help herself from asking, "And what about the children? What about me?"

His face softened then, if only a touch. "Maggie, love, I'm sorry. You know that I don't want to leave you, or the kids. But this – this is a once in a lifetime chance. I can't sit back and let it go." When Maggie's expression didn't change, his face hardened again. "Of course, you wouldn't understand. Women don't understand this sort of thing."

It was the sort of remark designed to get her blood boiling. "Oh, don't we? I understand well enough what this is about, Charlie McGill. I understand that you're wading into someone else's war out of pride, when you'd do a damn sight more good staying here with your family."

"Don't be stupid, Maggie."

"And don't call me bloody stupid!" Her voice was a low, violent hiss. The temper that ran like wildfire through her family, which she had fought hard for years to keep under control, was uncoiling like a serpent in her belly; her thoughts were inchoate and jumbled, and all she knew was that she had to get away from Charlie, before she did or said something irreparable. She turned, and had taken just two strides towards the door when there was a scuffle behind her and Charlie grabbed her hand. All thoughts of dignity long gone, she refused to turn, trying to wrench her hand out of his grasp, but he only held on tighter.

"Maggie," he said, and again, "Maggie," and the second time the sheer desolation in his hoarse voice got through to her; her anger receded as if it had never been and she breathed deeply, once, twice, before she turned back and took her husband into her arms.

So they were friends again, at least on the surface of things, but something had changed; Charlie's anger at his brother's fate, and his eagerness to finish the job that Martin had started seemed to lodge like a tick just under his skin. It wasn't that he was in a temper all the time – to look at him from a distance, he smiled and laughed as much as he ever had, if not more, as he took Elizabeth and Peter's sadness onto his shoulders like a weight that he seemed determined to lift. But Maggie knew her husband, and it was with inexorable sadness that she noticed the way his face had changed, the frown lines that were forming on his brow, and the way that, when he thought no one was looking, his expression fell into shapes of habitual melancholy and resentment. In her own quiet anger, she thought that this change in her happy-go-lucky husband was yet another thing that the war could be blamed for.

Chapter Twenty-Two

The recruiters came through three weeks later, and Maggie dreaded their arrival every day; in her imagination they changed from a group of probably very nice, decent, upstanding men to a Mongol horde, sweeping into town, taking all the men and liable to impale the children and rape the women while they were at it. At night, lying in bed beside Charlie, she could feel him vibrating with suppressed excitement at the thought of the fight ahead; they lay, side by side, not touching, eyes open and staring at the ceiling, locked into their own thoughts – they could have been hundreds of miles apart. Soon, Maggie thought bitterly to herself, they probably would be.

When the recruiters finally arrived, they brought the town out onto the street, cheering for the boys who had gone and the boys who were about to go. Their arrival had been anticipated and dreaded in equal measure. Bright-hearted boys longed for the chance to sign up, ship out and fight for a king and a country that weren't theirs; their more craven or timid or even thoughtful comrades, who had felt obliged to join in the excitable boasting about their excitement at the idea of joining up, knew that now was the time that they were going to have to nail their colours to the mast, and dreaded both the humiliation of saying that, actually, they didn't want to go after all. They thereby risked the scorn of their friends and the wrath of the rest of the town (some of whom had heard of the European practice of sending white feathers for cowardice to men who weren't prepared to sign up, and seemed keen to adopt it in Cottier's Creek); or the even worse alternative, being pronounced medically fit to fight and being whisked off to the other side of the world before they could manage to decently escape into the bush and hide out there until the recruiters had gone. The mood in the town was electric; in the few days before the recruiters came there were more fights in the town pub than there had ever been before, a stray word igniting the combustible atmosphere of fear, excitement and anticipation as men who had always been good friends came to blows and had to have buckets of water poured over their heads to calm them down.

When the day arrived, the town hall was transformed into the recruiters' domain. A Sergeant Major and a Corporal from Adelaide were presiding, holding court, ushering the men and the boys through the doors, pointing them in the right direction. A corner had been curtained off to create the illusion of privacy for the compulsory medical examination, though every word could be clearly heard through the flimsy fabric and some of the younger boys liked to linger nearby when their mates were being examined, dog-like glee on their faces as they waited, open mouthed, for any piece of sensitive information that could potentially be used to embarrass their friends.

The hall was rammed with a squirming mass of people. Charlie recognised men whom he hadn't seen for years, boys he'd been at school with who had vanished into the outlying properties and rarely if ever came into town, but somehow the recruiters had flushed them out with their promises of adventure and glory. It wasn't just the white Australians, either. Charlie was surprised to see some of the Aboriginal men who lived between the town and the Ghan Town, long-limbed, eyes downcast – and there were even some men from the Ghan Town itself, dark-skinned and grinning. A flush of anger came over Charlie for a moment, until he talked himself down. They weren't Turks, he knew; Maggie had told him that the only Turks in town were the two he sometimes saw on the ice cream cart, and that the rest of the Arabs had as much reason to be wary of the Turks as he had.

Zein approached him boldly. Charlie remembered his name; he'd employed him for a couple of seasons as a shearer, and he'd done a good job of it. He was a man of few words but he'd been cheerful and conscientious, always the first there in the mornings and never bleary or short-tempered with the after-effects of drink like many of the white men had been.

"Morning," he said, and Charlie nodded at him, a little stiff.

"You want to sign up?" he asked, and Zein nodded.

"Yes, of course!" Charlie noticed the increasing breadth of Zein's vowels and couldn't help smiling a little – the man had obviously embraced his Australian identity and was doing his best to cultivate an accent to match. "Wouldn't miss it. Lots of us from the camp want to join."

"You're happy to fight for Australia?"

"Of course, mate. This is our home now. I've been here for eight years; this country's been good to me. And besides – it's not just the Germans now, is it? The Germans have never done anything to me. But the Turks – I'm an Arab from near Damascus, me, part of the Ottoman Empire for years – they're trouble at home, the Turks, always trying to take what's not theirs, and now they're trying again. I'm looking forward to facing up to them this time, showing them who's in charge now."

Zein went first into the doctor's area, and Charlie did his best not to listen, not wanting to know any of the intimate details of Zein's anatomy. But it was over within minutes, and Zein pushed back the curtain, grinning triumphantly; it was clear that he was through, and one of his dark-skinned friends came over to him, clapped him heavily on the back, exclaiming in that dry, dusty language the two of them shared.

Charlie's turn now, and he walked inside with as much swagger as he could muster. The doctor barely looked at him when he introduced himself, let along shook the hand that Charlie extended and then hurriedly withdrew, embarrassed. In a routine that he had patently done hundreds, if not thousands of times before and that was oddly elegant, as perfectly choreographed as a dance routine, he looked into Charlie's eyes and ears, lifted his shirt and pressed his stethoscope to his chest and back, asked Charlie to bare his teeth, gave them a perfunctory glance, and then made Charlie remove his shoes. In his head, Charlie was already kitted out in his uniform, his rifle hoisted over his shoulder, upright and marching proud, a reverie out of which he was abruptly jerked when the doctor said, "No."

"What?" Charlie looked down at the doctor, who was still crouched by his feet.

"Sorry, mate. You're not fit. Flat feet."

"What do you mean?"

The doctor took one of Charlie's feet in his hand.

"See this?" He pointed to the underside of Charlie's foot. "What you're supposed to have here is an arch. But yours is flat. Flat feet, can't have those in the army."

"But I've never had any problems, doctor – I'm completely fit; I work bloody hard out on my farm, and my feet have never bothered me –"

" – and you've probably never marched thirty miles in a day with a twenty-pound rucksack on your back, have you? No. Sorry mate, but there's no way. Plenty of other boys with the same problem as you, and we've had to disappoint all of them."

Afterwards, Charlie could never quite remember leaving the recruiting hall. He found himself, twenty minutes later, marching along the main road out of town, breathing heavily. The blindness of rage was starting to lift – how dare the doctor turn him down; he'd never been turned down for anything in his life! – to be replaced by a bitter, corrosive sense of disappointment and shame. He couldn't go home, not yet – he couldn't bear to see the expression on Maggie's face, which he knew would be manufactured pity and sympathy, inexpertly concealing the relief beneath. Well, she'd got what she wanted, hadn't she? She'd have him at home for as long as she wanted. But not yet; he wasn't ready to accept his lot of sitting at home while that glorious carnival raged on the opposite side of the world. Turning in his tracks, he stalked back towards the town, and the bright banner of the pub that was reaching out to him like the hand of a saviour.

Maggie had never seen Charlie drunk before, not properly. He was generally a man of moderate habits, doing nothing more than getting occasionally slightly bright-eyed and slippery-voiced on special occasions like Christmas, his birthday and the births of the children, but that was nothing like this. Charlie was a flailing, shambling wreck of a man by the time he finally stumbled home; his shirt stained and untucked, his hair wrenched out of its customary sleekness and falling over his face in straggly hanks, dust all over his trousers as he'd clearly walked the three miles back from the town pub and fallen several times along the way. He could barely string a sentence together, his tongue flapping this way and that, the words running away from him before he managed to close his mouth around them.

All evening Maggie had known where he was. Gossip ran like wildfire around the town and so she couldn't avoid hearing first how Charlie had been turned down by the army – a bright flame of joy had ignited in her at the news, while at the same time she knew how terrible he must have been feeling – and then, later, how Charlie was sinking his disappointment into the bottom of a beer glass. As hour after hour went past with no sign of him, she had put her energy into building up a head full of righteous anger, all of which slipped away when she saw the piteous state her husband was in as he came stumbling up the path from the gate.

Hustling him into the house and up the stairs to their bedroom, before Elizabeth or Peter woke and came out to see what all the noise was about, she sat him down on the bed and started to unbutton his shirt, kneeling at his feet and unlacing his boots while all the while he swayed above her, pitching like a boat on rough seas, spouting a continuous monologue in which Maggie could only understand one word in twenty, if that. She had a sudden, vivid memory of her mother doing the same thing for her father when she had been growing up, but she was surprised to find that, instead of it provoking renewed anger towards Charlie, it brought forth nothing more than a small, aching nugget of sympathy for her mother, spending her life in a marriage where this sort of thing had been the norm, rather than the single glaring exception.

She gave up when it came to his trousers – the thought of trying to ease them off his long, thrashing legs, tight and corded with muscle, defeated her – and instead she pushed him back onto the bed. She expected him to protest, but he lay quietly, legs dangling, as if blearily intrigued as to what she was going to do next. She lifted his legs onto the bed, half turning his body as she did so, thanking her lucky stars for the broad shoulders and robust body she'd grown up with. He grunted in surprise, but otherwise seemed perfectly amenable as she nudged and rolled him over to the side of the bed, allowing herself a foot or so to squeeze in beside him. She briefly considered making up a bed in the nursery and letting him have the bed to herself – not out of anger, but so that he would be comfortable and they would both get some sleep – but decided against it, uncertain how he would react, in his addled state, to waking up and finding her not there. Charlie murmured something incomprehensible, and she made some sort of innocuous, amenable nothing comment in response. It seemed enough to placate him, so, daring to leave him for a moment, she slipped down the hall to the lavatory, splashed cold water on her face, and eyed herself in the looking glass with a sort of brittle hilarity. By the time she made it back to the bedroom to undress and put on her nightgown, Charlie was fast asleep, mouth yawning like the pits on the edge of the town, producing a series of dry, choking snores, and despite the pathos of the situation, she couldn't suppress the giggle that lurched up from her belly, unstoppable.

She woke with the blank, white dawn staring in at the window to the sound of sudden movement, which, on further examination, turned out to be Charlie lurching violently out of the bed, thumping, barefoot to the door, scrabbling at the handle and fleeing down the hallway to the bathroom. She grinned ruefully to herself; it was a scene that she'd seen many times with her father as a child, not to mention her older brothers – the maudlin drunkenness, the sudden descent into unconsciousness, the violent illness on waking, and the rest of the day spent, greenish, head in hands, vowing never to repeat such behaviour again, or not that day, at any rate. Sure enough, Charlie poked his head around the door a few minutes later, his face as wan and woebegone as Little Peter's when he was feeling unwell, and, any animosity forgotten, she opened her arms to him. Without hesitation, he came to her, lay beside her on the mattress, and rolled into her embrace. At that moment, it was as if the past few weeks hadn't happened, the awkward, uncertain truce between the two of them as they circled one another, weapons not quite drawn, in their marital home; they were back to the way that they had always been with one another.

"My poor boy," Maggie said quietly, as if she was soothing a tear-streaked Peter, and Charlie grunted a little and wriggled closer into her arms. He smelt of soap and cold water – he had always been fastidious – and, as his breathing started to slow, hers matched his. She was on the brink of sleep again when he spoke.

"I'm sorry, Maggie."

"It's all right," she said sleepily, hoping that he would take her at her word and that she could snatch an hour or two more before Mary started yowling for her breakfast.

"No, it's not. This is no way to behave. This isn't the sort of husband that I want to be for you."

"This isn't you, though. This was once, one night. You won't do it again, I'm sure."

He gave a short, mirthless laugh, his breath warm on her throat. "Not based on the way I'm feeling, no. I doubt I'm ever going to touch the stuff again." He fell silent for a moment, and then sighed. "You heard what happened?"

"Alma Corcoran told me. Came to gloat, more like – her husband's joined the 17th Batallion. Seemed to think that I'd be upset that you didn't make it through; she was very cross when she found out that I was glad. I think she's been trying to find an acceptable way of getting rid of Archie for years."

Charlie didn't laugh, and for a while he didn't speak, before finally he whispered into her shoulder. "I feel like such a damn failure."

Maggie tightened her arms around him, her heart twisting inside her. "Oh, love. You're not a failure, you're far from that. It wasn't your fault …"

"I don't understand it. I'm fitter than Archie Corcoran, fitter than half the men I saw signing up yesterday. Flat feet, he told me. Flat feet! What does that matter if a man's fit and young and able to fire a gun? I'm the best shot for miles around, I'm bloody strong and I'm fast. It's not right, not at all."

"They know what they're doing, love. They know what they're looking for."

"I just wanted… I wanted to do you proud. To do the whole family proud, to make up for what Martin's lost."

"But you can't do that, Charlie. Nothing's going to give him his leg back, let alone risking his brother in the same war that's nearly killed him. And the rest of us, we are proud. I'm proud, the proudest I could be – I couldn't ask for a better husband, and the kids couldn't ask for a better father." She ran her hand down his back, her cool fingertips smoothing the bunched ridges of his muscles. "I don't know what I'd do if anything happened to you. I never wanted you to go, and I don't care who knows it. I don't care about this bloody war – it's not our war, Charlie, it's being fought by men from the past, men who're looking backwards, and that isn't what this country's about. I don't care about the war, and I don't care about England, or Germany, or the bloody Ottomans, or any of that. I care about you and me and our kids, and this house, this town, this country. Nothing more."

For a long time he was silent, and she wasn't sure if she'd offended him – but so what if she had, she thought; at least she'd told him what she thought. But finally he took a deep breath, and lifted his head to look at her. His face was tired and ravaged from last night's excesses, his eyes dark-ringed as if they'd been bruised, the whites bloodshot, and his mouth was tight with pain – his head, Maggie thought with sympathy, it must be killing him. But despite all this, his expression was clearer than she'd seen it in weeks; the uncertainty and the anger that had been trembling just beneath his skin since the news about Martin had come was gone.

"I'm a bloody idiot sometimes, Maggie McGill," he said, and Maggie smiled. "And sometimes I need you to talk some sense into me. I don't know how I managed to get around before I knew you. I'm surprised I didn't end up trampled by a bull or dead in a ditch without you looking after me." He smiled at her with his old, charming, boy's smile. "I don't care about anything as long as I've got you," he said, raising his hand, which shook only slightly, and twining a loose curl of her hair around his fingers. "Nothing matters aside from that, nothing aside from you and the kids and my family. You're right, it's not our war, and I'm better off out of it."

It was a Sunday, which meant that there was nothing but church to get up for. The two of them lay silently, close enough to feel each other's pulses rippling their skin, as the house woke up around them – as Nancy tapped her way down the hall to get the children up, bathed and ready. This was something that Maggie normally helped with but today, feeling almost like a newlywed, she couldn't bear to leave Charlie. Peter's squawks soon roused them, though. Maggie slipped out of bed, threw a shawl over her shoulders and opened the door, calling to Nancy as she swished efficiently past. "Bring the children in here, when they're ready," she said, and Nancy nodded, her face not betraying any glimmer of what she thought of this unorthodox request. Fifteen minutes later, Charlie was propped up in bed, pale but smiling, Peter bouncing on his knee, as Maggie cradled Mary in the rocking chair beside the bed.

Normally they split up on a Sunday. Maggie made the trip into the town to attend the Catholic mass, and the rest of the family tricked themselves out in their best clothes and flocked en masse to the Presbyterian church – the McGill chapel was only used for the most special of occasions, and the average Sunday was seen as something more social than religious. But this Sunday Maggie decided to make an exception. She dressed with uncommon detail and care and, without a word, she joined the McGills as they climbed into their carriage on their way into town. Nobody passed any comments, but Charlie put his arm around her and pulled her closer, and Nancy passed Peter across to her so that she could hold him on her knee.

At the door of the church Maggie felt something swell within her – her husband, her children, her chosen family, presenting a united front to the town. Faces looked towards them, feigned pity when they caught Charlie's eye, and she squeezed his hand. He had nothing to be ashamed of, she thought with as much vigour as she could, hoping that he could catch what she was thinking even as she stayed silent. His head stayed up and his eyes never wavered, and she had never been prouder of him than she was then, never gladder of the decision that she had made to hitch her fate to this man.

Coming home that afternoon, Maggie realised that, without even wanting to, she had picked her side. Her fondness for Halim and Süleyman was a mere flicker compared to the shining beacon of love she had for her chosen family, and her muddled, unformed beliefs that everyone should just be able to get along with one another couldn't stand up against Charlie's certainty about the war's clear, burning rightness. She thought of the scene in the cinema, of the rumblings in the town that had been going on ever since, of the pure, uncomprehending anger that she had seen on Halim and Süleyman's faces, and she thought of her own horror of the war, and her utter rejection of the idea that it could spill over into her town. *I wanted to help them to stay*, she thought, *but that was my own vanity, my own desire to prove to myself that I could fix this – perhaps it's better for all of us if I help them go.*

Chapter Twenty-Three

The whole town turned out to watch the parade a few days later, and Maggie and Charlie turned out with them. It was clear to Maggie that Charlie would have preferred to be almost anywhere but there, hiding in the paddocks or in the sheep pens, pretending that the war wasn't going on without him. But, no matter how much he wanted to hide, he wanted even more to show the town that he didn't care about not marching with them, that he was proud of the boys going off, and pleased for them in an uncomplicated way that was in no way twisted up in envy and humiliation. Charlie had always been a man whose emotions showed plainly on his face – dissembling was alien to him – and Maggie watched him with sharp sympathy as he, in his turn, watched the motley band of new recruits in their ill-fitting uniforms, laughing and teasing one another, as far from the image of an efficient, disciplined army as could be imagined. After a while his face softened – she could see him convincing himself that he wouldn't want to be part of something as amateurish and ill-disciplined in any case, a fiction in which Maggie was more than happy to remain complicit. With a flurry of drums and the low, howling drone of the pipers, the band started up, and Peter, who always responded intensely to music, started squeaking with excitement, windmilling his arms, his mouth stretched wide in a grin that showed off his tiny milk teeth to their best advantage. Charlie gave his first genuine smile of the day.

"Come on, sport," he said to his son, who was clinging to

Maggie's hand, and hefted him into his arms and then onto his shoulders, where Peter sat with a sort of lunatic dignity, surveying the excitement around him. With his left hand Charlie steadied Peter's leg; with his right, he took hold of Maggie's, who was balancing Mary on her hip. "Let's see if we can get any closer."

The four of them pushed through the crowd, which was thrumming with excited chatter, the air above crackling with nervous energy. People were dressed in their best, the younger men and women and children draped in streamers of red, white and blue, handing out rosettes. Those towards the front were gripping flags, and Charlie soon spotted one of the men who was handing them out, procuring two, handing one to Peter (who gripped it stickily and waved it with an absorbed intensity, as if he was conducting an orchestra), and the other to Maggie, who let a fascinated Mary examine it carefully, only removing it from her grasp when she started to gnaw on it.

Spirits got higher the closer they got to the new recruits. Mothers and fathers were pointing out their sons to one another; old friends, the ones who had been turned down by the recruiters or the ones who hadn't even tried, pushed as close as they could to their mates in their uniforms, baggy or over-tight, taunting them – "Hey, Blue, how'd the boots fit you?" – demonstrating as publicly as they could that they didn't care that their friends were going and they were being left behind, and that the boys that they had grown up with, the same ones who had been fat or spotty, who had come last in all the sprinting races, who had clumsily fallen into creeks while trying to catch frogs, or who had flatly refused the challenge to climb the tallest tree in the village, who had been bucked off horses, who had been turned down by girls, who had wept at weepie films in the town picture house, who had wet themselves on the first day of school, these boys, standing straighter than ever before despite the odd pulls and bulges of their uniforms, were suddenly being fêted as heroes.

Maggie glanced in the opposite direction, to look at the dais on which stood the mayor of the town and various other luminaries, and had to stifle a laugh to see Süleyman's garishly painted cart parked right beside it. The reason was quite clear – it was directly in front of Mrs Bell's house, from which Süleyman and Halim collected the milk for their ice cream every week – but as Maggie turned back to Charlie, smiling, intending to share the joke, it became immediately clear that he didn't find it as funny as she did.

"Bloody cheek," Charlie muttered, his face darkening.

"I'm sure they didn't mean it," Maggie laid her hand on his arm, gentle and placating. "They go there every week to collect milk – to make the ice cream, you know. It's just coincidence."

"Still, they should have bloody known," Charlie said. "Two Turks like that, on a day like today – they should have known to stay away."

Standing just behind the dais, little did Charlie know that Süleyman and Halim were fervently wishing the same thing. Süleyman couldn't see a way out of this mess – pails of milk in either hand, he and Halim dithered, out of sight, watching as Sena grew increasingly restive, rolling her eyes with exaggerated histrionics, and the resentful mutterings of the crowd grew more and more angry.

"We should move the cart," Halim hissed urgently. He still bore the bruises that he had received in the abattoir the week before, and despite his initial sang-froid he had been plagued by nightmares ever since, waking up gulping down the thin night air, every muscle tensed for the next blow to fall. He hadn't been back to the abattoir since, and it had taken all of Süleyman's skills of persuasion to get him to come into town that morning, something that both of them were now bitterly regretting.

"How can we move the bloody thing?" Süleyman countered. "Best just to leave it there, wait until the parade's gone past and then get on with it. If we do anything now, we'll just be making a show of ourselves, and they'll like that even less than having the bloody cart there."

But it wasn't their decision to make. Minutes later, Mrs Bell came striding down the path with one of the mayor's aides who looked in a state of high dudgeon. With an apologetic shrug towards Halim and Süleyman, Mrs Bell pointed them out where they were skulking with their pales of milk, desperately trying to avoid notice, and he stormed across the grass towards them.

"You!" bellowed the aide. He was a small, skinny man with an unusually deep and loud voice, which he clearly intended to use to its best effect. "What the bloody hell are you doing? This is a parade, you bloody idiots! What the hell is your bloody cart doing there? Get it out of the way at once!"

"But – " with a roll of thunderous drums, the march began, drowning out Süleyman's mild retort. All three of them turned and looked over their shoulders to see the new recruits of the 17th Battalion lurch forward and start to make their ungainly way towards them. The aide's face was purple and apoplectic.

"No buts, I don't care about your excuses! Just get it out of the way!"

Süleyman and Halim exchanged a glance but said nothing more, just ran towards the cart, loaded the pails onto the back and hopped up onto the box. As soon as he was up there, Süleyman's objection became perfectly clear to Halim. The shaky line of new recruits was now only twenty yards or so behind them; any attempt to move the cart now was bound to attract more attention than doing nothing, and, judging by the hostile expressions of many of the people closest to them in the crowd, Halim could tell that the attention was not going to be positive. He leant closer to Süleyman to whisper his concerns, and Süleyman nodded distractedly.

"I know, I know! Look, I'm just going to try and move her past the dais so we're a bit more out of the way, not so noticeable."

Halim nodded, and Süleyman had just gripped the reins in his sweat-slick palms when everything seemed to happen at once. Now only ten yards behind them, the sergeant major at the head of the straggling line of troops opened his mouth and his throat and seemed to produce a shout from the soles of his boots:

"Eyes left!"

And at the same moment, the aide, puffed up and swollen with rage, standing by their cart, raised his hand and gave Sena a resounding slap on the rump. The combination of the slap and the shout snapped her last, frayed nerve; Sena shied and, to the speechless horror of both Halim and Süleyman, leapt out into the centre of the road. The ramshackle, brightly-coloured cart, the horse with her jingling bit, and the two Turks in their threadbare clothes – they were suddenly leading the procession.

His face frozen in disbelief, Halim turned to Süleyman. "Get her out of the road!" he ordered desperately.

"And put her where?" Süleyman's face was rigid with anger and embarrassment, and Halim saw his point. They were well past the dais now, where they'd originally planned to pull in. As far as they could see ahead of them, the street was lined with people, their faces blending into one another with a curious mixture of confused and offended expressions. There was nowhere they could stop. With the troops at their heels the only thing they could do was brazen it out and pray for it to end quickly.

Any hope that the townspeople may have just assumed that it was the simple mistake that it was, rather than a deathly insult, evaporated when the first tomato thudded into the side of the cart. Looking to his left, Halim saw a crowd of young boys descending on a fruit and vegetable cart, ignoring the protests of its owner. Eager young hands grabbed hold of anything that they could reach, and despite the muttered protest of the crowd around them – not out of concern for the Turks, but not wishing the parade to be any further insulted – arms went back, and the fruit and vegetables were flung. Behind them, Halim caught sight of Daniel's pale, freckled face, still cut and bruised from the previous week's beating, but no sooner had their eyes met Daniel turned away, elbowing a path through the mêlée. Halim and Süleyman ducked and dodged as much as they could, but the hail of vegetables was unceasing and soon Sena started to buck and shy; temperamental at the best of times the situation had utterly unnerved her and she lifted herself up onto her back legs, kicking furiously at the sky, performing a kind of delicate dance that skewed the cart sideways and brought it to an almost complete halt.

Halim could taste blood in the back of his throat and his pulse surged like waves in his ears. The group of boys, sensing their weakness, descended on the cart and a bony hand grabbed at Halim's shirt, trying to drag him off – on the other side of the cart he saw the same was happening to Süleyman, arms clawing at him, bone white and oddly inhuman. *This is it*, he thought; *I survived being beaten up in the abattoir only for it to come to this, torn to pieces while leading a parade of bloody troops.* Then the hand let go, he became conscious of shouts and squeals of protest and realised that, unlikely as it seemed, the police had come to their aid, wading into the crowd to break up the incipient riot. Wasting no time, Süleyman grabbed the reins and, with an urgent shout, spurred Sena into the swiftest trot of her previously sedate career. Looking over his shoulder, Halim almost choked with relief to see the angry crowd pulling further and further away. As soon as he felt it was safe to stop watching, he turned back and, unable to look at Süleyman, dropped his head into his hands.

Once back at Süleyman's house, the two of them took their towels in silence and cleaned themselves off as well as they could, picking cabbage leaves from their hair and wiping tomato juice from their clothes. Süleyman's face was still and set with fury and Halim didn't dare speak, though he eyed the parlous state of his shirt mournfully – his sleeve was practically detached from the body of the shirt. He'd had to throw out the shirt and trousers he'd been wearing when he'd been beaten the week before, as they had been torn and stained beyond repair; now he felt as if all his possessions were gradually being stripped from him, almost literally, and by people who had more than he had in the first place. He had a needle and thread in the small case that he still kept at the foot of his bed, and, not knowing what else to do but wanting to do something, he searched it out and went out onto the veranda, where the light was better, to mend his shirt as best he could.

An earth-shattering crash brought him to his feet and back inside within moments. When he had stepped outside, Süleyman had been sitting at the table, sponging the tomato juice out of his shirt with intense, furious concentration; now, he was standing, his face twisted to the point of being almost unrecognisable; one of the kitchen plates, the same ones that Süleyman and Halim washed so carefully every night, wiping until they squeaked before putting them away, was in a thousand pieces at his feet, and, as Halim stood in the doorway, Süleyman picked up another plate and flung it to the ground.

"Süleyman!" Of all the things that had happened that day, this was the one that frightened him the most. He had seen Süleyman angry before, of course. There was a bloom of anger inside Süleyman which only seemed to be getting bigger over the past few months, pouring out of him when provoked in bursts of unimaginable invective and vitriol. After the film, Süleyman had been angry; when they'd heard that Sadiq had been bad-mouthing Turks, Süleyman had been angry; when Halim had arrived back from the abattoir a week ago with his eye swollen shut and his teeth rattling loose in his mouth, he thought he had never seen Süleyman so angry. But, despite all of that, he had never seen Süleyman lose control; he had never seen him like this. This wasn't the man that he knew, the portly middle-aged man with his quick temper and expansive smile – this was something else; this was a person pushed beyond the limits of his endurance, and Halim didn't know what he could do to bring him back. But in the short-term, he did know that he should stop Süleyman from destroying all their crockery.

Grabbing Süleyman by the arm, Halim nearly overbalanced. He had half a head on Süleyman, but Süleyman was nearly as wide as he was tall, and not all of that was fat, while Halim was thin as a whip and, try as he might, weak enough to be blown down in a strong wind. Barely halted, Süleyman whirled around and Halim saw in his blank eyes that he didn't know who Halim was, didn't recognise him, only sensed that someone was trying to halt his destructive rampage and must be shaken off. Süleyman raised his fist and, resigned, Halim prepared himself for the blow, but when it came it was staggering, harder and more painful than anything he had experienced the week before, and it knocked him to the ground instantly. He couldn't be bothered to try and get up, but waited for Süleyman to drag him to his feet so that he could hit him again, or kick him while he was down; he suddenly felt impossibly, insufferably fragile, as if the merest touch would cause him to disintegrate, and at that point he would have welcomed it. But nothing happened. All was silence above, and after a moment Halim dared to open his eyes, looking first at the threadbare knees of Süleyman's trousers, and then at his horrified, concerned face restored to itself, as Süleyman squatted down in front of him.

"Oh God, Halim," he said, his voice breaking slightly, "I am so sorry. I am so sorry."

"It's all right," Halim said, and, though his very words opened a cut on his lips that spilt blood down his chin, it was. Süleyman had been returned to him; he could take anything, he thought, as long as the two of them were together. Süleyman rocked back on his heels and then sat clumsily on the floor, his legs splayed. He looked both comical and despairing.

"My God," he said again. "What are we going to do?"

"I was hoping that you could tell me that," Halim said, with a half-hearted attempt at levity.

"We can't stay here, not after today."

"You've been saying that for months."

"And it's time to take action at last. We have to get out."

"And how? With what money? The fine cleared me out; I don't have anywhere near enough to get back to Sydney, let alone all the way back home."

Süleyman frowned. "We'll think of something. We'll ask them, why don't we?"

"What do you mean, *them*?"

Süleyman jerked his head over his shoulder in the approximate direction of the town. "You know, them. They don't want us here, they couldn't make that clearer. We don't want to be here any more than they want us. So they have to help us leave. They have to send us home."

The idea, to Halim, sounded intoxicating and impossibly unlikely all at the same time – but there was something in the way that Süleyman spoke, in the certainty of his words, that made Halim believe him. He couldn't afford not to.

"I'm sorry about your lip," Süleyman said at last, and struggled to his feet, taking a cloth in his hand, wetting it with water from the kettle. "Come on, let's get you cleaned up."

Chapter Twenty-Four

These days, panic was constantly bubbling at the back of Halim's throat, threatening to overwhelm him, the rhythm of the mistakes that he'd made beating a tattoo, roaring on the inside of his skull. Back in the village, when he and Irfan had talked about the lives they would have, Irfan would talk of adventure, fighting and piracy and war and barroom brawls, and Halim would smile obligingly and agree, but he never came up with such stories himself. He tried, sometimes, but while in some ways he knew that his imagination was as vivid as Irfan's (he was always the village favourite among the children for retelling folk stories about djinns and demons), when the subject of his future was raised, he could never turn his mind to swashbuckling. If pressed, he could only say that what he hoped for in his future was a patch of land, a pretty wife, a couple of children and enough food for all of them. Facing facts, Halim knew that he wasn't cut out for adventure – he'd been dragged along in Irfan's wake – let himself be dragged, he corrected himself, because he thought that was what he was supposed to do; that fact had put all these other events in motion, and he didn't know what to do next, how to turn back. He supposed that he must go on, but he was unwilling, and spent his waking hours with his head hunched further and further down between his shoulders, his eyes on the flat earth in front of him, wishing himself into annihilation. The rest of the time, he slept.

The weariness came over him in great, crashing waves, and he surrendered to it eagerly, longing to be lifted and held in its swell, taken away from his small, craven self for a while. If there was an hour in the day that he didn't know what to do with, it didn't matter whether it was eleven in the morning or four in the afternoon, he would take the chance to curl up on the mattress that still lay in the corner of Süleyman's living room and sink down into somnolence. He had never slept so much – fourteen, fifteen hours a day – not even when he'd been eight and recovering from the measles, every step straining his energy to breaking point so that by the time he'd crossed the room his skin felt crackly, like paper, and his eyelids came crashing down over his eyes unbidden.

It was as if now he had not only his own allotted portion of sleep, but Süleyman's too, for Süleyman seemed to have stopped sleeping entirely. This was normal during the day, of course, but although Halim slept a lot, he never slept heavily, and he would wake in the night, bobbing like a cork out of the depths of his slumber, or skimming the surface like the flying fish he'd seen from the boat, to hear the pad of Süleyman's bare feet on the soft, pitted floorboards, the hissing bloom of the gas stove being lit. The moon and stars he could see in the scrap of indigo sky above his bed told him that it was two, three, four o'clock and yet Süleyman sat, monolithic, like an avalanche, his silhouette solid and immoveable, quaking from time to time with huge, silent sighs, lifting his glass of tea to his lips at such long intervals that Halim always thought that he would forget about it completely.

Occasionally, some shift in Halim's breathing would give away the fact that he was awake before he even fully realised it himself, and Süleyman would speak to him, always in a relaxed tone, as if he were continuing a conversation that had been broken by a few seconds' pause, rather than launching into some half-realised discussion that Halim could only faintly grasp at. It was like that the day that he'd been to the local council, to talk to them about repatriation assistance; when he had come back, his mouth so tightly shut that Halim could almost believe that it would never open again, his eyes glittering with a mixture of pride, anger and sadness, Halim had shrugged, silent, knowing that their hopes had been dashed once again, and hadn't bothered to ask. But at four o'clock that morning, Halim heard Süleyman say, his tone bright even as his voice grated with weariness,

"You see, Halim, all we have to do is get the money together."

As often as not, Halim ignored Süleyman's midnight ramblings, but he couldn't bring himself to ignore so direct an appeal, although he knew that speaking would cause the last strands of sleep that still clung to him to break. He sighed, and shifted onto his side.

"They won't help us, then?"

"Not with money. But they would help us leave. Put us on a train, organise our tickets from Melbourne or Adelaide or Sydney, back to Europe. They want us out of this town as much as anyone else does. It's that or the camps – incarceration. We have to be gone from here before it comes to that."

"But we're back where we started then, aren't we? We don't have the money. I have barely anything left over from when I had to pay the fine." With that, a thought occurred to him that made his body burn and flash cold at the same time. "You have the money, though, don't you? You wouldn't – you wouldn't go alone? You wouldn't leave me here?"

"Of course not." Süleyman sounded almost angry, and his tone set Halim more at ease than any gentle appeals would have. "You know that I wouldn't leave you here. We both go, together, or we both stay, together. You're more family than I have anywhere else in the world. No. But we haven't done all we can to raise the money, have we? We have things that we could sell. Little things – all these plates that we don't need – and big things. The cart – and this house. It's the sturdiest structure around, far better than any of the tents of humpies, and I've seen Sadiq eyeing it up; he's doing so well down the mines he's got ideas above his station, I think he sees himself moving in somewhere like here as a way to get Amir to give him his daughter as a wife."

Halim propped himself up on his side. "Would it be enough money?"

"Oh, I think so. Enough, or at least enough if we could sell the cart and Sena as well, and the business. It's a good business, when I'm not running it; someone else could do well out of it. But not yet. That should be the last thing to go."

"And where would we go, while we were waiting?"

"Well, perhaps Tariq – "

"No," said Halim, with a firmness that came from nowhere. He couldn't have explained it if he'd tried, but he felt strongly that to involve the Imam in the tawdry, foolish mess that they had stumbled into would be wrong. Besides, Halim thought, if Tariq wanted to help them, he knew where they were. He knew that Tariq was just being sensible, staying out of problems that could affect the whole community if he were to involve himself – and while it hurt a little when he remembered the kindness in the Imam's eyes, the warmth of his hand on Halim's shoulder when they had first met, it was just one more in a long line of hurts and indignities, paling into near-insignificance.

In the darkness, Halim saw Süleyman lift and drop his shoulders in an earthquake of a shrug.

"It's summer. The nights are hot, and it never rains here at this time of year. We wouldn't need much more than the cart and a tarpaulin to keep the wind off. We'd be all right. And I think – I think we would be better off moving away from the Ghan Town. People don't want us here any more. They know that we are bringing a bad image onto the people who live out here. They'd be more inclined to be friendly and helpful, I think, if we distanced ourselves a little."

Lying in bed, Halim stretched out his hand until the pads of his fingertips touched the warm, smooth wood of the wall by which he had slept every night since he came to Cottier's Creek, and he felt an unexpected tightening in his throat, a flood of tears at the corner of his eyes that he blinked angrily away. He would cry at anything these days, it seemed, even at the idea of leaving a place that he hated. *Stop it*, he told himself and, once again, as he had the other day in the abattoir, he heard Irfan's voice, as clear as a bell. He knew that he should be worried, that he should push Irfan away, but the comfort of his childhood friend was undeniable, his old buoyant spirit, and his unquenchable enthusiasm. *Sleeping out in the desert!* Irfan said now, and while Halim was still enough himself to know that Irfan wasn't really speaking, it wasn't really his voice that Halim was hearing, it was enough to make him smile. *Perhaps*, he thought carefully, trying to frame the idea in a way to make it less mad, *perhaps I could conjure Irfan up, bring him back, hold onto him like a talisman. He was the other half of me, the brave part, bright burning.*

Süleyman went to speak to Sadiq the next day, and Halim surprised himself by wanting to go with him – bolstered by the imaginary Irfan, he felt more able to take part in his life than he had for weeks. Sadiq's face was wary when the two of them approached his tent – he seemed worried that they were going to ask for a favour in the name of their former friendship, something that he would be unwilling to carry out but would feel obliged to do.

When Süleyman explained the truth of the situation, however, the change of mood came off Sadiq in waves of warmth. His shoulders relaxed, his smile deepened and broadened, and he hustled his way into the tent, returning with some of the pastries that Amir's daughters made so well, crusted with sugar and sticky with honey. Halim let them melt on his tongue, the oil flooding his mouth, the pastry as soft and delicate as eating clouds. Within minutes, Süleyman and Sadiq had entered into hard negotiations, discussing and refusing each other's offers with incredulous smiles and shakes of their heads, and Halim concentrated on the bittersweet savour of the tea, lulled by the rhythm of the conversation, the same rhythm he had heard his whole life as his father bargained his goats for money over interminable cups of tea. He didn't have to understand the words to know when negotiations had reached an end; it was as certain as the concluding notes of a song, and he looked up to see both Süleyman and Sadiq with rueful smiles on their faces, both acting as if the other had got the better deal, both secretly thinking that he came out of the negotiation on top.

"And so you're leaving?" Sadiq said, and Süleyman nodded.

"Not quite yet, but in a few weeks. Need to get a bit more money together first, sell a bit more ice cream maybe, just so that we'll be sure to have enough for the journey. Not safe for us round here anymore." There was a hard note in Süleyman's voice at that, and Halim noticed the flicker of shame that crossed Sadiq's face, knowing that he could have done more to help the two of them, and that Süleyman would have done the same for him.

"Look – I'm sorry about what's been happening here. I heard about the parade, and about what happened to you – " He turned to Halim " – down at the abattoir. I wish I could have done something. But you know how it is: you risk bringing their anger down on the whole community."

Süleyman nodded, but he wouldn't meet Sadiq's eye, and so Sadiq stumbled on with his apology that wasn't really an apology. "I mean – we want a quiet life, you know? All of us have come here from somewhere else. For many of us, we've been leaving bad things behind. We don't want to entice bad things into our community here. Some of us have been here for years and years, hardly any trouble. Nobody wants that to change now. Some of us have wives and children to – "

Sudden as a thunderclap, Süleyman was on his feet, his glass of tea in the sand, the liquid forming a viscous pool, and Halim's fist clenched, remembering how uncertain Süleyman's temper had been lately. But Süleyman did nothing more than take two deep, quick breaths in and out and force a smile. "You give us a few days to organise our things, yes? We'll be sure to have the house ready for you by the end of the week." And bending down, he picked up the sandy glass, dusted it off, and passed it to Sadiq, who looked nonplussed. "I'm sorry about that. Nothing broken, though. See?"

*

Their plans changed daily, sometimes even hourly, and were informed as much by idle fantasy as they were by the constraints of reality. The intended end was always the same – the final homecoming – but the means varied and went through as many permutations as went through their heads. One day, the plan was to leave as soon as possible, without even waiting for the money that Sadiq had promised them, to jump the next train going down to Adelaide or across to Sydney, evade the authorities and work their way onto a boat going home, and when they talked about that Halim's imagination flared. It was the right thing to do, he thought; who cared about the money and the risk? The only thing that they could sensibly do was to get out and get home as fast as possible.

But as soon as they had stopped talking about it and Süleyman's voice – for it was always Süleyman who drove these conversations – faded into silence, the fire in Halim's belly would start to cool, and the doubts would creep in. What would they do if they were caught on the train? The guard would throw them off, maybe in the middle of the desert – there was no point hoping for mercy and compassion from these people, not towards two penniless, itinerant Turks – and what then? They would die under the baking sun, every drop of moisture and goodness squeezed out of their bodies, their carcasses picked over by whatever things that lived out in the desert. Halim pictured dark, fanged beasts, emaciated from the privations of their surroundings, falling on their withered corpses with hellish fervour. Or, even if they made it to the city, to Melbourne or Adelaide or even Sydney, what then? Sydney might be all right, thanks to Yiannis and Maria and their extended network of friends and relatives… though Halim was bitterly aware that the gaps between Fotini's letters had increased to the point where they seemed to have stopped altogether, so perhaps he shouldn't be so quick to assume that his former friends would want anything to do with him, now that he had been deemed the enemy. And anywhere else would be even more of a struggle.

What if there wasn't a boat straight away? And were there even boats running these days, now that Australia and Europe and what seemed like half the rest of the world were at war? They could hardly smuggle themselves aboard a boat carrying troops to the front; but nor could they afford to wait around indefinitely in the hopes of a boat that would take them to their ideal destination; they would have to take the first they could get on, and work their way back from wherever it decided to turf them off. Halim's feelings were strongly against that idea. He wanted a full stop at the end of this story, a definitive finishing line that he could cross and know that he was safe; this harebrained idea of Süleyman's had their futures trailing away towards an uncertain, tattered horizon; there were so many potential hazards along the way, and if anything, Halim was more afraid of uncertainty than he was of death. A short, sharp end to his life he could anticipate almost without fear. A possibly never-ending journey through hostile climes made him shudder to think of it.

"Maybe," he would begin, turning to Süleyman, and they would move back to Plan B; that they would stay around for a while longer, a few weeks, that was all, they would find some way of earning enough money at least to buy their fare out of the town...but the practicalities let them down. Süleyman had barely sold any ice cream for weeks now. It was the height of summer, always the most popular season, but the animosity towards the two of them following the parade was so strong that barely anyone was prepared to even acknowledge them anymore, let alone buy from them. But what else could they do? All of their possible money-making options seemed to rely on the goodwill of people, the loss of which was the very thing that was driving them away.

Chapter Twenty-Five

When the men came, it wasn't a surprise; not really. For a while now, Halim and Süleyman had been wary of leaving the house together, leaving their possessions unguarded, but while Halim could no longer work, Süleyman still had to sell ice cream to the few people in the town who would still buy from them, so that he and Halim could eat. This meant that he needed to fetch milk, a two person job. He could have taken someone else from the Ghan Town, yes, but that would have meant admitting to one another what they were scared of, and they couldn't bear to do that. A few days later and they would have been safe – they had agreed with Sadiq that he could move in on Saturday, but Süleyman had wanted to stay for a few final days, to have the space to churn the milk for the ice cream (Sadiq had agreed that he could keep storing the ice cream there for the last few weeks they remained in town), and Halim realised that he was sentimental; the house may have been nothing more than a wooden shack, held together with inexpertly hammered nails, the boards never flush together so that the outside was always visible, carrying with it spirals of cool air in the winter and clouds of insects in the summer – but it was Süleyman's own, made with his own hands, and he was going to miss it.

When they returned that day, Halim's first thought was: *I'm just glad they didn't burn it*. The door was askew, hanging awkwardly and there was no telling what sort of damage was inside, but at least if the house was still standing, there was a chance of recovery. As soon as they realised that something was wrong, neither of them looked at one another; they simply climbed the steps, Halim after Süleyman, his boots heavy on the wooden boards. When he reached out to open the door, it juddered off his hinges, and Süleyman carefully took it in both hands and laid it against the wall, as gently as if he were holding a child. Halim remembered then, realised what Süleyman must have been thinking, the echoes that this experience brought back of another time when he returned to his house, in another place, to find it violated, and that time he really had been carrying a child in his arms.

When they got inside, both of them clung to the hope that the motive of the intruders had been destruction rather than robbery. It certainly looked that way. Chairs had been kicked over and curtains torn down, ripped into shreds; the kettle lay on the floor with its belly dented and bent, and those dishes that Süleyman hadn't broken days before were in shards nearby. Whoever had done this had done so with the intention of creating as much disorder as possible in as short an amount of time as possible; they must have known that Süleyman and Halim wouldn't have been gone for long, and feared interruption.

"As they should," Süleyman said tightly, when Halim suggested this to him. Süleyman's hands were drawn into fists and his eyes were darting, his breath coming in angry pants, but, Halim was relieved to see, he wasn't in the state of blind grief and rage as he had been the day of the parade. Halim feared that version of Süleyman nearly as much as he feared the actions of the people who had ransacked their home, or the men who had beaten him up at the abattoir. When Süleyman walked over to the doorway, his hands visibly trembling, then knelt down and lifted the floorboard under which he had stored his money, Halim couldn't even bring himself to feel upset or disappointed when he saw Süleyman's shoulders slump as he buried his face in his hands. The robbery now seemed almost inconsequential compared to the violation of their home. The air in the shack was foetid and noisome, and they soon tracked down the source of the stench as coming from a pool of piss in the corner, where the people who had done this had decided to relieve themselves on the tattered curtains they'd torn down.

Sighing, averting his face in disgust, Halim hefted the curtains into his arms and went outside to draw a bucket of water. Kneeling down on the veranda, he took the cake of carbolic soap they used for their own clothes to scrub the filth and the stench from the curtains. It was an oddly satisfying task, and Halim felt his mind detach a little, as he watched not only the piss but months', years' worth of dust and dirt ease itself out of the curtains, and a fabric that had once been a pretty floral print reasserting itself. He didn't question why he was doing it, given that the curtains were torn perhaps beyond repair, and that he and Süleyman would be turning the house over to Sadiq in a couple of days in any case; he simply knew that they had tried to destroy something and he wouldn't let them succeed. So he scrubbed, and rinsed and scrubbed again, lulled by the movements of his own hands, the sun on his closely shorn dark head, the mesmeric swish of Süleyman's broom inside as he swept up the last remnants of the broken crockery and carried them outside.

Knowing he was being obsessive and yet not much caring, Halim rinsed the curtains three times before he was satisfied with them, then spread them out to dry on the wobbly veranda rail. He kept noticing movement out of the corner of his eyes, people from the camp watching him, but he paid them no mind. If he allowed himself to think about it – which he wouldn't – he would have started asking himself why no one from the Ghan Town, the men who worked shifts, some of whom were always there during the day, had stood up and stopped the men who had done this; or indeed, why the men who had done this had known that they wouldn't be stopped. He didn't ask himself, and he knew the answer anyway: that no one likes to defend the person at the bottom of the pile, no one wants to put themselves between the boot and the person being kicked.

It was only later that Halim discovered the extent of the outrage. On arriving home, he'd given no more than a cursory glance to his own modest pile of possessions, which lay stacked up in the corner next to the place where he unfolded his mattress when it was time to sleep. It had seemed undisturbed, so he guessed that the destroyers had had larger forms of destruction on their minds, and had assumed his things to be untouched. It was only when he finally went to check that he realised the truth of the matter. His recoil sent him tripping back halfway across the room, and his shout of horror and disgust summoned Süleyman from where he was on the veranda.

"What is it?" Süleyman asked, but Halim couldn't bring himself to answer. Something very peculiar was happening inside his head, as if his brain was vibrating so fast that it was trying to escape through his ears. His vision was jumping as violently as if he was sat on the back of the cart going into town, and Süleyman's voice could barely penetrate the thick, high whine that filled his ears. It took several moments for him to identify what he was feeling to be sheer, blind, overwhelming rage.

"The Book," he finally said to Süleyman. It felt as if someone else was operating his tongue and his lips. "The Holy Book. See what they have done."

Süleyman looked, and as he took it in – the unidentified turd, animal or human, that had been placed with uncommon care on top of Halim's Koran, the one that his mother had kissed and pressed into his hands when he had been leaving the village, the one that he had read to Irfan from as he was feverish and dying on the boat, the one that he had slept beside every night since he had left his home and barely given a conscious thought, yet that, he knew now, had remained the safe repository of his faith and his hope since he had left his family. He watched as Süleyman picked up the book carefully between extended fingers and moved to take it outside.

"Halim, I am so sorry," he was saying, "but we can clean it, we can make it better," and Halim heard himself speak.

"No," he said. "Burn it."

Süleyman's face was a mask of shocked surprise, almost comical. "You can't mean that?"

Halim nodded. "They've defiled it. It's not – it's not what it was. It's nothing, now, nothing but what they've made it. Don't ask me if I'm sure," he went on, as he saw Süleyman open his mouth to protest further, "I'm sure. The only thing to do is to destroy it." An image came into his head, unbidden, of the act itself, of the man who had perhaps squatted over the Book, laughing, or perhaps placed on it with fastidious glee the filth that he had brought there for that very purpose. He wanted to look away from the image but it was inside him, behind his eyes, and he couldn't drop his lids to block it out. It was the smile that stabbed at him, more even than the act – the idea that someone had found this funny, that a mind inside a person who looked like everyone else had dreamt up something so horrific, something that Halim knew he couldn't have imagined in a hundred years.

"They are not human," he said to himself, and Süleyman stopped, his head down, silent, listening, so he repeated it again: "They are not human."

Halim watched dispassionately as the Book burned, its leather covers with the gilt script, delicate as a spider web, melting and warping, and then the pages themselves curling and crisping, the ashes bouncing round the yard with a pretence of exuberance. The two of them sat there, heads close together, eyes on the embers of the fire as it died down to a miserable glow; the sun bounced suddenly below the horizon as it did out there in summer, and the last dregs of the fire were the only light left. Neither of them spoke, not for a long time; Halim simply closed his eyes and felt things inside him shift, pieces of his past, his present and his future moving about and dropping into place. He seemed to himself to be unimaginably different from the boy he had been that morning, and he had an idea that Süleyman had sensed the change in him, too. He wasn't sure if it was respect, or worry, or even fear that he felt shimmering off Süleyman's skin, or perhaps a combination of all three, but he knew that things had changed. There was no fear in him anymore, and he was surprised to note that there was no anger now, either, or not the hot flare of sensation that he usually associated with anger. Instead, it was as if he had swallowed something solid, something that sat in the pit of his stomach and was cold and bitter and eating him up from the inside out, and the only way that he could survive it was to outrun it, to keep moving out of its way so that it couldn't devour him. He thought that perhaps he ought to find the sensation more unpleasant than he did.

Halim didn't even look up when Sadiq entered the yard, but Süleyman got to his feet. He heard Sadiq's apologies: "I am so sorry that they did this to you! I wasn't here, I was working, but you know that if I had been here I would have stopped them; I know that I haven't been the best friend to you but this – they have gone too far..." Halim thought that perhaps they even sounded sincere – it could be that Sadiq meant what he said, that he was just weak, as weak as most people were, rather than malign. He heard Süleyman describing the many indignities that had been foisted upon them, and he stayed silent. They had taken the best words that he had ever seen, the words most full of peace and love and understanding, and they had shat on them. Halim had no time for words anymore.

Chapter Twenty-Six

Halim had never expected to see Maggie again; the thought of her and the time that they had spent together barely crossed his mind, his whole self given over to the baser instincts of survival. When they caught sight of her one evening walking towards the ramshackle tent they'd constructed for themselves, both of them were speechless – her proud, white figure in its pale dress fluttering in the teasing breeze was like a vision out of another life, belonging to someone else. It was true that the last time Süleyman had been in the town, selling ice cream a few days after their unfortunate parade, she had greeted him with a flicker of her former warmth, but he had filed that away as evidence of the last gasp of their former friendship. The lines had been drawn – not by them, Halim and Süleyman would argue, they had never wanted it to be this way – and they had found themselves on either side of them, by virtue of their birth and their very skin, their flesh and their bones and the hearts that beat in the prison of their ribs, and there was nothing that any of them could do about it.

Maggie's greeting was tentative, as if she were uncertain of her welcome, but hospitality was ingrained into Süleyman, as essential a part of his very nature as his faith, or his language, or his fondness for mildly crude jokes. For a few moments, as Süleyman bustled towards her, seating her on a low stool by the fire, filling the kettle from one of the pails of water they had brought from the Ghan Town's pump that morning, as she looked at Halim and smiled her old smile, open and uncomplicated, it felt almost as if nothing had changed between the three of them, and that they were still the unlikely triumvirate that they had been months before. But Maggie's smile dropped from her lips as quickly as it had come, and her eyes skated away from Halim's own, and he felt himself harden towards her. She was one of the better ones, it was true, and she had been kind – but fundamentally she was still one of them.

"How are you, Halim?" she asked, but Halim didn't – couldn't – answer. It was a strange thing; with Süleyman, his tongue was still as free as it had always been, but although he still understood the English words that she spoke to him, he couldn't force his throat and his lips, his tongue and his teeth into the shapes necessary to make the words to answer her. English had dried up within him, the few thousand words that he had known rattling in his chest and his belly like desiccated husks.

Süleyman rushed to explain. "He – he isn't talking much at the moment. Not since the men came to the house." His tone noticeably cooled in the space of a sentence, as if he had moved from the person who was still eager to please Maggie and all she represented, to the person who remembered what had been done to him.

"It was that that I wanted to speak to you about," Maggie said, rushing into the words, still with half an eye on Halim's silent form sat straight-backed by the fire, eyes on the ground as he kicked at the soft sand. "I didn't want you to think that I had anything to do with it, or my family. Not Charlie, and not his friends."

"I saw him after the parade," Süleyman said. His voice was stiff and tight. "The last time I came into town. He was with you, and he wouldn't even look towards me. He crossed the road, Maggie, to be on the other side from me."

Maggie coloured. The flush didn't suit her, Halim thought coolly; it made her look like overcooked meat. "I know. I won't pretend. I know that he has felt differently about you, since his brother was hurt in the war, and since – since what happened at the parade."

"You know that was an accident!"

"I know, but – a lot of people in the town believe – with the parade coming so soon after the film that you saw – they thought that you were trying to get your own back. Mocking us. Making fun." Süleyman shook his head, mutinous, but Maggie continued: "That doesn't matter, anyway. What I want to tell you is that Charlie didn't have anything to do with what happened to your house. We heard about it and we were so sorry – and Charlie said… he said that although he's not happy with you being here, what those men did was wrong. Nobody should hurt you." She looked around, at the empty landscape and at their tent, cowering in the shadows of the slag pits, and shrugged. "We know that if you had a choice, you would rather not be here, either."

She had carried a small bag on her arm, which Halim and Süleyman had barely noticed when she placed it on the sand in front of her. Now she lifted it onto her lap and opened it, taking out a bundle that she passed to Süleyman. He looked at it blankly, not opening it.

"What is it?"

Maggie didn't make the obvious answer, that he should open it and find out. "It's tickets. Two tickets on the train to Melbourne that leaves on January 2nd, and enough money for two passages on a boat back to Europe. Charlie asked around; there's a boat leaving for Athens around the middle of January. You could be on it, and from there it's not far back to where you come from. There's enough extra money there for you to take care of yourselves while you're in Melbourne, and hopefully enough to help you make your way to Istanbul, though I don't know exactly how much it is."

Still Süleyman didn't open the package. All three of them were very still, none of them looking at the others. Halim probed himself for feelings – surely he should be feeling relief?

Happiness? – and found only a slight elevation in the base level of anger that he carried, buzzing and humming, around with him every day. They would take the money, of course they would, there was nothing else that they could do – but these blows against his shattered, shaky dignity just kept coming; that they had to be helped by the enemy, that they didn't even have the chance to make their own way home!

Finally Süleyman spoke. Halim had to lean forward to catch his words over the hiss and spit of the fire. "Are you doing this," he asked Maggie, his tone almost gentle in its courtesy, "because you want to help us? Or because you want us gone?"

She flushed again. "Does it matter?"

Süleyman cocked his head on one side and smiled a little. "Does it matter in terms of us taking the money and the tickets? No. We've come so low that we don't have any pride left to puff ourselves up with. But I would like to know."

"We were friends once," Maggie said. "Can you not take the money to remember that? It's for you, to help you, and it's to help the town, too, to help my husband and my family and – and even the people who have hurt you. It's the best thing, all round. Do you see that?"

"I see." Süleyman nodded, and said it again. "I see."

Maggie moved as if to go, but he reached out and put his hand on her arm to stay her. "Before you go, can you tell me one more thing? Do you know who it was who came into our house and ruined our things?"

Maggie looked unhappy. "I can't tell you."

"Please."

"Why do you want to know?"

Halim spoke without thinking, his tongue unexpectedly loosened. "If we know who to blame," he said, his voice wobbling and unsure, "then we won't have to blame the whole town."

Maggie looked at him steadily for the space of a breath, and then nodded. "It was the new recruits," she said, "the ones who will be shipping out to the front on New Year's Day. They're frightened and excited and they don't know what they're doing, and they – I suppose they wanted to take control of something. They wanted to start fighting before they left, so that they would know what fighting was like." She nodded with a level of decisiveness that made Halim remember her manner in the classroom.

"Now you know," she said, "and now you can forget it," and she turned and walked away.

Chapter Twenty-Seven

"Could we get a second one?" Halim asked, his voice loud in the close, fast darkness inside the tent. He had thought of little else since, when they were moving their paltry bundles of possessions from the house to their makeshift tent, he had noticed Süleyman carefully cradling a long, unmistakeable shape wrapped in a tatty blanket, and later, when Süleyman had been boiling the water for tea Halim had crept, heart crashing, across to Süleyman's side of the tent, unwrapped the blanket and found what he'd known was there, well-greased and shining. Now, outside, the desert was making the sorts of noises that seemed deliberately designed to frighten and repel. The sun had set over an hour ago, a line of burning red on the western horizon, and there had been nothing for them to do other than go to bed and lie, restless, wide awake in the dark. Halim heard Süleyman shift beside him.

"Another what?"

"You know." He paused, but Süleyman didn't seem to want to help him out, so Halim said impatiently, "Another gun."

Süleyman propped himself up on his elbow, his eyes searching uselessly in the thick, liquid darkness for Halim's face, trying to read it. Halim was thankful that he couldn't be seen. There was something in this question that made his insides burn with a mixture of fear and excitement and exultant joy and terror; he could barely keep his voice steady, let alone control the expression on his face.

"What do you want another gun for?"

"You know why."

"Maybe. But I want you to tell me."

"I don't want to let them get away with it," Halim said. His voice was steady now, his confidence growing with every word. Speaking about these things, and acting on them, seemed to be the only way to outrun whatever was tearing him up inside, that potent mixture of rage and helplessness. "Those men who did this to us. Everything they've done. You want to just sit here and take it? And now to leave town, sneak out of here quietly because that's what they've decided?"

Süleyman sighed. "Maggie's given us a chance that we didn't have before. Enough money to get away – "

"Get away from this town, yes. But what then? Then we're in the city. I've heard what they're doing there to men like us, putting them in camps. Maybe there's enough money there to let us get onto a boat home, maybe not. And even if there is, do you think they're going to let us go? They won't believe that we're just going home for a quiet life, away from this. They're going to believe that we want to fight for the Sultan, against Australia, and they won't let us go. And don't think that Maggie doesn't know this! You heard what she said. She wants us gone, she doesn't care what happens to us afterwards."

"Maybe you're right," Süleyman said. His voice was shaking, and Halim had a moment of sharp dislocation as he realised how thoroughly their roles had reversed – Süleyman the strong, sure man who had helped Halim, guided him in his uncertainty and assisted him to take his first wobbly steps on this land was gone, and the man left behind was old and broken, one more disappointment piled on top of too many. "Maybe you're right," Süleyman said again, "but then, perhaps we should just go quietly? We're strangers here and – "

"No," Halim broke in, with a violence that surprised both of them. "I'm sick and tired of thinking like that. Sick of it! Who lived here a hundred and fifty years ago? You taught me that – it was nobody but the black men. Certainly not any of them out there in the town. They've all come from somewhere else, from England or Ireland or other places in Europe. And it's not just us that they treat like shit. You've seen the way they treat the black men – the people who were there before them! If this country belongs to anyone, it belongs to them, and yet the Europeans treat them even worse than they treat us. And it's not about who this country belongs to, or about who came first. They just hate anyone who isn't like them, they think they're better, and they'll keep thinking they're better until somebody shows them that they're not."

"And we're going to show them?"

"The new recruits are going to be travelling to Adelaide on the first of January, Maggie said. We can find out when the train is going. And then…"

"And then what?"

"It's a war," Halim said simply. "It's beyond our control. The war didn't have to come here, they brought it here. And now it's here, we have to fight. For Allah."

His last word dropped like a stone into the dark silence. Both men lay side by side, not speaking, breathing out, letting go of hope. Halim knew that he wouldn't see his family again, wouldn't even see Fotini, would never have his own small farm on the hillside outside the village where he had grown up, would never have a shop in the city, would never marry and have children and die with them surrounding him. These thoughts had bobbed around in the heady soup of ideas and emotions inside him over the past weeks, and every time they had tried to assert themselves he'd pushed them down firmly, refusing to accept the hopelessness of his position. Now, he found himself welcoming it. He had never wanted to believe that he had come all this way, halfway around the world, only to fail and die, but he realised now that he had been looking at it in the wrong way, seeing it as a waste. Now he knew that he was dying for something, for his God and his faith, those things that were such a part of him that they ran through every organ, every fibre of his body like a steel thread, stringing all his disparate parts together and making him a man.

Beside him, he heard the dry, papery sound of Süleyman opening his mouth, wetting his lips, preparing to speak. "Jihad," was all that he said, and with a sudden rush of love for Süleyman, Halim knew that he was with him, that Süleyman had shrugged off the shackles of hope and embraced the power that came from hopelessness.

"Yes," Halim said softly. He reached over in the blackness and felt for Süleyman's hand, plump and calloused, shaking slightly. He gripped it tightly.

"Who in town is going to sell us a gun?" Süleyman asked the next morning. His tone was remarkably matter of fact; the coiled intensity of the previous night's conversation had dissipated in the pale blue cool of the early morning, as they brewed their first cup of the tea of the day. Reality had shifted, making their course of action inevitable, and Halim was powerfully relieved because there was nothing as horrible as uncertainty. A doomed action was better than no action at all.

"Nobody, not to us. But we can give money to Sadiq or someone else in the camp, and ask them to do it for us. None of them know that you have a gun, do they?" Süleyman shook his head. "Good. We can tell them that we want a gun so that we can hunt in the desert, find our own food. Maybe catch a kangaroo."

"Is that halal?" Süleyman asked, grinning. He seemed more relaxed than he had been in weeks; the uncertainty had been eating away at him, too, as well as the sense that he was responsible for Halim and should look after him, show him the way. He knew that on some level, the change of power in their relationship was wrong, that perhaps he should assert his patriarchal rights even though he wasn't actually Halim's father, but he hadn't the energy; the surrender of will was nothing but a relief.

In the event, getting a second gun was easier than they could have hoped. The two of them went to ask Sadiq, expecting to have to cajole and persuade, but, sitting on the veranda of what had once been their house, Sadiq agreed all too readily, with an eagerness that was redolent of guilt.

"Yes, yes," he said, "I see. You need to have something to protect yourselves, after what happened with this house. I understand. If you give me the money and tell me what you want, I'll go and buy it for you this afternoon." Halim didn't speak while Süleyman gave Sadiq his specifications, details of the type of gun that they would need, as well as ammunition; Sadiq nodded again and again with a touch of obsequiousness.

When they left, Süleyman grinned once more. "Selling Sadiq the house was the best choice that we made," he said. "He knows that he got a good deal, he knows he's doing well off the back of our own misfortune. He'll do anything to help us out now."

That afternoon, Sadiq brought the gun over to their camp, smiling happily. "Here it is!" he announced, with evident pride. "They had one just like you said. You'd seen it, hadn't you, back in town?"

Süleyman nodded. "I knew what I wanted. I just knew that they wouldn't give it to me." Smoothly, he broke the gun, slipped bullets inside, and brought it up to his eye as Sadiq looked on admiringly. "You know about guns, then?"

"I know enough. My father used to take me hunting when I was small. I hated it at the time, but it taught me a lot."

Sadiq nodded, seemed to think for a moment, and then asked almost impulsively: "Listen. Will you two come and eat with me tonight? I'd like it a lot. You know I feel bad about what's happened to you two, and I feel bad that – well, that you could say that I've profited from what's happened. With the house. I know that you'll be leaving soon, and I'd like to eat with you before that, one last time. What do you say?"

Instinctively, without thinking, Süleyman looked over at Halim for confirmation, and for a moment Halim felt as if he was choking: it wasn't right, surely, that he should be the one making the decisions now? But it was as it was, and he nodded. "Yes, please," he said to Sadiq, hating how halting his English sounded – in the past few weeks he'd spoken to so few people other than Süleyman that, while his understanding was still good, he felt that he was practically back where he started when it came to speaking the language. "We will come."

The food was excellent, beyond anything that either of them had tasted in a long, long time – better than anything that Halim had had since leaving Sydney, and better than anything Süleyman had eaten for far longer than that. It seemed that Sadiq had decided to make a proper occasion of it, and rather than preparing his own customary limp stew, full of vegetables with the life and taste boiled out of them in a tasteless, watery broth, he had drafted in some of the women of the camp to help – Halim had seen Jamila, the wife of Karim, making her way down the back steps as they had arrived, swaddled in her black abaya, tall, graceful and shy. There was felafel and fuul, hummous and tabouli, vine leaves, different kinds of rice and bread, as well as köfte and kebab, both of which Halim avoided – now that he was gone from the camp, he was certain that the meat wasn't halal – but which Süleyman tucked into with evident enjoyment. The three of them ate in silence, scooping up the juices of the food with pieces of bread, saying nothing but occasionally meeting each other's eyes with an appreciative nod.

When they were finished, Süleyman leaned back in his chair, slapping his expansive belly. "I can't remember the last time I ate so well!" he announced; his tone was jolly, but Halim reached for and grasped the melancholy behind his words. Smiling, Sadiq started to clear the dishes away, and then, with a flourish, brought in a tray of pastries, golden and glistening with syrup and honey. Even Halim couldn't hide his pleasure. This time, their eating was more leisurely. Sadiq boiled water for tea, and Halim nibbled and sipped slowly, savouring the tastes as he hadn't with the main course, concentrating on nothing but the flavours on his tongue, letting the conversation between Süleyman and Sadiq wash over him. Finally, with a mischievous look, Sadiq produced a clear glass bottle, at which Süleyman grinned appreciatively.

"Arak?"

"Karim's best. Made from grain, I think. Horrible stuff, it'll set your throat on fire, but it does the trick." Sadiq glanced at Halim, who had said barely a word the entire evening. "Drink?" But Halim shook his head, unsmiling. "He doesn't drink," Süleyman explained hurriedly, "but I'll have his share."

As they walked back together across the flat desert floor, the heat of the day rising up through the soles of their shoes, Süleyman weaved a little until Halim took his arm. They walked together in silence, Halim feeling the tug and pull of Süleyman's body as his feet tottered this way and that. He had never understood the appeal of alcohol; it was forbidden, anyway, but even if it hadn't been, he didn't see why people wanted to dim their minds in that way, becoming silly and raucous, garrulous and flailing. He'd tried it once, with Irfan of course; they'd been eleven or twelve, and Irfan had stolen a bottle of raki his father had hidden. They'd taken turns, one swig here, one swig there, trying not to wince as the corrosive liquid seared their gullets, and Halim couldn't remember feeling good at any point of the whole venture – he felt warm, and oddly hilarious, and then very, very ill, and the two of them had spent the rest of the day taking turns to vomit in the same way that they'd taken turns to drink. Looking sideways in the moonlight, though, Halim took in the slightly idiotic expression of good will on Süleyman's face, his mouth lifted at the corners in the shape of a smile he'd forgotten to wipe away, his eyes half closed, and wondered whether he was missing out on something after all.

"Süleyman?"

"Mmm?"

"How does it feel? The drinking?"

Süleyman stopped, unlinked his arm from Halim's and turned to face him, his wobbles not dislodging the beaming smile from his face. "It feels – warm. Cocooned, safe. Like nothing can bother you, nothing bad can touch you. Everything is friendly and good."

Halim smiled. "It sounds nice."

"It is. But I'll pay for it in the morning."

Abruptly, Süleyman let his knees buckle and sat down with a thump. At first Halim thought that he'd fallen and, worried, went to help him up, but Süleyman grabbed hold of his arm and pulled him down, saying, "Sit, Halim. Sit and enjoy, for once."

So Halim sat. At first, he wasn't sure what he was supposed to be enjoying – the ground was still warm from the heat of the day but the air was cool, the surface of the desert rippling with tiny cross-winds, flinging sand into his face like hundreds of miniature whips. He was cold and tired, uncomfortably full of food and wanted nothing more than to go back to the tent and lie down, rather than sitting cross-legged in the middle of nowhere beside a drunken fool. But Süleyman gripped his arm so hard that he had no chance of escape, and then flopped backwards onto the ground, lying flat and pulling Halim with him.

"Look at the stars, Halim!"

Halim looked. He'd never paid the stars much thought before – they'd been presented to him as nothing more than navigational aids – but at Süleyman's urging he forced himself to look at them for their own sake, thousands upon thousands of burning pinpricks of light, besmirching the calm dark perfection of the night sky. The moon was no more than a wink hanging over the horizon, allowing the stars to shine all the more brightly.

"There are so many of them," Halim said; his voice was hushed but nonetheless it sounded uncomfortably loud to him.

"There are. More on this side of the world, did you know?

More than you would ever see at home." Süleyman raised his arm and moved it in a wide, reckless arc, causing Halim to flinch slightly. "See that?"

"What?"

"Shooting star. Watch. You'll see one."

Halim watched, peering up into infinite space. He felt himself fall away, piece by piece, and was glad of it, until nothing remained of him but a bright, brittle skeleton and his eyes, looking. Peace settled on him for the first time that he could remember; he felt cupped in someone's hands, protected and nurtured.

Süleyman hauled himself back into a sitting position, then struggled to his feet, looking down at Halim's supine form with drunken sympathy.

"Come on, Halim," he said, and Halim's eyes swam back into focus. Süleyman extended a hand and pulled him to his feet.

Back in the tent, Halim stripped off his clothes and lay down on the bed without a word. The sleep he fell into was deep and abrupt, plunging into a warm, deep pool of water, and for once he wasn't plagued by dreams of death and disaster, as he had been for as long as he could remember. He awoke early, before Süleyman for once, and lay still in the early dawn light, feeling the unstoppable pump of his heart, the whispering of his breath in and out, in and out. They had two more days.

*

Halim had decided that they needed a flag. Süleyman and Halim had argued over this. "Why would we want something like that?" Süleyman had demanded. "We're doing something terrible; why should we announce our presence? Why should we make it so obvious that it's us? We'll be spoiling our chances of getting away."

Both of them knew that their chances of getting away were minimal, but they kept up the pretence, for each other's sake, that they would hide out for a few days in the desert, bribe one of the Aboriginal men to take them to the next town down the railway line, and board the train from there.

"But they have to know who's doing it, otherwise there's no point. If they think it's random, then it doesn't mean anything." Halim took Süleyman by the shoulders and looked at him searchingly. "Don't you see? You said it the other night – it's a jihad. They have to know what we're doing, and why we're doing it."

Süleyman had agreed, as he eventually agreed to all of Halim's decisions these days – but the next argument had been about what flag they should use. Süleyman had been in favour of a green banner, for Islam, and although Halim understood his reasoning, it didn't sit right with him. "It should be green, for a jihad," Süleyman declared, but the point that Halim kept coming back to and worrying at like a loose tooth was that, if they were fighting for Islam in a general sense, why weren't the rest of the Muslims in the Ghan Town beside them? And Süleyman had no answer for that. "It may be a jihad," Halim said at last, "but it's a private one, just the two of us. And so we should use the Ottoman flag.

The question was how to procure the material they needed; buying that quantity of red material was bound to arouse suspicion, although it would be nearly impossible for anyone to guess what they should be suspicious about. To start with, Halim insisted that the material be new, ensuring the flag was fresh and bright, but they reached a compromise – they each went through their clothing and put together a pile of things that they no longer needed. Meanwhile, Süleyman dispatched Sadiq to town for a packet of red dye – "We want to brighten up some of our clothes," Süleyman explained, with a smile, indicating his tired-looking shirt, "before we get to the city and everyone shuns us for being country bumpkins," and Sadiq found it convenient to believe him.

They read the instructions on the packet and soaked their clothes for as long as required, trying to ignore the fact that they came out patchy, the colours varying from pink to vermillion to burgundy. Neither Halim nor Süleyman was much use with a needle and thread, but they managed, sitting together for hours, Süleyman using the small knife that they used to cut vegetables, sharpening it often on the whetstone. Carefully and painstakingly, they unpicked sleeves of shirts. Süleyman took trousers apart panel by panel, before passing them to Halim, who eyed them up carefully, cut them into bits and pieced them together again to form a rough oblong, which he then sewed in the poor light of the tent, his face close to the material, tongue between his teeth in intense concentration. As a final touch, Süleyman produced the remnants of a can of white paint that had been used to hold down the canvas of the tent, and together they daubed onto the flag the white star and crescent, securing it to the desert floor with rocks. It was done. Sand had blown into the fresh paint, begriming it, and the colour looked fleshy and inconstant, rather than the vivid scarlet that Halim had envisioned, but nonetheless, from a distance it was clear what it was meant to be, and if you squinted, it almost looked like it was supposed to.

New Year's Eve and the air was still, the breeze that had been tossing sand and dust into the air slackened and died at nightfall, and the hot night seemed crisp with tension and excitement. All sounds carried in the stillness – the muezzin's call to prayer reached Halim and Süleyman easily as they sat outside the tent; they didn't have to strain to hear it as they usually did, and wordlessly they washed themselves, unrolled the prayer mats that they had brought with them and prayed, the words clearer in their hearts and minds than ever before.

For a moment, halfway through the muezzin's solemn, heartfelt recitation, the peace was broken by the sound of drunken singing, as a trio of farm workers from one of the outlying farms bounced along one of the dirt tracks on their way into town for the New Year celebrations. Halim and Süleyman noticed nothing, and after the prayers were over they sat in a fragile, brittle silence that neither of them dared to break for a long time. Halim's body ached from the day's activities, the long walk out to a gully on the far side of town where, with a patience that Halim never would have guessed he possessed, Süleyman had taught Halim how to shoot, and Halim, his hands steady and his eye cool and clear, had unerringly knocked tin can after tin can off the boulder that Süleyman had designated for target practice. He only hoped that his hand would be so still when his targets were moving.

"We could still change our minds," Süleyman said, as if he were suggesting something of no more importance than Halim trying a different type of food or a different style of shirt. "Nothing is final yet."

"I know," Halim said. A sudden, desperate desire for a cigarette hit him in the throat and the heart, although he had never liked smoking; something to do with his hands perhaps, something to stop them from shaking. Tiredness hung heavy and liquid behind his eyes and on the back of his tongue. He knew that they wouldn't change their minds, and that, even if he suggested it, Süleyman himself would be obscurely disappointed. Halim had never really understood when people spoke of pride – Irfan had used the word a lot, a flourish in his boyish rhetoric, and Halim had nodded and paid lip service to the idea, but he had never known in his guts what the word meant. He knew now that there was only so far you could be pushed down before you reared up fighting. The rights and the wrongs of the situation were beyond debate – there was only action and inaction, and Halim could no longer bear to be still.

Chapter Twenty-Eight

The New Year, 1916, dawned overcast, with dust-clogged clouds hanging low and dull over the town like a grimy tablecloth. Maggie woke early, before seven, although she and Charlie had been at the party in the town hall the night before. There had been a sort of forced, desperate jollity there that had made her uncomfortable, and she had demanded that they leave early, much to Charlie's disappointment. She couldn't explain it and, while he was normally tolerant of what she suspected he dismissed as womanly whims, this time he was annoyed. All the town's new soldiers were there, smiles too bright in white, stretched faces. Their bodies buzzed with excitement and gave off a faint whiff of fear, and their families thronged around them, plastering pride over loss and confusion, clinging to the good cause for which they were losing their boys temporarily, praying that the loss wouldn't become permanent. It was this desperation that Maggie had been unable to stand, even for Charlie's sake. He protested that he wanted to stay for just another half an hour, to have a chat with Robbie Cole, who was shipping out tomorrow and Charlie didn't know when he would be able to see him again. And Maggie relented, giving Charlie a final ten minutes as she stood outside the door swallowing mouthfuls of the cool, clear night air and feeling her heart still a little within her. When Charlie finally emerged – having taken a good twenty-five minutes rather than her allotted ten – he looked irritated.

"Aw, come on Maggie. It's New Year. What's up with you

tonight?"

"I'm just not feeling well, that's all. It's too loud in there, too close, and it's been too hot lately."

"That's not just it."

"You know what the rest of it is, too, and you don't like it. Why do you want me to spell it out for you?"

They walked another few steps in silence, towards the waiting buggy. Maggie hated arguing with Charlie; it gave her a special sort of pain, a dull ache just below her cheekbones, as if all her female ancestors were trying to remind her to respect her husband by holding her mouth closed. She told him silently to leave it, but Charlie had been drinking – only a couple of beers, he said, but she could tell the change in him by his loose-limbed walk and the way he held his head tilted slightly higher, pride evident in every inch of his body.

"Maggie…"

"Charlie, just leave it, all right? There's no point talking about it. I'm never going to love this war like you do – oh, all right, I know you don't love it. But I'm never going to respect it, and I'm never going to see eye to eye with the people who think that it's something to be celebrated. I can pretend for a while – a parade I can put up with – but it gets tiring, all right? Can we forget about it now?"

They had reached the buggy by now, and were facing each other in the close, clinging darkness, speaking in the hushed, hissing tones of angry people who don't want to lower themselves to shouting. Glancing up, Maggie caught sight of the clock on the town hall – quarter to eleven – and all the fight drained out of her. She put a reconciliatory hand on Charlie's arm, who was looking mutinously away.

"Look. Let's not fight about it, not again, not tonight. Anyway, who wants to spend New Year's Eve with that lot of bores?" Charlie's expression lightened fractionally, and Maggie felt herself relax. "Come on. You're the one I want to spend tonight with, not the – not the bloody mayor, or his boring wife, or Jack Connell from the shop, or any of them. Let's go home."

They found the house in darkness – Charlie's parents had travelled out to one of the outlying farms for a New Year party and wouldn't be back until late the next day, and Nancy had already put the children to bed. Noticing that Charlie still seemed a little terse and tight-lipped, Maggie did what she knew she could always do to cheer him up, and, ignoring Nancy's disapproving stare, she went to wake the children. Mary squalled for a moment, then quietened; Peter was wide-eyed and reverential, clearly noticing and appreciating the honour and import of his late night awakening. As she knew it would, Charlie's face cracked into a broad smile as soon as he saw Peter meandering his way down the hallway, toes turned comically in as they always were at that age, one hand in his mouth, the other clutching the ragged scrap of crocheted blanket that had comforted him since birth. Putting down the glass of whisky he'd been pouring himself, Charlie squatted on the floor and held out his arms to Peter, who made a wobbly, tumbling run into them.

"Hey, my boy, this is fun, isn't it? You know what we're going to do? We're going to watch the fireworks!"

The firework display was to be held behind the town hall; from the back of the top paddock they were afforded a perfect view. Mood spiralling dizzily upwards, Maggie held Mary in her arms as Charlie led the way, stumbling through the dark, Peter gripping onto his hand, stoutly striding out for as long as he could and being scooped up and hauled onto his father's shoulders when he couldn't go any further. The grass was wet from dew and brushed against her ankles, and the world felt wide and wild and belonging to them only. Voices floated up from the town below – the raucous, crude songs being bellowed from the pub veranda, and the more sedate, yet excited, tones that were coming from the party in the town hall as it spilled onto the back lawn, ready for the display. Maggie had thought that Mary would shout at the noise, but to her surprise she kept silent at the first bang; when Maggie looked down to check on her, she found Mary's face transfixed, mouth open, eyes bright and wide as the fireworks sailed into the sky and exploded there. The four of them watched in silence, Peter as engrossed as Mary, and, Maggie thought, looking across at her husband, Charlie was as entranced as either of his children.

It was nearly one by the time they made their way back to the house. Nancy, clucking and sighing at Peter's damp clothes, whisked him and Mary off to the nursery for a quick wipe down with a warm cloth and a change of attire before bed, as Maggie tiptoed into the kitchen to warm up some milk for them. The children safely in bed, Maggie padded down the hall and into the bedroom, to find Charlie sitting on the bed, shoes off, legs outstretched, his mood ebullient, completely changed from earlier that night. Thank God for the fireworks, she thought, and grinned at him.

"I must look a fright."

She made a move towards the mirror to examine her tousled and wind-whipped hair, but Charlie put out a hand to stop her.

"No, Maggie. You look beautiful."

She looked down at him as he drew her towards him, wrapping his arms around her middle and pressing his face into her stomach. She could feel the heat of his breath through the thin muslin, and her head felt suddenly and pleasantly light, in a way that it hadn't in some time. Pulling back, he looked up into her face.

"I'm sorry I was bad-tempered earlier."

"It's all right. I understand. I'm sorry I made you leave the party when you wanted to stay."

He shook his head. "It was the right thing. I had a far better time back here with you and the children than I would have had there. I suppose I just feel guilty, still. That they're going, and I'm staying behind."

"It's their choice, though. They want to go."

"And I want to stay." He tugged gently on her hand,

encouraging her down onto the bed beside him. "I've been telling myself that, but didn't really let myself believe it until tonight. It's the right thing to do. I don't want to put myself in the line of fire for this bloody Empire. This is where I want to be."

And so this is the end of it, Maggie thought; tomorrow, the boys would be off to the front – and though she didn't allow herself to think of it directly, only glancingly, the Turks would be leaving the day after, Halim and Süleyman on the train, slicing through the desert, towards the coast where they would leave for home. She hated to admit to herself how much her last meeting with them had disturbed her, their blank faces and the lack of life in their limbs, and she hated still more to examine the part of her that knew that she had failed them, simply by trying to protect her family by retreating into it. She wished them well, but not as much as she wished them gone.

December 21st, 1915

There was no way, Patrick decided, that you could make a pretty picture out of an evacuation. Nearly fifty thousand men evacuated with fewer than ten casualties and no deaths – that was a success, yes, but it was still an evacuation, it was still eight months of pointlessness, thousands of men dead, a military failure and the land blasted to bits and bound to be offering up horrors for dozens of years to come. Still, there it was, and, while he couldn't think of a single thing about this experience that he wanted to remember, he nonetheless took a leaf from a tree that was growing by the beach and wrote on it: 'The last of Gallipoli evacuated, December 1915'.

Chapter Twenty-Nine

The train station was as crowded as Maggie could remember it. She was reminded of the Central Station station in Sydney, the sandstone sweep and arch of it, where she'd stood under the great hanging clock in the centre and said perfunctory, embarrassed goodbyes to her family years before. The New Year's Day picnic train had never been so busy, and for a moment Maggie was confused, until she caught the eye of Anne Michaels. She'd taught Anne's daughter, Judith, a few years before, and she knew that Anne's son, Judith's older brother, Angus, was one of the ones who was due to depart for the war that day. Anne's eyes were red-rimmed and watery though her face was calm; a great act of pulling herself together was clearly occurring.

"Are you going to the picnic, then?" Anne asked. Despite the waver in her voice, her tone was friendly and conversational, but Maggie couldn't help herself from reading accusation into it where almost certainly none was intended: *How dare you celebrate the New Year when my son is leaving?*

"We decided we would, yes," Maggie replied, trying to keep the apologetic tone out of her voice. "I thought the boys had already left?"

Anne shook her head. "No. A few days ago they said that they were to leave first thing in the morning, but they changed their minds yesterday, and now they're not due to leave until just after the picnic train. Strange timing for it all, I think, all we mothers here saying goodbye to our sons at the same time as the rest of the town's going off for a picnic! Not that I begrudge you, mind," she added hastily. "Of course not. Life goes on. And I was grateful for a few more hours with my boy – " She laughed shakily " – even though he was raring to go himself."

Snug in the open carriage, the picnic basket between her feet and Charlie sat opposite, Maggie tried to concentrate on the conversations around her and not get distracted by the movements on the platforms, but it was difficult, particularly as Peter, standing in her lap, was enthralled by the scenes that were playing out below, and kept heaving his sturdy little body up to peer over the edge of the cart. When Peter wanted your attention he was hard to ignore; jabbering in a language that – as yet – only he really understood, he pressed his plump fingers against Maggie's face, turning her head to what he was looking at, insisting that she focus her attention on this thing and that thing, and so she ended up watching, drawn into Peter's fascination, as the recruits, clownish in their ill-fitting uniforms, laughing, joking, teasing, singing to mask their collective unease, were boarding the train alongside their own, barked at now and then by military personnel who were trying in vain to instil a sense of military discipline into the boys.

On the platform stood silent, diffident knots of people – the Michaelses, the McCrearies, the Logans – men, fathers too old to fight, pale but upright, hands bunched into fists; the women, mothers, sisters and wives, fighting back tears or succumbing to them, faces buried in handkerchiefs, hands held, shoulders rubbed, reassurance spoken in subdued voices.

Soon the recruits were seated – quieter now, tense and nervous, lined up like the tin soldiers in the box that Peter had been given for Christmas, a lifeless mimicry of the real thing. White faces were turned towards the windows of the train like petals, no one wanting to be seen to be straining for a last glimpse of their family, but the families on the platform had no such compunction and roamed up and down alongside the train, peering into this carriage and that, searching for their boys that they were losing. Any joy that Maggie had been feeling about the day was being gradually leached out of her, to be replaced by a thick, dragging misery, and she turned to Charlie and complained with uncharacteristic petulance, "Oh, why are we just sitting here? We should have gone ten minutes ago!"

Charlie lifted his eyebrows at her tone, but seeing the tension on her face, her hands twisted, white-knuckled, as she gripped Peter's arms, holding him upright, he held back from commenting. "I'll go and see if I can find out what's going on, then, shall I?" he asked, and without waiting for an answer, swung himself out of his seat and over the edge of the carriage, dropped down onto the platform and vanished into the throng. Moments later he was back, shaking his head.

"It's one of the Barker kids, the youngest one, Billy, is it? Mary Barker decided that they shouldn't bring the family dog with them, but I guess Billy had other ideas. He was in the carriage one minute and gone the next, run off back home to fetch the dog so that it could come with us today. Mary's absolutely fuming, bright red, embarrassed at the hold-up being down to one of hers. You know what a stickler for punctuality she normally is."

"So how long will it be until we can leave?" Maggie asked.

"Maybe another ten, fifteen minutes, something like that."

Outside the window, the Captain in charge of the new recruits was glancing repeatedly at his watch and looking first displeased, then angry.

"We're supposed to go before them," Maggie said. She could see Anne Michaels, one arm round fourteen-year-old Sarah, standing at one end of the platform; Maggie remembered suddenly that Anne had lost her husband the previous winter, in a riding accident – his neck had been broken; he had barely been in his forties. Her stomach twisted with something that was too sharp and painful to be sympathy.

The Captain was having words with the stationmaster now, a small, harassed looking man whom Maggie only recognised on sight; he always looked jumpy and nervous, as if he was only one or two wrong turns away from emotional collapse, and it had occurred to Maggie that it was probably for the best that he was stationmaster in Cottier's Creek, rather than in one of the cities; having to deal with more than one or two trains a day would have given him a conniption. Arms a-flail, eyebrows leaping about on his face, no amount of frenzied jabbing at the timetable he held in his hand could be any match for the Captain, a man evidently used to instant obedience, who looked as if he couldn't have been any less interested in the stationmaster's views. The stationmaster eventually shrugged, eyes down, and nodded.

"They're sending them off first," Maggie reported. Charlie shot her an odd look, clearly not understanding why she was so interested in the progress of the troop train, but she could let herself watch now, knowing the waiting was over. The whistle blew, a streamer of steam escaped from the train's chimney, and then the troops were on their way, gliding out of the station, their loved ones walking, then trotting alongside, and then the new soldiers were gone, steaming across the desert. She wasn't sure if she had actually seen him, but the last image that stayed in Maggie's mind was of Angus Michaels, his face pale and set and resolutely turned away from the glass.

*

Most of the other days of Halim's life had had some sort of linear structure; even if he couldn't remember the exact details of how he had got from one place to another, the separate pieces of the day fitted in together with one another, forming a coherent whole. Not this day, this final day; this day seemed to take place in a series of flashes, disconnected from one another, with nothing tying them together but a general sense of forward motion, irresistible and unstoppable.

He slept late, for him. Ever since they had moved out of the house, Halim had been waking with the dawn or even before, lying in the half darkness, trying to make sense of the unidentifiable noises around him, counting the minutes until it was an acceptable time to get up, accidentally-on-purpose waking Süleyman with his too-loud dressing, so that he would have company, albeit grumpy and moaning. It had seemed as if he had gone from sleeping as much as he could, to being unable to sleep for more than five hours a night, but that morning, the first day of 1916, he slumbered on with dense, unremembered dreams until Süleyman placed a gentle hand on his shoulder, squeezing it until he opened his eyes and stared straight at the glass of sticky, steaming tea in front of his nose.

Neither of them spoke much over breakfast, which was light; whenever Halim looked in Süleyman's direction he found his friend silent, gazing, seemingly enraptured, at some small, barely noticeable thing – the sinuous ruffles the night wind had made in the sand; the small, vivid red flowers that had punched their way out of the parched desert plants; the patterns of grey on grey on the blank morning sky. Halim could not bring himself to look at anything in any detail; it wasn't even as if he was consciously avoiding it, but rather that whenever he tried, his mind would glance away, like a horse shying at a gate. He didn't force it.

They had polished the bit and the bridle the night before until they were gleaming, and they had oiled the old leather of the reins until it was as smooth as butter and supple in Süleyman's hands. Halim had half expected Sena to be nervous; she had always been a little flighty, and her owner's moods were often passed to her down the reins, so that she would often be the stamping, snorting, outward expression of whatever anger or irritation or sadness that Halim or Süleyman were feeling; but this morning she was as calm and docile as the sheep that Halim used to lead to slaughter. She hadn't had the cart hitched to her in some time but she submitted to it easily, and stood still while the two men, still in silence, loaded their supplies into the back: the two guns, the ammunition, as much non-perishable food that they had been able to scrape together, several bottles of water, the tickets and money from Maggie and a change of clothes for each of them wrapped up in a careful bundle, and their home-made Ottoman flag, blotchy, lopsided and amateurish, folded into careful quarters in the bed of the cart.

They had walked out to the train tracks two days before, a five mile walk as the sun was sliding down behind the distant hills and the frogs from the creek were clearly audible in the still air, and had worked out their prime position, behind a jumble of boulders perhaps a hundred yards from the track, where it rounded a sharp curve to avoid the low hills on the outskirts of town. Halim had sat there, an imaginary gun held to his eye, watching the tracks for nothing, until he had finally dropped his hands, turned to Süleyman, nodded and pronounced, "This is good."

They were far too early, of course, when they arrived on New Year's Day and tethered Sena to a stunted, withered tree. For the length of their friendship, Halim and Süleyman had been able to sit in silence together, but suddenly, today, as the sun burst through the clouds, presaging the steady rise in temperature to the noonday heat, Halim couldn't bear the stillness and longed to fill the dull air with chatter. The present was unpalatable and the future impossible, and so they spoke about the past, the far past. Halim struggled to remember the story of the three orange-peris that his mother used to tell him, but the descriptions of the Mother of the Devils that used to strike terror into his child's heart only served to make Süleyman laugh. Then Süleyman, in his turn, dug up the story of the wind demon that Aygen had told their children, reciting it word for word as she had done, as much to himself as to Halim, who sat enraptured.

The shriek of a train's whistle roused them from where they sat, their backs to the warm rocks. Halim was on his knees immediately, peering over the rock at the silhouette of the train as it came charging through the high, noon sunlight, roaring and crashing, as his eyes narrowed against the glare. *We should have thought of this*, he thought irritably to himself, *perfect vantage point at dusk, and of course now we're half blinded by the light.*

"Is it – ?" he asked Süleyman, though he knew it wasn't, and Süleyman shook his head in confirmation.

"It's the picnic train." He had been to speak to the stationmaster the day before on the pretext of finding out when the train for which they had tickets departed, but really in order to double-check the time of the troop train. So the two of them watched the picnic train as it slid by beneath them, and Halim found his mouth quirked into an involuntary smile as he thought of the people inside, of Maggie tickling Peter's plump belly, perhaps, or of Daniel, dreaming of a few hours lying in the sun, looking at girls. All antipathy towards them had been eclipsed by the enormity of what he and Süleyman were about to do, and he could only hope that the townspeople below had a good day in front of them. "But we'd better get ready," Süleyman added, elbowing him. "The troop train should be ten minutes behind this one."

In the wake of the train, the two of them squatted down, their hands moving with the deftness of constant practice. This was something that they had done over and over, sliding the bullets one by one into the rifles' chambers, and Halim found that his hands were shaking less now than they had in practice. His vision had shrunk – from being able to see all around him, the shadows of the rocks and the wide, careless sky, the edges of his world had dimmed and then darkened completely, and he saw only what was straight in front of him in sharp, intense detail, as if he'd paid the price of his peripheral vision for this tight, relentless focus. His heartbeat surged through his body like waves, and he counted, just to slow it down, fasten it more tightly to the stem of his body, though he felt himself rocking to its beat. He counted too for the sake of timing, to try and work out how long he had to wait, although he knew the timing of the train was less than certain. Seven minutes to go, now, maybe... five... his hearing was going now, the background noise of the desert (he'd always been surprised at how noisy it was) flickering and then fading in his ears, all his senses sacrificed before the extreme violence of his concentration.

Halim barely heard Süleyman exclaim, but he felt the knock on his elbow as Süleyman leapt to his feet, and he himself looked up, irritated – this was no time to be jumping about! But then he saw what Süleyman was doing; he had run to the back of the cart and was hoisting the red mess of fabric into his arms, staggering a little under the unwieldiness of it. Of course, the flag; how had he forgotten? They hadn't wanted to set it up too soon, to alert people to their presence, but his earlier words clanged in his ears now: *There's no point without the flag, it doesn't mean anything if they don't know who's doing this*.

He cast his gun down on the ground with a hasty look over his shoulder – no sign of the train yet, slipping along the tracks like quicksilver – and ran over to help Süleyman. They had carefully, clumsily stitched a series of loops onto the edge of the flag so that it could be easily affixed to a pole, and they had remembered the pole, too, a pale, dried out limb of a branch that Halim had rescued from their stash of firewood, recognising usefulness in its unnatural straightness, stripping it of its twigs till it formed a perfect flagpole. Both panting, sweating, overexerted in the relentless midday sun that crashed against their skins, Süleyman held out the flag, its ends trailing unforgivably on the dusty ground, as Halim pushed the pole through the loops – done, now, and Süleyman heaved it upright, nearly tipping over when the weight of it caught in a light breeze.

The whistle came then, sharp and shrill and unmistakeable, and Halim recited every curse he knew, the fouler and more forbidden the better, as he struggled with Süleyman to balance the flag and its pole into the bracket that, years ago, Süleyman had welded onto the side of his cart to support the Australian flag when he flew it on Anniversary Day. Finally, their red flag stood unsupported, first hanging limp, then licked by a gust of wind and thrown into a storm of scarlet – and the two of them turned their back on it, flung themselves down onto the rocks, seized up the guns. The train was there now, closer and closer, now within their sights, the tiny dots of heads bobbing over the top of the open carriages, so small and so vulnerable, and Halim gave a quick prayer of thankfulness for the flag. He realised that if he had been given time to think about what he was doing, his finger would have frozen on the trigger and he would have sat there, motionless, until the train sped off towards the horizon and to war. As it was, there was nothing inside him, no doubts and no fears, nothing but the sense that this was what he was going to do. He heard Süleyman mutter a prayer beside him, his old tongue sticking to the roof of his dry mouth, and Halim took aim at the train, closed his eyes, and shot.

Chapter Thirty

Maggie was dozing. As soon as they had left the town, relief had descended on her with the weight of a heavy cloak around her shoulders, and she found that all she wanted to do was to close her eyes, basking as the heat of the sun soaked through her. She didn't sleep properly, though, listening to the lulling conversations around her, Charlie talking quietly to Peter, pointing things out to him as they flickered past, and Peter's answering babble, while she was simultaneously somewhere else – a shadowy dream world that was partly the park where she had played as a child in Sydney, and partly the location of the picnic, the soft grass under her hands as she sat, lying back in the sun, her feet in the cool water that lapped around her ankles.

The chat in the carriages of the train was raucous, bursts of laughter like gunfire, and singing, caterwauling and out of tune, and so at first she didn't notice the shouting, the subtle shift in tone from excited chatter to confusion and fear. She felt the jerk of the train, though, as the driver pumped hard on the brakes, and she heard the agonising squall of steel on steel as the wheels locked against the tracks, halting thousands of tons of speeding metal. She opened her eyes as Mary, in Nancy's arms, opened her throat with a wail that was as much about the affront to her ears as it was about fright, and met Charlie's gaze across the carriage. It was moments like this that she always realised anew how much she loved him, what a man he was, as his gaze was unafraid and unwavering and it steadied her, bringing her heartbeat back from a frenzied stutter to a regular thump.

"What is it, do you think?" she asked, trying to keep her voice steady for the sake of Peter, who was looking at her with round eyes that were still only curious, not yet alarmed – but Charlie was already moving, passing Peter to her and getting to his feet, when, with a sound like stones rattled in a tin can, the second round of bullets came.

*

The driver hadn't known what to make of it when he'd rounded the bend and seen that red sheet fluttering in the wind. *What a place to try and dry your washing* had been his first thought, and then he'd seen that the flag was attached to that gaudily painted cart that the Turkish ice cream sellers had used to ride around town. He'd thought they'd long ago left town, and his stomach soured. His cousin had left today for the war; to think that these Turks had the gall not only to still be in town, but to fly their flag so openly, identifying with the enemy...

"What's going on there?" Jimmy, the fireman, asked. At fifty, his eyes were starting to fail and he could only make out a smear of red against the dull brown rocks by the tracks.

"It's those bloody Turks. The ice cream sellers. Probably some sort of stupid bloody stunt to try and stop the train, sell some ice cream to the passengers. They'll be in a hell of a lot of trouble if they try to – "

His words were lost with the sound of a whip crack echoing across the broad empty valley. The sound seemed to come before any movement, certainly before any pain, but then he was no longer sitting at his seat, he was on his back on the hard metal floor of the train, staring at the ceiling. His first thought was that Jimmy must have grabbed him, and he had just opened his mouth to berate him when he was gripped by the clawing pain in his right shoulder, the hot, sticky feel of it. Then Jimmy's face, round and terrified looking, loomed over his, a stream of expletives coming out of his mouth, and he understood, if not exactly what had happened, then at least that something had gone very badly wrong. Jimmy went to kneel and, despite the pain, the driver shook his head sharply, and bit out a terse command: "The bloody train, you fool!" and Jimmy swore again, before swaying out of sight and shutting off the steam, and then the great shrieking of the wheels against the track seemed to fill the world.

*

It had been Halim's idea to go for the driver first – *I'll get them to stop the train*, he'd said to Süleyman, *otherwise they'll be just bound to keep going and they'd hardly get any decent shots in.* If they stopped the train, at least some of the men would be bound to come out and give them some clear shots – but when it came to it, it was Süleyman who remembered. Maybe it was sewn into his bones and sinews, from the long-ago training that his father had given him, shooting rabbits out in the fields – but whatever the reason, in the heat of the moment Süleyman remembered what they had meant to do, even though he, Halim, had forgotten.

Halim's mind was as blank as the cloudless sky above, a single imperative causing him to tighten his finger on the trigger, his eyes squeezed shut against the reality of what he was doing. Of course his shot went wide, far too high, sailing above the train, but Süleyman's hit home. There was a noise like the earth tearing in two, and Halim opened his eyes in time to see the train juddering to a halt beneath them, figures vaulting over the sides of the open-topped carts, passengers spilling onto the bright sand. *How did I get here?* Halim asked himself; for a second, the shadow of Irfan glimmered on the edge of his vision and then winked out with the suddenness of a candle under breath. The sun was glaring so brightly that, from their position, the people below were nothing but black matchstick men, leaping one by one from the carriages, not bothering to take the time to open the doors, running up the side of train.

"Come on," Süleyman grunted next to him; any reticence that he had had towards this project was gone with the single-minded determination he always showed when faced with a task at hand. "Shoot, shoot," Süleyman grunted, reloading, and so Halim did the only thing that he could do, although every instinct in his body revolted against it: he kept going.

*

There was nothing wrong with Charlie's eyesight, he could pick a single sheep out of the flock from a hundred yards – but there was something wrong with his brain, he thought, because he simply couldn't make sense of what he was seeing. When the train had shuddered into stillness, a number of possibilities had occurred to him – something blocking the tracks; the driver taken ill – and it was his natural instinct to take control, find out for his family what was going on, and help in any way that he could. Old Lizzie Matthews was stumbling out of her seat, squinting her eyes and peering towards the distant hills, and he put a comforting hand on her arm, moved her out of the way, gave her a few vague words of reassurance (he was sure it was nothing, he was just going to see what was going on) and swung his legs over the lip of the carriage, jumping down onto ground that was hot and hard under his boots. In front of him, feet waved at eye-level as a couple of men from the next carriage hauled themselves inelegantly to the ground; he couldn't see straight away who in the glare of the sun, but behind him he heard banging metal and the thumps of feet on dirt and knew that any number of men were doing the same.

It was the next thing that he couldn't quite understand; the way that Bill Paterson from the old Paterson farm (his eyes had started to adjust, and besides, Bill was easy to pick out, being three inches taller than the next tallest man in town) seemed to stumble and fall. He hadn't even been moving so he couldn't have tripped over anything, and Charlie felt a laugh choking his throat: bloody clumsy Bill, his head was so high up that he could never tell what his legs were doing. The bang that rattled the sides of the train was nearly an afterthought, lost in the yell of the man who had been standing next to Bill, and then that

273

noise again, a series of deafening cracks and then thumps as something hit the sides and the interior of the train, splintering the wooden seats. *Bullets*, his brain told him, but that was ridiculous, of course it couldn't be; who would want to attack a train on its way to a New Year's Day picnic? He couldn't argue with his body, though; his reflexes had always acted before allowing his mind to catch up with them, and before he could make a decision to do so, he'd leapt back into the space between two carriages, squeezing his way through to the other side of the train, the safe side, the side that was sheltered from the flying things that were certainly not bullets.

The bangs and cracks continued as he ran towards the front of the train, sounding in counterpoint to the slapping of his feet on the parched ground. The driver's compartment was in front of him now, doors on both sides, and he leapt up the steps and grabbed the handle, trying to banish from his mind the image of Bill's head as he'd fallen; that hadn't been blood, it was just the way that the shadow had happened to fall. The door swung open to reveal a frantic Jimmy bent over the driver's body, turning his white, ravaged face up to look into Charlie's own. "Those bloody Turks," he said, and Charlie couldn't fool himself any longer.

*

Maggie had never been particularly good at staying still, whether as a child in church or as an adult, when she felt that interesting things were going on without her. Curiosity had always been the main driving force in her life, and no matter how old she got, she was powerless to ignore it. She looked at Nancy who, with Mary in her arms, sat cowering in the corner of the carriage, and suppressed a stab of irritation at her fearfulness. It didn't occur to Maggie to be frightened, in the same way that it didn't occur to her that anyone would ever wish her harm.

When the word came rippling from carriage to carriage she didn't believe it at first. People shooting at the train? What a ridiculous idea! The war was thousands of miles away but it had clearly addled people's minds, to make them think that anyone would want to attack a picnic train. She supposed that the bangs had sounded a little like gunshots, but they could have been any number of things – though she couldn't quite work out what those things could be. If only Charlie would come back and tell them what was actually happening…

Then the screaming started, and it chilled her in a way that the banging noises hadn't managed – first one voice and then many. She saw Lucy Paterson leap from her seat, shrieking, two rows in front of where Maggie sat, with Mary Macarthur gripping her arm, holding her back, white as bone, her eyes darting until they caught Maggie's own. "They've shot Bill," Mary said to Maggie, almost conversationally, "She wants to go to him, she won't listen, it's far too dangerous."

Without thinking, Maggie deposited Peter in Nancy's spare arm and went to help, clambering over the backs of seats until she got close enough to grab Lucy's other arm and pull her back from the edge of the carriage. As she pushed Lucy down into a seat, her wailing was joined by the voices of both Mary and Peter, in tones of upset dignity. Maggie felt wild, almost unhinged. "What's going on, Mary?" she asked, but Mary just shook her head with impatience.

"I told you. They're shooting – "

"Who's shooting?"

"I don't know, I just know that Bill went out to see what was happening and he was – there was a crack and he went down, there was blood… "

Suddenly pale, and looking on the verge of fainting, Mary sat down next to Lucy. "What are we supposed to do? Do we just stay here and wait till they come to get us?"

The thump on the side of the carriage next to Maggie caused her to shriek out loud, much to her embarrassment when she saw Charlie's face gazing up at her. Her hand to her chest, trying to still her hammering heart, she turned to her husband. "Charlie, what on earth…? They're saying that Bill Paterson – "

"Bill's dead," Charlie said flatly, "and I don't think he's the only one. The driver's pretty bad too, may not make it."

"But who's doing this?"

"Your bloody Turks, that's who."

She was breathless. "It can't be! They wouldn't – "

Charlie shook his head. "Maggie, we don't have time to talk about this," he said angrily. "You have to get out. The children first – we're safe on this side of the train, they can't hit us over here as long as we stay close. Pass the kids out to me."

In silence, numb, Maggie lifted first Mary, then Peter, over the side of the carriage, and Charlie caught them one by one. They looked so small and helpless standing there, Peter staring up at her, his mouth enormous, rending the air with his misery. "Now you," Charlie said, but Maggie shook her head.

"Nancy should go first." She turned back to where Nancy sat in the corner of the carriage; she'd slipped off her bench and was pressed against the metal side of the carriage, weeping silently. Smiling in what she hoped was an encouraging way, Maggie reached out her hands to her, hunching her shoulders a little in response to Charlie's desperate entreaties to keep down.

"Nancy, love, we've got to get out." Nancy said nothing, and when Maggie touched her shoulder she flinched violently; Maggie couldn't help wondering what had happened to the tough, smiling girl that they'd employed two years ago. "Come on, Nancy; you'll be safer out there, it's just a little jump over the edge of the carriage, and Charlie will catch you." But Nancy just shook her head violently, even as, out of the corner of her eye, Maggie could see the whoosh and flurry of skirts as plenty of women were choosing to take Charlie's advice. Even pallid Alice Crawford was crawling over the edge of the carriage, albeit crying all the while, but Nancy spoke in a small, pinched whisper. "I can't."

"Oh, Nancy, of course you can! See, all the others are doing it, and it's perfectly safe." But Nancy shook her head again, and whispered, "My leg," and, with a lurch of guilt, Maggie remembered what she'd always been able to forget and overlook: Nancy's right leg, shrivelled and wasted by childhood polio. She barely limped, and of course the leg was well-hidden by her skirts, but more than once Maggie had been with her when she stumbled and winced with pain and exertion, and Maggie berated herself for forgetting that not everyone's body was as robust as her own.

"Nancy can't climb over," Maggie called back to Charlie, who swore loudly. "It's her leg," she explained, "She really can't, it's not her fault."

Charlie sighed. "She'll have to go out the door, then," he said, "but you – "

Maggie shook her head. "I have to stay with her, Charlie. She's scared. It's only right."

He pressed his lips tightly together in a way that showed he was worried, but to her relief, he didn't argue. "I'll tell you what to do, then. The door's at the front of the carriage, on the right hand side; keep your heads down, below the edge of the train – the way that the door opens, you'll be protected behind it, and you can drop down and slip through the gap between the coaches. You'll only be exposed for a split second."

"But Charlie…"

He smiled at her, startling in his white, drawn face, but his same old smile nonetheless. "Go on, Mags. You can do it."

The carriage was almost empty now, but for Maggie, Nancy, Lucy, still barely clinging onto her sanity, and Mary Macarthur, who was gripping onto Lucy's hand. So they went, the four of them, along the aisle, crouching down as Charlie had said, crawling to the front of the carriages. Another round of bangs and cracks came, unmistakeable now; Maggie didn't know how she could have ever thought they were anything but gunshots. As they reached the front of the carriage, a bullet bounced off the side and hit a nearby bench, blasting it into splinters that cut Maggie's hands, but she could barely feel the pain.

"You first," she said to Nancy, taking change of their little mission, wanting to see them all safely out of there. She explained to Nancy what to do, how to use the door as shelter, drop down, and then move into the gap between the carriages. "You'll be all right," she insisted, giving Nancy's hand a reassuring squeeze, and then Nancy had gone, tears on her face but doing exactly as Maggie had instructed, disappearing between the carriages, safe.

Lucy went next, handed down by Mary into Nancy's waiting hands, then Mary herself and finally Maggie. Behind the door, she slipped down the steps, balancing on the last one, about to drop to ground, and then curiosity got her by the throat. It wasn't the Turks, she knew it wasn't, it couldn't be, and she wanted to be able to tell Charlie so. The banging had been silent for nearly a minute now, so perhaps it was over; in any case, it wouldn't do any harm just to pop her head out for a second or two and look, and then she would have the satisfaction of telling Charlie that of course neither Halim nor Süleyman would do something like this. She dropped down, her boots hitting the ground, and she leaned to her right, her head out from behind the door, her eyes searching the rocks from where the shots were coming. She had just enough time to catch sight of the wooden cart, the red flag unfurled in the brisk afternoon wind, before she was hit.

Charlie, coming back between the carriages to find what was taking his wife so long, was just in time to see her fall.

Chapter Thirty-One

It had become a game to Halim; it had to be – to see how many of the black figures (who were not people) he could hit. Three were down now, two hit by Süleyman and one by himself, and he had another in his sights now, one that was leaning out from behind one of the train doors. He shot, the figure fell, and then he noticed the discrepancy; this figure wasn't shaped like the others, there was a skirt where the two legs should be, but it couldn't be, it couldn't; even as he thought it, he felt Süleyman's hand on his arm, staying him, and Halim swung round, looking at Süleyman's horror-struck expression.

"It can't be," Halim whispered. The silence seemed louder than the firing had been. "Why would they have women on the troop train? It doesn't make any sense."

They looked back. It was a trick of the light, maybe, but no, the new figure on the ground wasn't the same shape as the other three. More beskirted figures were appearing now, crowding round the fallen woman, trying to drag her between the two carriages, and as their ears returned to normal after the deafening gunshot blasts, they heard it – the unmissable sound of a child wailing.

"It's the wrong train," Süleyman said. His lips were white.

"It can't be," Halim said again. The gun in his hand suddenly felt impossibly heavy and he dropped it without thinking. "It can't be. You said – " He rounded on Süleyman. "You said! You said that the picnic train would be first, and the troop train second! You said!"

Süleyman shook his head. "That's what they said to me. They must have changed it at the last moment."

It had been almost two minutes now since the last shot was fired; with a lurch, Halim realised that people were moving in their direction. "We have to go," he said to Süleyman, who didn't move. Halim tugged on his sleeve. "Come on, old man! We have to go!"

Moving maddeningly slowly, as if wading through mud, Süleyman stumbled back to the cart and heaved himself up onto the driver's box. Halim vaulted in beside him. "Let's go," he said, but Süleyman just shook his head.

"Go where?" he asked. His voice was unfathomably weary, every syllable weighted down, and for a moment Halim didn't know how to answer. He knew that Süleyman was thinking that they should just wait where they were and take what was coming to them, but Halim wasn't ready for that quite yet. "To the hills," he said at last. "Out to the hills, we can hide out till nightfall."

*

They moved her, Nancy and Mary and Charlie, moved her into the space between the carriages but as soon as he saw her, Charlie knew that it was no use: she was dead, died instantly it seemed, her eyes still open (he closed them, his fingers on the smooth, damp skin of her eyelids), her mouth still in a half smile. She hadn't suffered, at least, and perhaps he would allow that to be a comfort to him at a later time, but not then, not yet. He had never felt like this before – anger, yes, he knew anger, but this was like being possessed by something infinitely larger than himself. He was swept up in a tornado of heightened, heady emotion and he surrendered to it gladly, because he couldn't face the thought of being Charlie McGill at that moment. Once he had ensured that Peter and Mary were safely in Nancy's care, and could be kept away from their mother's body, he took off for the driver's cabin. Now, too late, he remembered that there was a telephone there. Why hadn't he thought of it before, called for help? He was certain that no one else would have thought of it, either. When he arrived, he found Jimmy sat in the corner of the cabin, his arm around the driver who was grey and sweating but still alive, breathing in great, whistling gasps, no part of him moving except for his eyes, which tracked Charlie's movements, and the shallow hitching of his chest.

"The telephone?" Charlie asked, and Jimmy's eyes widened. "I didn't think – "

"It's all right." Glancing at the clock above the driver's seat, Charlie was surprised to see that it had only taken ten minutes from the firing of the first shot to now, which seemed to be the end of it. He lifted the receiver and dialled the police station in Cottier's Creek.

It took a few moments to get the message across to the police sergeant, so unbelievable was the story, but Charlie was forceful when he needed to be. When he hung up, Jimmy was still watching him. "How many dead?"

"A few," Charlie said, close-lipped.

"Your family?"

"Maggie." Just saying her name choked him; a buzzing seemed to fill his head and he shook it to clear it. Once out of the cabin, he took several lungfuls of the hot afternoon air, then walked round to the side of the train closest to the hills; it seemed fairly certain that the shooting had stopped, but even if it hadn't, it would have posed no fear for him. He wondered briefly why they had stopped when they did: out of ammo, perhaps, or was it more than just a coincidence that Maggie had been the last to die; perhaps they'd made a mistake, attacked the wrong train? He shook his head again, gulping back a sick laugh. Bloody typical, that'd be. Bloody typical of those useless Turks.

Help arrived from the town soon enough: the doctor and a few other men with transportation that could be rounded up. The dead were loaded onto a cart to be taken back to the town, but Charlie refused to go and watch; leave that to the others, he thought, he had work to do. Not bothering to listen to what anyone else was saying, he went over to Robbie McLean, who'd come with his two-horse buggy. Seeing Charlie approaching, Robbie stepped towards him, extending his hand.

"Charlie, I heard about Maggie, I'm so sorry – "

But Charlie stopped him with a terse shake of his head. "Did the police bring a tracker?"

Robbie knew Charlie well enough not to push when Charlie clearly didn't want to talk, and nodded. "Yep, over there." He nodded towards a tall, black-skinned man who stood, silent and still, outside the knots of people.

"You got your gun?" Charlie asked.

Robbie nodded again. "Yep."

"Good. Grab the blackfella, then, and let's go."

*

By the time Halim and Süleyman reached the hills, the Ghan Town was already burning, the smoke hanging low in the hot, still air. Halim wasn't surprised – nothing about this day could surprise him anymore – but Süleyman seemed shocked and asked, "What's going on?"

"They must have heard already, the people in the town."

"But it's not the people in the Ghan Town's fault!"

"We can't do anything," Halim said dully. They drove on, along the path of the dry river bed, but it became rockier and rockier, the cart jouncing unbearably, Sena starting to stumble.

"We should walk," Süleyman said at last, and Halim nodded. Their chances on foot were worse in the long term, but better in the short term, and the short term was all that he cared about at that moment; he couldn't think beyond nightfall. They slipped off the cart, and gently Süleyman unhitched Sena. He led her by the bridle to the creek where she started to drink thirstily. Süleyman pressed his head against her smooth, damp neck and wept silently for a moment, his shoulders shaking, before turning his back on the mare and nodding at Halim, his face tear-stained and resolute. "Let's go."

By four, they could go no further. They were dry and parched, having finished the last of their water, and the terrain was too rough to continue. Halim thought that perhaps he could have managed to go on, but Süleyman was staggering and stumbling, and Halim wouldn't leave him, no matter how many times Süleyman urged him to do so. They sat, then, in the crook of the rocks, huddled into the lengthening shade: waiting for dark, Halim said, when they could regain some of their strength and try and slip further away from the town, but both of them knew it for the lie that it was; they were waiting to be discovered. There was nothing left for them to say to one another. The weight of guilt they both carried was too heavy to allow them to open their mouths, and Halim felt sick with it. He was glad of Süleyman's weakness, which gave him an excuse not to try and escape – this was something that he didn't want to get away with. As the afternoon started to turn to evening and the last of the day's light leaked through the jagged cracks in the rock, Süleyman moved wearily over to their pathetic bundle of possessions – the money, the tickets, the scraps of clothing – and brought out the notebook that they had used to write down bits of vocabulary for Halim to learn, and the stub of a pencil. Curling his hand around it, he starting to write.

"What are you writing?" Halim asked.

"It's a confession."

A confession. It seemed the right thing to do, but Halim couldn't even begin to imagine what he would say. Süleyman had always had a gift for brevity and precision in his words, which Halim lacked. To explain how and why he had ended up at this barren outcropping in the harsh dusk light with the blood of so many people – he didn't know how many – on his hands, Halim would have had to go back so far, beyond Sydney and the boat and the long, footsore walk to Port Said to the first time Irfan had looked at him, sidelong and calculating, put a pebble in his hand, and said *I dare you*, and Halim, five-years-old, scared and thrilled at once, had shied the stone at Old Mehmet's donkey. Without that, and all that had come of it, his friendship with Irfan and what friendship had come to mean to him, and the fierce desire to protect those things that were most important to him, none of this could make any sense. A confession was impossible, then, but Halim needed to do something, mark his final minutes onto this land somehow, ensure that there was something left behind him that showed that he knew what he had done and that he regretted it. So he took out the one thing he had in his pocket, the one thing that he had chosen to bring with him that morning, without knowing clearly why: the small, silver crucifix that Fotini had given him. Halim took it, and he pressed it into the sandy earth, pressed it down hard so that it stood up small and proud, casting its long shadow across the ground, and his heart, clenched like a fist inside him, eased a little.

Chapter Thirty-Two

Charlie too saw the hanks of smoke rising from the Ghan Town, but his reaction was nothing more than a shrug.

"I guess they're going crazy back in town," Robbie offered. His words were met with such a stony silence that they might just as well have not been said. There were six of them in all: Charlie, four men from the town, all on horses they had uncoupled from buggies, and the Aboriginal tracker on foot, whose name none of them knew, but who, with professional disinterest, had led them unerringly on the trail of the Turks. They had found the discarded cart by the river, the horse still nearby, and while Robbie had gone over to try and catch her and tether her – she looked like a decent mare; someone in town'd probably pay a bit of money for her – Charlie went straight to the cart, rifling through the scant possessions in the back of it, leftover ammunition, scraps from the Turks' lunch, and the flag, limp and lifeless as a shot bird. He wished he had some gasoline, but his knife would have to do, he thought, as he cut into the flag, dismembering the star and the crescent moon, finally casting its scraps into the creek where its colour seeped into the water and dyed it red.

They found the Turks as the sun went down. Charlie hadn't known whether they were going to turn and run or stand and fight, but he didn't expect what happened, that the two of them, the older first, and the younger behind him, would stand, calm, blank-faced, and walk towards him, hands empty and open, their lips moving, making the same shapes again and again. If it was a plea for mercy, Charlie had none; the other men stood back as he lifted Robbie's rifle and with two quick, clean shots, took out the older one, then the younger one, bang, bang, as they fell without a cry.

*

Dusk had always been Halim's favourite time of day. When he had been a child of nine or ten, playing with Irfan, they'd felt that they owned dusk more than any other time. The day was for obligations, school and chores, and night time was ruled by adults, who demanded you stay inside – but dusk was magical, liminal, neither here nor there, wholly theirs. It seemed right that the men should find him at that time, too, and right that he and Süleyman should stand to greet them. The landscape around them shifted back and forth, Halim noticed, and he wondered if it was doing it for Süleyman, too: one minute the bare rocks of the Australian outback, the next the green hills he'd grown up with, back and forth, back and forth, like the one film he'd seen in the cinema, lurching from scene to scene. They'd been silent all afternoon but now he could think of a thousand things that he wanted to say to Süleyman, questions he'd never asked him, things he wanted to tell him about himself, things he wanted to show him: Do you see that eagle over there in the half light? What was the name of your wife, the names of your children? Did you know that my oldest sister was pregnant when I left? I would have a niece or nephew by now. He wanted to speak, but the only words he could think of were prayers, which were probably the right things, anyway. He was glad that Süleyman had written the confession. The world was wild and beautiful and hard, and he was ready for it to be over now.

The noise of the shot scared the birds from the trees, black shapes flapping against the red sky, but it didn't hurt a bit. As the lip of the sun slipped over the edge of the earth, Halim fell.

Acknowledgements

Thanks, as ever, to everyone at Legend Press/PaperBooks, as well as to all my family and friends who supported, nagged and cajoled me along the way. Extra thanks are due to Rachel Coldbreath, who housed me while I was writing; to Anne Pordes and Justin Sacks who, along with Rachel, were fantastic company in Turkey while I was carrying out initital research; and to Natalie and Colin Craig who put me up in Sydney while I was researching there. Huge thanks also to my father and Graham Rouse, whose original screenplay about the events in this book served as wonderful inspiration; and to Leda Glyptis, Turkey expert and all-round superstar, whose fact-checking and general wealth of knowledge was invaluable: any mistakes in the text are mine alone. Finally, all my thanks and love to Tom Harkness, for everthing.

 **PaperBooks**

This book has been published by vibrant publishing company Paperbooks. If you enjoyed reading it then you can help make it a major hit. Just follow these three easy steps:

1. Recommend it
Pass it onto a friend to spread word-of-mouth or, if now you've got your hands on this copy you don't want to let it go, just tell your friend to buy their own or maybe get it for them as a gift. Copies are available with special deals and discounts from our own website and from all good bookshops and online outlets.

2. Review it
It's never been easier to write an online review of a book you love and can be done on Amazon, Waterstones.com, WHSmith.co.uk and many more. You could also talk about it or link to it on your own blog or social networking site.

3. Read another of our great titles
We've got a wide range of diverse modern fiction and it's all waiting to be read by fresh-thinking readers like you! Come to us direct at www.legendpress.co.uk to take advantage of our superb discounts. (Plus, if you email info@legend-paperbooks.co.uk just after placing your order and quote 'WORD OF MOUTH', we will send another book with your order absolutely free!)

Thank you for being part of our word of mouth campaign.

info@legend-paperbooks.co.uk
www.paperbooks.co.uk